lick *of* fire

CLARA ELROY

Editing: Erica Russikoff
Proofreading: Nice Girl, Naughty Edits
Cover Design: The Pretty Little Design Co.

You can't escape fate, no matter how fast you run. That was a lesson hard learned for me.

I spent years trying to bury my past, but my future held skeletons bleaker than the ones I'd left behind.

Darkness follows me everywhere I go, hanging over my shoulders like a scythe. A byproduct of my bad karma.

For so long, I refused to even look at my hometown on a postcard. That is until trouble comes knocking at my door, and I'm forced to move to the one place I've been avoiding like the plague.

Ares Alsford, my deepest regret, and most painful memory is the one I need to stay away from at all costs.

But I'd be naive to think old wounds stay closed when you scratch them, and I fear my presence back in the city he ran me out of is going to cause more shock waves than I can handle.

One thing's for sure, though...

I might be broken, but I refuse to bend, regardless of how hard he tries to hurt me.

NOTE

Lick of Fire is a full-length, interconnected standalone that features strong language, sexual scenes and mature situations which may be considered triggers for some.
Reader Discretion is advised.

I'd prefer for you to go in blind, but if you would like a detailed warning list you can find it by scanning the code below:

PLAYLIST

"Bad Habits"— Ed Sheeran

"Animals"— Maroon 5

"Bad Girl"— Daya

"Ordinary Life"— The Weeknd

"Night Crawling"— Miley Cyrus, Billy Idol

"Addicted To You"— Avicii

"Like I Can" — Sam Smith

"Try Me"— The Weeknd

"I Miss You"— Adele

"Middle Of The Night"— Elley Duhé

"Someone To You"— BANNERS

"Power Over Me"— Dermot Kennedy

For everyone that harbors an untold story.
It's never too late to take control of your narrative.

Things are not always what they seem; outward form deceives many; rare is the mind that discerns what is carefully concealed within.

— PHAEDRUS

PROLOGUE

Five Years Ago

There was blood on my hands.

It dripped down my fingers in the same rapid rhythm as my heart, turning the mattress a deep shade of red as it soaked through the cotton sheets. I could smell the iron in the air, could taste the bitterness on my tongue, and could feel its heaviness set over my silver dress.

The weight of a memory I would carry for the rest of my life.

One more sin to add to my overflowing scoreboard.

Lifeless eyes stared back at me. His brown irises were duller than usual. Spittles of red stained his fatty cheeks, sparkling under the moonlight slicing through the square windows of the seemingly abandoned Brooklyn apartment block.

The neighborhood waiting beyond the doors of the brownstone building was less than stellar. Drug dealers littered the streets. Prostitutes looking for their next fix, bent over half-open windows, shielding the affairs of cheating husbands. And crooked cops turned a blind eye to the evil raining on their turf. The law enforcement acted like a cobweb, catching small flies but letting wasps and hornets break through.

So I served my own justice.

My tormentor was no more than a soulless sack of skin and bones. A life I'd robbed in his room while he was sleeping, digging the pocketknife I'd stolen from one of the other guys sixteen times into his lungs. Until his struggles turned futile and the blood rushing up his throat muffled his screams.

I did it.

I can't believe I've done it.

My muscles were sore, arms still shaking by my sides from the excessive force. I was fully prepared to die tonight if things didn't go according to plan. If I hesitated, if murder didn't come easy to me. I never should've doubted myself. Killing was in my blood, after all.

Thump.

My breathing stunted when a loud thud echoed in my ears, my gaze flying to the door. Fear bled into shock as my red-stained fingers clutched either forearm, curling my body inwards. A slight twinge of calm blended into the mix when my vision refocused, and there was no one at the threshold.

It must have been a door slamming shut downstairs.

My chest caved with a deep breath, and I counted to ten in my mind, turning around to palm the sharp blade I'd left abandoned by his head.

Maxon Wardwell.

That was the name my pimp went by. I didn't know his

real one. It was ironic since I knew other parts of him so well, as he did me.

Unwillingly, always unwillingly or unconsciously.

Some nights, my hair would hurt and my body would be bruised and sore after he'd rape me in his room. Others, I'd be so plied with drugs, I'd have no idea what was being done to me.

"I'm doing you a favor, little girl. There are about a dozen men out there willing to break you in if not me. And, baby, they'll be much rougher than I am," he said as he held his hand against my neck, cutting off my airflow. I clawed at his arm, but he was latched on. Maxon's other meaty hand traveled to the hem of my dress, and I couldn't kick out my legs to stop him. I was pinned to the bed, completely useless and weak—a vivid corpse. *"You've been here for five months now, but you might as well still be fresh meat. You haven't been easy to declaw, though I sure have fun trying."*

"I'm never letting you win," I spat with as much energy as I could muster.

His laughter made my skin crawl as it rolled over my exposed chest when he lowered his mop of unkempt brown hair.

I withered underneath him, struck out until he pinned my hands over my head, using his hips to drive my dress up. He had easy access to my entrance. We weren't allowed to wear underwear. Another rule meant to demean and belittle.

I was nothing but a walking entity with multiple entry points for men like him to take advantage of.

"Oh, honey, I already have." He breathed harshly in my ear, a second before I felt the sharp sting between my thighs of him entering me without remorse.

Fighting came easily to me, inflicting pain. But at that

moment, numbness spread over my limbs, something that happened when I was drugged, allowing him to move freely inside of me.

He was right.

He had won.

A fitting end for a villain, falling prey to another. My dignity was torn off excruciatingly, threads of it coming apart every time a different body was forced in me. And now they wanted to get rid of me?

Cigar smoke tickled my nose, and instead of scrunching my face and turning away, I walked closer to the half-open door at the end of the hallway. They had all the girls pamper themselves and dress well today, a treatment we reserved only for special guests. And he was currently in Maxon's office. They said curiosity killed the cat, but death didn't sound so bad when you were barely surviving.

The old floorboards that usually groaned under my weight were silent tonight as I took a peek inside the shadowed room. Max sat behind a grand mahogany desk. The other man referred to as Carlos leaned against a bookcase stacked with files, staring out the window next to him as he swirled the whiskey inside his crystal tumbler.

"Where did you shop the brunette with the big mouth from?" He arched a dark brow at Max, mouth set in a firm line.

"The one that looks like she needs a cock in her every hole to finally shut the fuck up?" Max laughed crudely, and the glint in his eyes made my blood chill. I had an inkling I knew who they were talking about if the new guy's frown was anything to go by, when I presented myself in pajamas when every other girl was shoved in a mini dress with sequins.

4

"*Yeah, that sounds about right.*" His tone was indifferent as he shrugged.

"*A druggie from Southie dropped her off. Exchanged his girlfriend for a bag of crack,*" Max explained, and the back of my neck prickled with heat when he reminded me who got me here in the first place.

Easton Smith was the first man I went on a date with when I moved to Boston. I was a stupid girl who looked at the wrong place to hide when she was shunned. I got sucked in by his charm and the abundance of white lines on his kitchen table that provided me with the relief my disturbed brain craved.

Sweat dotted my forehead when Carlos went on again, circling the desk and standing in front of Max, his broad build disrupting my view of him. "*Don't you think it's time to let her go? She's too much work for what she's worth.*"

Let her go? As in, set me free?

Excitement hit me so hard it felt a little bit like horror shook me to my core. I pressed my body to the wall and tried to remain silent as I peered through the crack.

"*I'm having Landon dispose of her by the end of the month, but I plan on getting my fun in for a few more nights. Their screams always taste sweeter when they struggle.*"

Pain radiated from my bottom lip when I bit down on it, holding back my gasp.

Why are you so shocked? *A little voice whispered in my head.* Wasn't this what you wanted? Death over a life of modern-day slavery? You worked for this. It'll all be over soon.

I had worked for it. Bit, scratched, punched, and repaid their treatment tenfold. No wonder this man wanted me gone.

I was hurting his business. But was I truly ready to die at the hands of my rapists? Let them live on and hurt more women?

"Not much value in terms of money, however. Our customers want to feel wanted, not a bitch screaming bloody murder whenever a man enters her room." Carlos's voice carried the edge of an ultimatum. "This week, Max, I want her gone by the end of this week."

Except, I'd beat them to it by five days.

A sharp sting in my palm had me refocusing on the matter at hand. Max blended into the background as I watched when more blood pooled in my hands. My own, this time, from the brand-new diagonal slash.

Bile rushed up my throat as my mind started processing the evening. But what accelerated my anxiety was what was yet to follow: the wild goose chase I'd willingly subjected myself to for the rest of my life. I couldn't kill one of theirs and live free, but most importantly, I couldn't know what I did and roam through everyday life with no repercussions. Names were ingrained in my mind, along with faces I wished I could forget.

Dawn would wipe off the stars from the night sky soon, and they'd know as soon as they saw him who did it. People had seen him pushing me in his designated bedroom—more people than I could ever kill with a single dagger.

Nausea rolled through me at the thought of taking another life.

I had no other choice but to run.

The window over a desk overflowing with used needles was my safest bet. I could survive with a broken pelvis; a bullet in the back of my head was a different story.

My gaze swept over the floor as I crawled out of bed, trying hard to ignore the bloodbath I'd left behind. I kept my injured hand cradled against my chest as I cracked open the window, taking in greedy inhales of fresh air and washing out the iron-like scent from my nostrils. I wanted to peel off layers of my skin to stop feeling so dirty, to get his essence off me, but I had no time to freak out right now.

Go. Go. Go.

I kept repeating the word to keep my mind clear of any other thoughts. A palpable thrill rushed down my spine as I gazed out at the streets shrouded in darkness. I was small in build; they wouldn't see me.

Hoisting my leg on the desk and gripping the windowsill, I couldn't help one last look back at the consequences of my actions. Ice-kissed December wind caressed my neck and chest as I let my eyes roam over Maxon's body one last time, and a sick feeling unruffled in my gut.

Satisfaction.

It wasn't me lying dead and naked, pale as snow, defeated in my own game. Something told me this wouldn't be the last time we met, but our next reunion would have to wait until I joined him underground.

"See you in Hell, Max," I whispered and leaped into the dead of night.

CHAPTER ONE
ARES

"How's the soundproofing of this house?" my tormentor for the last hour asked, tugging her curtain bangs behind her ear.

Usually, house showings stretched for twenty to thirty minutes, but she'd been wasting my time for over an hour now. Her kids weren't remarkably well-mannered either, screaming up a storm in the backyard as they chased each other. They would have more than a few problems with the neighbors if they decided to put down an offer.

"Are you planning on having many loud parties?" I asked as we walked into the master bedroom. Our interior designer had made sure to stage the house according to the neighborhood's demographic, going for a homey but modern look, perfect for a middle-class family. The white walls and dark wood trims of the furniture created a well-balanced contrast of light and dark, making for a pleasant atmosphere. Sans any personality, but having opinions was overrated in our day and age.

Elaine clutched the pearls around her neck as she spun

around in a circle, taking in the king-sized bed, half covered in throw pillows.

"Gosh, no. It's just that I don't want my kids to hear my husband and me..." She thumbed the lining of the bed, looking back at me with a suggestive smile on her face. "We can get quite loud. Especially when we have *guests* over in our bedroom."

I crossed my arms, and her eyes turned molten when my muscles strained against my blue dress shirt. I was far from ugly at six foot five, with a mop of brown hair sleeked over on one side, and hazel eyes that looked gold when the light hit them at the right angle (according to my ex-girl-friend's assessment; to me, they looked poop brown). I also had an athletic build, maintained by daily visits to the gym.

Getting hit on wasn't a rare occasion; getting hit on by a mother whose screaming kids were currently tearing down the living room *was* a first.

Her smile got wider, and paired with her vacant pale eyes, she reminded me of those porcelain dolls in horror movies that hoovered up kiddie souls for survival. Her stilettos clicked on the floor as she advanced my way, about to make her move.

At the last minute, I stepped aside, ushering her out of the room to avoid a scene, and we continued our path down the hall without a hitch. If dodging advances by desperate women was a competitive sport, I would've won a gold medal.

I didn't need to close this deal. Alsford Realty was on an upward spiral, after all. Still, it wouldn't be what it was, had it not been for our complete devotion to every deal, no matter how luxurious or minor. And I guess having a *my way or the highway* attitude when conducting business didn't hurt either.

"The house is equipped with insulation foam. You have nothing to worry about." I focused solely on her question, removing my hand from the small of her back as we slowly checked out the rest of the rooms.

"That's good," she said, a disappointing tinge coloring her voice. "Um, so, how old are you, Mr... May I call you Ares? You seem so young."

Already moving into first-name territory... I walked faster.

"Thirty-one, ma'am," I answered, my lips curling downwards. "Not *that* young."

I wish I was young again.

It was ironic, really. All I thought about when I was a kid was growing up. At fifteen, I couldn't wait one more year to get my license. At seventeen, college seemed like *the* dream destination with no overbearing parents, filled to the brim with older girls and parties that went on twenty-four-seven. At twenty, I couldn't take one more day of watching the girl I liked pine after my best friend. Then, at twenty-nine, everything slowed down. I had my dream company, my house, and great friends. On top of that, a girlfriend that was funny, intelligent, and independent—the holy trinity for me.

I was getting wary because life never flowed smoothly for too long. And later that year, it turned out I had a reason to be when my parents died in a car accident. They were driving to their vacation home in Cape Cod when a drunk driver took their lives. Their car was totaled, crushed in such a way there were no survivors.

I felt my chest constrict as a dark cloud settled over my shoulders. An obnoxious ringing noise sounded from deep within my ears. The light spilling from the first floor took over my field of vision as we came to stand in front of the spiral stairs.

With a head nod, I let Elaine pass first as I rubbed my hands down my gray cigar pants and grabbed onto the railing to combat the dizziness that tried to take over.

"Please, you've barely hatched," she continued, and for the first time, I was grateful for the annoying pitch of her voice piercing through the numbness in my mind. "This neighborhood is so nice," she gushed, looking through the floor-to-ceiling windows once we reached the end of the staircase. Suburbia was in full force here, with colonial houses dotted around the street, fully equipped with hulking SUVs next to every well-kept lawn.

"Sure is; Crestview High is three blocks south too, one of the top schools in the country. They have a hundred percent graduation rate." Hard not to when almost every parent belonged in the one percent. The money they donated every year didn't just go to building new facilities. After all, how many wings did a library need? "Your kids would fit right in," I said, trying to keep from cringing. The two boys were attacking the welcome cookies now, dropping crumbs all over the floor.

"And do you live nearby?" Elaine asked, and a shudder went through me when I faced her again. They looked exactly like her.

"Is that a prerequisite to you buying the home?"

She flushed, giggling as she smoothed down the wrinkles on her pinstripe dress. "You're so funny, Ares. No, of course not. I was just wondering since I've heard some rumors about Astropolis."

"Do tell." I raised a brow.

She leaned closer, as if she wanted to keep the rumors a secret. "They say once you move here, you never leave. People are so taken aback by the city's beauty that they instantly make it their forever home. *Traveler* magazine even nicknamed Astropolis as America's Amsterdam."

I failed to comprehend how this was a rumor when even news outlets had picked up on it, but I didn't dispute her logic. We indeed had a problem with over-tourism, and the locals were none too happy about it. Even those that left eventually found their way back after a few years. Like Killian Astor, who seemed to be hanging around more and more lately, much to his brother Saint's dismay.

Well, almost everyone.

My jaw flexed at the unwelcome reminder. Instead, I fixated on a flock of birds flying over Elaine's head out the windows, sliding my hands in my front pockets to stop the oncoming downward spiral of my thoughts.

"I guess there's some truth to that statement." I shrugged. "But I don't live near this area. Astropolis is quite spacious. The city covers a lot of land, *even though it might not seem like it.*" The last sentence came out hushed, causing Elaine to squint at me.

"What was that?"

"I said, people here are amiable"—*all up in your business*—"so even though the city is big, there will always be someone nearby to lend a helping hand when you need it."

"Great, that's what we're counting on!" She smiled, and her teeth looked a little too perfect not to be veneers.

I bet you are.

Before she could carry on with her interrogation, I was saved by my ringtone. I took a quick glance at the screen, knowing full well I would've answered even if it was a solicitor. Unfortunately for me, it was someone worse.

Taking a deep sigh, I smiled apologetically at Elaine. "Shoot, I'm sorry, I have to take this. Do you mind? I'll only be a minute."

"Not at all. I'll just take a look at the pool outside."

I watched her and her spawns exit through the back door before answering, and I didn't even have to speak. Saint's unamused voice greeted me as soon as the beeping stopped. "Where *are* you?"

"Hi, Saint. Oh, me? I'm great. How are you?" I replied sarcastically.

"About to pop if I have to blow one more balloon. The kid's turning *one*. I don't see the point in all this. It's not like he's gonna remember shit anyway."

I was not one to laugh at someone else's misery... except when that someone else was either Saint Astor or Leonardo Bianchi. I'd known the poor bastards since kindergarten, and while they got along fine on most occasions, they clashed more often than not. I imagined spending an entire day together, setting up a birthday party for Leo's son would've led to an argument or four.

"And you'd think being a professional athlete would've taught you a thing or two about breath control."

"Stop acting smart, Alsford. You were supposed to be here twenty minutes ago to help with Matt's birthday party, and you were oh-so eager to agree when Eliana said she wanted to DIY this whole thing."

"You know Leo hates it when you call him Matt," I reminded, heading over to the fridge, grateful to find it stacked with water bottles. My mouth was parched. I wasn't a big talker, part of the reason why I didn't take on any showings.

"All the more reason to call him that." I could hear the smirk in his voice and his wife's frustrated sigh in the background. Did I say four arguments? Probably up to ten. "Tell me you're pulling up the drive. We have to carry two tables to the terrace."

Suddenly, Elaine wasn't as unbearable as I initially thought. A sore back, however, was a whole different story.

"Sorry, man, you have to do it without me. One of my agents had to cancel last minute, and I took over her appointments as a favor."

"Since when did you start taking over appointments as a favor?" I heard a balcony door sliding open on his end, and the microphone picked up the slight whistle of the wind. "Is she hot?"

"She's in labor as we speak," I deadpanned.

"Ah, is the baby daddy in the picture?"

"Jesus." I laughed out loud. "I'm not *that* desperate."

"Aren't you, though? You haven't gone out with anyone since you dumped Sonia. You're losing your touch, Ares."

"You're keeping tabs on my dating life? Are you that bored?"

"You're the only wild card left. I'm living vicariously through you." An *ouch* soon followed his statement, and I didn't have to hear his following sentence to know Aria smacked him. "Babe, come on, it was a *joke!*"

I chuckled, chucking the empty water bottle into the bin and taking a peek outside. Judging by the way Elaine was chasing the brats, trying to get them to slow down, I had a little while before I needed to hang up.

"I'll have you know I was just indirectly invited to be part of a throuple."

"Throuple? I thought you weren't into that."

Yeah, sharing wasn't my form of caring, unlike him. Saint had been the talk of every gossip column during his single years and not without merit. The young heir of a billion-dollar high-fashion company, painting the town red with a different girl on his arm every night? The headline basically sold itself.

I thought I was dreaming when he announced his engagement to Ariadne Fleur. I believed he was set on having a Hugh Hefner kind of lifestyle, with his very own Playboy Mansion.

"There's always a first time for everything," I lied through my teeth, mostly to get them to stop riding my ass about my dating life.

"I love how you expect me to believe that," he snorted out.

Loud voices fleeted through the exit again, and I wrapped up the conversation. "Don't break your back carrying that table on the terrace, Astor."

"At least be here half an hour before the party starts. Eliana wants to take pictures."

"Tell her not to worry. I have one more showing after this. I'll make sure to wrap it up quickly," I assured.

With her hands circling the shoulders of either rowdy boy, Elaine met me in the middle of the hallway. "Ares, we'd like to put in an offer!"

I checked my watch one more time, tapping my foot on the ground as I rested my weight on an overgrown dogwood tree. The universe was set on me not attending Matteo's party today. My current appointment was fifteen minutes late, and I was giving her five more before I bounced.

A drop of sweat slid between my shoulder blades, and the time got reduced to two minutes.

Fuck, it was hot.

Winters were cruel in Massachusetts, but summers were unbearably humid...or maybe my ass was too spoiled to survive without an AC in the middle of June.

This place was very unlike the last house, a fixer-upper through and through. The price was a steal for this neighborhood, but renovations would probably cost upwards of a hundred thousand dollars. A realtor's job was never to repel people from buying, though, so as far as I was concerned, it could rival the likes of the White House.

Creeping ivy had taken over the exposed white brick exterior, spreading on the windows. The few front steps leading to the entrance could use some sweeping. And I already knew by glancing inside, a fresh coat of paint was non-negotiable. As was a functional AC system, hence why I was currently dying in ninety-degree heat.

At least a slight breeze was picking up...and with it, my need to hop on my bike and go. I blew out a frustrated breath, glancing at my watch.

Then, when my head was down-turned and facing the cracked driveway, a sudden screeching noise came from my right side, painting the image of tires skidding out of control.

My heart rate picked up, and my imagination wasn't so far off reality when I turned sharply, watching a tragedy unfold in slow motion. I froze in place, the blood in my veins icing over when a pink Beetle rushed toward the driveway, its acceleration too fast to break in time. It came forth with such speed, my bike was a goner, dragged across the concrete, and slammed against the garage door like a rag doll.

What the hell?

Fury danced along my skin, prickling it with rage. The car pulled to a stop, and it was all I could do not to rush over and punch whoever was sitting behind the wheel. Getting charged with assault wasn't on my bucket list, though, so I memorized the car's license plate as I rushed to my motorcycle to assess the damage.

"Oh my God," a female's voice sounded behind me. I barely heard her as I focused on the matter at hand. "Are you okay?"

"I'm not the one that's not okay," I snapped, touching the dented clutch cover. My eyes spread over the side of the motorcycle, seeing how it bent inwards in the middle and outwards on the sides, resembling a bowl.

Great.

Fucking perfect.

"Did I hit you?" she asked, and my jaw ticked as I picked up a sharp piece of glass, no doubt originating from the shattered headlights.

"Obviously, it wasn't *me* you hit." Sarcasm dripped from my voice, and I straightened my back as I looked at her for the first time.

There wasn't much to look at.

She was wearing a giant floppy hat and black sunglasses twice the size of her face that left...well, *much* to the imagination, along with her black sundress, which save for the dip across her chest revealing some of her firm breasts, ended right below her knees.

"You rushed in front of the car last minute, and I thought I caught you too." She gestured with her hands, staring at the wreck, the lines of her face set in harsh lines. "I-I'm really sorry about your bike."

I cocked my head as I assessed her, drowning the misogynistic part of me that screamed, *this is why women don't belong behind the wheel.* Of course, men were just as bad, but hell, being unfair came easy when you were wronged by a pink Beetle driver that looked like she was heading to a funeral.

"What *I* want to know is who goes fifty miles an hour in a residential area? And most importantly, doesn't slow down right before they're about to brake?" My voice came out harder than I intended, and she still hadn't looked up to face me.

Her head was tilted downwards, shoulders slumped slightly forward, like a sulky child that knew they fucked up and were in some serious trouble.

"This is my friend's car. I'm just borrowing it for the day. I'm not used to it," she explained.

"If you're not used to it, then maybe you shouldn't be driving it," I snapped.

"Look, I said I'm sorry. I'll pay for any damages."

"I hope your friend has some good insurance then, cause it's gonna be a hell of a bill, sweetheart. This bike was only in production for a year. Parts are tough to come by," I voiced, and her head swung up as if I'd hit her.

Finally, I could see a little bit past her hat, to her full pursed mouth, painted a berry red, the only bold choice amidst her drab fashion sense. She had cute tiny nostrils too that itched her glasses up when they flared on either side.

Her mouth dropped as if to say something, and my brows knitted when no words escaped her. Instead, she just stood there staring at me like she was encased in marble, every part of her body stilling until I was barely able to tell if she was breathing. I'd be worried if it wasn't for her fists clenching and unclenching on either side.

"Well?" I prompted, the silence getting to me.

"W-What are you doing h-here?" she stuttered, and the slight movement broke through the onyx surface of her sunglasses, her eyes fluttering rapidly.

"Excuse me?" I said a little too smoothly, a telltale sign I was being pushed to my limits.

"I was supposed to meet Amy for the house tour. Amy's a girl's name. You're not a girl," she replied, her tone robotic and a hint deeper than it was before, like it'd aged a thousand years in a single second.

I took a step back, the thumping in my chest shocking me into silence. A murky part of my brain reigned for a single second as I looked at her long and hard, trying to understand where this sudden case of déjà vu came from. Her thin shoulders seemed to curve inward, as if bending from the power of my stare. When she dropped her head once again, the feeling dissipated into thin air.

Weird.

"So you remember her name, but not the time your tour was scheduled?" I put some extra bite behind my words for some unknown reason.

"I'm a little bit late." She cringed.

"Explains you driving like a maniac," I sighed, rubbing

the sweat off the back of my neck. It was inexplicably sunny today. "Amy couldn't make it, so I'm covering for her."

Her face tightened, and my eyes took a dive when she crossed her arms, the most visible part of her standing to full attention. God, her chest was phenomenal, complete with silk-like skin that was begging for my teeth.

"Oh please, it's not like you don't have fifty more motor-cycles in your garage," she scoffed, tapping her heel on the ground.

"How do you know that?"

"'The Alsford Heir's One Million Dollar Motorcycle Collection'?" She posed the title as a question, referencing an interview I'd done a few years ago. "Do you forget your celebrity status, Mr. Alsford?"

"I'm a businessman."

"With a knack for showing off the finer things in your life. You also look like one of those guys addicted to green smoothies and the gym, and your jaw could cut glass. So that automatically elevates your status from an average busi-nessman to a rich man I wouldn't mind spending the rest of my days with because he has enough money to get me anything I want and is not seventy years old." She picked some lint off her dress, one side of her mouth tipping up. "Don't be coy. You must know almost every girl in this town is obsessed with you."

I wasn't one to complain about the struggles of belonging to the top one percent, but she was right. The scrutiny that came with being in my position wasn't something to write home about. Girls were already in love with the idea of me before even getting to know *me*. It sucked the fun right out of dating, and I found myself doing less and less of that.

Besides, being a phone call away from getting my dick wet every night sucked the fun right out of trying too.

"And I'm assuming you're one of those girls. Is that why you destroyed my vehicle—to make an impression?" I asked, just to spite her. I didn't know how she'd made a compliment sound like an insult, but I didn't like it.

"I said, *almost* every girl. I make do fine on my own, Mr. Alsford. And wannabe bad boys are not my type, especially when they're way too old for the persona they're trying to imitate."

To my utter annoyance, I noticed my ears felt hot. I resisted the urge to touch them. I wasn't blushing. That was a fact. I never blushed. Her lips puckered, and I realized the longer it took for me to respond, the harder it was for her to fight her smile.

Gritting my teeth, I strove to be a picture of nonchalance as I clutched one hand over my heart, reaching for my phone with the other one. "Your words wound me, truly. And as much as I would love to sit around and trade insults with you all day, I'm going to need your name and phone number."

That pulled the plug on the smile. "What for?"

"The police report? You know, for the accident you just caused five seconds ago?"

She blanched under my stare, and satisfaction rushed up my spine at getting to her. God, I hadn't cared about anyone's opinion since middle school. I didn't know why being considered *uncool* by this stranger mattered to me.

"Right, right..." She fisted the skirt of her dress, and the cinnamon scent wafting toward my face from her U-turn almost stunned me speechless. The sweet spice with a hint of citrus evoked memories I'd rather keep locked in Pandora's box where the rest of my sins lay. Alas, like the ocean, they ebbed and flowed whenever they pleased. Sometimes the water was calm, and other times it was overwhelming. It took me years to learn how not to let them drown me.

A vision of bold red lipstick and shiny dark hair flashed behind my eyelids at my slow blink. A siren's call, melodic and smooth, too entangled with my soul to ever leave.

It couldn't be...

I fixated on the woman's back when I regained my vision. Seeing voluptuous curves instead of a bony build. Light almond brown hair touched the arch of her ass and seamed tights with the black line on the back, starting from below her heels and disappearing underneath her dress. It was almost like they showed you the direction of every man's thoughts whenever they spotted a woman in them.

When my pants started becoming unceremoniously constricting over my dick, I turned to stone. *Shit*, I didn't know what was worse, getting hard at the remembrance of the past or over the woman that crashed my bike.

Both.

Definitely both.

I knew my place in a mental asylum was guaranteed when I breached the age of seventy and had made peace with that fact. So, shaking out of my stupor, I followed close behind her when she reached her car, shifting the fabric over my nether region.

"Hey, where are you going?"

She opened the driver's door, but instead of driving away, she bent over and reached for the armrest. I tried, I tried really hard not to look, but her backside was more impressive than her front. Even her nun-like attire couldn't disguise the jiggle of her ass as she rummaged through the interior. At one point, her leg came up, and it was game over.

My mouth was watering, and I was adjusting my pants again when she came out for air, a sleek black and white card clutched in one hand.

"Here." She extended her arm, but I didn't reach for it. I willed my dick to find the south as appealing as the north because if I let go of my pockets right now, I'd be left with a *very* massive and *very* obvious erection.

"What is it?"

Grandmas in walkers. Adult diapers. World hunger. Smoking. Septum piercings.

"My business card—all my information is there since I can't stick around for long." She shoved it in my direction again, and I widened my legs as I took it from her. "I actually passed by to see if we could reschedule the tour since I couldn't reach Amy's phone, but, um...yeah." Her eyes flicked to the scene.

My hard-on turned into a semi at the reminder, and a cruel smirk found its way on my face. "That's too bad, princess, I got places to be too, but I can't because of your ineptness to press the brake."

The corners of her lips rose, and instead of apologizing again like I thought she would—as she *should*—she said, "Call a tow truck and order an Uber, Mr. Alsford. I'm sure you can afford one."

"Oh, I can. Will you be able to afford the lawsuit I'll hit you with if you get in that car and drive away?"

In hindsight, what she was proposing would save me time too, but she inspired the asshat in me, especially when she shrugged, sinking in the driver's seat.

"We shall see, I guess. Again, sorry for the inconvenience. Can you tell Amy I called?" My nostrils flared at her nonchalance, and she had the gall to wave goodbye as she put her car in reverse.

To fight the urge to rush behind the Beetle kicking and screaming, I curled my fingers around her card, my sweaty grip glossing over the sans serif script that displayed her name.

Amelia Duante.

CHAPTER TWO

ARES

"Well, look who finally decided to grace us with his presence." Leonardo's emerald eyes glittered with inherent mirth as he clapped me over the back. He greeted me at the end of his sweeping drive, coupled with a meticulously cared-for lawn that decorated the way to his mansion.

Bianchi lived in a gated community on the hills of Astropolis, a few blocks down from me. The neighborhood was home to some of the biggest heavy loaders in the city. Property prices were set so high, new money could only dream of crossing past the two-feet-tall iron gates.

"Don't start." I passed by the huge-ass plants lining up each side of his double door entrance, so tired I was tempted to pass out in one of his thousand bedrooms upstairs. Waiting for half an hour under the blazing sun for a tow truck and then fifteen more minutes for an Uber had pretty much depleted any energy I had left to file a police report.

That didn't mean it wasn't going to happen. Ms. Duante's entitled attitude was pleading to be knocked down a peg or four, and I was entirely on board with being the one to do so.

If she'd thought she'd seen the last of me, she had another thing coming.

Lively chatter flowing down the long hallway, past the octagonal entry floor, reminded me I wasn't here for nap time. With a sigh, I fell into step with Leo. Running water ran along each side of the walkway, and butterfly koi fish swam through the filtered current. Navigating this corridor drunk, sure, was an adventure. And the bastard I liked to call my best friend may or may not have been holding on to embarrassing footage of me crushing the fishies' party by face-planting on the blue tiles after one too many glasses of sauvignon blanc.

"It's not me you have to worry about." He *tsked,* referring to his wife, who was the kind of person that come hell or high water, always showed up on time.

My face twisted into a grimace as I asked, "How mad is she?"

"From one to ten, I'd say about a solid six." Leo nodded toward the blue bag I was carrying. "What did you get him?"

"Moon sand in seven different colors since Bella wouldn't let him play with hers the other day." I held it up with a stupid grin. There were only so many things you could get a toddler that they couldn't choke on.

"Let's make that an eight. That's gonna be a mess to clean up." Leo cringed, looking at me with a *you're not so bright* expression before it changed to serene and utterly blasé in the blink of an eye as he asked, "So, part of a throuple, huh? That's what held you up?"

Rolling my eyes, I couldn't say that I was surprised he

was already clued in. "I see Saint's putting his big mouth to use."

"Eliana was telling Aria that if they were thinking of having kids, now would be the time, so they could be close in age with Matteo. He kinda freaked out and wanted to get the attention off himself."

"By throwing me under the bus? Got it." I was being dramatic, but if it bothered him, the huge smile that spread over his face when we rounded the corner of the living room and his kids came into view didn't let it show.

I bit my cheek to distract myself from the tightness in my chest. I shouldn't feel jealous of my friend's happiness, of his cozy home filled with first steps, tooth fairies, and childish laughter. He'd gone through the wringer to get to where he was at. But bitterness hung over my shoulder like a scythe. It was only a matter of time before Aria got pregnant, too, despite Saint's insistence on swearing off kids. And while being the designated cool uncle was fun, a certain distance was bound to follow as they both focused on raising their families.

Maybe it was loneliness influencing my ability to think straight because I'd never been so keen on having a built-in excuse to go to Disney World before. Mindless relationships and meaningless sex weren't cutting it anymore, though. Not when I got to hang out with these pussy-whipped asshats most days of the week.

"Judging by the stick up your ass, you did not partake in any Eiffel tower activities, did you?" Leo tilted his chin, tracking a little boy who offered his daughter a cupcake as if he was gifting her a ticking bomb.

It was safe to say the kid would have no dating life until she was at least thirty, and that was all good in my book.

"Eiffel tower activities?" An airy voice ambushed us from behind, and Eliana raised a blonde brow in question when we faced her. "Do I even *want* to know what that means?"

"Yeah, you do." I raked my eyes over her white shirt and velvet blue skirt, wrapping nicely around her curves. They had become way more prominent after giving birth twice. My suggestive tone got a little reaction out of Leo in the form of his elbow in my side, and I laughed, dodging him. "But the caveman you married wouldn't want you getting any ideas."

"You just made her ten times more intrigued," he snorted, and indeed her baby blues gleamed with unabashed curiosity.

"Little ballerina." I stepped forward, intercepting the line of questioning by taking her in my arms.

"Mr. Alsford, we missed you today." She returned the hug, her feminine scent encompassing me at the same time as her limbs.

"Well, if you took me up on my offer to run away together and leave this poor bastard behind, you wouldn't be missing me," I said over her head, loud enough for Leo to hear.

"*Oookay*, that's enough hugging." I couldn't help but laugh again when his hands came between us, separating us and tucking Eli under his arm. When she tried to pinch him, and he caught her hand in his, bringing her fingers to his lips, I swiftly looked away.

I was embarrassed to admit that the first thing I did at a kiddie party was check out the crowd for any single mothers. I was aware I'd hit rock bottom, but I needed some form of intimacy other than self-loving myself in the shower.

My eyes swept quickly over the space, starting with the

backyard first. The furthest I could see was the pavilion at the cusp of Bianchi's artificial lake. But, just my luck, I stumbled when I caught Sonia staring back at me—as in the girlfriend I'd dumped three months ago for no apparent reason.

I should've known she'd be here—she and Eli got the chance to bond while we were dating—but a little warning would've been welcome. I sent her what I hoped was a normal smile, but from the way she didn't return one back, probably meant I looked constipated.

"What happened to setting up the party on the terrace?" I asked, switching my attention away from my ex.

It made sense to have the party here. The open floor plan gave the kids plenty of space to play, and the wet bar conveniently tucked next to the kitchen gave the adults enough of a buzz to ignore their squealing responsibilities for a few hours. I couldn't imagine it wasn't hurtful seeing the handmade rugs covering cold French limestone floors being trampled on, though.

"Leo's back health is declining, and I thought it was best we stayed at ground level. Didn't want him pulling any muscles carrying heavy loads upstairs, right, baby?" Eli taunted, patting Leo's flat stomach through his polo shirt.

"Yup, only one of us carries heavy loads in this house." He smiled down at her, giving back tenfold. He groaned when, instead of a pat, she delivered a soft punch to his abdomen this time, her cheeks reddening at his innuendo.

God, they were unbearable—didn't even notice me slipping away because they were too busy making eyes at each other. After dropping off my bag at the gift table, I retreated to the bar, getting a scotch on the rocks since I was still partial to my life and couldn't throw myself down actual rocks.

Not even two sips in, blow number a thousand of the day came in the form of a blond man dressed in a designer suit, with a cute brunette plastered on his side. I heard him before I saw him—*even though he was built like a truck*—his words bleeding kindness as ever.

"What happened to you? You look like shit," Saint exclaimed.

Aria met my scowl with an apologetic grin. "Honey, that is not an appropriate way to greet people."

"Ares is not a person," he bounced back.

"Yeah," Leo joined in once he'd detached his mouth from Eli's. "We found him lurking around Area 51. Lord knows what alien planet he came from."

"It was one called your mother's pu—" I stopped abruptly when a curious three-year-old broke our little circle. She stared at me with curious blue eyes, so like her mother's, and I finished off by saying, "*Pumpkin.* Your mother's pumpkin."

Her brows knitted, and she made an *everything I thought I knew was a lie* face before asking, "You came out of a pumpkin, Uncle Ares?"

Now, how do I dig myself out of that one...

I scrubbed a hand over my five o'clock shadow, buying myself some time.

"Oh, this should be good." Saint chuckled into his wineglass.

"Hey, isn't that—" I paused for dramatic effect, bending down, so I was eye level with little Matteo sitting at the kids' table, sneaking his chubby fingers into his sister's frosting. "Isn't that Matteo taking a bite out of your piece of cake?"

Her head swung back so hard I thought she'd break her neck, and I held her from falling backward. Her hands turned to little fists, and in a few seconds, my pumpkin fiasco was forgotten as she stormed over to her brother. "You little brat, I told you to stop touching my things!"

Aria let out a slow whistle. "She's really not excited to have him around, is she?"

We all watched as she took her plate back while Matteo looked at her with puzzled eyes.

Leo sighed, shaking his head. "Her name is not the only thing she took after my sister. She's a little bully, just like her."

Eliana snorted, as if that was the most ridiculous thing she'd ever heard. "Please, I have a hard time believing you were bullied. You never run out of retorts."

"I had to learn how to be tough the hard way."

"And by *the hard way,* he means over strategically placed Legos when he was five and purposefully dumped tampons inside his shoes when they turned thirteen," I added, remembering his horrified gaze when he found out his twin sister started menstruating.

The rest of the night moved on without a hitch, if you counted out me lurking in the corner while Eliana blew out Matteo's candles, googling Amelia Duante's name like a creep. The composed energy she radiated stayed with me. One thing lingering on my mind was watching it dissolve under a wave of boiling hot water. I didn't know what I was hoping to find, but certainly a—*Your search - **Amelia Duante** - did not match any documents*—result wasn't it. My face scrunched. Who didn't have a digital footprint in

LICK OF FIRE

our era? An Instagram account, Facebook, Twitter, hell, I'd even settle for LinkedIn.

Breathing out my nose, I pocketed my phone and let the alcohol burn sweetly down my throat. I was doing fine, erasing the memory of her for a couple of hours until I had to relay what happened, and got mad all over again. What fucked with me the most was that she was probably cool as a mint while I was busy stewing.

"Ares..." A petite brunette interrupted my inner dialogue, quite literally the epitome of every *don't let size fool you* quote. Moira Lawson had a big personality and even bigger ocean eyes with long lashes fanning her cheeks, which gave her that innocent, ready-to-be-corrupted vibe as she stared up at you from her knees.

We had our fun occasionally.

"Moira." I straightened up. "How are you?"

"Great, I was wondering if you had any plans for tomorrow night." She was not one to beat around the bush.

I smiled. "My schedule's all cleared up for you, baby."

Even if I did have plans, I'd cancel. I needed to clear my head, and sex was the best kind of therapy there was. Mirroring my grin, Moira left a few minutes after we finalized our *date*, if you could even call it that.

I didn't expect to be faced with misty eyes and a scowl when I turned, but that was precisely what happened as Sonia brushed past me, muttering *"Asshat"* under her breath.

I glanced at Eli, standing off to the side, her face set in a frown. "What did I do?"

"Well, the general rule of thumb is not to flirt with other people in front of exes that still aren't over us."

"Fucking hell." I scrubbed a hand down my face, starting for the stairs that'd get me on one of the main balconies upstairs. I needed to smoke, and I doubted any of the parents present would be down with me doing so out in the backyard.

"Want to talk about it?" Eli asked as we stepped out into the fresh air. I knew she was following me. She had a thing for doubling as everyone's free therapist, the type of person to foster a stray, even if it was threatening to bite her hand off.

"Talk about what?" I lit my joint, and she came to stand next to me. We stared at the lush garden underneath, the green lawn neatly trimmed, cutting off and giving way to a bluestone terrace that held a kidney-shaped pool, in silence for a while.

"Why you've had that *someone ran over my puppy* look on your face the whole afternoon. Is it only because of your bike?"

"Yeah, I just had a shitty day, that's all." I shrugged, taking a drag and letting the ashes drop on the natural white stone below.

"But you've been broody every day this month. Come to think of it, every May, your panties are always in a twist."

I stiffened further, the weed running through my system but not acting fast enough. "Must be my unlucky month."

Eli shifted closer, resting her elbows on the railing and looking back at me with a raised brow that told me she knew a lot more than she was letting on. And indeed, her following words had me holding my breath. "Also, the month *she* left. You know, I always thought it was just some crush, that you were infatuated with the idea of something you wanted but couldn't have." She shook her head. "But the more I see you, year after year treating every relationship like it has an expiration date, I'm starting to believe you never really got over her."

I ignored the dip in my stomach. "Has it ever occurred to you that maybe they weren't the ones?"

"It did." She nodded. "But you and Sonia were doing so well. It was the happiest I'd ever seen you in a long time...and then you cut her off in the blink of an eye."

She didn't know what she was talking about.

My parents died, and I needed some time alone. That was all there was. No grand thought process. No hidden crush behind my decision to break up with Sonia.

"You're overthinking things." Smoke clouded my vision, and the relief I felt to be obstructed from Eli's gaze was damning. There was something terrifying about being in the presence of a woman that could crush you with the truth.

"I tried looking for her," she admitted, and my oxygen intake ceased utterly. "A few months after she left. Leo didn't speak to me for a week as a sign of protest. It didn't matter; what she'd done, who she'd become the past few years... I-I knew it wasn't her. Hurt people *hurt* people, and, man, thinking back, we were all a bunch of immature little assholes."

I was glad Eliana had someone like Leo to look out for her because a heart that big attracted every bloodthirsty bulldog in the area to chew her like a squeaky toy. Serena Laurent had bullied her for years, physically assaulted her, and tried to ruin her goddamn relationship. I didn't understand how she could be so forgiving. My expression told her that much, and she faced the open air again, sighing heavily.

"Don't get me wrong, the bitch deserves to suffer, but I couldn't turn off the part of me that worried about my childhood best friend, penniless, homeless, and left to fend for herself. The government seized all of her father's assets after the trial, and Serena's mom came from virtually nothing."

I hated myself for knowing how she felt like, for having experienced that concern for someone that didn't deserve an ounce of it. Serena was a master at making a mess out of her personal relationships, taking until you had nothing left to give. Disappointment would follow you like a shadow if you expected people to act as you would, though. So, at the end of the day, it was no one's fault but my own for licking the wounds Leo inflicted, for expecting her to choose me, for letting myself be treated as nothing more than a second choice when I wanted more.

Looking for her crossed my mind once or twice, but I didn't believe she wanted to be found, especially by me.

My cigarette's accumulated ash fell on my other hand, and the sting was enough to snap me to the present. I didn't wipe it off, letting the pain spread as it had on a pair of haunting brown eyes the last time I saw her.

You know what? Fuck her.

She didn't deserve any sympathy.

"Why are you telling me this?" I asked harshly.

Eliana wasn't intimidated by my tone, glancing back at me, unimpressed. A single peek that said, *I've known you for years, who are you trying to fool?* My jaw tightened, and that was the only answer the unspoken question got.

"Aren't you going to ask me what I found?"

"No." I crushed my half-finished joint under the tip of my boot, this time actually starting for one of their guest rooms. I was in no position to be alone tonight. "I don't want to know. She could be dead for all I care."

Eliana didn't come after me this time, but she didn't have to. What she said next had me stopping dead in my tracks, my heart climbing up my throat like it wanted to take permanent residence there.

"She might as well be because..." Worry simmered under her tone, and I could detect a tiny bit of guilt too. "The P.I. couldn't find anything on her."

CHAPTER THREE
AMELIA

"Don't you look positively ravishing," Elliot, my coworker Elsa's younger brother, said as I reached their table inside the bustling Ruby's Corner. The name was fitting, given that the bar was tiny and packed this Friday night but charming with its fairy lights and cozy wood countertops.

"I know, right? Training with Sloan is starting to pay off." I hung my crossbody clutch on the side of my chair, not lingering on how weird the words felt coming out of my mouth.

It had been about two months since I moved to Astropolis and started a new job at an up-and-coming electric vehicle and clean energy company. I applied on a whim, not expecting to gain anything out of it. My resume wasn't all that impressive. I was missing all of the years of experience companies required an applicant to have fresh out of college. My nonexistent work experience was hard to explain without any kids or a husband (or, as I liked to call them, adult toddlers).

I didn't even want to be here. It wasn't my first choice, but it *was* my only one, so I sucked it up.

"You know what would make you even more attractive?" the twenty-year-old asked as I kissed his sister on the cheek, settling next to her. They had similar laugh lines, deep dark skin, and beautifully braided hair. "Some humility."

I wrinkled my nose, thumbing the strap of my red leather mini dress. "Humility has no place in a body this hot."

His feline eyes traced my strategic move, and despite my finger wobbling to abandon my self-paved path at the spark of interest behind his browns, I didn't remove it. Tonight was a test for me. A test of shedding off my layers and getting comfortable with wearing any outfit I liked both inside and outside the house.

"There are genuinely good people out there, Amelia. I know it's hard, but you shouldn't let your trauma define you. Slowly but surely challenge yourself to take a step out of the box."

My therapist's advice played in the back of my mind like a broken record, and I breathed steadily through all the smells and noise. A mix of sweat, perfume, and alcohol topped off the chatter of the crowds and Dua Lipa's voice singing softly in the background.

"You're right, someone else does, but you're playing hard to get." Elliot sent me a charming smile, and tension ebbed off my shoulders.

Elsa choked on a sip next to me, and I scoffed. "Find someone your own age, squirt."

"Can't." He shrugged. "Cougars are more up my speed."

"My God," Elsa jumped in, hiding her face behind her hands. "Remind me again why I let you tag along with my friends and me?"

"I've heard there's a retirement home a few blocks south," I played along, mildly offended that he called me a cougar. I was about to close in on thirty-one, still in my prime...only with some added back pain. "They have bingo nights every Friday at seven. You might still make it if you run."

"You think you're so funny." His eyes narrowed, and I smiled sweetly.

"I don't think so. I know so."

Elliot pretended to pout even though there were about five women in our vicinity eyeballing the hell out of him, and I pretended not to be jealous. Not because they wanted Elliot, because they were *attracted* to him. Because they had feelings. Because they were fucking normal.

I couldn't get past the friendship zone with any guy out of my own volition. I mean, who the hell would settle for damaged goods, anyway? I was fucked in more ways than one.

"Don't be so glum, Elliot," Elsa comforted him, her voice dry as a chalkboard. "You wouldn't have been able to date her behind bars either way."

I groaned when she brought it up again, regretting even telling her in the first place. I couldn't escape it, though, not when the car belonged to her, and I had to apologize profoundly for involving her in this. She was kind enough to lend it to me when mine was in the shop.

Elliot's face sparked with interest as he faced me, scrubbing the five o'clock shadow on his chin. "What'd you do, Duante?"

"Nothing worth discussing for the millionth time," I bit out. "Besides, I still haven't received a phone call from the police."

Elsa's eyes rounded. "It's only been *one* day."

"Maybe he realized one missing bike wouldn't hurt his collection of a thousand."

"Maybe you're way in over your head."

I bit my bottom lip, knowing she was right, but hoping otherwise. Fate was cruel, getting me into an accident with the one guy I was trying to avoid the most since coming back.

I shifted in my seat, crossing my legs tight at the memory of his piercing gaze. Heavy lashes bracketed stormy eyes that held depth unlike I'd ever seen of him before. He'd grown up a lot, some of that boyish charm replaced by an overflowing intensity that was apparent in his cutting replies and body that screamed, *I'll support your weight with one hand while eating you out on the saddle of my bike.*

A pulse networked its way up my body, and I gulped, wetting my parched throat. You could count on me to always go for the worst of the worst. Maybe I hadn't found anyone to treat me badly enough. That was why I hadn't been able to commit to a relationship. Maybe I liked being treated like dirt, and that was why my body reacted to him when it hadn't for anyone else for the past five years.

"Okay, someone needs to clue me in," Elliot piped in again, prompting an eager Elsa to start explaining. I wasn't in the mood to sit and listen again, mainly because my mind would wander off to territories it had no business re-entering.

"I'm getting a drink. Do you guys want something?" I interrupted, mentally jotting their orders down before starting for the bar.

The lighting became more intimate the closer I got, instead relying on the illuminated shelves supporting several hundred bottles of alcohol. None of which I was allowed to have.

Relying on liquor to take away the critical moments of my past was something I'd gotten too reliant on. Trading white lines for amber liquids made sense at one point. They were cheaper, widely available, and not as damaging in the short term anyway. So whenever I craved coke, I had a drink instead. Once a day, twice a day, until I was drunk all twenty-four hours of a day and forwent my rule of having either alcohol or drugs.

It was easy until it wasn't. Until I had to get my stomach pumped and my priorities checked. I'd narrowly escaped one evil. I didn't want to kill myself after all that hard fucking work. I guess it was my narcissistic tendencies that helped save my life. I had no one else to live for other than me.

Ordering two gin martinis and a virgin cocktail for me, I drummed my fingers on the countertop as I waited. Of course, I couldn't help but overhear the pretty loud conversation the couple next to me was having... Okay, it wasn't loud. I was just nosey.

Tucking my hair behind my ear, I turned my body at a sixty-degree angle, seeing a tall blond man and a much smaller Asian woman in my peripheral vision.

"What's the matter, Ava?" he asked, leaning closer. I couldn't make out his face, but something about his voice and the straight slope of his nose struck a chord with me.

"I-I'm just wondering if meeting *here* i-in public like this is wise," she clarified, throwing sly glances over her shoulder. "Goldberg has stringent anti-fraternization policies."

Goldberg.

I rolled the word in my mouth, spelling it out against my

teeth. *I knew that name.* A sixth sense swooped in like second nature.

"Coworkers meet for drinks all the time," he reasoned, and I could tell he was getting frustrated with her.

"Yeah, but we're not just coworkers."

"I'm the CEO's son. There's nothing they can do to me."

That haughty tone, that blind self-confidence... *Aaron, Aaron Goldberg.* My eyes turned into saucers when I realized who he was.

Digging my nails into my arms, I fought every instinct in me, screaming to turn around, to see how my biggest competitor was coping.

I didn't need to look to know the answer. We'd graduated at the same time, but unlike me, he actually started working at his father's law firm. A trust-fund baby's future was already mapped out, but life liked to throw curveballs sometimes. Such was the case of *moi.*

They were my father's biggest competitors, and I was starting to believe the only reason my dad managed to stay ahead of them was due to his criminal business practices.

Karma caught wind of it, though, and the dropkick from the top to an early grave was swift and brutal.

Just what he deserved.

"Yeah, but there's plenty they can do to me," the girl echoed, and I had to agree. Aaron had a tendency to go for his biggest rivals, wear them down with an approach specifically catered to each person. Some liked fluffy pink clouds of love, and their guards dropped, others' intimidation.

He'd tried both on me, and to this day, probably still walked stiffly from when I introduced my knee to his balls. My best guess was, she was pulling more cases than he was, and he wanted to get rid of her.

Of course, people changed, though.

I hoped he had.

"Don't worry, no one's firing you, no matter what happens between us."

Those cocktails must have been made of gold with how long it took the bartender to get them done. In the meantime, I tapped my stiletto on the floor in a staccato rhythm, my brain doing its best impression of Anakin from *Star Wars* as it yelled *liar*.

It wasn't my problem. I shouldn't get involved.

You're gonna keep your mouth shut if you know what's good for you. We wouldn't want you following in your mother's footsteps, now would we?

I almost dove for the drinks once they were handed to me, eyeing Elliot's martini like it was my enemy. It was too tempting to take a sip, especially when my father's threats escaped the Pandora's box I'd locked them in.

I walked blindly back to the table, but there were so many people along the way, one of them ended up nudging me, and I rushed forward. Unfortunately, I liked my heels a tad on the tall side, and it came back to bite me when I almost face-planted on the floor. A strong hand on my elbow held me up, though, and only the drinks sloshed a little bit in my grip.

"You okay there?" A man's voice registered, holding a prominent Australian accent. Intrigued, I turned to find kind blue eyes smiling at me, with swooped-up golden hair, crouched so he could support my weight. The wrinkles on either side of his mouth betrayed that he was way past his twenties and on to his mid-thirties.

"Yeah, thank you." Standing up, I blinked when he let

me go, seeing him stretch to his full height, easily measuring over six feet.

He was something, that was for sure. I could appreciate his good looks. His skin glowed from within as if he took the *one apple a day, keeps the doctor away* advice seriously, and he filled out his suit jacket well.

He looked like a less ripped version of Chris Hemsworth.

The handsome stranger continued smiling at me, but before either of us could say anything, Elsa swooped in, taking her drink out of my hand.

"Amelia, this is James..." She gestured to him, introducing us. "One of our new software developers. He came in on Thursday, so you haven't had a chance to meet yet."

Oh, I'll be seeing more of him.

"Pleasure to meet you." I extended my hand to shake his.

Instead, he gripped it, bringing my skin to his lips, heating it with his touch. "Likewise."

Elsa snickered at the over-the-top greeting, and I couldn't help but mirror James's infectious grin as we all made our way back to an abandoned Elliot.

James went for some extra brownie points by pulling out my chair and sitting next to me. Muttering a *hi* to Elliot, he turned his focus back to me. I raised an inquisitorial brow, and he led with a question.

"So, what do you do?" In response to my puzzled face, he added, "At the company, I mean. Which department do you work in?"

"Ah, my job is not half as exciting as yours, just an in-house lawyer."

"Not as exciting, but definitely more lucrative. Didn't they steal you away from some big law firm in Manhattan?"

Elsa jumped in, reminding me not to get too invested in this fantasy.

I am Amelia Maria Duante.

A lawyer, originally from Albany, New York. Hiking and skiing on the Catskills was my favorite pastime. I dreamt of owning a cabin in the mountains and took a job in Manhattan to make my dream come true. When I'd gathered sufficient funds to afford to do so, I drove back home to surprise my long-distance boyfriend, only to catch him in bed with my best friend. Devastated, I looked for another place to call home, and that was how I ended up in Astropolis. My parents were begging me to come visit, but I needed to be alone for a little bit.

Easy enough to remember, relatable enough to believe.

"Jack & Sons," I confirmed, taking a sip of my cocktail. Mango and passion fruit bloomed on my tongue as James and Elliot's eyes widened.

"That's the highest-grossing law firm in the U.S.," James stated.

"The world," Elsa corrected.

"What the hell possessed you to leave? You must have been paid a pretty penny. They take on so many high-profile cases." Elliot looked at me as if I had an extra limb.

I felt Elsa's hand rubbing comfortingly down my back as if to give me strength. I figured lying about my situation would make my case more believable in her eyes. After all, who'd share their dirty laundry with practical strangers?

"I wanted a change." I kept it vague.

"A change?" Elliot's nose wrinkled. "Females usually say that after a rough breakup."

His sister gasped at his forwardness. "You're very obnoxious, you know."

"But with valid points." He fixed her with a pointed look, continuing his grilling. "Was there anyone special in your past you wanted to forget? That's why you moved?"

"No, it usually only takes a pixie cut and dye job for me to move on." I laced my tone with enough sarcasm for them to be wondering if I was joking or being serious.

"Your hair's super long," James commented, his finger reaching up as if he was going to touch a lock. Thinking better of it, he let his hand drop by his side again.

Throwing my locks over my shoulder, I drew my attention to him. His eyes were still on my hair. It was overdue for a trim, but I liked it this way, almost touching the arch of my ass. It made me different from who I once used to be.

"I was the one doing the breaking." I didn't know where the wink came from, but at that moment, it felt right and gratifying when a faint wash of pink marred his cheeks.

I ate up the sight like I'd never seen anything like it before because, well...I hadn't. I couldn't remember any occasion of a man blushing in front of me. They usually had a disgusting amount of confidence.

It was endearing of James. The low light also did wonders for his pale eyes, making them appear brighter in the dark.

"Of course, you were," he said under his breath, but the others didn't hear him either way. The siblings had begun fighting about some vinyls Elliot had stolen and never returned, and I angled my body toward James.

"What's that supposed to mean?"

The blush burned fiercer, but he looked me in the eyes and said, "I don't see how any man with working brain cells would let you go."

A knot formed in my throat at his words. He was hard-core flirting, especially since it was our first meeting, and I couldn't figure him out. Did he mean it? Or was he telling me what I wanted to hear?

With some men, you knew you would get your heart broken, and you went in because you were willing to brace the hurt if it meant you'd get a minute of their time. Others whispered sweet nothings in your ear, led you astray, and dropped you the minute you weren't valuable to them anymore.

I'd experienced both.

Few (if any) men fell in between.

"You just met me, James. How do you know my character is not terribly flawed?" I cocked my head, indulging in his game. If he was indeed playing, I knew I'd win.

"I'm a good guess of character."

He bit his lip while I leaned closer, as if I was about to divulge my deepest, darkest secrets. "While I was a delivery food worker, I would purposefully spill the food on the orders of people that had a history of not tipping."

James's eyes widened, the corners of his lips twitching. "Really? What other flaws are there? Lay it on me thick."

"I'm into healing crystals and can't leave the house without checking myself out in the mirror at least twice."

"Healing crystals? All right, yeah, I'd dump you on the spot."

I laughed, mock punching his arm. "What's so wrong about healing crystals?"

"You mean other than there's zero scientific proof behind them actually having any powers? They're just highly ordered ionic solids. They can have interesting properties, but magical healing abilities are not among them."

48

Hot and into science... Well, duh, he was a software developer.

"You must be fun at parties," I said drily.

"The funnest." He nodded, letting a huge grin spread over his face.

"That's not a word, smarty p—" A big hearty laugh faded out what I had to say next, and I snapped my mouth shut when the sound registered in my brain.

It held the kind of abashed self-assurance that sent my heart spinning, happy as if the person had no care in the world, and so utterly male, the hair on the nape of my neck stood to full attention. It was painfully familiar, too, because I used to be the recipient of that laughter. I was the one that caused it.

Like a moth to the flame, my eyes began their search, filtering through faces as fast as my heart was beating, relentless until I found the source of it all. When I did, the sucker punch to the gut was no lesser than when I saw him yesterday.

Ten years was a long time, but they had been kind to Ares Alsford. So kind, I could barely control my breathing as I stared at his straight white teeth, sharp with promises of love bites and body tight as a drum. He was no lankier version of Chris Hemsworth. He was Thor himself. A darker version, with caramel hair, and honey eyes, just as sweet and addicting too, causing a burst of sweetness to explode in your mouth whenever you looked at them.

You could tell that he belonged in high society from how he carried himself. Still, he was definitely one of the more approachable amongst them...the one that would smile at you whilst he twisted the knife in your back.

And I always appreciated bluntness over fakeness.

"It sounded right," James said, but I barely heard him once I realized Ares wasn't alone. A girl was feeling his abs through his black shirt, looking at him with stars in her eyes.

Simmering contempt came boiling up when he took her hand in his and kissed her knuckles, along with a wave of bile because I knew they'd fuck tonight. I knew his tells when he was horny. After all, I was the one girl he couldn't have for the longest time.

Until he did.

He had me and threw me away.

Brutally and painfully. He didn't know what awaited me, and I doubted he'd even care if he knew. He would probably do it again in a heartbeat since he lost nothing, and I, everything. Not only my past and present, but my future too.

And Ares Alsford didn't know a thing. That was why he was happy, why he could laugh with no care in the world and bed whomever he pleased, start a family without a haunted conscience.

James was still talking in the background, albeit I wasn't listening. All I could think about was how much I was craving to wipe that stupid smile off Alsford's face. Make him feel even an ounce of the hurt I did when... *No.*

I cut the thought off, yet the damage was done. My sick mind had already crafted a plan within seconds, and the sentence was out of my mouth before I could stop it. "I don't really like my drink. I'm going to get another one real quick." I blew the rest of James's words into the air as I pulled my chair back.

Ever the gentleman, James made to stand up with me, asking, "I'll get one for you. What would you like?"

If there is anything called "How to let go of grudges and

jealousy," *I'll gladly take it. Been needing it since I was thirteen.*

I could still bow out of this, but ultimately the fire fueling my bloodstream was really striving to disappoint my therapist. I bit my lip, trying to hold off on what I wanted to say, but then Ares laughed again, and it was game over.

"No, it's fine, really. I'll get it." My self-control snapped like a twig, and I might've been a bit harsh on my delivery.

"All right, then." James held his hands up in an *"I surrender"* manner, settling back in his seat.

Elsa pulled my arm when I stood, asking me to get her a specific drink that I was too pumped up on adrenaline to remember.

I had five targets as I made my way through the crowd. Thoughts of *you're better than this* were overpowered, as I put all my energy into observing my victims. A set of friends, standing opposite each other. One of them had his back turned on a woman in a red blazer whose glass of wine was perched conveniently over Ares's head. All I had to do was bump on the guy to the left, and the rest would fall like dominoes.

Honestly, I was doing the poor girl a service. There was nothing more that Alsford could offer her other than Don Julio bottles and empty promises.

I pacified myself with that thought as I walked ahead. The space was so cramped, I honestly didn't have to do much other than glare at Ares's moving lips as he talked to his lady friend. They looked so smooth. I wondered if he used Chapstick.

Fuck.

He didn't even recognize me, and I was daydreaming

about how fucking smooth his lips were. Not that my get-up had made it easy, or altering my voice, but still.

As it turned out, I didn't need to intentionally bump into the guy. When Ares leaned forward, giving his date his signature *come fuck me* eyes that had girls climbing him like a tree in college, before aligning his mouth with hers, all I saw was red.

Do you really love her?

Does she make you crazy like I did?

Blind envy gripped me so intensely, my next breath was a rasp. I wasn't paying attention to my path, and based on a yelp behind me and my body being shoved toward my initial target, I'd probably stepped on someone with my heel.

I watched it all unfold in slow motion almost, all the puzzle pieces falling together. The man I was trying to steady myself on rushed forward, causing his friend to bend from his weight and hitting the female behind him. She, in turn, let go of her wineglass as she tried to balance herself midair, and then—

"*Fucking hell!*" Ares's date released a girlish shriek.

"*What the fuck?*" he followed up, and I couldn't help but look at them as I straightened myself up, even though it was risky.

His hair was soaked in red liquid, dripping down his eyebrows and into his eyes, which he wiped furiously. I couldn't see her since her back was to me, but I didn't believe she was fairing any better in her blush pink dress. It was a nice one too; too bad she wouldn't be able to wear it anymore.

As if feeling my gaze on his, Ares's eyes snapped up, but I quickly turned my head before he could notice me. Mumbling a *sorry* to the guy I was supporting myself on, I rushed to the bar before people put two and two together and found I was the culprit of the whole ordeal.

"Took you long enough." Elsa snatched her glass from my hand, but I had to wait until after Ares had retreated to the bathroom to return.

The initial satisfaction of ruining his night was short-lived. I ruined mine too. We all had skeletons in our closet, but mine was overflowing with bad decisions and, most importantly, terrible personality traits.

I wasn't proud of who I was, and I didn't think I'd ever be if I kept resorting to my old habits of lashing out because I felt bad, because I was lacking attention. Even though part of me believed it was unfair he got to live unscathed, it wasn't my role to serve justice.

Whatever was meant for him would come for him, as it did for me.

The rest of the outing passed by like a blur. I refused to look in *their* direction again, and after a lot of prodding from James and a bit of *not-so-subtle* nudging from Elsa, I agreed to give him my number. The least I could do was try to have some sort of dating life. Having such a strong reaction to someone I hadn't seen in so long wasn't normal.

I wasn't normal.

Splitting with my friends at the parking lot entrance, I made my way to my car. Head tilted down, I felt unexplainably emotional as my self-loathing reached an all-time high. On days like this, I considered my existence a miracle. The simple fact that I still kept breathing after looking in the mirror and not liking a single thing about myself was nothing short of wondrous.

Why?

Why do I choose to keep living in hatred when death sounds so appealing?

My answer came in the form of shadows spreading over my back and bleeding over the gravel of the parking lot when someone rushed up to me. I froze for a single second, and it cost me.

I gasped as rough hands—*male hands*—encircled my wrists, and I was pushed against the nearest car, face forward. A body settled behind mine, stiff and rigid, and I all but lost it as I thrashed against him.

No. No. No.

This isn't gonna happen again.

"Siren."

One word.

All it took was one word to immobilize me, uttered by a silky voice that held way too much power over me to ever be considered healthy.

I was stunned into silence and could only shudder when his face slid between the strands of my hair. His minty breath spread over the side of my neck as he shook the very core of my fragile existence with a single question. "Did you really think I'd let you run away for a second time?"

CHAPTER FOUR
AMELIA

Ten Years Ago

"I'm heading out," I announced to my father and his fiancée while they were being waited on at the dining table. The only response I got was a flick of the wrist from him and Claire, palming her swollen belly as she watched me leave with a creepy smile on her face.

I swear she got the high of her life from reminding everyone she was pregnant all the time. Talking about how beautiful their baby would be. How she hoped it would inherit my father's fair hair and icy eyes. How there was no chance the child would ever come out short because both of them were over six feet tall.

How she basically wanted her kid to be everything I wasn't.

I was pretty for an *exotic* girl (her words, not mine). The south Italian genes on my mother's side were too dominant on my face to be considered attractive in her eyes, and she was sure I had *some* Middle Eastern in me. I guess if you were going for the trophy wife look—short, curvy brunettes didn't fit the bill.

It was either that, or she didn't want to be reminded of her blood-stained hands. Their relationship was born out of a concoction of sins—greed, fueled by envy, and ultimately wrath. My mom and Claire's husband had to be axed for them to get together. Amelia Laurent overdosed, but it was her husband's infidelity that led her to find solace in drugs. While Francis Roux got imprisoned for a crime he didn't even commit, conveniently losing his life after getting stabbed by another inmate.

It killed me living in the same house as them, breathing the same air as two killers and adulterers. I got hit with the need to wring their necks every time I heard them laughing or talking. I wanted both of them gone more than I wanted my own life, but I had to be smart about it. Wait until I got my degree and was self-sufficient.

I didn't have the luck my ex-best friend did. Claire wouldn't win any mommy of the year awards, but Eliana's father made sure to leave her with a hefty inheritance. Why she didn't use it to start fresh was beyond me. I would've left this place behind in a millisecond. But of course, Eliana Roux couldn't survive without her prince charming. Not that there was anything pleasing about Leonardo Bianchi or the way he abandoned you after stealing everything you had to give.

Sighing, I headed to my car, pretending like I didn't know what drove me to talk to them. I never did. These past few months, my dad and I weren't even pretending to be a family anymore, but I wanted him to stop me. Stop me from my continuous perusal of mistakes.

I was big on leading myself in situations I couldn't get

out of, and wearing a black corset tube top, complete with tight dark jeans and thigh-high boots, was just asking for trouble. Especially when the person I was painting my lips berry red for before starting my Mini Cooper was Ares Alsford.

Leonardo's long-time friend and the one I should be staying the hell away from.

I tried. So damn hard.

I gave him the cold shoulder every time he helped me up after Bianchi's countless rejections. I refused to meet his eyes when he sent me those signature panty-melting smiles of his and met his flirting with sarcasm.

Not because I wasn't attracted to him, because I was— way too much for my own good, but I didn't deserve Ares.

Leo wasn't my first contender for a boyfriend, but his life was in shambles already, so I didn't fight when I was told to go after him. He was as messed up as I was, with a drug-addicted mom, absentee dad, and dead twin. I didn't fear I'd alter him. He was as scared as they came already. Whereas Ares really didn't need me fucking up his life.

He had a good thing going, and getting between my legs was going to ruin that.

But he'd texted me earlier today, saying he wanted to talk to me about something, and I was fairly sure it was a bullshit excuse to see me, but I was curious... *and* I might've missed him a little bit.

I limited our interactions to only when Leo was around because the last time he wasn't, well... we both had had way too much to drink, and hands slipped in places they weren't supposed to as our mouths did everything else but talk. I couldn't be trusted with alcohol in my system, so when Leo cut me off as favorite flavor of the year, I cut his insistent friend off too, who took the saying *one man's trash is another man's treasure* to heart.

My belly twisted in knots as I took a left, cutting through the middle of a thick New England forest. The address he'd sent me was a bit far from the city, and my curiosity piqued as I watched the cars on the road lessen with each turn I took.

I didn't cut Alsford as the type to kill a woman because she rejected him, but it was starting to sound probable when I pulled up in front of a cottage surrounded by nothing else but trees for at least several miles. It was cute, don't get me wrong. It had a natural stone finish, a tiny blue front door (I'd love to see Ares squeezing through that, that was for sure), and warm yellow lighting that was starting to seep through the windows as the sun set, painting the sky orange.

It was the no civilization for a couple of miles part that creeped me out.

The front door swung open as soon as I got out of my car like he had a built-in radar that detected my presence. I took a deep breath when I saw him coming down the stairs with a massive smile on his face, excitement stomping through my middle like a stampede of wild horses. He had the most basic attire on, a tight blue long-sleeve, and some gray sweats, but of course, my brain released hormones as if he was dressed in a full-blown suit and was asking my father for my hand in marriage.

His pearly whites were on full display when I met him at the bottom of the staircase, grinning at me like a boy obsessed. "You came."

Sweat made my hands slick with the urge to touch him, but I kept them firmly planted by my sides. "I decided to take mercy on your poor soul. Who knows what you would've done if I didn't."

"Probably gorged on some s'mores and downed the bottle of Glenfiddich I brought."

"That's my favorite whiskey." My mouth parted.

"Is it?" he asked, his honeyed eyes full of mirth. "What a coincidence."

"I'm sure." I pursed my mouth in order to keep a smirk back. "So, what is this place?" I glanced over his broad shoulder, taking in the cottage again.

He followed my gaze. "Well, seeing that it has a door, walls, and a roof, I think some people would consider it a home."

"Ass." I delivered a small blow to his rock-hard stomach, instantly regretting it when I felt the hard ridges of muscle underneath. We both sucked in a sharp breath, and I avoided his all-consuming eyes as I asked, "What are we doing in a home in the middle of the woods?"

"My family owns it, and I thought you could use some separation from your day-to-day life." His tone lost some of its humor.

"What gave it away?" I released a dry chuckle, and he responded with a searing stare that seemed to look through my soul.

Is it the fact that everyone stopped talking to me when Leo picked Eliana over me? Is it the fact that I was once invited to more parties than I could attend in a day but am now viewed as a social pariah if I step foot in one? Or that I spend all my time at the library on campus? Or that I eat lunch in my car?

Fuck, I'd turned into a nobody, and my fall from grace was so public it was painful. I thought I had more power than I did, but it turned out Bianchi was holding all the cards and took back the ones he'd lent me without a second thought.

Ares didn't bother with a verbal response, just threw a glance at me over his broad back when he turned, asking, "You coming in?"

Against my better judgment, I followed him into the cottage.

All my brain could register was light stone walls brightening up the otherwise rustic interior, fully equipped with a leather couch that looked ready to swallow you with comfort when you sat on it, and it did as we sunk on opposite sides. Ares's tour was eclipsed by the fact that I kept staring at his ass as he showed me around, so the crinkle of wood had me wrinkling my nose when I noticed he had a fire burning.

"A fire in May?" I questioned, suddenly feeling stuffy in my puffer jacket. I removed it, throwing it over the back of the couch, and my ogling was returned tenfold as Ares pinned his eyes on the swell of my breasts aided in volume by the tight corset.

I shivered, and he chased the litter of goosebumps all the way up to my bottom lip, trapped between my teeth. An insatiable hunger painted his face, and we both leaned slightly closer as we continued our conversation.

"It's considerably colder up here than the city."

"It's definitely more peaceful, is what it is." I cleared my throat, placing one of the throw pillows in my lap to anchor myself in place.

"I'm surprised you don't recognize the place. That slope right there"—he pointed to the window behind me, and I twisted in place to look—"is where you broke your foot after I helped you put your ski gear on, and you accidentally rolled down the mountain."

"Oh my God, it is!" My eyes widened as I looked at the snowy peak, its powdered sugar-like top slowly giving away to darkness as dusk took over. "That's one painful memory." I winced, caressing my previously injured foot automatically.

His stare was unimpressed when I turned back, and he handed me a tumbler half full of amber liquid. I took it graciously, taking a small sip and letting it warm up my body —not that it wasn't already hitting record temperatures with the way Ares's gaze kept drifting to my exposed décolletage.

"It was more painful for me than it was for you. I had to carry your ass all the way up again, so you could receive first aid, and you never said thank you."

"If you're expecting gratitude now, don't hold your breath. You threatened to drop me because I was crying." I smiled sweetly.

"You were being hysterical. I was helping you calm down," he said matter-of-factly as if his reasoning had an ounce of logic.

"I was in pain," I replied incredulously.

"It worked, though. You stopped crying." Ares shrugged, reaching for a plate filled with delicious smelling, pre-made s'mores. He'd had to have gotten here way earlier than I did to make them, and I was just now realizing (since my brain had been rid of some of its lust-induced haze) how much effort he'd put into this.

String lights were hung on the walls (and I doubted they were part of the usual decor), he'd made snacks, took care of the drinks, and there was even a bouquet of fresh Marigolds —my birth month flower.

It was either a freaky coincidence, or he remembered when I'd told him I thought the future was set in stone.

Though their bright orange color made them appear cheerful at first sight, Marigolds symbolized grief over a loved one, and my mom left a hole of despair in my soul that would never fill up since she killed herself.

What hurt worse was the thought that I, *her own child,* wasn't enough to make her stay.

I blinked when he handed me a s'more, my hands shaking as they wrapped around the tissue paper. Something akin to affection and sadness smothered my body all at once, and all I wanted was to sink into the arms of the guy that had tricked me into a date.

I settled for hugging the pillow closer to me, frowning. "Because I was too busy throwing every curse word in the dictionary your way."

"I can't believe I actually tolerated your ass and didn't leave you there to die."

I was a bit ungrateful, but I was injured, so I got a pass.

I took a bite of the chocolatey, creamy goodness and sighed pleasantly when the concoction of flavors exploded on my tongue. He followed suit and seemed to make fun of my sigh with an even louder one, sounding borderline orgasmic.

I kicked his shin with the tip of my boot, and he choked on his bite, making me smile.

"You're always so patient with me," I commented, reaching over and patting his back lightly.

"Yeah," he coughed. "It's turned into a toxic personality trait."

I knew an undercurrent of truth topped his humorous statement, and my palm resorted to smoothing up and down the length of his back until he regained his breathing as a sign of silent apology. Not one of my wisest moments, but I handed him his glass of whiskey to wash down the food stuck in his throat, and he drank it without protest.

In another not-so-wise move, I remained planted right next to him for the rest of sundown. The space between my thighs was uncomfortably slick, and it didn't make sense because the rest of our conversation progressed into us roasting each other and disagreeing on various other topics. We had different opinions on almost everything, from if we really ever stepped foot on the moon to if Tesla was as environmentally friendly as Elon Musk claimed.

At some point, the way his eyes glittered whenever he won an argument had me rooting for him. Or it could have been because his vivacity had my attraction flaring whenever he made a compelling point. Or because of the fact that his ocean musk scent had been tickling my nose for the past hour and a half, and his food filled my belly.

And I hadn't had that in...well, ever. No one I liked had ever doted on me with this much attention.

Our shoulders brushed as we discussed the *Game of Thrones* finale, and he rolled his eyes at me, saying, "Are you kidding me? It makes no sense why she burned down King's Landing. She'd already won when the bells of surrender went off."

"What she did wasn't right, but it *did* make sense. Cersei killed one of her closest friends, and she saw that Jon's claim to the throne was stronger and snapped."

"You're saying you'd kill thousands to avenge your closest friend?" He raised a brow, eager to call me out on my bullshit.

"No, because I'm not in a *TV show*, Alsford. The person responsible, however..." I gulped, remembering past me.

"There was a time when I would've done anything for my friends."

"What changed?" His tone got a shade deeper, and I shrugged, examining my manicure.

"I realized that there are no friends, only moments of friendship."

"And you got all that because you lost a boy to your best friend?" Ares got straight to the point. It wasn't rocket science to figure out I was talking about Eliana.

"It started out that way, and it stung, I'll admit." I rolled my stiff shoulders back, thinking about my brief crush on Bianchi. "But by the time I got over seeing the two of them together, too many things went down for Eliana and me to go back to being friends. I thought she..." *Knew.* I thought she knew about what a cunt her mother was. That our parents were sneaking around together and didn't tell me until it was too late. Until my mom died, and I'd willingly taken up the role of being someone's puppet.

"You thought she what?" Ares pressed, and I shook my head. There was no point in saying anything. It was too late anyway.

"Nothing."

He heaved a deep sigh, throwing himself back on the couch as he crossed his arms. "How long do you think you'll be able to bottle things up for, Serena? No one can survive on their own, and secrets breed nothing but loneliness."

His judgment made the tips of my ears burn, but I stood my ground. "I don't see the bad in that. No one has ever loved me more than I love myself."

"Because you cut down anyone who tries to get close to you," he bit out, and I could tell he wanted to say more when he rubbed his palm over his mouth as if to hold back his words.

"I can see that you have to get some things off your chest. You might as well say them before you graduate." I mirrored his pose, crossing my own arms and tapping my boot on the floor. I was planning on moving as far away from this town as physically possible.

"Everyone has been wronged by someone else, but if you continue prioritizing karma over your own happiness, you're going to be eighty, alone, and miserable before you know it."

"And I suppose the happiness you're referring to is yourself," I scoffed because we could never happen, not as long as he remained Leo's friend.

"I'm just saying that I could get you off way better than your fingers do after every time you see me, and that certainly comes with a healthy dose of serotonin," he replied, all pompous, spreading his arms on the back of the couch.

"Your arrogance is outstanding." I faced the crackling fire, but my cheeks were extremely hot for an entirely different reason.

"It's not arrogance. It's the truth, baby." He reached out, trapping my chin between his fingers, and I stiffened when his minty breath tickled my lips. "Don't you think I heard you in Astor's bathroom after we hooked up, taking care of the mess I'd created between your legs? You weren't particularly quiet."

If I thought he looked pompous before, he was dripping with the kind of confidence a man possessed after he'd made his woman come at least three times. I hadn't let our hookup progress past second base, but him hearing me come all but defeated the purpose of my resistance.

He knew I wanted him.

I tried to turn away, so Ares didn't see the embarrassment on my face, but he kept me in place, his eyes locked with mine. My hands twitched down on my lap, my stomach rising and falling like an avalanche, and I fisted his shirt, partly to pretend like I wanted him to set me free and to appease another part of me that was dying to touch him.

"You brought me here to antagonize me? Is that what this is?"

"I brought you here to see what's right in front of you. While everyone else wants nothing to do with your bitter ass, there's someone still here that likes your flaws enough to stay when you've given him every reason not to."

My eyes watered, much to my dismay, when the truth of his words reflected all around me. Ares was the only one left when I insisted on pushing him away the hardest. He progressed to cupping my cheeks when he saw the vulnerability on my face, and I let him, smoothing out my palms on his shirt and feeling his heartbeat against my skin. For all his calm demeanor, it was racing as wildly as mine, and that put me at ease.

"I would never put my foot down on this if I didn't know you were craving me as much as I am you. Why do you insist on pulling away?" he asked, and I felt inclined to be honest with him for the first time. Ares ought to be happy, not pine after something that would never happen.

"You don't want me, Ares, trust me. I'm the raging dumpster fire everyone is scared of, and for a good reason. Don't let me take you down with me."

"Your lows are as much of a part of me as your highs are, Serena. No one is perfect; they just know how to hide their imperfections better than you do. Don't let them brainwash you into thinking there's something wrong with you. You're not going to take me down. On the contrary, you're going to make me extremely fucking happy if you agreed to give us a chance."

My face had scrunched up by the time he finished his sentence to hold back the tears that stung my eyes as a result of his words, but it was no use. A few stubborn ones escaped, and a low growl came from Ares's chest as he kissed them away. My breath hitched when his hot lips touched my cool skin, and I closed my eyes, soaking up the feeling of being cherished because that was what he did. He kissed all my tears away, lingering on every cheek as long as he could as if he dreaded having to pull back, but when he was done, I kept him in place, lacing my hands behind his neck, our faces only inches apart.

I didn't notice who breached the slight gap first, but next thing I knew, our mouths were on each other like we were starving, and fireworks were going off behind my eyelids. His lips moved on mine, and a bone-deep sigh escaped me. I'd been dreaming of this. Ever since that first time he kissed me.

This.

This.

This.

Ares Alsford was a work of art, and his kisses were no less magnificent. A shiver shot up my spine, and urgency filled my core when he licked my lips, urging me to open up, and I couldn't deny him. Unadulterated need filled our moves, and our kiss was nothing short of filthy when our tongues met, tangling as if parched for each other. There was no tact, no elegance when his hands fell from my face and gripped my hips until I was straddling him on the couch, feeling the hardening length in his sweats.

He didn't let me adjust, eating up my gasp like he lived off my breathy moans. Our mouths made wet noises every time they disconnected, and it only encouraged us to dive back even more eagerly, loving all the dirty noises we produced. His lips were the perfect amount of soft mixed with enough roughness to let me know he was enjoying this as much as I was. Sipping from my lips, feeding from me like he couldn't get enough.

Ares's grip turned bruising on my ass as he groped me over my jeans, moving me over his hard length. He captured my bottom lip between his teeth, and we both took a moment to breathe in deeply as he gave it a little tug before letting it go. I opened my mouth to protest, but his lips found my jaw and traveled down my throat, leaving wet trails in his wake that cooled when the air touched them.

"This is really not a good idea," I rasped to the ceiling when he kissed me in places no other man in the past had paid so much attention to.

"I think it's an excellent idea." He fought me as always.

"Does it turn you on? Fucking girls your best friend has had first?" I tried to hurt him with my words, but my actions spoke the opposite when I ground on his lap, seeking friction from the bulge in his sweatpants. "Is that what this is, Alsford, some weird, kinky fantasy?"

"If Bianchi had fucked you, his balls wouldn't be attached to his body right now." He bit my neck, and I gasped in pain, pushing him away.

Ares's lips were red and his hair wild, and he gave me a lazy grin as he kept my hips moving over his while I asked, "What's that supposed to mean?"

"It means your bullshit show together was just that. *A show*. We both know you were more into torturing Eliana by pretending to be together than you were into each other. And as long as he didn't truly like you, he wasn't allowed to touch you."

"Who are you? The hookup police?"

In an unexpected turn of events, one of his hands traveled between my legs, and my mouth dropped open when his thumb put extra pressure on my clit, and he winked. "For select pussies only."

"You're sexist. That's what you are," I said, but the bite backing my words was weak. "What gives you the right to dictate what *I* do with my own body?"

"Look me in the eyes, and tell me your panties aren't soaked, baby. That your cunt is not dripping for me. Look me in the eyes, and tell me that kiss wasn't the best one you've ever had." He paused, waiting for me to say something, but I knew anything I voiced, other than admitting what he told me, would be a bald-faced lie. "Finally, look into my eyes and tell me how much you'd loathe my lips on other parts of your body."

I shivered, the circular motion of his thumb unrelenting over my nub, and all I could think of was shedding my clothes so he could really touch me. "I can't."

He took my admission as a green light and attached his mouth to my neck again, the scruff on his face scraping delightfully against my delicate skin.

"Can't *what?*" Ares barked, his tone holding a silent order.

"I can't tell you that," I whimpered, and my eyes rolled to the back of my head when he spanked my ass.

"Then you've got your answer, Siren. As long as I'm the only one you get wet for, you'll be on a one-dick diet." He sucked on my skin hard enough to bruise, and we both shuddered when he came up for air. "Don't worry, I promise to feed you plenty."

"Siren?" Through the haze in my head, I wondered if he'd called me another woman's name.

"You sing like one when I touch you," he explained.

"I do no—" I started, only to finish my sentence with a bewildered moan as I threw my head back when he lifted my ass in the air and brought me down on his dick with enough force that made my womb quiver. "That was *definitely* not melodic."

"Your screams sound like music to my ears." The logic behind his words was faulty, but I didn't mind as he twisted us, laying me on the couch and settling his weight on top of me. The fire illuminated the side of his gorgeous face with unfulfilled promises, and he was dead serious when he said, "And I think I should make you do it some more."

"Well, then..." I gulped, tangling my hands in his silky hair before giving him the go-ahead he craved. "You *should* make that happen."

CHAPTER FIVE
SERENA

Ten Years Ago

I knew I'd face repercussions for my words, but we deserved a chance. Our chemistry was explosive. I couldn't stop thinking about him when he wasn't around, and he turned me on like no one else. I could try to be better for him—*no*, I *would* be better because Ares Alsford deserved nothing but the best.

He fed me a guttural groan when he kissed me again, mouthing *thank fuck* against my lips, making me feel more needed than I ever had before, and I hooked my legs around his waist.

"Ares," I breathed, pecking him. "As much as I love dry humping you, I think you should take off my pants."

His eyes darkened as he lifted slightly and watched me, pecking my cheek, my neck, and biting the swells of both my breasts popping out of the corset until I moaned, arching my back. I tugged on his hair when it stung a little too much, and he let go of my skin with a wet pop after suctioning a bit of fat in his mouth, a groan rumbling from his chest.

"Take off your shirt, Siren," he ordered. "Undress for me."

My fingers fumbled with the buttons of the corset, and by the time I reached the second one, Ares let out an impatient noise. His hands covered mine, and before I had any time to process what he was doing, a line of tiny popping sounds filled the cabin's living room.

I gasped, my eyes flying to his. "What the hell, Alsford?"

"You were too slow." He shrugged as if that gave him the right to ruin my clothes, but he distracted me from continuing the argument by opening either side of the corset. My nipples pebbled once free; either from the air or his wanting gaze, I didn't know.

I perked up when he choked on his next breath, looking at my tits like he wanted to *love* them... *intensively*. I stretched underneath him, knowing he liked what he saw. My boobs weren't too big, but they were enough for his cock to slide between them and disappear, and from the look on his face, that was precisely what he was imagining.

"Goddamn, Serena, you're perfect." He sounded awed, his hand stretching toward my tits as if compelled, and he glared at me when I slapped it away before he could make contact.

"No, no, no." I *tsked*. "Take off *your* shirt..." I cocked my head, thinking about it for a second. "And pants, and then *my* pants, and after that, you can touch them." To highlight what I was talking about, I cupped my boobs, circling my fingers over my nipples, and watched him with a smirk.

Ares couldn't just tear off my clothes without some kind of repercussions.

He smiled in return, and the predatory look on his face promised he was going to make me pay for every little rebellion. "What a bold little Siren."

"The kind that drives men mad." I winked.

Like the wise man that he was, he listened to me, tugging his shirt over his head and removing it in one go. Not wasting any time, he unhooked my legs from his waist, taking care of my thigh-highs first, but I took my sweet time staring at all that hard-packed muscle, imagining sinking my teeth into his inviting pecs and feeling the ridges of his V-line that led to his crotch with my tongue. Fire consumed my chest when he lowered his slacks, revealing his hard, thick cock. My mouth watered, and I reached forward on autopilot to taste him, but I was forced down on my back again when Ares yanked my tight jeans and panties off all at once.

"Oh, baby, don't I know it." He spread my legs, studying me there, and my wet center cooled a tad once exposed to the elements. My breath caught as I watched him lick his lips, and my thighs trembled when his finger caressed a trail of wetness. "You're fucking dripping down your cheeks."

This wasn't my first time, and I could say I was way past the awkward, blushing phase whenever a guy saw me naked, but something about Ares's gaze on my bare pussy had me shying away like a virgin. Inches before my knees connected, though, he roughly tugged them open on either side, his palm coming down with a slap on my wet pussy.

I yelped as evidence of my wetness echoed around the room, and I looked at him in shock when he said, "Keep your legs open, or there's gonna be more where that came from."

My God, can this man get any more perfect?

I was even more excited to get this show on the road when his rough palm made contact with my wet arousal and, doing as he said, I spread my legs wider, taunting him in a way that'd drive him wild. "Well, if you're gonna stare at it, you might as well lick it."

"Demanding vixen." He slapped my pussy again, and fuck if it didn't make me moan like crazy. But I needed more. These little one-second stings were driving me wild. "I wanted to taste your tits first, but you'll let me do anything I want with them when I'm balls deep inside you, won't you, Serena?"

"God, yes." I watched as he leveled his face with my cunt, and the promise of his tongue easing some of the fire built in my core would have me laying down my life for him.

"You've been hiding such a pretty pussy away from me," he muttered darkly, a faint hint of anger coloring his tone. I was all lost when he kissed me there with an open mouth, and I nearly jumped from the couch. His hands came around my thighs, and he held me open, his head settling between my legs like he was about to feast. He indulged himself in another languid lick, and I watched transfixed as his tongue coated with my juices and his eyes closed in pleasure.

Somehow, knowing that he was doing this for himself as much as he was for me made me giddy. He loved it, enjoyed my taste so much so, he whispered, "So good" to himself as he fed from me.

I reached down, lacing my fingers through his strands when he began picking up his pace, alternating from probing my entrance to swirling his tongue around my clit. He did it a couple of times, and lava pooled low in my belly, ready to explode. It was really his attention to my sweet spot that got me going, though, so with my hand in his hair, I guided him in place, making him focus solely on my nub.

"Grind that cunt all over my face. Make yourself come," Ares growled, his breath burning hot against my sensitive center, and it was all the encouragement I needed to go feral.

I didn't have the mental capacity at that moment to feel any sort of embarrassment about how I decorated his face with my wetness, his beard glistening under the low light of the room. The sounds that came out of my mouth were downright inhuman, but he was loving them if his mirroring groans were anything to go by.

Ares let me use him to get my pleasure. He was confident in giving me control, allowing me to set the pace this once, and he obliged with everything I required him to do, sucking, licking, scraping his bottom teeth over my sensitive folds until I saw stars behind my eyelids.

"Fuck," I cursed when my lower stomach tightened, and I knew I was seconds away from coming. My energy always depleted as I rode the high, which meant I couldn't guide him anymore, so I warned him by voicing his name loudly, "*Ares*," and he didn't let me down, taking over again.

He built up the perfect pleasure, his licks fast and circular around my clit, just the way I loved it. His entire face was wet with my arousal, and the man basked in it, smiling at me like he could be eating my pussy for an hour on end without getting bored or complaining.

He was fucking perfect.

His enthusiasm, and the fact that he began to flick his tongue in a practiced move, set my belly off in a series of contractions that made my body buck as I finally let go and carried the wave of one of my most intense orgasms. The kind only my vibrator had been able to deliver in the past.

It hit me with the magnitude of a 9.0 earthquake, and while I usually voiced out my releases, I was shocked in silence by its intensity. I let it work its way out of my body, throwing my head back. My legs quivered, and my mouth formed silent screams as my eyesight went black. I came apart like a skyscraper knocked down by a blunt force, and by the time I was able to regain my senses, I believed more than three minutes had gone by since my orgasm started.

Ares got off his knees when a last satisfied sigh escaped me. His chest puffed up with pride as he gazed down at my body, twisted and sweaty as a result of his expertise. It should annoy me that he was so good at this, but I didn't have any room to talk. I was the one that had pushed him away.

"You look beautiful coming and screaming my name," he said, and my heart cracked a little. He didn't call me sexy, pretty, or hot. He called me beautiful. I was beautiful to him. Leaning down, he wrapped my hair around his fist and pressed a filthy kiss on my mouth, letting my salty taste bloom on my tongue. "Do you like the way you taste on my tongue, Siren?"

"I think I'll prefer the way I taste on your dick," I replied, and I was sure it was the empty feeling in my core that had me sprouting such bold statements. I wanted Ares Alsford to fill me up, and I wanted it now.

He sucked in air between his teeth, then gripped my jaw, his fingers delving in my mouth as he aligned our bodies. I sucked his index in, and he shuddered. "That mouth of yours will be the death of me. Take me in, give your pretty pussy what it has been aching for."

He fit himself at my entrance, and we both palpitated

with anticipation as I held on to his shoulders when he thrust upward, pushing himself inside me.

Yes.

I popped his finger off my mouth, my legs circling his waist and aiding him in inserting all of his dick. I craved every inch of him inside me. When he was finally all in, he remained still for a bit, and I was grateful because his length took some getting used to.

"Fuck, this is where I want to go after I die." I heard the pleasure/pain in his voice, and it made me beyond giddy. "Not Heaven, not Hell, not earth. In your cunt."

"Ares, my God." I hugged his shoulders, pressing my tits against his chest, and his head dropped down to the crook of my neck. "You're so big it's painful."

"Oh, but you like a little bit of pain, Siren. You go wild for it." To prove a point, he took my earlobe between his teeth, pulling out and slamming back in again. I hissed at the double bite of pain, but it gave way to searing pleasure soon enough. "Tell me, do you want my teeth around your pink nipples when I suck them?"

I nodded, not trusting myself to speak without sounding like a dying seal when he pumped his hips again.

"What was that?" he asked, just to be annoying.

"Yes, you bastard," I groaned when he picked up his pace.

He got his routine down, pulling out all the way, and pushing back in again with blunt force. I hadn't had sex in so long, it took a while adjusting to it, but the longer the sound of our skin slapping together filled the room, the longer Ares kept licking my breasts like they were his personal lollipops, the more and more I was enjoying this.

I was so wet, my essence dribbled down my thighs and

made a mess between us. You could hear me sucking him back in my body every time he pulled out and slammed in again. He was thorough, his thrusts hard and measured, but I could tell he was holding back, and we had to rectify that.

"Ares." I tugged on his hair, unlatching him from my breast. "I need it harder."

The gold specks in his eyes flared, and he kissed me on the mouth once, muttering, "Your wish is my command," against my lips, making my stomach flutter, and then shift as he flipped me on my knees with no warning.

I squealed, my hair smacking the small of my back, and he took it as an invitation to grip it, twist it a few times in his fist, and hold me up, leaving my chest exposed, as he rode me hard and fast from behind. He hissed as he slid in deep, and my body shook with the force of his thrusts.

"How's that, beautiful?" he asked, and I feared if I gave him anything but a positive answer, he'd split me in half with his dick.

"You're fucking me like you hate me," I voiced because it was true. Passion was spilling out of us in waves. His grip on my hair was damn near painful, his hips were pistoning in me like a man possessed, and his other arm was wrapped underneath my tits, just to feel them bounce on his skin.

"That's because I do. I hate you," he growled in my ear and lost it, slamming into me repeatedly, with no tact or rhythm, just pure need. My poor insides melted like liquid to accommodate his intrusion, and I didn't know how something so violent could feel so fucking good. "I hate you for all the times you denied me when I could've been blowing your brains out years ago." *Thrust. Thrust. Thrust.* "I hate you for flirting with my best friend right in front of me when you knew what it did to me." *Thrust. Thrust. Thrust.* "In fact, I fucking despise you for that." He peppered his last sentence with a slap on my left tit, and my head fell back on his shoulder with a moan.

He let go of my hair, wrapping his palm around my neck and squeezing, feeling my wild pulse. Every part of my body tingled, and my world shrunk into this one room. For a second, I forgot anything else existed. It was just me, Serena Laurent, and Ares Alsford, lost in each other, taking what we weren't allowed to have for so long. The embodiment of Heaven and Hell coming together and creating pleasure so raw my ears rang and my lungs burned.

"Take my cock like you were born to ride it." He kissed the side of my face with a tenderness that contrasted everything else about him. "Apologize for acting like a bitch."

"Don't call me a bitch." A moan came out of my mouth simultaneously, weakening my defense.

The mocking lilt of his laugh went unmissed, and his hand on my breasts scaled down, running over my stomach, and worked my clit as he whispered, "How about a whore? My dirty little whore."

My hips bucked at his filthy words and touch. No woman in their right mind should like being called a whore, but coming out of Ares's mouth, it felt more like praise than an insult. I liked it way more than I cared to admit, and he knew when he chuckled at my responsive body.

"I'm sorry," I whimpered, knowing he deserved the world, and I'd thrown him scraps for years.

"Apology not accepted. Tell me you're mine, Serena. Tell me there's no one else you want fucking you until tomorrow." He backed every single sentence by driving deeper into me, his fingers pressing down harder on my clit, his teeth biting into my shoulder as if they were looking to draw blood.

My orgasm started building for a second time, like receding waves right before a tsunami hit. I didn't know what it was about this man, but he ruined my body from the inside out in a way only natural disasters could.

"I'm yours, Ares. No one else's." My words rang true because there had been no one else I'd fantasized about more than him. He was always on my mind, be it for good or bad. "Every time I was with him, I wished I could be with you," I admitted. Ares made everything bearable. Every time I saw him next to Leo, a part of my soul sighed with relief.

I didn't know how much he needed to hear those words until he gasped, his warm breath cascading over my skin like a soothing balm. A tortured sound came from within his chest, and I almost fell face-first on the couch as he transitioned his hands to capture both my wrists behind my back, using them to hold me in place, like a prisoner for his own enjoyment. My head bobbed wildly as he bounced me on his dick.

"Say it again," he ordered.

"I'm yours," I screamed into the dead of the night, smiling before finishing my sentence with words that would ultimately break the dam he kept over his release. "Only your dirty little whore."

I thought I heard him roar behind me, but I didn't know. It could have been the blood rushing to my ears.

"Fuck yes, you are. My beautiful girl." He delivered a slap to my ass, and my skin cracked by the force of his hit, making me cry out. "Come, baby. Come with me."

I didn't need any more encouragement. I was on the verge of release already, and with those final words from him,

I stepped off the cliff and surrendered my soul to the handsome devil. I was free-falling, suspended, as satisfaction unlike I'd ever felt before took me on a ride I would remember for the rest of my life. It wasn't just the sex that obliterated me. It was who I was doing it with, the charged atmosphere and emotions that ran between us like an overflowing current.

Waves of light flashed by me on my descent, and I knew it was Heaven closing its doors on me because there was no way bliss this intense wasn't the ultimate sin. Ares Alsford might have been God sent into this world, but together we were Hellbound. A recipe for disaster so good, you enjoyed every bite on your way to ruin. And that was what I did. I enjoyed every second of this orgasm like it was the last because if there was one thing I was set on never doing again, it was taking him for granted.

"Serena," he said my name in a broken whisper as we both collapsed on the couch, our bodies too heavy with sweat and aftershocks to be nothing more than a tangle of limp limbs. "You're it for me, baby. My endgame."

His voice was so hushed it was challenging to hear, but I did, and my heart squeezed painfully. My well of energy was depleted, yet I still found it in me to twist in his arms until we were face to face and chest to chest, still connected in all the ways that mattered.

I smoothed my finger up the crease of his eyebrows, swiping his messy hair back on his head and cupping the side of his face, kissing each shut eyelid once. "And you're mine. My endgame," I mirrored his words, and his eyes popped open to catch them as if we were exchanging vows.

The air charged with our pledge, and Ares sealed our promise with a soft kiss to my mouth. I didn't know what tomorrow held or what would happen to us because we were bound to face opposition from either side. But one thing I knew for sure was that after tonight, he would always have a permanent place in my heart.

I woke up the next morning in a bed, not the couch, naked under the comforter, the events of last night slowly coming back to me. The food, drinks, and finally, Ares Alsford and his magical dick.

Yeah, I called it magical because he'd made me come five more times with it. There was a lot of unresolved sexual tension between us and years of mutual pining that led to a whole lot of extra energy keeping us up throughout the night.

I broke out in a smile, blissfully exhausted, but more awake than I'd felt in a long time. I reached over but didn't feel him in bed, nor did I when I patted his sheets and pillow.

Where is he?

Cracking my eyes open, I squinted against the sunlight streaming in from the windows and rested my elbows on the mattress as I looked around. A decorative vase by the door was knocked over, still intact thanks to the soft Persian carpet underneath. Throw pillows were arranged neatly on the floor from when he took me from behind again and was considerate enough to think about my knees. And the curtains on one side of the window were ripped off— partially my fault, but primarily Ares's for wanting to try acrobatics against the wall.

The man of the hour was nowhere to be found, though.

His side of the bed was cold, but the indent of his body was still there, so at least I was sure I hadn't dreamt last night up.

Throwing the covers off me, I winced at the general soreness of my body and the frigid morning air that rushed around me. Tiptoeing to the bathroom, I emptied my bladder, brushed out my knotted hair, and guzzled some mouthwash. I didn't plan on having a sleepover, so I had to make do with what was already available.

My eyes turned to tiny moons when I saw the state of my neck and boobs, blooming with purple hickeys. Out of curiosity, I peeked at my backside in the mirror, and of course, when I squinted, I could make out faint handprints on both my ass cheeks. Fucking hell, no wonder I felt sore all over. He'd better be making it up to me with some pancakes, heavy on the maple syrup.

The cottage was eerily quiet when I stepped into the living room, shrugging what was left of my clothes on. My corset top was completely unsalvageable, but Ares's undershirt lay beside it, so I put that on instead, not missing the way my nerves eased. He wouldn't leave without his shirt, right?

"Ares?" I called, and my heart hammered in my chest when I received no response. I checked the kitchen, and it was untouched, and the breakfast I hadn't had somehow still found its way rushing up my throat.

God, I was being a drama queen. Maybe he stepped out for a second.

A muffled ringtone came from the living room, and the way I rushed for my phone was pathetic. I had to dig it out of the couch's cushions that had gotten quite a show last night, and when I did, my face fell.

It wasn't Ares.

It was my father.

"Hello?" I answered, my voice flat.

Why was he calling me? He hadn't cared when I'd gone missing for days on end before.

"Where the hell have you been?" Carter blurted out. "I've been calling you since last night."

I swallowed down the sarcastic response on the tip of my tongue. My sperm donor had ignored my calls countless times before, too busy doting on his mistresses or attending business trips that were more important than me, but I was supposed to come running every time he needed me.

I'd once made the mistake of cussing out Claire in front of him, and he'd locked me in my room for an entire day with no food. He never let me forget the power he had over me. I was his lackey more than I was his daughter. When he found out Leo and Eliana were getting closer, he all but blew up on me, and I was forced to try to split them up because them being together triggered him.

It was the day I started having doubts if Eliana's father had indeed murdered Leo's twin sister.

"I'm sorry, my phone was off," I told him. "What's the matter?"

"*What's the matter?*" He mimicked my voice. "The matter is that that boy toy of yours and his father are completely out of their minds."

I stilled, my mind flying to Ares. "What are you talking about?"

"Oh, please, do I have to spell out everything for you?" he hissed. "Leonardo and Alessio Bianchi showed up yesterday a few minutes after you left, accusing me of all sorts of wild stuff."

My legs faltered, and I sank onto the couch before they gave out.

It happened. Way sooner than I expected, and that was a problem.

"Like what?" I asked, even though I knew he'd never answer me.

"It doesn't matter right now. I need you to contact Elijah and bring him to the Astropolis Police Department. You'll find his number in the first drawer on my desk in the office."

"You were arrested?" The shock in my voice was surprisingly real for being one step ahead of him.

I was the one that provided the locations of the sex-trafficking ring my father was involved with to the police after snooping through his office one day. But even with actual hard facts against him, he was Carter Laurent. One of the best lawyers in the country. I never thought they'd actually nail him.

Obviously, I'd underestimated Leo's need for revenge.

"Yes. And everyone who had a hand in this is getting sued, don't worry." He raised his voice as if warning the people around him, and the urge to tell him I couldn't give less of a shit was intense. "Just do as you're told and hurry up and bring Elijah here. Claire is getting stressed, and it's not good for the baby."

My nails dug into the couch, and while I didn't care about Claire, especially after the confirmation that she was involved in the cover-up of Isabella's murder, the baby was innocent.

"Okay," I said and hung up on him without waiting for a response.

The situation sunk in as I stared at the brown coffee table, the silence around me deafening. While Ares had asked me out on multiple occasions in the past, I hadn't heard a peep from him ever since I kissed Leo on my birthday. I was forced to do it, but he didn't know that, and I gave ground to his anger. So it was suspicious that he decided to put the past behind him the day Leo apparently raided my house.

Even more suspicious... he was nowhere to be found today.

My chest caved, and I fell to my knees as the world came crashing down around me.

It was a lie.

All of it was a lie.

Leo wanted me out of the house for the day, and Ares, being his good friend, agreed to keep me busy by feeding me empty promises. Top-shelf liquor for a broken girl.

A loud sob escaped my mouth, and I let myself crumble on the same couch I thought I'd gotten my happy ending.

He didn't want me.

Contrary to his lies, even Ares Alsford had given up on me.

CHAPTER SIX
SERENA

Present

His touch seared my skin, and our proximity made me pant. Shivers sprung up my arms as I came to peace with the fact that Ares Alsford was pressed against me in an almost empty parking lot.

Not quite the reunion I'd dreamt of.

A thousand words sat on the tip of my tongue, but none of them expressed my thoughts very well. They sounded a bit distorted, foolish compared to the depth of my infatuation with this man.

So I settled for a warning, twisting my wrists in his palms. "Get your hands off me, right now."

My voice echoed, and Ares stiffened behind me as if he couldn't believe it was really *me* that had spoken. *I* couldn't believe that I was talking to him when I never thought I'd see him again, and I had a lot more time to get comfortable with the fact that he was only a few miles away from me on a daily basis.

It took some time for my words to sink in. It felt like hours went by as he squeezed my body against his, and my treacherous mind sang with happiness after getting pumped up on the feel of rough-textured palms, scratching familiarly against my much softer skin.

My front was pressed against a Mustang, and I welcomed the coolness of the hunk of metal, trying to eradicate the heat that emanated from my back. Unwelcome tendrils of secret, terrifying beauty spread down my spine like vines, more concentrated on the parts where we connected. His face was still shoved between my strands, and he took a deep breath from my neck, as if my scent gave him the fuel he needed to speak.

"But I know how much you love it when my hands are all over you." His reply had me shaking again, but for an entirely different reason. The tension was so stifling I struggled for my next breath. My brain was caught in the crosshairs of my indecisive heart, craving to hurt him but feeling weak next to the memories he alighted in me.

But I had to remind myself that was all it was: memories, beautifully crafted lies by the hands of a master deceiver.

I couldn't let them overwhelm me.

Ignoring the irrational burn weaving through my veins, I knocked my shoulders back with all the power I could muster, and from his muffled groan, I realized I caught him on the jaw. I tried to ignore the empty feeling that rushed around me as soon as his body wasn't on me anymore and turned around, catching him stumbling, his eyes wide and hooked on mine.

He still had the same clothes on, a patch on his shirt darker than the rest of the fabric. It told me he'd come straight back here to catch me after dropping off his date home. Something green burned through my veins like a lit wick, and I smoothed my hand down my dress. It shouldn't have, but knowing he wouldn't spend the night with her elated me.

"Jesus Christ, it really *is* you." Cupping his jaw, he looked at me like he was seeing me for the first time, and in a way, he was. I wasn't the same girl he'd abandoned the morning after a one-night stand. Far from it, actually.

My face carried wrinkles that weren't there the last time we were together. My vanity wouldn't let me not take care of myself, and while I did get regular skin and beauty treatments, years of substance abuse couldn't be entirely erased by a micro-needling pen. My breasts weren't as firm as they used to be, and the bottom of my stomach jutted out slightly, despite the daily set of crunches I performed religiously. The changes under my clothes were prominent, but he'd forever lost access to that part of me years ago.

I refused to cower under his perusal, refused to think about if he found me as attractive as he once did, or if even that had been a lie. I was still a knockout at thirty, and I wouldn't get in my head about it because of him.

"Did you think you were seeing ghosts or something?" I cocked my head. "If so, you should really get that checked."

He didn't bother replying right away, his eyes running down the length of me like a caress. There was familiarity in them. They burned like a meteor, but this time, instead of wanting to encase me with warmth, they turned me to ash.

"I didn't think you'd be stupid enough to show your face back here." His voice was measured, too controlled to be considered laidback. He ran a hand over his mouth as if to cage in any more words that craved to escape the tight-knit control he had them under.

He had nice hands. Big and masculine, with clean, blunt nails. I wished I could find something I didn't like about this man, but it seemed it would have to be with his personality and not with his appearance.

Annoyance bubbled to the surface, and I wondered what it would take for my body to understand that Ares Alsford was a walking red flag. He'd already killed a part of me I'd never even thought I'd mourn for.

A smirk graced my lips, disguising the hurt his words caused. "I'm sorry, I missed the part where it said I had to ask for your permission to return to my hometown."

"What hometown? You have no home here," he said, unimpressed, and I blinked at the bluntness of his words.

Now, *this* was the Ares underneath all those sweet words. This cold and aloof version of him was the true him, and I'd do well to remember it.

"I will," I replied with steely resolve, even though I knew he didn't mean a physical home.

I didn't realize my mistake until the words were already out of my mouth. Ares had no way of knowing I was still alone after all these years. He'd simply made a guess, and I'd confirmed his suspicions by running my big mouth.

I dug my nails into my palms as a form of punishment for falling for his trap, and he ran his teeth over his bottom lip as if to rein in a smile. My eyes narrowed on the corners of his mouth, and his gaze imitated mine. A look shouldn't feel so intimate, but his eyes taunted me as if he had X-ray vision and could see beneath the red fabric of my dress.

My nipples pebbled in response, and I held back a frustrated sigh. It was hard to win a battle when all the odds were stacked against you. When you insisted on remembering all the good and divine and burying the ugly and the bad. It was a defense mechanism to keep me from descending into total insanity, but I preferred dancing with madness over letting anyone walk all over me ever again.

I shifted my hair over my chest before he caught on to my body's betrayal, and the plague of thoughtful silence was sliced when he lingered on my strands before pointing an accusatory finger at me. "It was you. You were the one that showed up at the house showing."

Well, now you remember me.

I crossed my arms and took in the parking lot. Only a few people lingered, and they were too far away to see us. Where the hell was everyone, all the Ubers and Lyfts? It was the end of happy hour. Surely the universe hadn't aligned, so we'd have an uninterrupted conversation.

I lifted a shoulder. "I don't know what you're talking about."

"You crushed my bike," he drawled as if we were discussing the weather.

"You shouldn't have parked it there," I replied in that same bored tone of his, holding a smile back when the annoyance he was trying to hide peeked through his mask.

Of course, when a snake was backed into a corner, it struck.

"Amelia Duante? That's the name you're going by now?" He made a sound of dry amusement. "What happened, Siren? Are you too ashamed of your actual name?"

"Amelia *is* my middle name, and Duante is my *mother's* last name, asshat, so technically, both are still *my* names."

I resisted the urge to add a *"Ha, take that!"* at the end of my sentence because it would only make me look like a five-year-old, but when the feds told me to go with something other than Serena Laurent, I'd felt like a genius when I took on my mom's name. She was barely in any of my records. My father had made sure to wipe every trace of her existence, and my identity wouldn't be a lie.

"And what drove you to use your middle name?" he asked, and when I didn't immediately respond, he added, "I mean, I get it, being related to a murderer is not something to be proud of."

A cold sensation settled in my stomach, and his dry as gin gaze didn't feel so lovely anymore on my skin. I wasn't only related to a murderer. I was one. If he was still so caught up over what my father had done a decade ago and judged me for it, who knew what he'd think of me if he caught up on my life events ever since.

This whole night was a mistake. The desperate twenty-year-old in me hadn't thought about the repercussions of her ex-friends finding out she'd been under their nose this entire time, too busy starving for drops of Ares's attention.

Poking holes at my past had been a mistake, and Ares served as my lesson once again. These people thought they were angels with their holier than thou attitudes. A low-life demon like me was perceived as worse than dirt by them.

"It was *not* so great to see you again, Ares." Venom coated each sweetly spoken word like candy. "Hope you have a lousy night."

I made to turn, but a second later, he had my forearm trapped in his hand, anchoring me in place. The atmosphere grew heavy as I glared at his square jaw from below and became claustrophobic as his large body closed in on me.

"If you think I'm going to just let you waltz back into town, you have another thing coming." His breath coasted over my cheeks, leaving a faint dusting of pink wherever it touched. Anger buzzed like a live wire beneath the layers of my skin, and I couldn't help but wish I had the ability to shock his hold off me with a single touch.

"You forget who you're talking to, Alsford. If *you* think I'm intimidated by the likes of you"—I took a deep breath, shoving my arm from his grip but not backing down and letting him have my personal space—"*you* have another thing coming."

The corners of his lips tipped up with fake amusement. "You can put up a big front all you want, Siren, but you've been gone for so long, you have no friends here."

"I never did. I never had any true friends here, anyway." Something akin to hurt flickered on his expression, but it was so quick I thought I'd imagined it. "And the only way I'm ever going to be your Siren again is if I'm drugged, or out of my mind, so you might as well stop calling me that."

"I'll call you whatever the hell I want." We were almost face to face now, and while to an outsider, it might have looked like we were seconds away from ripping each other's clothes off in the parking lot, what we were truly doing, however, was squaring off. "I'm only going to ask you once, and your reason better be good. What are you doing here?"

"None. Of. Your. Business." I smiled as I punctuated each word of my sentence, and his hands turned to fists by his sides as he persisted.

"Why are you back?"

"Oops, that was the second time you asked." I held up two fingers, making it seem like he was dumb and needed a visual representation of what I was saying. His gaze singed my cheek, but I kept going. "Paraphrasing the question doesn't make it a new one."

"Do you remember what happened the last time you tested me, Siren?"

He asked indifferently, as if the question shared the same merit as my favorite food. Nevertheless, my cheeks filled with heat before I could stop it. He was referring to our night together, and I forced myself to think about the morning after instead.

I inhaled slowly and then released it.

It did the trick. Resentment poured off me, mixing with the scent of wine and salty ocean waves as I shook my head. "No. You were so insignificant to me. I barely remember anything about you other than you being Leo's friend and number one ass kisser."

I knew mentioning Leo would twist him up inside, but he hid it well. The only tell was his hands flexing a second after he shoved them in his pockets.

"That's cute," he commented, his jaw squaring. "Well, this ass kisser is doing you the favor of warning you to leave before you're neck-deep in rent payments, because the only way you're ever going to get a house here is when I'm six feet underground."

A drop of sweat rolled down my spine, albeit I was unsure if it was from the high temperatures as of late or his threat.

He couldn't do that. He couldn't take away the one thing I stood to gain the most out of since moving back to this godforsaken place. I wouldn't allow it.

"And how exactly do you think you're going to accomplish that?"

"I do own the number one real estate company in the city. It's my job to know which houses are for sale and which buyers are to be blacklisted." His tone was threatening, and a subtle glow of amusement lit his eyes up when my face dropped before I could stop it.

I used to love sneaking peeks at his face because—if I could be honest—he looked like God himself had molded him into existence. Like he had taken extra care to make him as beautiful as possible with his high cheekbones and heavy lashes, but contempt so deep it dripped like slime down my throat filled me as I stared at him now.

I tried to keep it from bleeding into my expression because if he knew how much this turn of events bothered me, he'd fight me tooth and nail on it. It was a losing battle, though, and I had to get out of here before he caught on.

"You're insane." I gritted my teeth, this time genuinely turning my back on him. "Every house sale in Astropolis doesn't go through you."

"We'll see about that."

"Take your empty threats elsewhere, Ares," I said and forced my limbs to move, taking it one step at a time. He didn't stop me this time, and I didn't allow myself to linger on the disappointment that suffocated me like a thick fleece blanket.

"Oh, and Siren?" I kept a steady pace, but his mocking words still reached me. "If you ever come after me or one of my dates again, destruction of private property is not going to be the only thing I'm going to have you charged with."

ARES

"We don't hit people just because they annoy us, Ares," Mama said, standing in front of a red punching bag hanging from the basement's ceiling. Dad was next to her, staring at me stoically. They were both disappointed in me since I

95

shoved an asshat that kept bugging the hell out of me against the lockers and knocked two of his front teeth loose.

It had resulted in my suspension and a lot of nagging from both of them, but if I could turn back time, I'd do it again. Especially when I remembered I'd caught him looking up Serena's cheerleading skirt while on the field the other day.

Bastard had another thing coming if he thought I'd let his predatory ways and running mouth fly.

Mom patted the punching bag, trying to recapture my attention. I blinked, refocusing on her concerned brown eyes, preferring them to my dad's disappointed ones. Fucking hell, they were acting like I'd become a delinquent from a single punch. It wasn't my fault the guy was a wimp and cried to Mommy because I'd cost him a trip to the dentist.

"Whenever you feel angry at school, you can come home and take it out on this punching bag. Look, Daddy and I set it up just for you."

Her patronizing tone grated on my nerves, and I gritted my teeth. What was this? Rehabilitation for their troubled son? It was just one fucking punch. I opened my mouth to say so, but my father cut me off with a single look, followed by words that would stay with me for years to come.

"Listen to me, boy. In this world, if you act like a brute, you get treated like one. Brains win over fists every day. You hit someone? That gets you sued. You injure someone badly? You get sent to jail." He stated every sentence like it was the rule of life. "Don't mess up people's faces. Mess with their minds. It's harder but more effective in the long run, and most importantly, it doesn't get you suspended."

Mom gasped, glancing between us like she was hoping she could use a neuralyzer to erase what dad had said from my brain. *"That's not really the lesson we should be teaching our teenage son, Christian."*

"He's going to figure it out anyway when he gets older, Quinn. Might as well give him the tools to succeed now." Dad shrugged, clasping my shoulders and nodding toward the swinging, oblong sack of sand. "Do you see this right here, boy?"

"Yes."

"It's the only thing you ever get to punch again for as long as you are under my roof. If I get one more call from your principal again about you being involved in a fistfight, you're grounded." He looked me in the eyes, before finishing his sentence, serious as a heart attack. "For life. Do I make myself clear?"

"Yes, sir."

I would love to say from that point on, I never used my fists unless absolutely necessary, but that wouldn't be the case. I'd just learned to be smarter about it. While my father had been right, and messing with people's heads got you places faster than your fists did, some people's minds were as empty as a used fountain pen. Violence was the only language they understood, and I was a sexually frustrated teenager with too much pent-up energy.

His teachings came in handy now, though, as I strained my muscles to go as hard as they could on *Bob*, otherwise known as my body opponent bag. He was an unlucky little man that got to bear the brunt of what Serena Laurent did to my body and mind. I needed to keep busy not to think about her. I'd been going crazy for the past week.

What is she doing here?

How long has she been here for, and I haven't noticed?

How is she still perfectly intact?

How had Eliana's P.I. not found anything on her when she was still alive?

Why does she get my dick even harder now than before?

Questions about her spread like fungus on my brain. If I wasn't immersed in the mystery of her sudden appearance after ten years, I fell back into old toxic habits of thinking about fucking her. Or staring at her, like a day hadn't even passed. I'd take whatever scraps she'd give me. And wasn't that just pathetic?

She lingered on the walls of my head like mold. Her voice was imprinted in my memory. Her little breathy gasps of shock, sounds I longed to hear every second. The scrape of her nails down my hand the other day, when she threw me off her, reminding me how they felt tugging on my hair when my tongue was attached to her cunt.

It was like my echoes of her were shoved in a little box in a corner of my head, secured by a fucking hair tie that was struggling against the overflow of my spiked obsession with the one thing I couldn't have. With the one thing I shouldn't want, but craved like a man starving for his next meal.

The fan whirled overhead as sweat dripped down my back from the rapid swing of my arms. I performed two jabs in a row and followed them up with an uppercut that sent the dummy tumbling to the floor despite its reinforced bottom.

A boom sounded, and the other two guests in my home gym stopped what they were doing, their eyes wide as they watched my heaving chest go up and down like I'd run a marathon.

"Boy, who hurt you?" It was Killian Astor who spoke first.

A manipulative witch with eyes that know how to play

the strings of my soul like a fucking harp, and perfect chestnut hair I'd like to wrap around my fist as she chokes on my cock. She took off and is now back, looking to make my life miserable again.

I didn't bother answering, just took a swig out of the water bottle I'd abandoned next to the treadmill. I should tell them, warn Leo that *she* was back in town, but I was feeling particularly possessive over the information—*over her.*

First, I needed to know for sure what she was doing back in Astropolis. If she planned on staying for a while or would be gone after a couple of weeks. I prayed it was the latter, and if it was, I didn't need to hurt anyone by scratching old wounds.

Sure, keep telling yourself that.

A snide voice in the back of my mind snarked, and the force of my fingers curled the hard plastic bottle inward. All right, so I might've wanted some time to explore this new turn of events by myself because as soon as everyone else learned Serena made an appearance, I'd be pulled in a thousand different directions at once.

"I thought you got laid last weekend," Saint said, and they both abandoned their weights as they came to stand next to me. The brothers looked very similar with their sandy hair and nearly identical facial features. If it wasn't for Killian's tattoos and blue eyes instead of gold like his brother's, I would've had difficulty telling them apart.

I glared at Saint for bringing up the topic of my struggling love life once again, and he sent me a blinding smile in return. The bastard could've done an ad campaign for Crest. He was that clean-cut as opposed to me and Killian. "Apparently not."

"What are you smiling about?" Killian punched Saint's

thick forearm. "Not everyone has a hot piece of ass waiting on them every night when they return home from work. Don't knock a man while he's down."

The look on Saint's face said he was ready to pull him limb from limb any second now as he faced him. "Kid, if you call Aria a hot piece of ass again, I'm going to introduce my fist to your face."

"Sorry, I meant to say a beautiful piece of scrumptious curve—" Saint did as he warned but missed when Killian ducked at the last minute, chuckling. "All right, all right, stop it, I'm sorry. I'm never looking at your wife again. I prefer her sister's ass anyway."

"Killian!" Saint almost roared and went after him again. This time, the squirt that was turning out to be a pain in his brother's ass didn't back down. "You are to stay away from Irena!"

"Goddamn." Killian squared up to Saint, the ink on his neck stretching with his movements. "What happened to your sense of humor?"

"It knows when you're joking and when you're hiding behind a joke."

The two were constantly up each other's throats ever since Killian dropped out of college in California two months ago and started hanging around more and more. At first, I thought it was brothers being brothers, but I sensed some underlying tension between them as more time went by.

I was no shrink. Hell, I was a fucking only child. I had no idea what all this meant, but I knew they needed to figure some shit out. And if it involved swinging punches and blood, it wasn't going to happen on my expensive parquet floors.

"Will the both of you shut up?" I got between them before things escalated, and being so close to two other sweaty, shirtless dudes at seven in the morning wasn't a position I thought I'd be in today.

I had my own damned life to fix.

They backed away reluctantly when I pushed them in different directions. Killian retreated to his phone, and Saint stole the water bottle from my hand.

"So, what *did* crawl up your ass?" he asked, taking a sip and making my left eye twitch.

I sighed, my nerves getting tested today. "Why are you both here? I remember canceling our workout quite clearly."

"We asked you what other plans you had, and you said nothing," Killian explained, his face still shoved in his phone while he texted away, sitting on an expandable bench.

"That was still not an invitation for you to show up anyway," I stated drily, but neither of them paid any attention to me.

Saint opened his mouth again, no doubt to say something obnoxious, but was cut off by my ringtone. I peeked at the screen, and a sardonic breath escaped me at the way my heart sped up in my chest, even worse than when I was kicking the hell out of the dummy.

God, I was playing with fire, and I had to be careful not to get burned a second time.

"Can I trust you two not to kill each other while I take this call?" I addressed both of them, and the only response I got was a glare at each other and identical scoffs as they started working out on opposite ends of the gym.

Running my tongue across my teeth, I ignored the lot of them, slipping my phone off the floor and retreating to the backyard flooded with sun rays and calming ambient sounds from the artificial waterfalls of the pool.

Good, I needed all the calm I could get for this phone call.

Sliding to answer, a warm, feminine voice greeted me on the other end, my assistant chippy as ever to be working on a Sunday morning. She had to be—her salary was three times higher than that of an average assistant, but she also filled in for other roles that didn't fit her job description and had connections I needed.

"Good morning, Mr. Alsford."

"Good morning, Yael," I returned her greeting, settling on one of the bamboo sun lounges, spreading my legs, so the sweat on my basketball shorts dried off.

"I've gathered the information you requested, sir. I'm calling to inform you I just emailed it to you since it seemed quite urgent," she commented, and I stilled, pressing the phone harder against my ear to refrain from putting her on speaker and delving into everything Serena Laurent. "I'm sorry it took me a week. It was hard to get anything on her. And even what I did manage to find is not much, just mundane everyday stuff. Did you say her name was Serena Laurent prior to this name change?"

"Yes."

My skin warmed as the sun rays came down harder when the fresh morning weather slipped off little by little, but inside, my bloodstream cooled as I braced myself for the worse. Something deep in my gut twisted when I remembered the way her eyes darkened when I asked her why she went by Amelia Duante now.

There was a story there that extended past her shame,

and I was determined to uncover it. Uncover every single little detail about her.

I'd been good—the fucking best. I hadn't sought her out when everything in me screamed to do so. To find her and shake her for bailing on me. I'd set her free because while our demons danced with each other, we weren't healthy. This maddening obsession that filled my pores every time I thought of her wasn't typical.

But then she'd gone and twisted my hand.

She ruined my date and dropped back in my lap like a kitten begging to be declawed.

I'd give her something to remember and send her back to where she came from for good this time. I didn't need her here messing things up.

"Well, according to my contacts, Serena Laurent overdosed four years ago in a motel in Boston. From there, she was rushed to the hospital where she ultimately lost her life." My heart skipped a beat, as if not bearing the thought of envisioning her dead. Yael hesitated on the other end of the line before leaving me with more questions than the answers I wanted. "So, either you have the wrong girl, or she's in a buttload of trouble and someone really powerful is covering for her."

CHAPTER SEVEN
SERENA

"How have you been, Serena?"

The man slouched on my tiny green sectional would have anyone running for the hills at first sight. Bodybuilder big, with broad shoulders, buzz-cut hair, and deep brown eyes that had seen their fair share of atrocities in this unjust world and carried extra weight every time they looked at you. His nose was crooked, giving you the perception that he'd broken it one too many times, and in all honesty, given everything I knew about Samuel Duante, that was probably the case.

"Fine, and you?" I questioned as I handed him the doppio espresso he'd asked for and placed my cappuccino on the glass coffee table.

He was pleased to see the brand-new Nespresso machine in my kitchen. Last time he'd visited me, I'd made him instant coffee, and he all but revoked my Italian heritage. It was safe to say, I kept the fact that I broke my pasta before boiling it to myself after that.

His stare was emotionless as he examined any part of my

body that wasn't covered by my white Valentino dupe dress (because maturing was realizing you didn't need to spend five thousand on a dress when you could get something similar and just as good for a hundred bucks), coasting over my bare skin with cold precision.

"You know what I mean." He lifted a brow, and if it wasn't for his words, I would've cracked a smile at how ridiculous he looked, taking a sip out of a tiny cup with his pinky sticking out and all.

He had been searching for bruises on my skin, needle marks. I didn't blame him. I didn't have the best relapse record.

Taking a deep breath, I inhaled the sweet scent of the lemon cake baking in the kitchen and let calm wash over me. Sam was a man of few words, and he rarely handed out praise, but I could tell he was pleasantly surprised by my spotless apartment and its colorful palette. Not to mention the fact that I wouldn't be caught dead cooking about a year ago and now had taken up baking.

Did I step it up a notch because I'd been privy to his arrival? Maybe. I kept hoping I could replace all those horrible memories of me begging him for a hit while I retched my guts out in a bucket with this new put-together version of me.

The wary spark in his eyes told me it was never going to happen, though, as I took my sweet time responding.

"Sober as a nun, Samuel. I told you, you have nothing to worry about anymore." I uncrossed my legs, crossed them again, and then blew on my coffee, so it didn't burn my tongue.

All this nervous twitching wasn't making my case any stronger. He got under my skin, though, because, unlike everyone else, I craved his approval. That pat on the back from a little girl that never had a father figure.

"Good, that's good." He nodded, and I knew that was the best I'd ever get.

"How is Gracie holding up? Everything went well with the delivery of the baby?"

"She's doing better every day. We're really excited about this latest addition to our family." His eyes lit up like the fourth of July when I asked about his wife, and he grabbed his phone from his pocket, showing me both her and their newborn cuddled up together in a hospital bed. His wife, looking down on the bloody, wrinkly baby on her chest as if she was a miracle, tears rolling down her flushed cheeks like jewels.

I was ecstatic for them. They'd been trying for a baby for the longest time and had finally managed to have one after so many failed IVF attempts.

"Evie is a lovely name," I pointed out, and he turned to me with narrowed eyes, pocketing his phone again.

"I never told you my daughter's name. How do you know it?"

"I can read minds," I deadpanned, then pointed to the tattoo on his neck when he crossed his arms. If he looked buff before, he resembled a tank like this. His fingers flew over his inked skin, and he grimaced when I asked, "Do you think it's wise? Tattooing your family's names on your skin with the work that you do?"

It was risky. If he was ever kidnapped, his enemies would know where to strike first. And I imagined he had made plenty after twenty years of working for the Federal Bureau of Investigation.

"I'm retiring next year, so I think we'll be fine."

"Oh." I blinked, not having known that. "But you're so young."

"It was always Gracie's and my plan to retire young." He shrugged, downing his coffee like a shot. "We worked our asses off in our earlier years to have the luxury of retiring whenever we wanted. I was actually going to hand in my resignation when she got pregnant, but..." His voice trailed off, and my grip became sweaty on the cup's handle.

My stomach tightened with nerves, and I glanced away from him toward the sparkling city lights from my balcony door. I lived on the thirtieth floor. It was easy to distract yourself with a beautiful view when you didn't like what was transpiring in your head.

"But you have to deal with my ass," I finished his sentence.

"It's not like that—" He started, but I cut him off.

"You don't have to sugarcoat anything, Sam. I know my life is not the only one I derailed with my actions."

"Using the word *derail* is a bit of a stretch because I get to retire at forty-one instead of forty." His voice was bone-dry, and the corners of my lips tipped up. "I'm staying because I want to; there are many incredible detectives I trust with my life that I could've assigned your case to, but I promised myself I would be the one to put an end to this."

Swarms of butterflies went off all at once inside me, and I realized why I always felt warm and fuzzy whenever Sam was around. He had been searching for me, and when I finally escaped, he was the one that found me and didn't run off when I greeted his head with a baseball bat after he knocked on my shitty motel door in the middle of the night. There was a lot of crying involved, mostly from me, because I couldn't believe someone had cared enough to look for me.

Sam was my protector in more ways than one. He did the impossible and carried me out of a ditch I thought I'd die in. If he asked me to lay my life down for him, I would.

"Because I'm your sister's daughter?" I asked, and anger simmered beneath his irises at the way I described our relationship.

"Because you're my *niece*," he corrected, taking my cappuccino away from me when it didn't seem like I was all too interested in drinking it. He glanced down at it, his brows furrowed. "And I wasn't there to protect you when I should've been."

"It wasn't your fault, Sam." He stiffened when I touched his arm, but I didn't take it personally. He had been through a lot in his career, and people touching him was a big no-no. I let my hand drop with a swallow. "I never told anyone how Carter treated me. He knew how to get me to keep my mouth shut. There was no way you could've known. And besides, you showed up when it mattered."

And stayed when I was a second away from knocking on death's door voluntarily.

"It wasn't anyone's fault, but Carter's." Sam's tone got gravelly. "I hope you know that. I hope you don't sit around blaming yourself."

I didn't blame *only* myself, though I could've spoken to the police sooner. I could've done something without waiting for Leo and Eli to take the first step, yet I'd acted like a coward. I was all about self-preservation, and I guess it was what had kept me alive and why I avoided looking in the mirror for too long.

"Oh, don't worry, I blame him plenty, all right? He got what he deserved, though." I balanced the truth on a double-edged sword because if I'd outright lied, Sam would've caught it. I doubted I was a better liar than the career criminals he interrogated for a living.

The oven's timer went off at the same time my stomach growled, and my mouth watered at finally getting to eat. I hadn't had anything since lunch, and it was nearing seven in the evening.

"Cake's ready." I got up, throwing him a look over my shoulder. "Do you want a slice?"

"How's that even a question?"

He followed me to the open-plan kitchen, setting some utensils on the onyx countertop, filling two glasses with water, and watching me with a frown on his face as I ducked in front of the oven when hot air rushed for me. Performing acrobatics because I got too excited for food was a daily occurrence.

"So why didn't you bring the girls? They aren't ready to be on long journeys yet?" I asked as I scooped out three slices for him, then one for me, and we sat on clear stools opposite each other. I waited for his thoughts on the cake expectantly as he took a bite, and he gave me a satisfied smile and a thumbs-up after swallowing.

I wasn't the greatest cook. Being in the kitchen just relaxed me, and I was getting better day by day if I could say so myself. Plus, I hated eating takeout...or opening the door without prior knowledge of who would be on the other side.

"I didn't feel comfortable bringing them here."

"Blunt as ever, uncle."

"It is what it is, Serena." Sam shrugged. "We're doing the best we can to keep your location a secret, but it's still not safe."

"So I'm guessing a trip to Hawaii for my birthday this year is out of the question?"

His answering look told me it was out of the question for at least two more years. I wasn't dying to go or anything like that, although not being imprisoned for six months in one location and then uprooting my life and being relocated to the next would be nice.

"We still have one name to cross off the list, and until then, you're staying put. The names you gave us..." He shook his head, and a chill went down my spine. They were only ink on paper for him. They'd been my daily reality for a year. "These are individuals with a lot to lose and will stop at nothing to eradicate a potential problem."

A familiar pang of regret hit me square in the chest, and guilt came swirling right along with it. I was a paradox. Sometimes I regretted ratting the bastards out. High-ranking officers and crooked politicians that beat women bloody to get their high, yet the thought of letting them continue thriving in fortresses made out of other people's suffering made my skin crawl with contempt.

There had been other girls that escaped the bordello. I wasn't a trailblazer in any way. They'd kept their mouths shut, though, and were allowed to go on with their lives. I'd let mine flow like a river, and now they were eager to drown me in one.

"Do I trust everyone at the agency?" I forked some cake in my mouth and shifted in my seat.

Organized crime was layered like an onion. It went a lot deeper than the average person thought, and I had no doubt in my mind they had tons of puppets shoved in governmental positions.

"You'll always get your news first from me." His eyes held a warning, and I nodded silently.

"Is there anything I can do to help?"

"Keep yourself out of trouble."

I didn't know why my mind immediately flew to Ares when I heard the word *trouble*, and I chewed slowly to delay my response. I didn't want *trouble*, yet *trouble* was dead set on following me around; damned be the time and place I unleashed the green monster in me on him. It was my own fault the bloodhounds in this town had caught wind of my scent, all because I couldn't keep my jealousy on a leash. When he didn't even deserve that.

I would try to keep myself out of trouble, as long as *trouble* kept his big nose out of my business. I had the element of surprise this time. As the saying went—*when you stare at darkness, it stares back*, and Ares Alsford didn't know just how dark I could get. He'd already destroyed a part of my soul I'd never get back. I wasn't going to let him claim another.

"Seems easy enough to do," I croaked, sipping some water to wet my parched throat.

"I heard you were looking to buy the house your mom and I grew up in."

I appreciated the subject change, even though there was no tact in it. This man was as graceful as a baby dinosaur on roller skates.

"Did a little bird whisper it in your ear?" Irony made its presence felt in my tone as he reminded me once again of my lack of privacy.

"You can't," he said, and it sounded a lot like an ultimatum.

My back turned ramrod straight. "And why the hell not? It's a good investment."

"And a very traceable transaction, which is something you can't afford to do right now." He rubbed a hand down his scalp as if I was giving him a headache. "Besides, it's best if you don't own your own house. Make sure your address is not in any documents."

My face scrunched up. "How do I do that? Do I give someone the money, and they buy it for me?"

Sam heaved a heavy sigh of disappointment. "You've got a lot to learn."

I smiled, seizing the window of opportunity before he drove back to Boston. "Then teach me your ways, master. I don't have to be at work for at least"—I glanced at the analog clock on the wall—"fifteen more hours."

ARES

"Oh my gosh, I'm so sorry to hear you didn't get a chance to view the house."

I stopped dead in my tracks on my way to my office on Monday afternoon. It had been a long day full of meetings, Excel sheets, projection predictions, and about a ton of different problems I'd go insane trying to solve in one day. Yet my brain somehow remembered that one of my realtors, Jenna, had taken over Amy's clients now that she was on maternity leave. The metal door was cracked open, and a sliver of light spilled over my Oxfords as I shifted closer, a whole-ass adult eavesdropping on his employees.

She wouldn't, would she?

She wouldn't call after I warned her off.

It was Serena we were talking about. The girl could turn more vicious than a Rottweiler when it came to getting what she wanted. As much as I disliked her, she had more balls than ninety percent of the men in my life. And that was precisely what had attracted me to her in the first place: her ability to spill her blood, bare her teeth, and go down fighting.

Of course, she would. She'd come back for more, and the fact that that knowledge sent a spark of excitement straight to my dick was concerning.

"Of course," Jenna's voice echoed again, a bit distracted as she scrolled down her computer screen. "Yes, we can absolutely set up another date for you to come by. It says here the house is still on the market—"

I pushed the door open before I even had any time to process what I was doing, cutting Jenna off mid-sentence. She jumped, but I made a shushing motion and mouthed for her to give me the phone.

Her expression told me she thought I was losing it, and mine replied that I was about to if she didn't do as I said. Grimacing, she slowly handed her phone over as if it was a ticking bomb and any sudden movements would cause it to explode.

Palming her phone, a smooth, feminine voice floated to my ears, repeating *hello* over and over again, much like the one I often tried to silence in my head.

"*I'll have the phone back to you as soon as the call is done,*" I mouthed to Jenna and was out the door before she could reply. Blowing down the hallway, I headed straight for my office, where no one could bear witness to how this woman tweaked my nerves like guitar strings.

"Is anyone there?" A frustrated sigh came through the other end.

"Ms. Laurent," I greeted, her name slipping off my tongue like silk. "Do you like testing my limits? Seeing how much you can probe before I show you back to your place?"

I imagined her mouth dropping open and closed, that confused expression that looked borderline like sexual frustration, painting her face as she questioned if it was indeed my voice coming through the speaker. She wasn't used to me speaking to her this way, so coming up with retorts for people that were only just recently added to her permanent shit list took a second.

"Mr. Alsford, I'd appreciate it if you could put Jenna back on the phone," she sputtered, and I waved my assistant off as I closed the door to my office. "I have nothing to say to you."

"That's too bad, sweetheart. Jenna is not available anymore. In fact, no one at Alsford Realty is," I purred as if delivering life-altering positive news. "If you are interested in one of our properties, I'm afraid I'm your only point of contact."

An unexpected sharp curse traveled through the line, and I gave my tie a tug as I settled on my spinning chair, drumming my fingers on the Oakwood table. A coffee cup since early this morning lay abandoned next to my keyboard, and I chugged whatever was left of it to combat some of the sweetness that bloomed on the back of my tongue. It did the trick, and Serena's following sentence added to the bitterness of the black liquid.

"Look, I've been here for three months, and you just found out about it last week, so I think it's safe to say I'm not looking to bother you, nor do I want to be bothered." She had a point, but for some reason, the fact that I was simply ignored by her for so long heightened my need to want to get under her skin and bury myself so fucking deep she felt me in her lungs every time she drew a breath. "So could we please go on with our lives and pretend each other doesn't exist."

"Really?" I scoffed, my eyes rolling to the back of my head. "Then why did my date end up wearing the contents of her wineglass instead of drinking it?"

"That was an accident," she said a little too quickly, and a sick part of me took pleasure in knowing I evoked some type of emotion in her despite the ice-queen persona she was trying to convey.

Serena Laurent was an enigma I was going to crack open come hell or high water. The second you let your enemy wander through your territory unattended, you'd lost the entire war, and I'd simply built too much of a grand life to let it crumble under her feet.

"Nothing's an accident with you. I've known you since kindergarten, Serena. You spent a night in jail because you couldn't handle rejection."

"When did you become so ignorant?" she snapped back at the mention of her worst of days. "So comfortable in living in your clear-cut, black and white world. The Ares I remember wasn't like this."

"The Ares you remember is dead, sweetheart." *You buried him single-handedly.* "This is the only version of me you're getting from now on."

"Bummer. Seems like a downgrade."

"Our latest models are reserved for people with actual value."

She sucked in a breath, and I banged my head against the

headrest, wanting to feel something—*anything* other than contempt, lust, and hidden insecurity. I was usually better at leashing my emotions, but with the death of my parents and Serena's reappearance, the dam over my control was cracking open.

"What the fuck do you want from me, Ares?" She ended with my name on a higher octave, and I blinked when genuine pain traveled through her voice.

Everything.

Everything you can't give me because you always felt less than I did. Because you bailed at the first sign of a deeper connection, like I wasn't worth your effort.

"Last time I checked, you were the one calling my place of work, so it's you that wants something from me."

"You know very well what I want." She sighed as I started typing a text I'd probably regret on my phone. I didn't allow myself to linger on it, though, and sent it off to my assistant.

"That house is not on the market anymore."

Serena scoffed, and I could almost hear her rolling her eyes. "One of your realtors said it still was *five seconds* ago."

"I bought it." I paused, the sound of her wings being clipped, echoing like a fucking symphony in my ears. "As of *five seconds ago.*"

Not exactly true. I put in an offer five seconds ago, but you had to be a bit of a liar in order to tell a story the right way. Besides, no one else would put in a higher offer for that shithole.

I felt good taking something from her, punching a hole through her plans.

Was it petty? Yes.

Did I care? No.

Serena's frowns interested me more than her smiles. I warned her to leave; she'd stayed, called my place of work, and fought with me over the phone. She wanted to get nasty but seemed to have forgotten how good I was at painting her every shade of filthy under the sun.

"*What?*" Her high-pitched voice pierced my eardrum, and I held the phone an inch away from my ear. It still didn't stop me from hearing her next statement, clear as glacial water and just as cold. "I fucking hate you, Ares. I hate you with all my heart."

She meant it, I knew she did, and her words stayed lodged in my throat like fragments of glass. I almost snorted when I thought twenty-year-old me got what he always wanted...a place in her heart. It was true what they said: be careful what you wish for, or at least be very specific with your wishes.

"How much do you want this place, Laurent?" I relented, breathing hard through my nose.

"Badly," she whispered, sensing the shifting winds and hopping on.

"Why? Its asking price is good but not worth it for all the cash you'll have to fork out for renovations."

Nothing but silence greeted me, and I pinched the bridge of my nose, frustrated more so with myself than anyone else. I'd fucking get those answers out of her, so be it the last thing I did. Stubbornness was a negative personality trait, but satisfying my curiosity ranked higher than worrying for my deteriorating mental stability.

"Come by my office on Thursday, and we can discuss this further."

There was a pregnant pause after my offer, as if we both couldn't believe what the hell I'd said. Was I really going to leave this up for discussion? For the moment, yes, but come Thursday, I couldn't change opinions like a leaf caught in the wind. I had two goals:

1. Cracking her open and learning what she'd been up to and why Yael couldn't get almost any information on her.

2. Driving her out of town when all was said and done because I didn't need the added distraction that was breathing the same air as her.

"I work until five," she said, confirming that she was indeed planning to stay.

"Then come after work."

"I have a date planned after work."

"Fucking cancel it, Serena." My throat felt coarse when the sentence came out of my mouth, and I cleared it, remedying my outburst by adding, "Or don't, see if I care when I raze your little passion project to the ground."

CHAPTER EIGHT

ARES

Thirteen Years Ago

Furious green eyes tracked me down as soon as I entered the kitchen, and I smelled the confrontation in the air before Leo even had a chance to open his mouth, looking forward to it since Eliana sat on my lap.

Notorious for making things messy, Leo threw a party in honor of her father's death in prison, and the asshat took it a step further by sending her an invite. I couldn't believe my eyes when she showed up, though, looking like a fucking wet dream in a crushed pink mini dress, all tan and dewy as if she'd just flown in from Ibiza.

Cunty brunettes might've been more up my speed, but any guy with working eyes in that room was adjusting their pants when Eliana showed up. And when she came up to me with a smile, notes of a peach scent lingering in the air as she threw her gold locks over one shoulder and offered to make Bianchi's life as miserable as he was making both of ours since Isabella passed, I didn't even have to think about it.

I got a bombshell warming up my dick with her generous curves. Leonardo blew up. And Serena's eyes lit with jealousy, lingering on my hands palming the front of Eliana's dress.

I smiled at him as I opened the cooler, and he saw it as an invitation he was all too happy to accept. I let him have at it as he grabbed me by the collar, slamming me against the silver fridge doors. My head banged against the metal, and I laughed as my vision spun.

"I should have your dick skinned." Leo's forearm pinned me in place, his face set in a snarl.

"Go for it," I taunted, hands dead by my sides. I didn't try to push him off. Watching him like this pleased me more than it hurt me. We'd been boiling up to this moment for months, and it was finally coming apart. "It's probably the closest you're ever going to get to Eliana."

A growl bubbled up his throat, and my head snapped back by the impact of his punch. A metallic taste filled my mouth, and I spat on the floor, my head swimming as I turned back to him, pushing until his spine hit the island behind him. "What's the matter, Bianchi? Can't handle the taste of your own medicine?"

"I never fucking touched Serena, bastard," he roared back, and ice filled my veins. He may have not touched her, but he was fucking playing with her head, and she deserved better. "But you know what? Maybe after today, I will. There's only so many times a man can say no to a beautiful pair of *come fuck me* eyes."

It was like my brain short-circuited. One moment I was looking at the arrogant smirk on his face, and the next, his blood stained my knuckles. The fact that we'd been friends since we were in diapers was all but forgotten as darkness spread in the pit of my stomach like ink, taking over. "Go ahead and try it. Put your hands on her and see what happens."

A shudder worked its way through me at the thought. The only reason I was even letting this happen was because Serena's mother passed not long after Leo's twin sister did, and I knew he could understand her grief better. He could bond with her on a level I couldn't, and that knowledge made my chest burn with jealousy, but I'd rather her be happy than belong to me.

She would eventually. I'd make sure of it.

At the moment, I was trying to learn the art of patience and was failing miserably.

"She likes me." His laugh was dry as a chalkboard, red liquid mixed with saliva running down his chin and staining his shirt, and the urge to cause even more damage came over me when he said that.

My fingernails bit into my skin as I fought to keep a clear head. It wasn't easy under the high of weed and anger, but today wasn't about me. The bastard had an innate ability to turn everything around as if he carried an Uno reverse card in his back pocket at all times.

"She relates to you. She doesn't like you. The only girl that has ever liked you for you, and not what you can give her, is Eliana, and you've pushed her so far away you'd need a miracle to win her back."

Like mirror images of each other, our chests fluctuated with sharp breaths. Awareness charged the air between us with static violence I could taste on my tongue. I'd given him a wide berth many times because he was my brother before he was my friend. Because he needed all the support he could get not to sink under, but I wouldn't allow him to parade Serena on his arm like she was his.

Leo nodded once, as if reading my mind, and I forced my limbs to loosen. I resisted the need to knock his head back one more time and abandoned him in the kitchen, grabbing the fucking beer I came in for in the first place. Bumping shoulders through masses of sweaty, glittery bodies, I started for the pool to get some fresh air and escape Ariana Grande's high-pitched voice that had my pulse echoing in my ears.

Alcohol mixed with blood as I took the first sip, staring at the red Solo cups floating off the surface of the infinity pool. It was a good thing Leonardo had uninhibited access to his father's oil money because the cleanup would cost him a pretty penny.

Holding the beer bottle to my chest like a newborn, I lay on a lounger, trying to map out constellations in the night sky, when a small voice came from my right. "Your lip is bleeding."

I ran my tongue over my teeth and found blood there too. I didn't even feel the pain. It registered as a dull throb in the back of my head that lightened every time I took a swig of alcohol. Swiping my mouth with the back of my hand, I smiled bitterly at the dark line of trees up ahead, sensing the apologetic nature of her visit.

"Are you here to kiss it better, sweetheart?"

She gulped audibly at my question, and even though I didn't want to look at her, it didn't matter. Serena moved in my field of vision, and the eye-catching lace on her black camisole caught my attention first as she sat next to my legs. Distracting floral patterns decorated the swells of her breasts, and I felt like leaning forward and mapping them out with my tongue.

"You need to stop, Ares," she sighed tiredly, and my brows furrowed.

Could she read my thoughts?

"Stop what?" I shook my head, but the lingering haze remained.

Serena's hand squeezed my thigh, and a current of electricity traveled all the way up to my crotch, making my dick twitch as she looked at me through heavy lashes. "Stop actively trying to hurt yourself. This isn't a game you want to be involved in."

"Fucking up other people's lives for the sake of revenge isn't a game, period, Serena." My lip curled, and for the first time, I didn't like her touch on me. Shaking my leg, she got the point and placed her hand in her lap, her glassy eyes an emblem of guilt. I turned away, not wanting to tarnish my view of her even more, stubbornly holding on to a piece of the fierce, intelligent version of Serena in my mind because a part of her was still there. "Why do you lower yourself so much for another's sake? This isn't you."

"Maybe you don't know me," she mused, her tongue swiping over her bottom lip as she faced the party in full swing past the sliding doors.

Oranges and spice tickled my nose from being so close to her, and I fought not to dive in and find out if her skin tasted as it smelled. Serena was beautiful in an ethereal way, like a Roman goddess with glowing skin, plucked straight from the shores of Sorrento. Traces of summer lit up her energy in bright blue hues, and when she smiled at you, you saw a bottomless ocean reflected in her eyes.

I hated that she shared the same smiles with others. I felt strangely possessive over them, as if I wanted to lock them in a box and be the sole recipient of her pearly white teeth.

Leaning forward, I captured her chin between my fingers, my rough pad gliding over her supple flesh, and her mouth parted slightly. "Oh, I know you plenty, all right. You've always been a bitch, but never one without reason."

Serena was mean to mean people and didn't hesitate to stand up for herself. She had that *don't fuck with me or else* aura that you were either born with or didn't have. No one messed with her because she didn't pull any punches. She let you feel her full impact, and it hurt like a ton of bricks. Her decisions were final, and if you crossed her, that was it. You could kiss your place in her life goodbye.

But she also had a soft side she kept to herself. It was as if she was scared to let anyone see the Serena who volunteered at the animal shelter at least once a week and played the piano for the kids at our local children's group home. The only reason I knew was because I pressed her to tell me why she was never available every Friday night, and despite her vehement denial, I tagged along one time to spend the evening with the little kids and her. Their eyes lit up like tiny moons when she entered the room, and I begrudgingly accepted that that was probably what I also looked like whenever I was in her presence.

I was so whipped for this girl it was embarrassing.

"Well, aren't you just so charming?" She snorted, pushing my hand away.

"If I was, you'd be bored of me, babe. You don't do charming."

"What do I do, then?" She crossed her arms under her chest, raising an inquisitorial brow.

A smirk spread over my lips. I took a sip of my beer and then answered. "A six-feet-tall guy in battered boots, with brown hair and gold eyes, whose leather jacket you always steal when you're cold."

"Hey, you willingly give it up!"

"Because I don't think you'll look pretty as an icicle."

She let out a little outraged gasp, punching my shoulder lightly, and even though I saw it coming, my sluggish brain dropped the bottle I was holding, and beer fizzed, rushing to the top and spilling on the grass below. My lips split with a laugh, but Serena's brows creased, and I felt the steady drip of blood down my chin.

"Jesus, Ares," she gasped, getting on her feet. "We need to get you fixed up."

"Where are you going?" I asked when she started walking away.

"To get a first aid kit from the bathroom," she called over her shoulder.

Either I was super out of it, or she moved like the Flash because only a few seconds passed from when she left and when she came back, sitting by my hip this time and touching my face with her soft fingertips. My eyes drifted open as she wiped my skin with a cold cloth, licking her dusky pink lips in concentration.

"Your little boyfriend is in worse shape than me. Why don't you go take care of him," I said huskily, looking at her through my lashes.

Her cheeks flushed under the moonlight, and she dropped the cloth to the ground, tilting her head down and rummaging through the medical supplies. "If you don't shut up, I just might."

My hands twitched at her response, and not giving a shit if anyone saw us, I used them to haul her up to my lap. Serena squealed, holding on to the first aid kit as I settled her sideways, smoothing the back of her green skirt with my thumb.

"What are you doing?" she breathed, fisting my shirt with one hand.

"Helping you reach up," I explained coyly, tugging her even closer when she seemed unimpressed by my excuse, my finger exploring the exposed sliver of skin between her skirt and shirt.

She shivered in my arms and tried to proceed as if unbothered, but I saw through her. The slight tremor in her hands, how antiseptic went everywhere but the cotton ball she was trying to drench. My eyes closed of their own accord when she started swabbing my wound, afraid of what I might've done by having her so close.

"I'm not a midget, you know," she whispered, and her breath touched my lips.

"Just related to some, eh?" I laughed and hissed when she purposefully pressed harder on my skin.

"Fucking witch." I ran my nails up her back and under her shirt, my pinky toying with the edge of her bra. She shivered in my arms, and I knew for a fact she could feel my hard-on against her ass. Serena shimmied her shoulders a little, and I let my palm drop back to her waist. It was so fucking tiny, my fingers almost touched on either side—or I just had large hands.

"And don't you forget it, babe. Now, stop talking," she ordered, and I remained silent, simply enjoying the feel of having her in my arms. A luxury she didn't allow very often. The last time I held her like this was a few days after her mom's funeral, when I'd found her crying in her parked car, her face red and splotchy. My heart twisted itself in a knot at the sight, and at that moment, I would've done anything to see her smile again.

I'd gotten all versions of her, aloof, happy, mad, horny—each more beautiful than the other, but sad Serena had me wanting to rub gasoline on whoever hurt her and set them on fire.

She finished cleaning me up, setting the kit on the ground, but when she made to move, I held her tighter, pressing her chest against my own. Her hands rested on my shoulders, and despite the loud music and shouting voices from the inside, I caught her slight gasp as if fine-tuned to hear everything that came out of that full mouth.

"Ares..." She said my name as a warning, but her cheek touched mine, fingers diving in my hair like she'd found her forever home in my arms.

"Thank you for taking care of me, beautiful." I spoke as if in a trance, lulled in utter tranquility under the stars, her chest brushing over mine with every breath.

Why her? I thought, glaring half-heartedly up at the sky in a one-sided conversation with God. *Why does it only feel this way with her? Like I'll combust every time I touch her and won't survive every time she leaves. Why no emotionally available girl?* I had Eliana on my lap mere hours ago, known her as long as I had Serena, yet she did nothing for me. I was eighteen, for God's sake. I was supposed to want to sink my dick in any semi-pretty girl I saw, yet I only chose this one.

"You're still not one hundred percent fine. How much have you had to drink?" she asked, and I didn't have the heart to tell her I lost count during the first half of the night. "You need to go home and sleep it off."

"No," I said like a petulant child, and damn, I *was* fucking wasted. "I want to be here with you."

Her laugh sounded like harmonious wind chimes. "I'll drive you, pretty boy."

"Hmm..." I hummed, shifting enough so my mouth was level with her ear. My lips brushed against her erratic pulse, and she made one of those little sounds that drove me crazy when I pressed a kiss on her feathery skin. "Does that mean you'll stay overnight and be my naughty nurse? You have before."

"When?" She entertained me, angling her neck and holding on to my hair so tight, pinpricks of pain filled my scalp, but I wasn't complaining.

"In my dreams." I kissed her earlobe this time, sinking my teeth in just a little to tease her. I felt her pebbled nipples even through layers of clothing, and if I was hard before, my dick was fucking weeping for some action now. "Plenty of times."

"And what do we do in those dreams?" Her question made my eyes roll to the back of my head. I wished we were alone, so I could've been selfish for once, claimed her as mine, despite her not being ready yet.

"They usually involve you on your knees, and your pretty mouth wrapped around my dick." Her nails formed crescents on my neck as I tangled my fingers in her satiny strands, my fist closing in on a handful. "My hand is in your hair, and you let me guide myself deeper." I tugged her head up roughly, catching her half moan with my teeth on her bobbing throat. "And you drink me down like a champ, even when your gag reflex starts acting up, even with spit and precum hanging from your tits like a filthy necklace." The raw need to leave purple marks on her creamy flesh overwhelmed me as I completed my detour on her neck with a parting nip and kiss under her chin.

I eased up my grip on her hair just a little, and she brought her head down until we were face to face, our breaths mixing, hearts pounding to the same rhythm. Dilated pupils greeted me, the brown in her eyes so sweet I wanted to drown in it—*in her*. Our noses touched as we shifted even closer, inch by fucking inch, and I stared at her lips like a man starved. The air grew humid, and my nostrils flared, taking in as much of her scent as I could as our eyes fluttered shut.

We were millimeters apart when it happened.

A loud crash like a thousand windows breaking all at once from within the house slashed through the heightened tension between us, making us jump. Our foreheads banged together so hard, every sexy thought fled from my brain like evacuation sirens were going off through it.

"Ouch," Serena complained, hanging on the edge of my lap.

"Fucking hell." I shared her sentiment, rubbing my pounding head.

Twisting in place, I glared at the wasted asshat that had decided to walk through the glass doors leading to the patio. People scattered around him like ants, with Leo breaking them apart like a bulldozer to reach the guy first. Everyone held a collective breath. Fear so palpable danced amongst them, the glass spread on the floor could cut through it. They all breathed out at once, though, when the injured guy held up a hand, repeating, "Fine, I'm fine."

Anger simmered beneath the surface when I turned around to see Serena, miles away mentally already. Her appearance was all over the place, but she stood up cool as a mint and patted her shirt and hair down like she was exiting a bad business transaction.

"All right," she said, taking mercy on me and offering her hand so she could tug me up. "No more mixing weed with alcohol for you or anyone else at this party. Let's go."

Being the sober one out of the two, I let her drive me home, abandoning my bike at Leo's. Any of the previous desires didn't follow us on our short journey. Both of us remained cold and standoffish as we digested what had transpired tonight, between me, Serena, Leo, and Eliana, a mess of fucked-up friendships and broken bonds.

It was ironic how the four of us teetered on the edge of constant love and war, utter peace and total damnation.

CHAPTER NINE
SERENA

Present

What are you doing here?
　　The question repeated itself in my mind for the thousandth time. It had been on constant loop since the moment I slipped into my silk blue dress and strappy black heels, did my makeup, and drove to Ai Fiori. I refused to meet Ares at his office. Only the two of us, together, in a confined room...that did not sound like my idea of a good time.

So, despite my better judgment, I'd let him drag me to one of the most upscale restaurants in town, where the meal portions did not match the price tag by a mile, and old acquaintances lingered. It had been less than a week, and I was already breaking my promise to Sam by entering the gold lobby with luxuriously heavy chandeliers and black marble floors.

A classy blonde in a navy suit met me at the entrance, insisting on showing me to my seat when I dropped the

Alsford name, but I declined. "That won't be necessary. I can see my..." I glared at the back of Ares's head, his teal T-shirt and those unruly brown curls a dead giveaway amongst a sea of fancy-dressed individuals. The sole reason a leather jacket wasn't hanging over his seat was because it was hot as balls. "My date. I can see my date from here."

She nodded at me, and a weird tingle spread in my mouth as I stepped past her, like I'd sucked on peppermint candy. Shifting my thick hair, so it spilled over my chest and covered half of my face, I came up behind Ares, his head turning sharply when I spoke.

"Alsford," I greeted, holding my tongue back when he glanced up from his phone, all indifferent, as if this meeting was beneath him.

He didn't even raise to... I don't know. Give me an awkward half hug or pull my chair back for me. He just sat there, laid back on his seat, legs spread under the mahogany table, eyes running over my exposed skin like I was made for his viewing pleasure. It felt weird seeing him in the flesh. I was still not over being in his presence. His energy buzzed against mine like a power source.

I ignored his lack of manners with a huff, pushing the plush white chair back myself, and plopping down.

"Laurent," he said back, his voice loud, and I discreetly glanced around to see if anyone had heard him. Thankfully, the nearest table was seven feet away.

"It's Duante, now," I instructed, narrowing my eyes.

"Not to me, it's not." He shook his head, setting his elbows down on the table. "It has always been Laurent, and you can't fool me with that Amelia bullshit."

I opened my mouth to argue with him, only to slam it shut again. He stared at me, brows high and expectant. And even though I'd just sat, I made to stand up again, scraping my chair on the floor. As much as I wanted my mom's house, I wanted to not have to deal with this asshat even more.

"Where are you going?" Ares's brows met.

"I've been here for five seconds, and you're already not respecting my wishes. I think it's best if we end this now." I squared my shoulders.

"Stay seated."

I stood.

Annoyance flared in his eyes, and he added a word I didn't think I'd get to hear coming out of his mouth. "*Please.* We could reach a middle ground."

Every word was stressed, as if it pained him to say so, and I relented begrudgingly, sinking back down. Buying my mom's home must have been a terrible investment if he was so eager to get it off his hands.

"What are you proposing?" I clasped my hands on the table.

"Siren," he said smoothly, and I should've known by the smirk on his face this wasn't going to be good. "You can't expect me to call you Amelia Duante. I will slip up."

But calling me Siren was easier? Stirring up memories of a night I'd rather forget probably elated him, but I refused to show him that it got to me. Whatever, anything was better than my actual name, and no one would recognize this one.

"Well, you've always been one fry short of a Happy Meal, so whatever, I guess." I shrugged, reaching for the thick brown menu. "Go for it."

"Did you just use a Happy Meal reference to call me dumb?" His voice was unnaturally flat, like he was trying to figure out how old I was.

I flipped through the pages with sweaty fingers. No

prices, anywhere, figures. "I certainly wasn't calling you smart."

"My, my, Siren, I see your claws are still intact."

"Very much so." I drummed my red nails on the back of the menu, looking at him over it. They were long and fresh. I'd gotten them done yesterday. His responding smolder had the tips of my ears turning pink. He adopted the same look when I used to run them down his back.

The silence that wrapped around us was stifling as Ares got comfortable in his chair. Crossing his legs, he threw an arm over his backrest, unbothered and confident as he studied me. We were locked in some kind of staring competition, and while he was cool as a cucumber, I was sweating underneath my dress and trying not to squirm. He was much more comfortable in his own skin than I was in mine. He got to live unbothered while anxiety was my middle name.

It was a throat clearing from our right that broke us out of our stupor, and I slammed the menu in my hands shut by accident. The loud bang had the waiter's gaze shifting awkwardly from me to Ares before asking, "Are you ready to order yet?"

Ares hadn't even touched his menu, but it seemed he had been here plenty of times to already know what he wanted. He probably brought all his dates here—not that this was a date, of course; I was forced to be here.

"I'll have the prawn linguine, and she'll get the pesto pasta with garlic and rosemary chicken. Could you also bring a bottle of Sancerre pinot grigio?"

"Um—" I tried to cut in, but the menu was taken off my hands, and the waiter was already nodding and walking away.

"Pesto sauce has nuts in it," I gritted, elaborating when he gave me a blank stare. "I'm allergic to nuts, Ares."

"Are you?" He cocked his head to the side as if he didn't already know. "That's too bad. I guess we're going to have to send your dish back."

I bit my lip to keep from lashing out because he was not worth it. Instead, I imagined us as two warriors on opposite sides of the battlefield about to wield our swords on each other. Hunger made me do mad things, including daydreaming about cutting someone's head off, because he knew I wasn't the type to refuse a dish. The staff already worked hard enough, and I didn't want to pile on more tasks.

I started bouncing my leg nervously under the table when our waiter brought us a chilled bottle of wine. He took way too long to pull the cork out, and the squeaking sounds made for an unpleasant atmosphere. Finally, Ares took over, pouring the white liquid into two big glasses while the pasta was placed in front of us. At least they were fast, not that I could have any of the mouthwatering food without resembling a pufferfish afterward.

Ares forked his pasta unbothered, though, skirting around the prawns on his plate for some reason. Sighing dejectedly, I asked, "Why am I here, Ares?"

"As in this restaurant?" He took a bite, taking his time to chew. "You refused to come by my office, and I was hungry, so here we are."

That wasn't what I was actually asking, but I took it easy, seeing as he still hadn't done anything to rectify the accident I'd caused more than two weeks ago. Bringing *that* up was not wise, but I couldn't help myself. I was curious. "Is there a reason the police still haven't contacted me about your motorcycle?"

"I took mercy on you, Siren. It costs at least five hundred thousand dollars to buy a new one since you totaled it. If you had that kind of money lying around, you wouldn't want to purchase that dump of a house."

I almost choked on my own spit at the amount. I was raised around people with more wealth than they could spend on five extravagant lifetimes, with some costly hobbies added to the mix. It still struck me dumb, though, how he was willing to waste that much on a motorcycle.

It shouldn't have since I was a notorious spender myself when I thought I was set for life. Everything was easy when you were a trust-fund baby. It was true, money didn't bring you happiness, but it certainly topped being broke and worrying about your next meal.

You truly got a sense of how well-off someone was when they didn't care about their precious belongings being ruined.

"I think it's charming." I didn't taste my fate by continuing to comment on the incident. He'd found something new to hold over my head, and I preferred this to being sent to jail for a hit and run.

"You used to say that about those hairless cats too," he said, unblinking.

"I'll have you know the Sphynx cat breed is one of the friendliest around."

"If I have to apply sunscreen on my pet, then I don't want it."

"Well, since you *bought* the so-called dump right under my nose, there must be something you like about it," I argued, gripping the butter knife next to my plate. The urge to jam it into his throat was real. I was hungry, and he was waging psychological warfare on me.

"I liked that my decision annoyed you," he replied with a half shrug, and blood rushed between my ears. I was considering throwing the butter knife at him like a dart when he continued, "See? That's called being transparent, Siren. Something you're going to have to learn if you want the house."

His voice crawled in my ears like sweet poison, and I froze. "What do you mean? You're selling it to me?"

"Under some prerequisites." He swirled the wine in his glass, the slight green in his eyes churning like the heart of a murky swamp as the wheels in his brain worked.

He put his mouth at the edge of the glass, sipping like it was the best thing he'd ever tasted, stalling. I liked when people got to the point fast, and he'd done nothing but waste my time since I sat down.

"Stop drinking and elaborate, Alsford." I felt my teeth grinding together when he tilted the glass ever so slowly, leaving no trace of wine in it. It didn't help that I couldn't have any. "Fucking hell, you're annoying."

He poured some more wine as he answered, eyes flicking to mine for a refill and frowning when he saw that I hadn't had a sip. "I'm giving you two options, so you can't say I wasn't fair."

I rolled my eyes. If only he knew what his *unfairness* had led to. "Get on with it."

"You can either fork out a cool mill, and we'll call it a day."

"One million dollars?" My eyes bugged.

"No, pesos," he deadpanned, making fun of me.

"And the second option?" I bounced on my seat impatiently.

He rolled his lips in his mouth, keeping the tension alive

by taking his sweet-ass time. He shrugged as if to say, *it's simple, really*, then hit me with it. "I ask you some questions, and for every one you answer, I lower the price tag by two grand."

I blinked.

He blinked back, as if in response.

Then I tossed my head back and laughed, no trace of humor in me.

I was fucked. I wanted a piece of my mom with me. My dad burned all her belongings after she died. I'd hid a tiny gold pendant I'd stolen from her, but one day it fell out of my school bag. Carter found it, and he destroyed that too. The only thing I had of hers were my memories and some pictures Sam had lent me. The thought of losing this last chance I had to connect with her to the man that had stolen another big part of my life killed me.

"You have got to be kidding me." My laughter died quickly, but my pulse still drummed wildly. "That's about five hundred questions, or three-fifty to get it down to its original price."

He'd have five hundred chances to find out the truth. To peek at the dark beneath the fancy dresses and stiletto heels. To know I couldn't stand a man's touch unless I absolutely felt one hundred percent safe with them. Even a simple question like *"How did you sleep last night?"* had the power to ruin the illusion of the resilient front I tried to paint.

I didn't sleep well. I never slept well. I always dreamt of white lines and rough hands, blood and tears, tiny fists, and small feet. All that could've been.

"You were always good at math, so I'll take your word for it." His mouth twisted into something that resembled a smirk, but it failed to last when my stomach picked the perfect time to growl. Glancing at his plate, he fought some internal struggle before pushing it in my direction. "Here, can't have you passing out on my watch."

I gave it a blank stare, even though I hadn't had anything since breakfast. My stupid pride, though, was louder than my appetite, and Ares Alsford made me understand why people went on hunger strikes.

"Why? I thought you didn't care." I sounded bitter even to my own ears.

"Oh, I don't," he confirmed. "You fainting would be an inconvenience, though; I have somewhere to be at nine." He checked the Tudor on his wrist, his face a painting of apathy. I didn't have to think hard to figure out his other endeavors this late on a workday. It was a phrase consisting of two words: booty and call.

I bit my lip, feeling weak all of a sudden. If I could choose one superpower, it would be to turn back time. I would've done so many things differently, starting with never feeding into whatever Ares and I had.

"How would this work exactly if you are so repulsed by my presence?" I entertained the idea since he didn't seem all that into having me around, and the feeling was mutual. Plus, if I put my brain to use, I could come up with a decent lie. I perked up, seeing the bright side in this. It was just a few questions, and I was a lawyer, for God's sake. Half-truths and untruths were part of my job description. "Are you going to email me all the questions you need answered, and I'll have to fill in a form?"

He cut that down quickly with a shake of his head. "We'll be in each other's presence. That way, I can make sure you're answering the questions truthfully."

What makes you confident you'll be able to tell? I wanted

to ask but didn't. Why should I be the one to ruin his dream when he thought he had it all figured out?

Truth of the matter was, I stood to gain more out of this than lose. But all good things came with a cost, and if that was seeing more of Ares's face and being put under a microscope for my answers, then so be it.

"If I agree to this, I have some stipulations of my own," I offered, swirling some water in my mouth to trick my stomach into thinking it was food for a second.

Ares crossed his arms, looking at me through unfairly long lashes. "Let's hear them."

I held up my pointer to start my countdown. "No personal questions, no—"

"No." He cut me off, his stare intrusive. "I get to pick whatever questions I like. Nothing's off the table."

My nostrils flared, and I continued on to my second point without arguing. I knew it had been a long stretch to begin with. "Then I get to pick when and where we meet."

"It has to be at least twice a week. There's no need to stretch this out for longer than necessary," he intervened, and I agreed. The sooner we were done with this, the sooner I could go back to forgetting his existence.

"And last but not least, if I feel uncomfortable with your line of questioning, I get to call it quits for the day. Basically, when you ask me a question, I have the right to answer at a later date."

He pursed his lips, and I straightened my spine. I wasn't budging on this. I was stupid enough to agree to planned interrogations, but I wouldn't be locking myself in that position. Finally, with a resigned sigh, he said, "Fine."

I wanted to shake the winning smile from his face. He really had that much faith in himself. He thought he'd be able to break me down when I wasn't contractually allowed to say anything. The only questions I could answer truthfully were ones he'd never think to ask.

Ares could be cruel and had the tendencies of an asshole, but I knew what I had to say had the power to break him into a million little pieces like it did me. And the fact that I wasn't all that put off by the idea concerned me. He already had big enough reasons to want to make my life a living nightmare.

"I want this all in writing," I said, picking the edge of my nail until the skin was raw.

"You don't trust me, Siren?" He raised a brow, mock offended.

What was there to trust about someone that lured you out of your house, fucked your brains out, promised you forever, and broke said promise the very next day?

"I'd trust a car salesman trying to talk me into buying a Range Rover more than I do you." They looked good, but *you* wouldn't when they left you stranded in the middle of the road.

"Now, that hurts my feelings, Sere—"

"I'm also putting in a clause that you're not allowed to call me that," I interrupted him, and the space between his brow pinched.

"*You're* putting in a clause?"

"I can draft a contract, Alsford. I graduated from law school."

"I thought you dropped out."

I had—*sort of.* I did finish my undergraduate degree, and as part of Sam's plight to set me on a straight road agreed to go to law school later on. I was grateful he made me do it. Piling on something challenging when you're already having a hard time might sound counterintuitive, but it was just what I needed to keep my brain busy.

"I'll write the contract; have your lawyer look through it." I dodged his attempt at getting me to spill information from now. I wanted to chew on this for at least one more day. It was Friday tomorrow, and he was bound to get his two days over the weekend.

"Give me your phone," he instructed as I pushed my chair back, ready to go home and gorge on whatever leftovers were in my fridge.

I wrinkled my nose. "Why?"

"Because Jenna might file a complaint for employee harassment if I continue using hers to contact you." He gave me a blank stare, and I sighed, pulling it out of my bag. Our fingers brushed, and he licked his top lip when I almost dropped the phone on the pasta he'd left for me. Ares started typing his number into my phone, occasionally glancing at me as I toyed with a fork. "You're not eating," he observed, his eyes then flicking to the full glass of wine. "Or drinking."

"I have to drive, and seeing your face made me lose my appetite." I smiled sweetly.

He gave me an unamused once-over, handing me back my phone. "Well, I hope you get over that sooner rather than later, since you're gonna be seeing a lot more of me."

"I'll be waiting for our next meeting with a bated breath." It turned out to be a challenging feat, keeping a smile on my face, so I dropped it as I got up, straightening my dress and hanging my bag over my shoulder.

"I bet." He ran a hand through his hair, his eyes never straying far from me. "Good night, Siren." His voice was like black velvet, caressing me in places it had no business being.

Either that or knowing his plans following our meeting

gave me enough courage to spew my next sentence. "Oh, it's gonna be. Thankfully, my date agreed to reschedule." There had been no hot date to begin with, although I had a feeling James was crushing on me. Still, watching Ares's face sour filled me with unparalleled joy as I bid my farewell. "Goodbye, Ares."

Guard your heart because there is no breaking mine this time.

CHAPTER TEN
ARES

The couch dipped next to me as a warm body settled between Leo and me. The patio doors were open, and a natural breeze had picked up, combating the overbearing summer humidity of the East Coast. Eliana stared at me, eyes big and expectant, as she held a bowl teeming with popcorn in her arms.

I raised a brow in question, and she thrust the bowl at my chest, looking a little guilty. "I made some more popcorn just for you."

Leo spread his arm on the back of the couch as the movie playing on the flat screen mounted on their living room wall got louder when an action scene came on. Good thing their kids were off with Leo's parents, something about spending the weekend at the beach. "Why does he get preferential treatment?"

I took a handful of popcorn, smiling at Leo. "Because I'm cuter than you, Bianchi. Suck it up."

He scoffed. "You wish."

I shoved a bunch of it in my mouth, somehow still

hungry even though I'd had dinner less than an hour ago. I glanced at Leo and Eliana as I chewed, wondering what their reaction to finding out Serena was back would be.

Leo would understandably be less than pleased, and Eliana...fuck, I didn't know. I didn't think she'd be happy, having to deal with Serena again, but she'd be glad she was safe and sound. It didn't seem like Serena wanted much to do with them—or me, for that matter, either, but you could never trust her. Beware of still waters—wasn't that what they said?

My chest squeezed with guilt when I thought about the information I had but was withholding. It was especially hard when Eliana tiptoed around me all day, trying to make up for what she had said to me on the day of Matteo's birthday party. Her words came back to bite me in the ass, too, because as soon as I saw Serena, it was game over. I was set on finding out everything she wasn't sharing. Her secrecy was like a virus spreading inside of me, and only the truth was going to make it go away.

"What's with the prominent ticking noises in the background?" Eliana snapped me out of my thoughts, and I focused back on the movie.

We were watching *Interstellar*, and its premise was pretty generic for a Sci-Fi movie. Earth was dying, and they needed to find a new home for humanity. Still, the execution was terrific. They were currently exploring a planet with nothing but oceans, and there was indeed a clicking sound in the soundtrack.

"One second on this planet is a whole day on earth, and I heard that the ticks symbolize how many days go by back home," I explained.

"That's brilliant." Eliana gasped as a massive tsunami

wave made its way toward the astronauts and their spaceship.

"Christopher Nolan is amazing," I agreed. "This is one of my favorite movies."

"Are you sure it's not your favorite because Anne Hathaway is starring in it? Sci-Fi was never your thing," Leo commented.

"It started after I realized this planet was doomed." I gave him a once-over, over Eli's head, and he met my eyes with an amused tilt of his chin.

"You're looking at me like I'm to blame."

"Aren't you the CEO of an oil company?" I deadpanned. He held the majority of the blame on a global scale.

"So? The company was a thing long before I was born. Blame my ancestors." He shrugged as if he made perfect sense. "Besides, we're looking at ways to go renewable. We'll run out of dead dinosaurs to mine for fuel eventually, so might as well stay ahead of the curve."

"Really?" I raised a brow, having a hard time grasping how an oil company could go green, but who was I to know? "That's fucking great, man. Sustainable energy is the way to go."

"Hm, I don't see you preaching the same thing when you drive your Harley Davidson instead of a Tesla."

"That's called do as I say, not as I do." I threw some popcorn in the air, catching it with my mouth.

He chuckled. "I'm getting you an electric bike for Christmas this year since you like freezing your ass off that much. It'll be good for your wrinkles, too, since you won't have to wear a helmet, right, Eli?"

I almost touched my face with my greasy hands because I didn't understand what the hell he was talking about. What wrinkles? I didn't have any wrinkles. My face was wrinkle-fucking-free. I was only thirty-one. I guessed that meant you were halfway to the grave by today's standards.

"Mm...what?" Eliana asked, distracted.

"Didn't you say that cold weather reduces the appearance of wrinkles?"

"Yes, it does." She nodded absently.

I handed the bowl of popcorn to Leo, who was making grabby fingers, deciding not to continue this conversation. It would lead to a well I was not too keen on uncovering. "Where's your mind at, blondie?"

"Watching the movie and not having a full-blown conversation during one of its key moments," she quipped, annoyed, hugging one of the throw pillows to her chest.

"That sounds a lot like you want us to shut up." I exchanged a look with Leo, and she blew out a frustrated breath, eyes still glued to the TV because we were, in fact, not planning on shutting up. I'd watched this movie before, and Leo had the attention span of a gnat.

"She is the type of person that thinks Netflix and chill actually means *Netflix and chill*." Leo stressed the words as if they had an entirely different meaning than the first time he said them, and they did. Everyone knew Netflix and chill meant having a movie playing in the background while you fucked.

"What do you expect me to do? If you put on a Timothée Chalamet movie, I *will* watch him." Eli rolled her eyes as if it was common sense.

Leo's face fell. "He looks like a fucking teenager."

"He looks like you when you were young," Eli countered.

"I was never that scrawny." He straightened up now,

balancing the bowl on his knee, genuinely offended. I could see it, though. He did have some of the same harsh lines on his face and dark, wavy hair.

Eli stole the popcorn, hiding a smile by popping three pieces in her mouth and chewing. She'd successfully managed to rile him up like she always did. They said things got boring after marriage, but these two always kept each other on their toes.

It was sickening because you could see fighting was like foreplay for them. And the longer I stayed around them, the urge to suck on a box of cigarettes got bigger. In my opinion, the "smoking kills" label they put on them was attracting more people than it was repelling.

"Take it as a compliment. Chicks go crazy over this guy for some reason," I advised, shifting in my seat and standing up. I did feel the need to have a smoke and empty my bladder. "On that note, I'm gonna let you argue about that. I need to use the bathroom real quick."

Eli's head swung to me like I'd just said I was going on a murder spree. "Sonia is up there."

My face soured.

I hadn't forgotten that my ex had once again been invited, but I couldn't very well order Eli to stop hanging out with her. Instead, I took it as a lesson to keep any future relationships private unless I was certain I only wanted to fuck that one person for the rest of my life.

"I can handle being in the same premises as my ex." *As I've proven before.*

Sonia and I hadn't met privately after the breakup, and I wasn't so keen on having any one-on-one time. To say we hadn't ended on excellent terms would be an understatement. But nothing would happen out of bumping into each other on my way to the bathroom.

"Just giving you a heads-up," Eli warned, and I waved her off, climbing the stairs to the second floor. Not before grabbing my phone, though.

It stuck by my side like glue since I left the restaurant a few minutes after Serena. Somewhere in the back of my mind, I was aware I was making the biggest mistake of my life by involving myself with her again. I figured that out when her hemline left ninety percent of her legs on display, and I couldn't stop staring at her ass as she walked out on me.

I came to the conclusion that my fixation was under control, but I had to feed it occasionally, and as much as I hated myself for it, eye-fucking Serena Laurent did the trick. I had no intention of *actually* fucking her, but imagining pulling her silk dress up and sinking inside her pussy with those strappy stilettos still on, didn't hurt anyone—other than myself, that was.

She still hadn't sent me a contract, and I was fighting the nervous twitch my fingers got whenever I thought of texting her, which was every fucking second. She would text, I was sure. Serena wouldn't normally put herself in such a vulnerable position. The fact that she did so with little opposition told me she had a lot to lose.

This time, I had the upper hand, and I needed to start acting like it.

Lost in my Serena-induced fog, I didn't notice the bathroom door opening until it was too late. A small body hit my chest, a grunt filling the air as we both staggered back from the impact. Sonia's back hit the open door, but I managed to keep my balance as I cringed, watching her slide to the floor.

"Shit," I cursed, rushing forward to offer her my hand.

Giving me a dirty look, she smacked it away, fixed her skirt over her lap, and got up without any assistance. "Watch where you're going."

"I'm sorry, I was thinking and—" I tried to explain, but she cut me off with a short, sarcastic laugh.

"Wow, you do that now?"

I frowned as she smoothed down her black, pin-straight hair. It was gleaming, like the type you saw in commercials, and one of the features I liked most about her. Most people separated men into three sections. Most preferred either big tits, a bouncy ass, or long legs. Well, if I had to add a fourth one, it would be hair.

It could be used for a multitude of reasons. It was aesthetically pleasing for one. There was nothing more satisfying than watching a girl's locks smack against the small of her back as she rode you cowgirl style. It was practical, in a way that you had something to hold on to while *you* rode your girl. And last but not least, it smelled like Heaven. Women smelled like Heaven.

"What's that supposed to mean, Sonia?"

"Nothing." She picked some lint off her shirt, but her tone told me it was most definitely *something*.

I took a step forward, forcing her to look up. She did, her jaw hardening under my perusal. "If you have something to say, say it."

Sonia crossed her arms and bit the inside of her cheek, trying to hold back, but when you pushed someone in a corner, they tended to bite. "It means you have a history of acting stupid." She huffed before asking suggestively, "How was your date?"

My mind blanked, and for some reason, the first person I

thought of was the one that'd run for the hills instead of ever having a date with me. *Pretty good,* I wanted to respond. *We glared at each other for most of the time, her insults were pretty creative, and I starved her.* Our hatred for each other was so deep and raw, it sometimes felt enjoyable, getting all that excess negative energy out on the person you disliked.

So yeah, *pretty fucking good* until I started thinking about how she could use a gag to shut up, and my mind took a sharp turn I hadn't anticipated. Serena was both my sickness and my cure, but I was trying to get more efficient in curbing her out of my thoughts.

"With who?" I blurted out the question without thinking it through.

Sonia's mouth dropped, and her usually intelligent eyes turned blurry with jealousy. "With Moira! Have you been on more than one date since we broke up?"

"I'm sorry, I must have lost the memo that said I was supposed to wear a chastity belt from now on," I deadpanned because she was getting on my nerves.

A sharp laugh escaped her, but it lacked any joy. Her hands fisted by her sides, curling and uncurling as she gathered her thoughts.

I didn't like hurting Sonia. She was one of the best women I'd dated, but if being mean would finally get her to move on, then so be it.

"I haven't dated anyone else, Ares," she said in a broken whisper, and my throat tightened. Seeing someone's heart break right in front of your eyes wasn't a pleasant sight, or maybe I cared too much. But I didn't know how you could spend so long with a person and revel in their misery when you moved on and they didn't.

Shuffling closer, I forced her chin up when she faced the

ground. "You should. You're a catch, Sonia. Men will flock to you."

"I only want one man flocking to me." She took the opportunity to clutch my forearm, desperate eyes touching my face. "You said we were taking a break, Ares, because you weren't feeling happy after your parents died. Breaks mean you eventually get back together."

"Breaks only make the distance stronger between a couple." My words came out robotic, as if I was trying to convince myself.

Then why the fuck wasn't I over the latest re-addition in my life? It could've only been love that faded, and hatred glowed in its stead. After all, hating someone felt surprisingly similar to loving them.

"I didn't want there to be any distance to begin with, but you froze over like the Great Lakes during winter whenever I crossed the imaginary boundaries you kept drawn between us."

My jaw ticked at her observation. I wasn't what you'd call emotionally available, or stable for that matter. Something about connecting with a partner on a deeper level, other than just a physical one, repelled me. I'd been through it once, gotten attached to someone that wasn't even mine—didn't *want* to be mine. It hurt like a bitch, and wasn't something I wanted to feel ever again.

I *trained* myself not to act like that ever again with a girl, but then she returned in the knick of summer, and I was oh-so fucking eager to fall in line behind her. I *was* fucking frozen, and the fact that only Serena Laurent knew how to melt my ice made my nerve endings light up with agitation.

It made me do stupid things like forget about Sonia's hurt feelings as I allowed her to step closer to me, run her hands up my chest, and give me that *I want to be fucked* look that would usually turn my dick to stone.

"Ares, kiss me," she sighed into the gap between us.

Sonia was good. She was young and successful, and life with her was easy. Other than lacking that sort of chemistry that filled the pages of a romance book, I didn't have a solid reason for breaking up with her.

Maybe I should give this, *us*, another chance. A fair one this time.

Her warm breath coasted along the bottom of my chin, and I held on to her hands gliding on my pecs. Her nose met mine in an Eskimo kiss, and I promised myself, the second her lips touched mine—this would be it. There would be no half-assing it anymore.

I wasn't the manwhore.

Nor was I the heartbreaker.

I was brokenhearted, and I needed someone safe.

Sonia was that someone.

She raised on her tiptoes, and I tilted my head down. We were sharing air when I felt a buzz in my back pocket before a sharp pinging sound made my mouth slam shut, mere inches away from hers. A sense of déjà vu filled me as the chemistry allying us evaporated in a few seconds.

I pulled back, gazing at a different face than the one I expected. Harsh angles instead of soft, and an overbearingly sweet vanilla perfume, very unlike the spicy orange one, flowed to my nose.

I can't do it.

Not to her, and not to me.

"What?" she asked, her eyelids fluttering open. Her cheeks were flushed with need, and her pulse pounded beneath my thumb as I let her wrists go. "Why did you stop?"

I took a step back, then two, ignoring the hurt glimmering in her gaze and sucking in some fresh air. "You deserve someone better, Sonia. I cannot be the man you're asking me to be."

"What, *committed?*" she spat, tired of my hot and cold attitude.

I nodded, taking on the role of the jackass of the century as I said, "Not to you."

Sonia gasped, eyes shining with unshed tears as she finally pushed past me, muttering, *go fuck yourself, asshole,* under her breath and taking the stairs two by two in her attempt to run away from me. She didn't know it, but her wish was likely to come true.

I was losing thousands in this deal, all to satisfy my curiosity.

Not wasting a single second, I pulled my phone out, scrolling through my texts, when I saw Serena's name glowing with a notification badge. I pressed it, and an attachment with the subject *"Will you pay for the renovations too, Alsford?"* stared back at me. I snorted as I clicked at the contract tying her life to mine until the countdown was over.

I had five hundred chances to get this right. To crack through her hard shell for the first time.

CHAPTER ELEVEN
SERENA

"*Get on your knees for me, and I'll think about it.*"

My body flared to life when I opened Ares's reply and saw what he'd titled the attachment in response. I read it with his voice in my mind, husky and wanting as if he was saying it to me in real life, and my breath hitched. He'd signed it, I'd signed it, and it already felt like we were dancing in a burning room.

We weren't getting out of this completely intact. I was sure of that.

"Crude asshat," I mumbled, shutting off my phone entirely, so I resisted answering him immediately.

"Who's a crude asshat?" Elsa asked, and I jumped, not noticing she'd come into my office, even though it was pretty easy to see everyone through every modern company's obsession: glass walls.

She raised a brow and walked closer, placing a stack of files on my desk. When I took too long to answer, she took it upon herself to sit down on one of my gray office chairs.

"Oh, it's just my..." Dammit, why did I never know what to label him as? I decided to blend some truth with fiction and settled for, "My ex, being a dick again."

Elsa's forehead creased as she got ready for all the juicy gossip, and she stole some colorful M&Ms from a clear bowl on my desk, asking, "He's texting you? I thought you'd blocked him."

I wished, but now I wasn't contractually allowed.

"He emailed me. I didn't think to block him there too." I gave her an awkward smile, turning my spinning chair to my PC, but Elsa kept at it.

"I swear all men are the same. They don't realize what they have until it's gone." She shook her head, chewing thoughtfully. "And even then, if you give in, they'll treat you like a queen for maybe three weeks, tops. After that, they get bored, and we're back to square one."

I nodded. There were many regular customers with tan lines on their ring finger at the brothel. Sometimes they didn't step foot for a month or two, but ninety percent of them always came back for more.

"The best relationships are rooted in friendship. In my opinion, only if a man can handle the weight, they're worth the risk."

Or sometimes they still proved you wrong even after you kept them waiting for years, but oh well, all that was semantics. What Ares and I had wasn't friendship. It was sexual tension. I guessed I pulled short on his expectations of me, and he dipped out.

"That's true, I'm not into the whole sex after marriage ideology, but I wait at least a good four months before taking someone to bed," Elsa said, and my eyes widened comically.

"That's probably decades in a man's eyes."

She fluffed out her hair, her face turning coy. "Is that what you're doing? Waiting?"

"What are you talking about?" I asked, confusion and nausea swirling in my stomach. Had she seen me with Ares?

"I'm talking about James, salivating all over you whenever you're near."

I slumped back in my seat, my chest warming with relief. The fact that my de facto answer to everything was Ares should worry me. Just like with his voice, his name was something I made daily requests to whatever higher power there was to erase it from my memory. He could only breed ruin. It was in his name, from the Greek God of war and all.

Now, James. James was perfect. There was a reason it was one of the most popular baby names. It was welcoming, pleasant, and didn't sound like the person who had it would rip your heart out of your chest and have it for lunch. Our James was very much all of those things too, and I'd have to add fucking gorgeous on top, as well, like a hot summer day spent on the beach. His hair reminded me of the wet sand and his light blues of the crashing waves.

He was the opposite of Ares in so many ways, and maybe...just what I needed at the moment. I wondered what would happen if I stopped watering these insidious thoughts about him.

Would they go away?

"He hasn't even asked me out yet." I spoke more to myself than Elsa, as to not get excited over nothing. He did hang around me longer than necessary, though, and made little comments on how much he liked my outfits or the shoes

I was wearing (although I had an affinity for high heels, and all men had a weakness for them), or that he loved how I styled my hair.

I'd given him a blank stare the last time he said that because I hadn't even had any time to brush through it in the morning. So he was a bit of a kiss ass, but not everyone's default mode was *asshole*.

"Maybe he's shy." She shrugged, and I pondered it, and then I got an idea...a terrible idea that would undoubtedly land me in hot water.

I wasn't going to make this easy for him, though. If Ares Alsford was looking to break me down, he had to expect I'd put up some resistance. And what better than a six-feet-tall hurdle with the face of an angel and the manners of a gentleman?

"You know what, you might be right," I said as I latched on to my phone again, scrolling through my contacts until I found *his*.

Elsa made an audible noise of surprise. "Well, that's a first."

Serena: Can you meet tomorrow at Bella's Pier, at 6 pm?

I clicked my heel on the floor as I sent the text, nibbling on my nail. My brows rose to my hairline when his response came through a few seconds later. He either had a lot of time to waste today or was waiting for my text.

Ares: Wanna share some candy floss while we watch the sunset, Siren? Aren't you a little romantic at heart?

I snorted, and Elsa looked at me curiously, but gave up

on asking me what I was doing when she spilled some of the chocolate discs on the floor and tried to cover it up by acting cool.

Serena: No. I'd prefer wrapping you with it, throwing you in the Atlantic, so the sharks have at you, and *then* enjoy the sunset and the show with a bucket of popcorn.

Ares: Ah, it was the candy floss, wasn't it? I should've remembered that you prefer savory things.

Serena: Why do I feel like there is an innuendo somewhere in there?

Ares: Because you have a dirty mind, Siren.

I bit down on my tongue, recognizing that he might've had a point.

Serena: Stop wasting my time, Alsford. Tomorrow, yes or no?

Ares: I'll meet you there.

I slammed my phone on the table so hard, Elsa's head snapped up, startled.

"Maybe he *is* shy," I said, rolling my chair back.

"What are you going to do?" she asked, a wary look coating her eyes.

"I'm going to ask him out." It wasn't the Middle Ages anymore. Men weren't the only ones that could make the first move. "You think he's gonna say yes?"

Elsa nodded. "So fast I fear he might swallow his tongue in the process."

"Good," I echoed, wiping the sweat off my palms on my dress pants as I stood on shaky legs. I had nothing to be worried about, though; why would Ares mind if some more people crashed our outing? It was about time he expanded his social circle beyond Leo's ass. "Do you want to come?" I asked Elsa.

"As a third wheel, on your date?" She pouted. "Thanks, but no thanks."

"No, it's going to be a double date. I know this guy, and he's just *so sweet*." The lie tasted anything *but* sweet coming out of my mouth, but I shoved any trace of guilt away. Ares was only cruel with me. He could be fantastic with other people, depending on his mood swings. "And single at the moment. I know he'll be down for this."

He might even wring my neck from his excitement.

Elsa worried her bottom lip as I rounded my desk. "Is he cute? Do you have any pictures?"

"So cute." I dug my nails into my palms because Ares was as cute as a murderous lion. He was intimidating, with a larger-than-life presence, and so fucking gorgeous it was annoying. "But I don't have any pictures. You'll just have to take my word for it."

Her cheeks flushed pink with uncertainty, and she sighed. "Uh, okay the—"

"Great," I chirped, cutting her off. "The date is tomorrow at six pm. I'll tell you all the details later," I barked over my shoulder as I rushed to the door and out into the hallway.

What a way to doom a relationship of great potential, a little voice in my head chided, but my strides remained determined as I made my way to the elevator. James worked on the second floor and me on the fourth; he always used our restroom, though, and it was high time I paid a visit to his.

So what if I wasn't in it for all the right reasons? In the words of Samuel Beckett, we were supposed to dance first and think later, and that was what I was doing—following the natural order and clinging on to the potential. Ares's attention was confusing. I wasn't sure if it was salve, or just a deeper kind of wound, that had my lungs aching to catch up with his pace for years.

Yet, amid all the chaos he bred, I'd never thought of using a distraction. An actual one this time, not one that was forced on me by my father, to forever close that chapter of my life and start a new one.

Ping.

The silver elevator doors slid open, revealing that I didn't have to walk far to find what I was looking for. James stood on the other side, stopping mid-step when he saw me, and I took it as a sign. The universe was looking out for me for the first time in, well, ever, and this man was the answer.

I quickly stepped inside, pulling on his arm so he didn't exit, and pressed the button that shut the doors. He turned to me, with confusion written all over his forehead in bold letters. "Amelia, what—"

"Hi," I cut him off, painting a smile on my face.

Frown lines marred his otherwise perfect features, but he returned my greeting. "Ehm, hi?"

My hand was still holding on to his forearm, but instead of dropping it, I squeezed it, peeking up at him through my lashes. *Just like a Band-Aid.* "Do you like me, James?"

A current passed through his eyes, mimicking the luminance of a moonstone charm. So bright, so blue, so refreshingly different. James's sigh came out as a shudder, and it was the most wholesome thing I'd ever seen as his muscles flexed beneath my skin. "I do."

"As a friend, or do you see us becoming something

more?" I pressed on, holding on tight to the sudden burst of confidence rallying through me.

It seemed that with every question I spewed, James's eyes became a fraction bigger, and his chest rose and fell at a rapid pace. "I *definitely* see us becoming something more." He took a deep breath. "Do you...do *you* like me?"

My heart stalled, but I ignored it. I did like him, maybe not as much as he liked me, but judging from my parents' stellar relationship, that should be preferred. The guy should always feel a little more fondly for his partner, love her just a tiny bit more.

"Very much so." I nodded, fissures forming over my chest at the huge smile that formed on his face. "I was wondering if you wanted to go out with me tomorrow. We're going on this double date with Elsa, and I wanted you to take me. Will you do that for me, James?"

"Amelia, I'm not doing it for you." He tucked a strand of my hair behind my ear, and I remained planted in place, focusing on his face, his voice, his smell—clean and sterile. I was okay. James was good. "I'm doing it for me."

"Should I take that as a yes?" I breathed, and his brilliant white teeth blinded me with how bright his smile got.

"Of course, I'd love to go out with you."

James's arms widened, and as soon as I saw the hug coming, my stomach lurched. *Do it. Stay in place. It's just a freaking hug. Lord knows you have no freaking hang-ups when it comes to Alsford touching you.* My mind fed me poison, and I had no other option than to drink it. It festered in the bottom of my liver, but I wasn't ready for a hug yet, and expertly sidestepped it.

"Don't get too excited now." I patted his cheek when he blinked at the empty air, pressing to open the elevator buttons again, turning to him with a wink. "I'll see you tomorrow, handsome."

"See you tomorrow, beautiful," he returned my compliment, disbelief hanging over his features at what had just occurred.

I had a feeling I'd be seeing Satan personified tomorrow too.

CHAPTER TWELVE
ARES

The combination of the sweltering heat with the salt of the ocean made my skin feel sticky to the touch. It also didn't help that the pier was so crowded. People kept brushing against me and making it even worse. There was a reason I avoided this place at all costs, yet Serena wanted to meet here, and of course, the word *no* fled my vocabulary.

I wouldn't even be able to hear her talk over the crowd's chatter. Dogs barked, children squealed on the Ferris wheel, and the laughter floating over from large friend groups pierced my drums. I'd have to lean pretty close to listen to her and wasn't that just a bummer.

Standing next to the lamppost, I propped my elbows on the sun-rusted railing, staring out at the blue ocean as I waited. Spittles from the waves crashing against the gathered rocks below wet my shirt, but I welcomed the freshness they provided against the dying rays of the sun.

"You lied. You said he was cute." Hushed whispers came from my right side, and I strained to listen.

"He's not?" a bored feminine voice replied, and goose-bumps spread down my back. If it was a product of the slight breeze cooling down my skin or recognizing who that tone belonged to immediately, I didn't know.

"No." The other girl had a higher pitch I couldn't recognize. "He's *smoking fucking hot*, way out of my league."

"Oh, honey, trust me," Serena snorted, making the most ungraceful of sounds seem fucking classy coming out of *her* mouth. "You're out of *his* league."

"Stop playing with me, Duante."

"Come on, Elsa." I heard the slap of skin, and the footsteps on the wood grew closer.

I straightened up when I saw them in my peripheral vision. Even though I'd recognized her voice, I was unsure if it was her. Because what the hell was she doing, showing up with one of her friends? Did she need moral support or something? I *was* prone to biting, but I wouldn't put my lips on any part of her body even if she begged me for it.

A throat cleared next to me, followed by my name. "Ares."

I turned, indeed finding her next to another woman. Both of them were dressed well, her (I was assuming) friend with the afro-styled hair in a button-down white dress with blue stripes, and Serena...*fuck, what the hell was she wearing?*

I mapped the expansive fair skin that stretched from her face to the swell of her breasts, disappearing under a thin, bustier shirt whose color resembled her skin tone so much, I had to blink twice to make sure she wasn't naked. It had thin straps that gave the illusion of bare shoulders drenched in some kind of body lotion that glittered in the sun like some Edward Cullen type shit. Her hair was up in an elegant twist, allowing me to clearly marvel at the betraying blush that spread on her neck and down her décolletage the harder I stared.

But perhaps it was her tiny, cropped shorts and clear lip gloss that stuck out the most. Serena thrived in expensive outfits and bold colors. Seeing this toned down girl-next-door version of her was a change of pace. An unwelcome one since my mind took the opportunity to develop a full-fledged fantasy of jumping through her window at night to fuck her while her parents lay in bed a few rooms over, thinking their daughter was sound asleep.

"S—" I cut myself short when her eyes flashed in warning, gritting my teeth. I peeked at the other girl again, noticing that objectively, her features were more eye-catching than Serena's, yet I'd coasted over them. "*Amelia, who's your friend?*"

I wondered when she would stop shining like moonlight in a quiet garden in my eyes. It didn't make any sense. I hated what she represented, the person that she was, but my eyes interpreted her appearance separately from her shitty character.

Her friend didn't wait to be introduced, and despite what she'd said about me, she met my gaze boldly, going in for a handshake. "Hi, I'm Elsa, pleasure to meet you."

"Pleasure to meet you too." I gripped her hand and kissed the back of it, a slow smile spreading over my face. "Ares."

Elsa's grip tightened, and Serena's soft huff danced in my ears. She knew my moves. I'd used them a thousand times on her.

"Oh, I know." Elsa mirrored my grin. "Amelia briefed me on the basics."

"Did she, now?" I raised a brow, catching Serena's laser-focused gaze on my thumb, circling Elsa's inner wrist before dropping her arm. "Because she forgot to brief me."

What the hell are you playing at, Laurent?

"Duh." Serena's laugh was a lot awkward and not even a bit humorous as she wrung her fingers together. "I know how you like to be surprised, silly. Ares is such a romantic at heart. He doesn't care about looks. All he sees is personality. That's why he was all in when I invited him to this blind double date."

The word *date* struck out at me like a viper, followed by *double* flowing into the inflicted wound like venom. I stiffened, like a pillar of salt amongst the lively energy of the crowd, my eyes burying on the side of her head like I was trying to burn a hole through her skull. Judging from their not-so-subtle conversation before walking up to me, she was most definitely trying to throw Elsa in my arms.

I should've expected she'd pull something like this. I thought I could pull a fool's mate, but I'd forgotten I was battling a seasoned player. Dodging my attempts to get her to open up was second nature to Serena. Throwing other people in the line of fire to avoid getting shot, practically a personality trait at this point.

The question was, who had she invited to taunt me with?

And how fast could I manage to regroup?

My smile slipped into a smirk as I took hold of Elsa's eyes again. Pure joy unburned by life's struggles met my line of sight. I treated her like the most crucial painting in a gallery, letting Serena fade into the gray zone she loved to cling to.

If she wanted a show, I'd give her a tragedy to remember.

"*Amelia* is right, but I can't say you pull short on the looks department, sweetheart."

Elsa's straight white teeth sparkled in the sun. "Oh my God, charming and hot? Where have you been hiding all my life?"

"Chasing the wrong girls, I guess." I winked, blatantly checking her out. She was attractive, tall, with rich deep skin and no hints of scars or wrinkles. Where Serena's energy sizzled through the air like a condensed fire licking at your skin in warning, Elsa's glided vividly around you in muted colors, down to earth, and approachable.

From the corner of my eye, I watched Serena's throat bob as she frowned in our direction. And for the first time since her ambush, my veins buzzed with excitement, realizing I didn't lag as far behind as I'd initially thought when she cleared her throat loudly, begging for our attention.

The intensity of her glare singed my skin, but when Elsa and I turned, her features smoothed back into the old, nice, and *very* fake Serena, she pretended to be with everyone else. There were a couple of reasons why I called her Siren, and her ability to lure people into a false pretense of security when they were around her was one of them. Before they knew it, they were swimming in *her* sea, following behind her blindly, even though the lethal waves hit harder the deeper she led.

"Where's James? Is he running late?" Elsa asked, and I snuffed out the flare in my chest before it had any time to develop.

Serena looked over her shoulder, troubled, and I felt the urge to wrap my hand around her swiveling neck and *squeeze* until she turned purple. There would be repercussions for her actions today. The Ares that held her hand while she sucked on his best friend's mouth was long fucking gone.

"I told him we were meeting in front of the souvenir shop. Maybe he's lost—"

"I'm here." A lanky, blond guy weaved through the crowd, considerably taller than the rest, even though he was bobbing up and down in his Baywatch-inspired jog. He looked like a washed-up Marvel hero, and I blinked at him like he was an alien when he stopped next to Serena. His chest heaved like he'd run a marathon when the parking lot was just a three-minute walk up here. "I'm here. Sorry, I got stuck in some traffic." He smiled apologetically, and the girls rushed to meet him.

I was still trying to connect the dots and not break his fucking arm wrapped around Serena's bare shoulders when he faced me. She didn't go for the heroes. She went for the misunderstood villains, and if the constipated look on her face as she tried to remain in his half embrace wasn't a plea for help, then I didn't know *what* was.

I shook his hand so hard I almost dislocated his shoulder when he reached out to me. Dudebro winced, removing his other paw off Serena and cradling his right arm. "Woah, you got a strong grip, man."

"Sorry," I said drily, void of remorse. Judging by the arrows Serena kept shooting at me through her eyes, it translated.

I offered Elsa my arm as we made our way down the pier. Serena was at least clever enough to position herself between the phony hero and me, and my hands trembled so hard, wanting to reach out and throw her in the ocean, I pressed them to my sides until perspiration dampened my clothes.

"Did you guys all meet at work?" I asked casually, noting that none of the questions today would lead to any price reduction, regardless of who answered them. If she could make up new rules out of thin air, so could I.

"Yes, Amelia and I are in-house lawyers, but you probably knew that already." Elsa laughed, fixing a flyaway in place. No, I actually didn't. I didn't know who this Amelia version of her was at all. "And, um, James is a software developer."

Well, wasn't that just adorable? He was a geek too.

"Cool," I exclaimed, feeling anything but.

I was on edge, like a live current sparked in me whenever he said something, and I hadn't realized how much an Australian accent bothered me until that very moment. At least when it came out of him, it sounded like he was chewing his damned words.

"What do you do, Ares?" James asked, and I took in his hand entwined with Serena's, my teeth slamming into each other.

"I'm in real estate."

"He owns a real estate company."

Serena and I spoke simultaneously, and I spared her a cold glance. I liked keeping things vague. Real estate was a lucrative business, and people treated you differently when they saw they had something to gain.

"You own your own company? How old are you? You look like you're in your mid-twenties," Elsa marveled.

"Your parents retired, didn't they?" Serena said, snidely, like she wasn't a trust-fund baby not too long ago.

"I'm thirty-one. Have been selling houses for as long as I can remember. My father put me to work early on, but yes, I stepped up after they passed away last summer."

"Oh, I'm so sorry for your loss." James and Elsa's voices blended together, delivering the perfect octave of pity and fake grief.

"They-they did?" Serena stuttered, and I didn't acknowledge her, my jaw ticking as we paused for a screaming kid to pass through.

"Um, it sounds like you two really know each other," Elsa assumed, trepidation coloring her tone. And I felt sorry for her, for having a friend with such a lousy track record. "Didn't you just recently move here, Amelia?"

I raised an inquisitorial brow at her, her squirming form holding the attention of all three of us. "Uh, yes, we—"

"We met at a bar on her first day here, actually." I cut her rambling off, almost deciding to tell them the truth when she sneaked in a little pinch on my ribs but settled for something better. "She had a little too much to drink and threw up all over me. You'd be surprised to know how much a person loves opening up after a drink or seven."

Elsa and James snickered, and the blood vessels on Serena's cheeks expanded their reach, painting her face scarlet. For a moment, I considered she might tell them I was lying. But that wasn't her style. It was an easy way out, and she was the kind of woman to take the long, winding road to victory.

"Yes, and poor Ares gave the entire dance floor a good view of his backside when he bent over to hold my hair back while I was vomiting my guts out." She grinned up at me, patting my back with a little more force than necessary. "I felt so bad for his pants ripping. I took him shopping to buy him some new ones."

"It's so weird, imagining you drunk." Elsa shook her head, and I tuned in to her words like a shark catching on to a scent. "I haven't seen you take a sip of alcohol whenever we go out."

Serena's face blanched, and her lashes fluttered rapidly as she responded, "Yeah, I don't really enjoy the taste of alcohol. I drink only occasionally when I'm partying to let loose a little."

Since fucking when?

She used to love the taste. Craved the burn of liquor traveling down her throat. Come to think of it, she hadn't drunk a drop last Thursday either. The only eye contact she had with a glass the entire night was when she glared at it while I was pouring the liquid in.

A sense of unease settled in the pit of my stomach as I watched her fidget with her gold rings, Yael's words coming back to haunt me. Obviously, they weren't fucking true because she was standing right next to me, tempting me to drown her in the ocean every time she drew a breath, but it was evident something had happened to her. As much as her motives drove me crazy, at the end of the day, she'd hurt her case more by dropping such valuable sources of information in my lap.

"No, I can't stand the taste of Vegemite." Serena made a sour face as if she was reliving tasting it for the first time. "I tried it when I traveled to Sydney for my eighteenth birthday, and let's just say it wasn't an enjoyable day for me."

"It's a spread. We don't have it straight out of the jar," James argued, showing more passion about fucking Vegemite than I'd gotten from him so far into the night.

They'd stopped to get ice cream, and we were standing

around a red round table. I just got water because there was only so much sweetness I could handle in a day. They were so engrossed in their conversation, homeboy had *vanilla* cream running down his fingers and dripping on the table and hadn't even noticed.

"Still, there are better things that come from your country that you could advertise more," Serena said coyly, and the urge to throttle her only got stronger.

"Like what?"

"Except for hot, young Thor lookalikes?" Serena asked, her voice loud. My limits were being pushed, especially when James chuckled like she'd said the funniest joke in the world. "I had some Pavlova and loved it. It's one of my favorite desserts. I make it at least once every few months."

"You make it?"

"Yes." She nodded. "I love to bake."

My time was valuable, and the more Serena was wasting it, the steeper her punishment got. She didn't know it yet, but every laugh, every smile, and every fucking blush she wasted on Thor's stick figure, she'd have to pay back in spades. Or maybe in spanks, if Elsa kept yapping in my ear about how her married neighbor was fucking the yoga instructor, all the while licking the ice cream cone like she'd been starved for a month straight.

Maybe I was being a little bit unfair, and on any other occasion, I might've even been a little turned on by the impressive suction she had on that freaking cone. But I was a little preoccupied with thoughts of prying the stick figure's fingers off of Serena's skin when he reached over to tuck a curl behind her ear.

My body turned to ice when he leaned in, and my skin stung as if it was frostbitten. I did not fucking like her. I did not fucking care for her. And I wished she'd never come back and left as soon as possible. But over my dead body would I allow for this to happen again—watching her fall for someone else while I stood on the sidelines.

If she wanted her happy ending, then she'd have to get it elsewhere because, in my presence, she was doomed.

Abandoning Elsa mid-sentence, I rounded the high top until I cast a shadow over both the lovebirds. James paused, staggering back to take in my presence, and Serena turned wide-eyed when I gripped her arm.

"I need to talk to you." The warning in my voice was unmissed as James blinked like he was meeting me for the first time, but, of course, Serena had to challenge me for it.

She cringed, motioning to the stick figure, and said, "We're in the middle of something."

Right, that was it.

"Now," I growled low.

I was fucking done with this charade. If my limit was situated at the top of my head, I was now drowning in a pool of her making, and by tugging at her arm and dragging her with me, I was pulling myself out of the water. I tried playing her game, mainly for Elsa's sake, but I didn't care. Not when she thought she could play me to the beat of her drums, and I'd sit in the middle and belly dance for her enjoyment.

"Ares, let me g—" She tried to twist around, but I was already weaving through the crowd like I was a professional kidnapper. James and Elsa's voices were sharp in the background, but it was her problem to sort through, not mine.

"I swear to God, Serena," I whispered in her ear, my grip tightening. "If you utter one more word right now, I will not be held responsible for the things I do to you."

"You're being beyond rude," she said haughtily, as if I gave a shit.

I saw my opportunity and took it. The crowd was dense and noise loud, but the crack of my palm connecting with her ass echoed as much as her shocked gasp did. A passerby whistled, shouting, "*My man*" but I paid him no mind. The surface of my palm didn't tingle just because of the impact, as I kept my hand glued on her ass. I dug my fingers deep, kneading her fat, until she whimpered in pain, and I hissed, "Shut up."

I was surprised when she actually kept quiet and didn't try to body slam me to the floor. She followed my drift, loosening her body until I didn't have to drag her around, and followed willingly as I started for the Ferris wheel, away from prying eyes and all the sounds that activated my misophonia. I patted her ass before reattaching my hand on her waist, just because I fucking could, my lips twisting in a grim smile when she shuddered in my arms.

There was another reason why she'd brought James here, and it wasn't just because she wanted to get on my nerves. Serena did what she always did. Tried to put a marathon between her and her feelings because living in denial was better than getting hurt.

It was smart.

She was smart because that was exactly what I intended to do: shove her heart through a meat grinder.

When we got to the Ferris wheel, we were blessed with a small line. Serena got fidgety when I shoved her in a gondola, eyes frightful as they stared at me while I took a seat next to her. There was almost no space between us, with her entire left side pressed into my right, and I was starting to realize why couples loved Ferris wheels. It felt like we were alone in the universe, isolated.

"You're scaring me," she said breathlessly, and a wave of euphoria crushed me.

"Good," I noted, stretching my arm behind her back. "You should be scared after all the shit you've pulled today. You blindsided me."

Her nails bit into the edge of the metal bar strapping us down, but she stared at the blinking sky on her left before I could decipher the expression on her face. "I just thought I'd invite some friends; just the two of us would've been boring."

"I bore you now?" I leaned over, and our cart rocked dangerously as I cupped her chin, her fearful exhale coating my lips. We were so close, I could see the tiny freckle right next to her eye, and I shoved the urge to touch it in the pit of my stomach.

"Ares, we're going to tip over." Serena held on to my hand, scratching the hell out of it in protest.

I didn't feel any pain as I pressed forward, the world blurring as I focused on her next answer. "And him? *James* gets you all excited?"

Lights reflecting off the infinite ocean danced on the side of her face, and with disgust, I realized that she had that same kind of demeanor, looks, and tortured soul that was the subject of many poems of lonely men written about the women that didn't give them the time of day.

She nodded sharply, a fake smile spreading on her face. "He does."

"You don't sound very convincing, Siren. Let's try this again." I tilted her head down until we were only separated by a sliver of air. Her dark eyes were alluring, but not enough to hold my attention as I snuck a look at her full lips. "What is it about him that excites you? His stick-thin figure? The fact that he couldn't keep your attention for two seconds? Or that he couldn't stop checking out every girl in a V-neck within a five-mile radius?"

"He wasn't checking out any other girls," she denied, but the bite behind her words was nonexistent. She'd caught on too.

"My, my, things must be very dire if you're willing to stoop that low." I let go of her chin when I got the crazy idea to bite down on her plump skin and make her apologize. By the way she scrambled back, I knew she would. Deep down, Serena was obedient. She just required a little push to get her that way. "What is it that you don't want me to know that badly, Siren, that you resort to throwing other people under the bus?"

"I didn't throw anyone under the bus." She squeezed her eyes shut as she said it. Her world was built around lies, and I sought to shatter her glass castle.

"Oh, but you did. Because if he'd leaned in and kissed you in front of me?" I kept my voice low, a lethal calm possessing me like the dead silence right after a scream on the top of a snowy peak, seconds before an avalanche hit. "He'd be leaving here in an ambulance."

Serena's breath hitched, and the look she gave me was one of pure loathing. If she didn't appreciate her life, she'd probably unlatch the metal bar and push me down. She poked my chest with a pointy nail, baring her teeth. "You're such a hypocrite."

"I don't give a rat's ass what you do when you're alone, sweetheart. You can pretend it's not my mouth on your pussy you're dreaming about while playing with your clit, and attend a fucking orgy for all I care." I enveloped her hand, throwing it off me when I started getting used to its warmth. Her lashes fluttered shut as if my indifference physically impacted her. Weird, she'd done everything to gain it. "*But. Not. In. Front. Of. Me.* We're not teenagers anymore. I won't sit around while you waste my time with bullshit games. We have an arrangement, and I expect you to stick to it. Otherwise, it's off. Am I clear?"

She jumped at my bark, concealing her moment of weakness immediately as she raised her chin in defiance. "Yes," she agreed, yet it was anything but reassuring. A storm was brewing between us, and it felt dangerously like adventure in the wind as we reached the top of the wheel. "And by the way, you'd be the last person I'd dream about sexually."

"That's cute," I commented.

"What?" She narrowed her eyes.

"How bad of a liar you are." Her throat bobbed when I settled back, making the cart rock again. "I advise you not to try your luck on Saturday because if I figure out you're bullshitting me, Siren, there will be hell to pay."

"Saturday?"

"I'm giving you a week to gather your thoughts and apologize for being a shitty friend to Elsa and stringing her along. Although, I doubt you'll ever make a good one, based on your track record."

If my statement affected her, she didn't let it show. The wind picked up, and her knuckles whitened as she held the metal bar. "No one asked about your opinion."

"Good thing we live in a free country, and I can share it anyway." I *tsked*, stuck in torture town for five more minutes as her hair brushed against my face, and her chest looked extra shiny under the glow of the moon as we descended.

I didn't make a move to help her out when the ride

ended. The operator offered her his hand instead, and her tiny legs worked twice as hard to keep up with me. When she saw that I was heading toward the parking lot, she stopped me by grabbing my arm.

"Are you leaving?"

"Well, I certainly am not entertaining this clownery any longer." I glanced down at where we connected, communicating through my eyes not to touch me. She was sure getting bolder about that. "You lost all your privileges. From now on, we will only meet on my terms."

"Ares, please, Elsa—" she pleaded, but I wasn't in the mood.

"Is a big girl and can handle my departure." I winked, giving her my back. "Enjoy the rest of the night, Siren, but not *too* much."

CHAPTER THIRTEEN

ARES

Thirteen Years Ago

"I'm concerned," I voiced as Serena took a sharp right turn, stretching her Mini Cooper thin by taking on an impressive hill. White pine trees stretched on either side, a thick mist coating their top and obstructing any view of the city.

She released a heavy sigh, turning on the fog lights. "How is it that you always have something to say?"

I wasn't the type for silent car journeys, and ever since I forced her to pick me up so she could show me what she did on her elusive Fridays, I hadn't let her enjoy a moment of peace. Besides, she kept blasting Lana Del Rey, which made me want to die a slow, depressing death.

A smile curved over my lips. "The sky fairy blessed me with a smart brain."

"It's usually the people that speak *less* that are the smartest."

"Well, that's not the case this time." I shrugged.

"What is it you're concerned about?" Serena sighed again, her thighs on full display in her green sweater dress as she shifted gears. Women that could drive stick shift were extremely attractive in my eyes. Being confined in a cramped car with one in a short dress and boots made out of some type of shiny leather had me and my boner wallowing in misery.

I cracked the window open a bit, not caring that it was freezing outside. Christmas in Astropolis was no joke, but I needed some fresh air. Serena's perfume acted like a drug, muting my senses. "This road leads to Breezy Peak. There's nothing to do there but stop at the observation deck, stare out to the city, and contemplate suicide."

I was being dramatic, but at the same time, there was truth to my words. That observation deck had seen its fair share of people plunging off it, especially since the neighborhood nearby was less than stellar. Drugs and homelessness ran rampant around this area. It was a beautiful place with a dark history.

I twisted my head in Serena's direction, my eyes flying to her wrists. I'd caught a brief glance of them before she'd covered her whole hand in those oversized sleeves. Bruises that eerily resembled fingertips decorated her olive skin, and it felt like lava spilled out of every crevice of my body when I asked her what happened, and she said she just fell, refusing to divulge more.

Serena reminded me so much of the moon, capable of such light and beauty. Nonetheless, it was very apparent she had a shadowed part she kept to herself. No matter how much you pried, she was locked tighter than a clam.

"Yes, that's exactly what I do." Her fingers flexed on the wheel, and she scoffed. "I waited so we could take the plunge together. It doesn't get more romantic than a *Romeo and Juliet* ending."

"*Romeo and Juliet* is a tragedy, and if I ever find you with poison in your system, I'm shoving my fingers so deep down your throat, you'll be puking for the rest of your life. You're not dying on my watch, babe."

Her throat worked with a gulp, and I wondered if she was thinking the same thing I was. That every time that we were together, and I couldn't touch her how I wanted to *when* I wanted to, it very much felt like a slow death eating me up from the inside out.

"Because life's not exciting without me?"

I watched the trees zoom past us, my legs aching from keeping them pulled in for the past thirty minutes. "Duh, if you're gone, who's going to be leaving homemade cupcakes in my locker every time on my birthday?"

I'd gotten attached to the chocolate cupcakes with the raspberry whipped cream she always made. It had become a tradition of sorts, but there was so much more than that. Even if I wasn't getting a hundred percent of her, she couldn't cut me off cold turkey without some repercussions.

"You only want me for my food," she complained, but we both knew it was bullshit. Still, I entertained her.

"Haven't you heard? The way to a man's heart is through his belly."

"I thought the way to yours was through horror movie marathons."

I released a sharp laugh at her trembling voice. I'd been in charge of movie night, and as much as the bastard was grating on my nerves lately, only Leonardo appreciated my choices amongst our friends. "Obviously, it's not a one-way road."

"Well, good, because there's no way I'm subjecting myself to that kind of torture ever again." She shook her head, and the car swerved slightly with her movement. I threw her a glare, and she smiled sheepishly, straightening up.

"You weren't even scared."

"Yeah, I was *bored*. Horror movies are super predictable and boring. I don't get what you like about them."

"And *A Walk to Remember*, wasn't? The cancer trope is so overdone it's not even sad anymore." I rolled my eyes. "I think I zoned out for the last half of that movie."

"You didn't just zone out, you fell asleep with your head on my shoulder, and I got a stiff neck for like a week because of you," she accused, taking another right. The hair on the back of my neck prickled when I took in the shady street. "And besides, the book is based on a true story, which is what makes it all the more heartbreaking."

"You could've thrown me off at any time," I reminded her.

"I felt bad. You stayed awake all night to study for Ms. Warner's test." She glanced at me with judgment in her eyes. "Of course, that wouldn't have happened if you hadn't procrastinated for like the entire week you had to prepare for it."

"Tell me, what's smarter, cramming all the knowledge in a day before, or spending long hours studying for seven days and ending up getting the same grade as me?"

"I think I'm *actually* going to push you off a cliff."

"Oh, don't be mad, babe." I reached over, twisting one of her caramel locks around my finger and smoothing my thumb on her jawline. Shivers broke on her skin following the trajectory of my finger, and she gripped the wheel harder. "Not everyone is on my level of awesomeness, and there's nothing wrong with being average."

"You might be craftier, but there's nothing average about me." She gave me a mean side-eye that had my dick stirring. There was something seriously wrong with me for finding her bitchiness as attractive as her soft side, if not more. It was hard not to when I kept picturing how well I could shut her up with my cock.

The rest of the car ride was short and uneventful. The neighborhood got progressively better, which I was pleased about. There was no way I was letting her walk out a few blocks south. I straightened up when we came across a large building. It looked kind of out of place with its Spanish archways, crisp white finish, and clay tile roof. Like a house belonging in the suburbs of SoCal rather than New England.

"What is this place?" I asked as we drove past a Christmas tree in the middle of a sprawling yard.

"We literally just passed the welcome sign, Alsford." Serena gave me a blank stare, but I hadn't noticed. "The Astropolis Children's Home. It's a group home for orphaned kids."

I pulled at my seat belt, glancing at the array of windows on the building before looking back at Serena. I did it a few more times, and she squirmed under my puzzled gaze as she parallel parked between two other cars. I'd thought of everything, college parties, a sneaky link I was prepared to maim, a fucking spa day, or a pottery class, but this...this never crossed my mind.

"This is what you do on your Fridays?" I unbuckled my seat belt, a bit stunned.

Serena kept her head low as she turned off the engine.

"My father donates a lot of money to this place, so he forces me to visit at least once a week. He says it'll look good on my college applications."

"Since when do you do what he says?"

A bitter laugh that had me concerned followed my question. "Trust me, there's no saying no to Carter Laurent."

"What's that supposed to mean?" My brows knitted, and when I didn't make a move to get out of the car, she shrugged, opening her door.

"You know how parents get. They're very annoying when you don't do something they ask you to."

Serena had many things going for her, but a poker face wasn't one of them. Or maybe I'd become so attuned to her tells, like how she bit her lip when she didn't like a topic or never looked into someone's eyes when she wasn't being genuine, to fall for her lies. She shut the door on my face before I could call her out on it, though. And a woman with a bright smile and even brighter cerulean gaze halted all of my interrogation plans when she met us behind the trunk.

"Jessy!" Serena squealed, mirroring her grin as they threw their arms around each other like they were old friends.

They hugged for what felt like an eternity before Serena and the young blonde turned to me. The difference between their styles was stark side by side, one business casual and the other teenage chic.

"And who do we have here?" Jessy quirked a brow at Serena, glancing at me.

"My lackey for the day, Ares Alsford." Serena winked as she passed by me, popping the trunk. "I brought him to help me carry some gifts for the kids."

"Pleasure to meet you," I greeted, going in for a handshake, but Jessy gave me a hug too.

Damn, the people at this place sure were touchy-feely. I eyed Serena in a way that said *you could sure learn a thing or two from them* when we came apart, but both women ignored me, focusing on the bags in Serena's trunk. And there was a ton covering every inch of the plush surface. My arms were sore already 'cause I knew I'd be doing most of the heavy lifting.

"Serena, you didn't have to do this. They already don't use all the clothes you brought last time, and we already have so many toys."

"Please, Jessy, it's almost Christmas," Serena said exasperatedly, handing me four bags and fluttering her lashes at me, so I took them. I did with a sigh. "I had to get the little cuties gifts."

Carrying our shared loads, we all made our way inside, and for all the grandiose space and high ceilings of the group home, it was decorated modestly, with string lights and the smell of cinnamon buns filling the air. Jessy led the way, and Serena walked next to me with a pep in her step and a smile that hadn't left ever since we got here. It was the longest her eyes had stayed crinkled in the corners ever since before her mom passed.

"Yeah, it feels a lot like you're forced to come here, all right," I whispered at her, almost regretting it when her smile vanished immediately, as if caught. My heart ached at the sight of her suppressing her kind side because the world had taught her it was a weakness meant to be exploited. "It's okay to show your vulnerable side sometimes, Serena. I promise your heart will not thaw out overnight. You can still cling on to the ice coating it."

"It *did* start out that way," she murmured back. "But I grew attached to them. They're brilliant, Ares, especially little Arta. She's going to be selling out stadiums one day." Stars shone in her eyes, and all of a sudden, I couldn't wait to meet this Arta that Serena was so fond of. It wasn't hard to understand why Serena loved being here. Kids usually had a lot more love to give, especially when it was robbed from them.

"With that kind of name, I believe it," I said. "It seems like all the big stars have unusual names."

Serena nodded, flexing her fingers around the bag's handles. "I was told it means golden in Albanian, so you're probably not wrong. Her dad was from there, but he died before she was born, and her mom decided to give her up for adoption because she didn't have the necessary funds to raise her alone."

Her voice held an undercurrent of pain for the girl, and it knocked the breath out of my chest, watching her care for others.

"You seem very fond of her." My voice came out breathless, and I cleared my throat. It was exhilarating. Getting to know this other part of her when cracking her surface required a DEFCON one level of attentiveness.

"Oh, she is. Arta and Serena are best friends. The little girl clings to her leg every time she visits," Jessy spoke out, and for a second, I'd forgotten she was even here. She turned on her heels as we rounded up the corner of a large living room, eyes on Serena. "She's been doing those vocal exercises you told her, and it drives everyone mad, but she said she wanted to make you proud."

The crushing smile was back on Serena's face when the kids came into view, about a dozen of them all scattered around a fluffy beige rug, a bucket's worth of toys spilled all around them. They were in their pajamas, seeing as it was six pm, and they'd probably go to sleep soon.

A girl whose chestnut hair was shoved into two pigtails noticed us first and nudged her friend next to her. Slowly, a hum of noise built as Serena stepped farther inside, dropping off the bags by the entrance.

"Serena!" they all collectively called out her name, and she lowered to the floor as they rushed around her, giggling.

She came alive here around the kids, warmth radiating from her like never before. Of course, my mind couldn't help but marvel at the fact that she'd make a wonderful mother—I shut it all down, though, before it started conjuring up wilder ideas. Dropping the bags after her, I stood next to Jessy.

It was easy for everyone to label Serena as a bitch. That was certainly how she presented herself. Her world was drenched in gray, with black and white labels, as if she was shallow and superficial. It was all intentional, though. All along, that was the image she intended to paint for herself. I guessed it was easier to hide a bleeding soul in neutral colors.

But here it was on full display as she took her time hugging the kids, all probably aged from four to twelve. Serena was an orphan too, so I was sure she could identify way better here than her snotty friend group.

The little girl that had initially recognized Serena stepped up to me, looking up with curious brown eyes, asking, "Who are you?"

I crouched down on her level with a grin she recipro-cated, her red nose turning up. She couldn't be older than six. "Hi, I'm Serena's friend. My name's Ares."

I extended my hand, and she eyed it curiously, but ultimately put her tiny one in mine and shook my arm so hard I chuckled. "I'm Arta. She's never mentioned you before."

Twist the knife in my heart, why don't you, kid?

"She avoids talking about me because she gets shy." When Serena was done, she turned to us, and I leaned into Arta as if I was about to share a big secret with her, but my voice was loud, and my eyes were glued to Serena's. "You see, she has this huge crush on me she can't get rid of."

"Do you like her too?" Arta asked, wide-eyed.

"Very much so." I screwed up my face as if not wanting it to be true, and I didn't. Life would be so much easier if we got to pick the people we fell for.

"So you're not her friend, then. You're her boyfriend," Arta deadpanned, and I laughed.

"I wish the grown-up world was as clear-cut as you make it out to be, kid." I flicked one of her pigtails before Serena swooped in, clutching Arta's shoulders and pressing her against her legs.

"What are you two talking about?" she asked, her eyes narrowing on us.

"Serena, why isn't he your boyfriend when you two like each other?" Arta didn't beat around the bush and went straight for the kill.

I curled a brow in question at her, and her chest fluctuated with sharp breaths, her gaze floating between Arta and me. Indecision sat over her slumped shoulders as she considered her words carefully over this age-old inquiry.

Finally, she focused on Arta, taking the easy way out with an answer that bred more doubt than it gave clarity. "Because sometimes that's not enough for two people to get together."

I ground my molars together, holding my roiling anger

back as she whisked tiny Arta away, disregarding me completely. It was hard to hold on to that resentment, though, as the night went on and the frost that made Serena one of the most composed women I knew melted little by little, revealing a big heart that was capable of so much love and affection.

Her whole face lit up as the kids opened their gifts, spending hours playing with each one of them. I helped out too, but it wasn't me they were interested in, and I didn't blame them. The brunette with the windswept hair and big eyes that helped you escape reality when you stared at them was hard to beat.

But Arta and her angelic voice gave Serena a run for her money when they performed a Christmas carol. Serena took her place behind the portable piano, and Arta belted out notes that seemed too high to be coming out of her tiny frame. The pride and love etched on her face for the little girl had me wanting to invest all my life savings into furthering her career.

"Tell me why it's not enough?" I asked into the dead of the night as we exited the group home, shocking Serena into twisting around, her brows pinched together.

I couldn't hold it in anymore. This limbo hell she'd placed me in was exhausting, eating away at my soul one bite at a time when I would've preferred if she'd annihilated it over this slow torture.

"What?" Her breath fogged up the air in front of her face. I still saw the puzzlement in her expression, though, as if she couldn't believe I was doing this right outside of the children's home.

Boo-fucking-hoo.

She'll have to get with the program.

"Why is liking each other not enough for you?" I clarified, walking closer in short, measured steps, like a predator stalking its prey. For every step I took forward, she took two back until her spine hit her car. Her gaze darted from my lips to my eyes before she rolled her shoulders back, that wall I wanted to take a sledgehammer to holding up strong.

"Come on, Ares, I need to be home by nine. I have an English test I've yet to study fo—" She tried to escape my line of fire, but I held on to her elbow, pushing her back in place before she could, slicing through whatever she had to say with a sentence that had her choking on her next breath.

"What if I told you I more than liked you?"

"What's that supposed to mean?"

The frigid air grew humid as our faces aligned, and I tipped her chin up. Usually, people looked uglier up close. Exposed pores, scars, visible wrinkles all added to the tally of what was deemed unattractive, but I disagreed. It made someone so much more real, unfiltered, and it was beautiful, watching them bask in their imperfections, holding their head high and saying a fuck you to all societal norms.

"That describing what I feel for you as simply *liking you* is a fucking joke." I exhaled, and she took in my air with a shuttered breath. I could almost taste her on my tongue this up close. Sweet, deceptive, and oh-so alluring. "You were amazing in there, finally free to be whoever you want to be, after repressing yourself daily to fit into a role that doesn't suit you."

Her eyes closed as she soaked in my compliment, palms

flattening on my chest like she was gathering her strength to push me away, but we both knew she liked me exactly where I was.

Allowing her this moment of peace was a mistake because when her lashes came apart, it was apparent she'd drawn from her bottomless well of self-control and shoved me back. Regardless of the fact that I didn't budge, her mind was miles away from mine, thinking of all the reasons she wasn't allowing us to happen and sharing none of them with me.

"A person has more than one side to them. It's not a role. It's a part of me you're not yet ready to accept. So you can't say what I think you want to say," she snapped, and I laughed bitterly.

"I can't, now, can I?"

"No, you can't." She shook her head vehemently. "I won't allow you."

My mouth was dry, as if I'd stuffed it with ash. There was so much I wanted to say, but nothing came out. For the longest time, I used to joke that she was just playing hard to get, or that she needed time, but she couldn't even fucking accept *my* feelings for her.

Insecurities swarmed around me like a pack of wolves scenting blood. The thought that she actually liked *him* made my lungs burn with my next inhale. Even though I'd psychoanalyzed the entire situation more than five hundred times and every time concluded that she was just flirting with Leo to make Eliana jealous, a shadow of doubt remained in the back of my head.

It was hard not to, and it hurt like a motherfucker.

"Get into the passenger seat. I'm driving," I instructed, retreating. She blinked a couple of times, confused at my abrupt change of subject. I was drained, and the last thing I wanted was to fight with her.

"It's *my* car."

"You drive like a fucking sloth, and I'd rather cut this journey home short. That way, we don't have to be in each other's presence for longer than necessary."

"Ares—" she started, but I held out my hand, cutting her off.

"Keys."

Reluctantly, she handed them over. There was an apology on the tip of her tongue the entire way home, but it didn't fucking matter since she never fucking uttered it.

I was teeming with unreleased energy once out of her sight, and my sick mind got the brilliant idea to invite Serena's best friend over. Caroline was more than down for anything as long as it involved pleasure. I wasn't proud of myself for what I did, and Caroline's fucking skills were mediocre at best, but it wasn't an orgasm I was after. It was the high of payback.

It felt good until it didn't.

Until I lay in bed staring at a head full of bleached hair, and a sickly-sweet floral fragrance tickled my nostrils when all I wanted was her cinnamon spice.

CHAPTER FOURTEEN
SERENA

Present

"Chips? Processed meat? Not a single vegetable in sight?" I sighed deeply, gazing at Ares's shopping cart. "How does it feel to be God's favorite? I didn't know it was possible to eat shit like this and still look like... well, *that.*"

I let my eyes roam over his body while he picked a bag of Doritos from the shelf. His muscle tee had deep cuts underneath each of his armpits, and it allowed me to see part of his chest every time he turned sideways. It was distracting, and the way my mouth watered whenever I caught a peek of all that tight skin was downright annoying and weak of me.

I wasn't expecting his ambush today. He'd cornered me into telling him my work address and had shown up all decked down in his workout gear and loud Harley that attracted more attention than I was comfortable with. Unfortunately, I'd done this to myself. My brilliant idea to invite

Elsa and James to the said double date had turned out pretty dumb after all, and not without repercussions.

Elsa had been giving me the cold shoulder the entire week, and I didn't blame her. My excuse that something urgent had happened to Ares, and he needed to leave immediately sounded stupid even to my own ears as well when I remembered the scene he'd caused. James was kinder, but he was definitely acting distant too. But what hurt worse was my lack of care.

It was as if he'd served his purpose of reassuring me that Ares was at least still partially interested, and now I could dispose of him. I didn't set out for it to be that way, but controlling one's thoughts was pointless. No matter how hard I tried to steer my mind to the lighter end of the morality spectrum, it stubbornly remained wedged in that gray area between devious and pure.

I was acutely aware that I'd just called Ares attractive indirectly, but he was already so far up the ladder he had nowhere left to climb. Sometimes it was hard hanging on to that resentment I felt for him. The more time we got to spend together, the more exhausting it was being mean all the time, but that didn't mean I had forgotten all the wounds he'd inflicted on me. To this day, they were bleeding, and I didn't think they'd ever stop, but I decided to allow for these rare moments of a ceasefire as I figured out his angle and followed him around the grocery store. A pit stop before heading for his house.

That cocky grin made an appearance as he cannonballed the bag into the cart. "My chef's on vacation. I'm just making do until he comes back."

"Of course. Why didn't I think of that?" I rolled my eyes for missing the obvious.

While successful by societal standards, if you put Ares in charge of cooking his own food, he'd die of starvation within a week. Or because of a self-induced fire. He was a hazard in the kitchen. He'd once tried to fry an egg and had almost burned his apartment down in college. After that, he'd strictly stuck with takeout.

I pushed the cart after him as we made our way down the line of the massive fridges. He pulled one of the doors open, grabbed a pint of Häagen-Dazs ice cream, and aimed for my chest. A hiss fell past my parted lips as I struggled to catch the slippery container, not accustomed to its frigid temperature in mid-July Massachusetts. I shot laser beams at him with my eyes when he chuckled.

"What the hell, Alsford?"

"Thought you'd want your favorite flavor," he said, and I twisted the container in my hands, brows furrowing.

"Vanilla's not my favorite."

"Hm, but you were loving it just last Friday," Ares replied slyly, tapping his fingers over the glass.

Giving him a blank stare, I let the ice cream trickle from my hands to the cart and pushed abruptly, catching Ares's toe under the wheel. "Is there a reason why I'm helping you shop?"

"I needed someone to steer the cart. Obviously, I made a mistake." His jaw ticked as he rubbed his thigh but fell into step with me shortly after. "How's our little *James* holding up?"

"Perfectly," I snapped, something about the way he said his name grating on my nerves. "He was very sympathetic when I told him about your regular bipolar episodes. Even told me I should follow you and make sure you're okay, like a man not easily intimidated, and comfortable in his own skin."

He hadn't told me any of that, but Ares didn't need to know.

"Otherwise known as a pussy," he challenged, not impressed.

I sucked my lips into my mouth in frustration. It shouldn't be normal that I somewhat enjoyed Ares's blowup, not in this current social climate where toxic masculinity was on the tip of everybody's tongue. Not when I'd lived through it. It was fucking weird, and I'd let him manhandle me when I should've kneed his balls. But what was stranger was that I didn't shy away from his touch. I didn't find it repulsive. In fact, my skin heated up whenever we came in contact, as if basking under his attention.

That'd only happened with Sam before, and I was starting to believe I'd only ever be comfortable with men I had positive memories with. Because before Ares was a thorn wedged in my finger, he used to be crimson fireworks and birthday wishes.

"You made Elsa tear up," I accused him, but he didn't bite into my trap.

"No, sweetheart. *You* made her tear up. It was your brilliant mind and need for attention that always makes an avalanche out of snowflakes."

Grounding my teeth, I ignored his judgmental look, swerving left at the last second and heading toward the cereal aisle.

"Where are you going?" he asked and almost bumped into me when I stopped abruptly, grabbing a box of Lucky Charms. I hadn't had them in a while. I liked taking care of my body and was the type of person who counted calories.

But compared to other poor decisions as of late, this was the least of my worries.

"If you're going to kidnap me straight after work, you might as well feed me." He circled in front of me, biting his lip, a look I wished I didn't remember so well overtaking his dilated pupils. "You see this milk carton?" I pointed at it. "It'll be on a straight trajectory toward your face if you say what I think you're about to say."

He paused, then his face broke into a terrible smile. Terrible because it pulled at my heartstrings like nothing before. "Why so violent, Siren? I was just about to ask if you still picked out the marshmallows and left the rest of the Lucky Charms intact."

"I'm sure." I smiled, sickly sweet, playing into his charade.

He opened his mouth to reply, but the sound that reached my ears was way different from his usual rough, husky voice. It was sweet, girly, and definitely not one that would come out of a grown thirty-one-year-old man's throat.

"Uncle Ares."

A tiny thing appeared next to him, all but reaching his mid-thigh, and I held my breath when I got a good look at her. It was like I was suddenly transported back to my child-hood, staring at a pair of bright, frosty eyes that knew all my secrets. Her face shape was small and round, mouth full and pink, and nose as upturned and aristocratic as my ex-best friend's—*Eliana's*. The only thing I could really say set them apart was the girl's wild curly hair, a delicious chocolate brown.

I was already pretty sure that this was Leo and Eli's daughter, but got my complete confirmation when Ares snapped his mouth shut, his face blanching like he was caught red-handed, being with someone he wasn't supposed to be. Shame oozed out of every pore in my body when he first looked behind the little girl, confirming that she was alone, and then sliced his gaze to hers.

"Hey." He sunk to her level, his hands hooking underneath her arms, tugging her up with him. "What are you doing here all alone? Where're Mom and Dad at?"

"They're home. I'm here with Grandma. I convinced her to make me Rocky Road, and she's picking the ingredients." The girl's fingers clutched his shoulders, her curious gaze floating to me. My throat loosened under her perusal, and I remembered to breathe as she glanced at me from the tips of my cream heels to my beige bell-bottoms and dark purple tee like she was examining a bug under a microscope. She poked Ares's sternum once satisfied, saying, "That's not Sonia."

"No, um..." Ares grappled with finding the right words, and I was thrust back to reality with a vicious slap to the face.

Who the hell is Sonia?

I'd assumed he was single because...well, he'd acted like he was. Going on dates with other women, touching me ina-*fucking*-ppropriately in the case that he had a girlfriend, both with his hands and eyes. I didn't peg Ares as a cheater, but I'd been gone a long time. Blind fury made my ears buzz, and something akin to jealousy corroded the surface of my heart. This Sonia chick must have been important if even Eli's daughter knew her.

Reminding myself to skin his balls later for keeping it from me, I plastered a painful smile on my face, doing Ares this last favor and introducing myself.

"I'm Amelia. Nice to meet you..." My mouth pursed in thought, and I took a wild guess. "Bella?"

Her eyes narrowed, and I saw a flash of her dad there too. "How do you know my name?"

I know your parents too well, kid.

"I guessed. A beautiful name for a beautiful girl." I placed my elbows on the plastic handle of the cart. "You look exactly like your mommy."

Despite all that went down between us, Eliana was gorgeous. I understood why Leo was so enamored by her. Hell, I'd be too if I was attracted to women. Unfortunately, I only got a lady boner for lying asshats of the opposite sex.

"Thank you. My dad hates it when people say that." A bright smile spread over her face as if annoying her father was one of her favorite pastimes, and I could already tell they'd have their hands full with this one. "Are you friends with my parents too?"

"No, I don't know them." I thought fast. Little kids were notorious for running their mouths. They didn't know any better. If Bella could comprehend how the news of my return would shake her parents, she'd try to erase my face from her memory. "Uncle Ares has shown me pictures of them."

Frown lines marred Ares's face when I included him in my fabrication, but he didn't dispute it, tightening his hold on Bella and glancing behind them in case her grandma figured out where she'd run off to. And I doubted Leo's mom had forgotten about me, so it was best we left before she found us.

As if reading my mind, Ares hoisted her up higher and scolded her. "Come on, Bella, let's go find your grandma. She's going to be worried. You can't just run off like that."

"Fine," she heaved a dramatic sigh, clutching Ares's shirt, eyes hooked on mine over his shoulder as he turned. "It was nice to meet you too, Amelia. You're so much prettier than Sonia."

Ares's shoulders shook with silent laughter at the kid's sharp tongue, and I was glad one of us found this funny. I'd admit it was an ego boost, but it also rubbed salt on the wound, reminding me that Ares was in a relationship, and I hadn't known shit.

On top of that, he'd made me feel like the bad guy for inviting James.

I waved goodbye at Bella, and she waved back with a massive grin sans some teeth, vowing not to let Alsford off the hook that easily.

CHAPTER FIFTEEN
SERENA

"We're here." Ares's voice was muffled underneath his helmet, but I already knew we'd arrived when the motorcycle stopped rumbling beneath me.

I thanked the Lord for making this ride a short one and tried not to feel at a loss when I removed my arms from around him. My bare skin was pressed against his in multiple areas, and I'd forgotten how intimate riding behind someone could be. He was basically my anchor, and it was summer, so less clothing meant more contact.

Tucking my hair behind my ears and placing the helmet beneath my armpit, I hopped off. I stood off to the side as Ares gathered the two fabric bags hanging from the handles during our entire trip. He raised a brow at me when I snorted, stretching tall before me. Our height difference was stark, and I added one more thing I didn't like about him to the list.

He was too freaking tall, and I needed to crane my neck up to look at him every time.

"This is so inconvenient. Why don't you just take your car if you know you have things to carry?" I asked.

Transitioning the heavy bags to his left hand only, his biceps bunched under the weight, and I allowed myself a quick peek when he grabbed the helmet from me and placed it on the handle.

"It wasn't a lot of stuff," he reasoned, and I didn't push it.

Letting him lead the way, my eyes roamed over his house. The brick and limestone Georgian colonial was much smaller than I expected. Of course, it was still way too huge for just one person. Big enough to probably fit seven bedrooms and every type of entertainment room you could think of. But compared to the fucking castle he grew up in, this was modest by comparison. It had ionic pillars guarding the entrance, tall windows that allowed a ton of natural light in, and award-winning pink skies as a backdrop.

The next home wasn't until a few miles away, so I imagined the uninterrupted view of the sunset was even better from the backyard. And because my mind was cruel, it played with my neurons until I saw him very clearly soaking in his Jacuzzi with *Sonia* and enjoying some chilled white wine.

Envy twisted me up inside in knots as Ares unlocked the Oakwood door. I barely registered all the modern furniture but did linger on the James Turrell piece hanging smack dab at the end of the hallway, facing the mirror. There was no grand tour of the place; he led me straight to the kitchen, and I didn't protest. I was busy dealing with the cowardly side of hate and all the bleak and desolate feelings it brought along.

Sighing through his nose, Ares gave me the side-eye as he

touched the bags on the pristine black marble counters. "Is there something you'd like to get off your chest, Siren?"

Biting the inside of my cheek, I propped my ass on the back of a cream stool, trying to rein in my green friend before the interrogation started. I guessed my jealousy acted to my advantage this once because it deviated from the attention from the reason I was here in the first place. "Who's Sonia?"

Raising a brow at me, he lined up all the groceries on the counter and folded the bags. "I thought I was going to be the one asking the questions."

"Not when you might be cheating on your girlfriend." My nails dug into the material of my pants, and I considered knocking the can of beans he held in his hand.

Unimpressed with my outburst, Ares continued sorting things in their respective places, his tone holding a mocking lilt as he asked, "I'm cheating on my girlfriend? How?"

Poison drifted in my soul like black ink being dumped in water. "So you admit it? You have a girlfriend?" My voice sounded shocked even to my own ears, as if I hadn't truly believed it until he'd confirmed it.

"So what if I do? What's it to you?" he challenged.

"I just find it ironic that you had so much to say about James when you are in a committed relationship." I straightened, having a death grip on the counter, when Ares met my gaze head-on, abandoning his current project. There was a kitchen island separating us, but the scathing glare he threw my way burned through my clothes. "I mean, does she even know you're spending time with me? I wouldn't be that comfortable if my boyfriend was spending one-on-one time with a girl he'd previously fucked."

Something about that last word sparked a lazy smirk on his face, as if I'd been caught red-handed. "*Fucked?* I thought

I was so insignificant to you. You didn't remember anything about me." He laughed bitterly, and a rush of nerves shot up my spine. "Clearly, some memories broke through the brain fog."

Ares cocked his head, silently asking how much of our time together I replayed in my head at night when I was alone. I diverted my gaze, my answer as *way too fucking much*. Most men were more interested in their own pleasure than their partner's. Ares was the only one that had made me feel like more than just a blow-up sex doll. Then again, the men I hung around with weren't upstanding citizens of any kind.

"I think what you're doing is disgusting." I gave my two cents, even though he hadn't asked for them.

"Thanks, Mother Teresa," he mocked, stepping out of the staring battle first, but I knew I hadn't won in any way, shape, or form. I was the one brewing in anger while he skipped about the kitchen. "I really value your opinion."

I snatched the Lucky Charms off the counter before he had a chance to grab them. He watched, amused, once done with his chores, as I shoved a handful of marshmallows in my mouth after saying, "Let's just get this over with."

I kept my gaze anywhere but at his, because even though Miss Sonia was living the life I used to crave with my whole heart, which automatically made me hate her, I felt like a homewrecker every time I looked at him. Because I wasn't just *looking* at him. I admired God's gift to women (outwardly at least), and it low-key felt like cheating.

"I don't." Ares's soft admission made me pause my chewing, my body locking up. "I don't have a girlfriend."

"But—"

"Sonia is my ex." He cut me off. "We broke up recently."

"Oh." I blinked, dusting my hands as I abandoned the cereal box. Immediate relief washed over me like a waterfall. "Why—"

Ares placed his fists on the marble, shaking his head, and I pictured the impressive view of his bunched back from behind. "That's none of your business. We're not here to psychoanalyze my life, but yours."

"Fine." I hopped off the stool, a bundle of nerves swirling low in my belly. "Step away from the kitchen, then. There must be something I could use in that fridge of yours. I'm hungry."

It turned out, Ares's chef had already stocked the fridge with vegetables, hence why he hadn't picked up any. So, I used the leeks, eggs, and goat cheese I found to whip up a quick frittata for either of us. I considered letting him starve, but that was too cruel, even by my standards, especially when I heard his stomach growl. He got his laptop out as I used his stainless-steel appliances and enviable French gas stove. It was unfair that he had a kitchen this grandiose when he didn't even cook, but that was life for you.

As I poured my mixture onto a skillet, he poked around as we waited for the food to cook, starting with some basic questions that didn't really put me at ease. We'd specified at the beginning that each question, no matter how minor, would count as a reduction, but I found it weird that he got to waste some away on inquiries like, *Is Harry Potter still your favorite book series?* I went with a yes, even though I'd upgraded to reading more rated-R content. Happy childhood memories were hard to beat. *Have you finally moved on from your Taylor Lautner phase?* I rolled my eyes, also answering with a firm yes, and took pride in informing him Keanu Reeves was my newest obsession. *Why do you find jellyfish so fascinating?*

"Um, because they survived five mass extinctions. They don't have a brain, or a heart, or bones, *or* blood, and are the only animal that can claim biological immortality," I gushed, but his lack of response told me he wasn't all that impressed. "They also glow in the dark," I quipped, and he nodded in an *aha* manner as if that was the most impressive thing about them. Swallowing an ironic reply down, I made peace with the fact that not everyone was as into knowing random facts as I was.

As Ares set up the cutlery for us, I'd admit he'd made me feel much more at ease with being here than I initially was. Wariness still lingered in the back of my mind, though, because I'd seen this interrogation technique in many detective series. Be friendly with the criminal and make them so comfortable enough around you, they put their faith (and fate) in your hands.

Ares remembered enough details about me to know that I wasn't the kind to open up willingly. He'd have to push, and push, *and push*, and I'd have to make sure I didn't break under his direct line of fire. He had a face you wanted to trust—*and ride.*

"Favorite drink?" Ares asked innocently, illuminated by the fluorescent lights of the fridge. He had a beer in hand for himself and was just waiting for my answer.

"I'll just have water, thanks." I gulped and began cutting into the frittata after sitting on one of the barstools.

"No alcohol? *I'm* taking you home."

"Nope, not in the mood." I stiffened. "And I'm taking an Uber. You're not driving me home."

I didn't want him to know my exact location yet. Except for Sam and the FBI team handling my case, no one did. I was advised not to invite anyone in case they ended up in danger through association.

After retrieving some bottled water, Ares shut the fridge door with more force than necessary and sat beside me. Our elbows brushed, and I took a bite, way too attuned to his movements as if he was an extension of me.

"You seem to never be in the mood for alcohol these days," he observed, cutting his food with calm precision. "Why's that?"

Cold sweat ran down my back as I shrugged. "Evolving tastes. I've become a bit of a health freak, and alcohol has pretty bad effects on your body."

"Actually, moderate drinking has some benefits, such as reducing your risk of developing and dying of heart disease. The more you know," he said conversationally, and I could hear my pulse in my ears. "Are you sure there isn't another reason why you don't drink anymore?"

My fork clattered on my plate, and he matched my blank stare with one of his own. It was like a battle of who had the best poker face, and mine started slipping when I realized he was playing me.

He knew.

He'd already seen through me, and I couldn't half-truth my way out of this.

I blew out a breath, pushing my food around on my plate. "I might've abused my limits for alcohol once or twice, so I decided not to drink anymore."

"Only once or twice?" he asked carefully.

"Yeah, booze wasn't my main addiction," I admitted, and

he sucked in a breath, almost fooling me into thinking he cared.

"What was?" he prodded, and I took a deep breath.

There was no reason to hide this. It gave him some of the insight he craved, and it wasn't like my substance abuse problem was unique. Millions of people suffered from it. If he thought of me as less than for my past, then that was his problem, not mine.

"Coke or heroin, depending on the day. One time I combined both, and it nearly ended up being the last thing I ever did." My voice was thick and cracked and not mine.

The table disappeared from my line of sight, and the view of a dirty motel carpet replaced it. I had a shot in my hand, sinking the needle into my skin. That feeling, the rush, the euphoria I was going to experience as the substance mixed with my bloodstream made me shiver with anticipation. But then I got on my feet, took one step, and the last thing I saw was the yellow ceiling as my skull banged against the floor, and darkness enveloped me whole.

If Sam wasn't there, if he hadn't heard the commotion, that would've been it.

I would've died.

My shoulders shook, and I stopped pretending like I was interested in eating anymore. I spread my palms flat on the marble, focusing on my manicured nails. They used to always be cracked and painful not too long ago. Even in the most minor of things, I saw testaments of how far I'd come.

"After I survived," I continued, before I lost the nerve to finish the story. "I made a promise to myself to never put my body through that kind of stress again. It was easier said than done, but I've been clean for the past three years now, and I'm proud of my progress so far."

Drugs were the easy way out, but that brief serotonin boost wasn't worth all the repercussions. Instead, I'd learned through therapy that focusing on filling my days up with activities that made me happy had the same effect without the deterioration of my body and mental health. If I was having a shitty day, I could always go for a walk on the beach, breathe in all the salt. Volunteer at the local animal shelter, and play with the cute puppies. Or cook something that tasted better than an orgasm felt.

Ares's skin brushed mine, and I turned into a block of ice as his fingers shifted through mine, his much larger hand engulfing mine. His touch spread like poetry on my skin. Thoughts and emotions, memories of how many times I dreamt about how my life would've turned out differently if he simply hadn't left me that morning, etched their way between us.

It was unfair to put that much responsibility on his shoulders, but I couldn't help how I felt. It was terrifying, knowing how he could make or break me, and part of me wondered if I deserved everything for all the hoops I'd made him jump. Giving him hope, then ripping it away brutally.

"I'm proud of you too, if it means anything. I've always envied your strength, and stubbornness isn't always a bad thing. Especially when it keeps you alive because if there's one thing I hate in this world more than you being back..." His thumb caressed my wrist, leaving behind trails of electricity. "It's living in it without you."

My breath got stuck in my throat as if someone had tied an invisible noose around it. My eyes burned with unshed tears as relief spread over my chest like a soothing balm. Even though he'd prefer there to be an ocean's distance between us, he cared enough not to want me dead.

I was scared to look at him because I knew I'd go soft. Ares Alsford had this innate ability to melt me with just a few words. He was good at them. I believed he must've been a poet or diplomat in another life because he opened his mouth, and you just wanted to lay your soul at his feet to make him happy.

But of course, like every diplomat at the end of the day, you couldn't forget that they had an agenda.

"Don't get all sappy on me now, Alsford." Reluctantly, I freed my hand from his grip, the tense atmosphere heightening when I kept my gaze low, and it snagged on his lips. They were berry red, and the urge to lean in and taste them shook me to my core. I worked my way up to his features, molten gold eyes liquifying with an emotion I couldn't pinpoint. "We still hate each other."

If my heart was a balloon, his nod pierced through the latex, and it floated to the bottom of my stomach with a sad thud. "I'm not sappy. It's true. I'd hate for any young person to lose their life before they've even lived it."

Any young person.

Of course, the passing of anyone was a tragedy, but especially young people that had their whole life ahead of them. His words felt like a low blow, though. They confirmed I didn't mean anything to him anymore. He just wasn't a psychopath and displayed his pity and empathy openly, even for his dearest nemesis.

It shouldn't have, but it stung, considering I was having such a hard time clinging to the side of me that wanted to dip him in a pool of fire.

"Yeah, well, if anything, I'm like a cat with nine lives. Not many people would've survived what I did." I shrugged, diverting my attention back to my plate. "So I don't take every day for granted anymore, and most importantly, don't take chances with anything that might lead me down the rabbit hole again."

Except for you.

The biggest reason why I fell into the rabbit hole.

Surprisingly, Ares didn't try to squeeze any more answers out of me for the rest of my stay. I believed it was because of the dark clouds that glimpse into my past had brought forth. We just ate in silence, and once our bellies were full, he thanked me for cooking.

I was waiting for my Uber to arrive, much to Ares's annoyance, when I caught a glimpse of what was in his living room after walking back from the bathroom. It seemed so out of place amidst all the modern furniture, yet it only enhanced the beauty in the room with a strategic pop of color placed over his dark blue modular sofa.

The psychedelic art called to me, and I neared, despite having Ares breathing down my neck and observing me like a hawk. He was nervous at my discovery, but he wanted me to see this because if he hadn't, he would've taken it down before I arrived—or *wouldn't have hung it up in the first place.*

Was he purposely trying to hurt me?

Crossing my arms, I swallowed down the bile that threatened to rise up my esophagus and studied the framed painting. A mermaid sat at the edge of a pond, surrounded by a bunch of lilting yellow flowers I recognized as daffodils. Her back was turned, the edge of her tail breaking through the water as she gazed far into the distance at a shadowed couple, kissing and embracing each other, ignoring an outstretched hand that tried to get her attention from behind.

It was all very...lonely and heartbreaking. Isolation and bitterness dripped from the painting, as if I was reliving it all for a second time.

"Mermaids are supposed to be in the ocean. Why is she in a pond?" I asked, an edge to my voice when he came up behind me. "And the feathers seem very out of place." I reached up with my pointer, but before I made contact with the few floating ones in the water, I pulled back.

"It's not a mermaid. It's a Siren," Ares voiced, his breath touching the top of my head now, so close if I turned around, I'd probably stumble into him. "They were rumored to have wings, and she's in a pond because that's how it came to me."

"You painted this?" I breathed, the knife twisting deeper in my gut.

"Yeah, a few years back. I got it done within a week."

"I don't remember you being this good." I gulped. Even though I hated it because of what it symbolized, it was indeed a work of art. "You only painted once in a blue moon."

"I still don't do it that often. It was just something I had to get down."

"Does it mean anything specific to you?"

His silence spoke plenty. He didn't even have to say anything. I already knew what it meant. For some fucking reason, Leo always called Eliana his Narcissus—pretty lame nickname if you asked me—the flowers and the pond were a testament to that. I was the siren, Ares was the one reaching out, but I didn't notice him because I was too blinded by jealousy.

Oh, how ironic.

The one person that knew me the best also knew me the

least. Technically, it wasn't his fault, but if he would've dug just a little bit deeper, he would've saved himself a lot of heartache.

"Ask me what you truly wanted to know all these years. Stop beating around the bush," I ordered, turning around to face him. We were chest to chest, and I had to crane my neck all the way back to look at him, but I stood my ground. A bitter smile slashed across my face like a scar, and my heart jumped in my chest with adrenaline and recklessness. Fed up with everything. Everyone. "Instead of eating yourself up inside, one-upping me to hurt me, ask me why I consistently kept choosing Leonardo over you. Why I couldn't keep my eyes off you but kept running to him. Why all the mixed signals?"

It hurt that he always pinned the blame on me, and it was concerning how he claimed to care about me, yet was so inclined to believe the worst. Even now, his face remained the picture of boredom, not giving in to my demands.

He gave a lazy shake of his head. "I don't want to know. Unlike you, I don't live in the past. I've moved on, and you don't belong in the plans I have for my future."

Yeah, the painting speaks plenty of how much you've moved on.

"No, you live in your head, and you're scared," I taunted and took a tiny step closer, not caring that our bodies were flush. I wanted to feel his heart beat in tandem with mine, the one indication that I was getting to him. "You're just a scared little boy with rejection issues."

His eyes were unnaturally blank as his hand came up, cradling my jaw, and I made an audible noise of surprise when he locked me in place, his elbow against my breasts. His hold was dominant, but gentle. The slight pressure he

---

applied was like a caress on my skin. "Watch your mouth."

"Or what?" I licked my bottom lip, throwing my sense of danger out the window.

He smirked, and my stomach swooped and dove when he used his thumb to wipe the wet trail I'd left behind. I didn't miss his touch when he retracted his hand because my lips tingled—*my everything tingled*—as he brought that same thumb flat against his thick tongue, his voice drifting to a dark rasp as he said, "Or I'll put it to good use."

A myriad of emotions slammed into me at once, and for the minute it took me to collect myself, I didn't know how to act. Part of me wanted to jump him, and the other one, knock him flat on his back—and not in a fun way.

My nostrils burned as I breathed out, taking the courage to admit what I had never to anyone other than Sam before. It was embarrassing and personal, but I couldn't stand him treating me like I was Satan's spawn anymore. My secrets were eating me up inside.

"I kept choosing him because I was forced to," I said softly. "Because I had a father that used his daughter to cover up his tracks."

"Here we go with the bullshit," he scoffed, moving back, and hurt flared in my chest. Was he so set on the idea he had of me he refused to believe the truth? "Just say you were jealous and get on with your life, Serena."

Yes, yes, he is.

Anger bubbled up in my throat, and I had no control over my actions when I shoved him. Ares stumbled but caught on to the edge of the couch, almost getting whiplash with how fast he twisted his furious face to meet mine.

"On my twenty-first birthday, I kissed Leo in my room

215

for the sole purpose of having Eliana witness the whole thing." My voice was way too loud, and it echoed. I kept going, though, riding the streak of confidence to the bitter end. "Contrary to popular opinion, I do have some self-respect, but time after time, I was forced to shove it down and prioritize other people's interests. The whole thing was organized by Leo's and my dad. They both had different intentions but a similar end goal, and it was to separate the two because, together, they were dangerous. Together, they could uncover the truth both he and Claire tried to hide. That they were the ones that had Isabella killed, and if I tried to refuse..."

I paused, gulping, and some of the annoyance had melted from his expression as he watched me intently, fists curled on his sides, eyes fostering a volatile fire that, if unchecked, could spread.

"What?" he prompted. "What could have possibly happened if you'd simply said *no*."

I folded my hands under my chest, my chest caving. It was too late to take it back now, so I let the tap run free, baring my soul and telling myself it didn't matter whether he believed what I had to say or not.

"What always happened when I told him I didn't want to make a fool of myself by pursuing Leo anymore when I didn't like him like that. It was a simple fucking childhood crush that he exploited for his own benefit," I breathed out harshly, keeping my gaze on my shoes. "He'd force me in my room and wouldn't let me eat until the hunger pains got so bad, I had no choice but to agree. And before you say it, I didn't think anyone could help me; that's why I never said anything. Carter Laurent was the number one lawyer in town. He knew every loophole so well. He could shut me down in two seconds."

"Serena—" Ares tried to interject, but I was on a fucking roll.

"And who knows, if I'd gone ahead with it, and no one believed me, maybe he would've actually let me starve to death."

A pregnant pause filled the room, and I dared to look at him again, my curiosity killing me. His brows were high in astonishment, mouth moving, but no words were coming out. Ares's knuckles were white; his body a marble statue as utter disbelief drew all color from his face.

Of course, he hadn't expected that, despite having all the clues. My father wasn't only horrible with a select few, he was horrible with everyone, and that was why I didn't hesitate to twist the knife in his back at the first chance I got.

It was so easy to draw conclusions with minimal facts, but unlike Hollywood loved to portray women, not all of us were fine with acting like man-eating, life-ruining cunts. It killed me inside little by little every day, taking on the role of the bad guy and still paying the price today.

"I-I—" he stuttered, hand shifting through his hair as he tried to gather his wits. I'd rendered him speechless. Would you look at that? There was a first time for everything.

My phone buzzed in my pocket, piercing through the heavy silence, and I retrieved it to see what it was. I blew out a relieved sigh when I saw that my ride was here.

I shifted uncomfortably on my feet as he digested my words. This evening had taken a turn I hadn't expected. My anger got the best of me, and to be honest, I was glad I'd finally admitted the truth. I didn't care if it made me seem weak.

It felt liberating to get everything off my chest.

It felt good not to be the villain in my own story anymore.

"Don't waste your words," I said patronizingly, pocketing my phone again. His head snapped to me when I turned, rounding the corner of the living room. "I've had enough of you today."

Some of the chains that weighed me down disappeared as I made my way down his hallway. My steps were lighter and soon turned brisker when I heard Ares's heavy ones closing in on me from behind.

He'd finally woken up from his vegetative state, but I wasn't in the mood for whatever he had to say. At least not today. I needed to retrieve and lick my wounds because if I stayed, I feared the can of worms would keep getting deeper and deeper.

"Serena, stop," he hissed from behind, and I was full-blown running now, twisting the front door open quickly and spotting the white Lexus in his driveway. "Fucking stop," Ares yelled, hot on my heels.

My lungs burned, but I kept going until I reached the car.

No, he didn't get to set it all right in a single night.

I wanted him to suffer. A lot.

"Fucking practice track more," I yelled back, meeting his crazed eyes as I sunk into the seat and slammed the door in his face. The driver looked at me wide-eyed, probably wondering what kind of soap opera he'd stumbled across, but took off as soon as I said, "Go, go, go."

CHAPTER SIXTEEN

ARES

How do you forget a monumental mistake?

You get your brains knocked out.

Pain spread on my left cheekbone like a thousand fire ants had taken permanent residence on my face, and my body was sore in several other places as I rested on the floor, thanks to none other than Saint.

That's what I got for boxing with a hundred and ninety-pound ex-football player. It wasn't his fault; I'd asked him to go as hard as he could, and he'd made good on my request. I didn't regret it. It erased Serena's words from my head even for just five fucking minutes.

It all came rushing back, though, as we caught our breath. The hurt in her voice. The tremble as she relived what she'd survived. The raw truth of what she was saying was painted all over her stance, and it left no shadow of doubt in my mind.

She was being genuine, and I'd had basically my whole life to put two and two together. But for some reason—jealousy, if I could be honest—I hadn't managed to connect the dots and taunted her with that damned painting that I ripped to shreds after she ran out on me.

She ran out on me.

I'd lost count of how many times she'd done that by now.

But I was starting to get fed up, and nice Ares was bound to fly out the window next time I saw her.

"How do you apologize to Aria when you fuck up?" I asked Saint, sprawled next to me on a blue mat.

His face twisted in thought, and I almost cracked a smile when I realized he was probably shifting through a mental library full of bullshit he'd done. "How big of a fuckup are we talking about?"

I gulped, wiping the sweat off my neck with a dry towel. What level would one rate acting like an asshat that couldn't handle rejection for fourteen years and taunting the girl of his fucking dreams for running away when things got real, thinking she would've one hundred percent stayed if she'd had his best friend's dick inside her? It was pretty bad to begin with, but factor in that she never even had a say in the first place, and I was in some enormous pile of shit.

So, definitely top-tier level bad.

"The worst you've ever done," I said, and even the grunting men going at it at the boxing ring on our right couldn't divert my razor-sharp focus on Saint.

His blond brows bunched, eyes filled with questions he surprisingly kept at bay as he sat up, giving me his undivided attention. "There are two ways to go about it, depending on the woman. First, you either wait it out a few days and then go after them if they're the kind to soften up with time. That's what works best with my wife." He laid down the rules. "Or if they're overthinkers, then you need to strike while the situation is hot because if they sit on it, it's going to turn into lava-level hot."

"So, the second option is out of the window," I sighed, resting on my elbows. One of the trainers gave us a pointed glare for resting for so long, but we blew him off. Saint kept biting his lip and fiddling with his hair, and I was surprised he'd kept the lid on it for so long. "How come you're not asking me any questions?"

He scoffed, as if the answer was obvious. "You get all prissy when I do."

"I don't get *prissy*." I spat the word out like it was an insult.

"Yeah, you do. It's like you're on your period twenty-four-seven, and the slightest thing will set you off," Saint argued, his golden gaze glowing with conviction. "Are you going through some sort of midlife crisis?"

It was my turn to scoff. Honestly, how could I *not* be prissy with friends like mine? "I'm only in my early thirties, asshat. Not anywhere near a midlife crisis yet."

"You're no spring chicken either," he said with a stupid grin and shrugged. "I'm just saying, some people start out young."

I caught his technique a little too late for my liking because I'd already fallen into his trap—of getting me so annoyed I had no choice but to tell the truth. It was weird he hadn't caught up already. There was only one person that used to get me this worked up.

The need to say something, talk with someone, burned in my chest like a toxic bubble seconds before popping. I couldn't admit that she was here without some repercussions, but I couldn't find it in me to care what people thought. I didn't care when everyone believed I was stupid for pursuing her then, and certainly not now. It was my life, and the hollowness in my stomach when Serena wasn't around hurt me more than every rando's opinion.

"Can you keep a secret?" My throat felt hoarse as the words came out, and Saint's face sparked with interest. The truth was bound to come out, but it was going to be on Serena's terms. "As in, you won't open your mouth to anyone, not Killian, not Eliana, and certainly not Leonardo."

"As long as Aria is out of the question." He negotiated and sucked on his teeth as I glared at him, unrelenting. "Okay, fine. I can. Are you going to tell me what has you acting like a cunt for the past month?"

"Promise," I insisted.

He rolled his eyes, mocking me by crossing his fingers over his heart. "I promise."

I chewed on my bottom lip, thinking about how to phrase it carefully. *The girl that broke my heart is back?* No. *The girl that's most likely going to break my heart for a second time is back?* Fuck no. *A brunette that you may or may not know, whose name rhymes with Selena Durrant, is back?* Triple no.

I blew out a breath, my mind going into hyperactive mode, producing more stress hormones than a law student about to take the bar exam.

"Spit it out, man." Saint gave me a blank, *what did you do* type of glare.

Oh, whatever, even if he didn't keep his mouth shut, it was just a means to rip the Band-Aid off quicker. Serena had never explicitly told me not to say anything. I'd done so, mostly because I was a selfish bastard that wanted her all to myself before shit hit the fan. If I'd managed to give her the boot in the process, all the better.

Now?

I'd had a week of radio silence from her, and let's just say the last thing I wanted was more of that. It was fucking crazy how easily I could unlearn all the past years of being without her in a single month of seeing her on and off. It was fucking mental how she'd managed to shift my entire perspective of her in that short period of time too.

Somehow, I felt both validated and dumb. I knew Serena's heart, but I'd villainized her so much in my head, she resembled a red-headed devil. She was no angel either, but we all had our flaws. That was what made us human.

"Serena Laurent..." I started, exhaling slowly before I continued. But when I opened my mouth again, I didn't get the chance to finish my sentence because Saint stole the words right out of my mouth.

"...is here," he finished for me, and my head snapped up.

"What?" The knot in my throat loosened despite the turn of events. Saint's fleeting gaze met mine, eyes wide as if he just came to the realization himself. "How do you know?"

"She just walked into the gym." He gaped at something over my shoulder, and I almost twisted my neck, turning to see what he was so enamored by.

I almost swallowed my tongue when I saw her.

Serena had a phenomenal body, and her violet lululemon tights and matching tank top did nothing to hide that. I could've sworn one of the guys going at it in the ring got punched just because he wasn't paying attention by staring at her. Her hair was up in a ponytail, slender neck out in the open, and my mouth watered at the sight.

Old Serena would've basked in the attention. She loved

eyes on her as much as she loved her designer clothes. But this new one...despite not losing her fashion sense, she walked in, shoulders hunched and pace quick as she made her way to one of the private training rooms in the back.

"Wait a second. You don't seem surprised." Saint hit my shoulder as we both watched her disappear down the hallway. His shocked face greeted me when I stumbled back, my elbows almost giving out. "Holy fuck, Alsford. Is this what you've been keeping from us? Leo will go insane when he finds out."

My stomach twisted up in knots, and I rubbed a hand down my scruff. It didn't matter that he'd react. That was a given. It mattered that I'd have to choose sides, and even though Serena would rather set fire to a billboard with me on it than see my face every day, I could be persistent.

And I also needed to know *why* she left if not liking me wasn't the problem.

Suddenly all the fucking thoughts and feelings I was trying to keep on lock, were coming back—all the *hope* I felt thirteen years prior—and I had trouble focusing on the matter at hand. You'd think I would've learned my lesson. But no, I wanted to talk to her.

"That's why he won't. You promised, Saint."

"Fuck." He threw his head back. "What is she even doing here? I thought she left after college."

"She works here." I shrugged, and his eyes narrowed at my casual tone.

"You better not get involved with her again, Alsford. You acted like a zombie for months after she left. We had to force food down your throat." The veins down his neck bulged, and I should be grateful I had friends that cared about me, but the parasite, otherwise known as Serena Laurent, was already in my system. "You already are. Is she the one you want to apologize to? What for? Not kissing her ass enough during high school and college?"

I stiffened, getting off my ass and dusting my hands. "Don't talk about shit you know nothing about."

Even looking at me from below, Saint had a powerful presence that rivaled my own. "I lived it with you, asshat. How are you going to tell me I don't know shit?"

Grinding my teeth together, I held back, starting toward the direction Serena had disappeared to. "I'll explain later."

"Where are you going?" he echoed behind me, but I didn't deign him with a response.

When I opened the door that led to the private training rooms, I heard him cursing harshly, but he knew better than to follow. On my way down, I stumbled across one of the personal trainers when he opened his office door. I recognized him as the one handling most of the one-on-one lessons. We'd been going to this gym for the past five or so years, so I was well-versed with the environment and its people, enough to know this guy was gullible.

"Alsford," he greeted, a smile plastered on his face. I mirrored his expression as he went in for one of those bro handshakes, bumping his shoulder with mine.

"Hey, Sloan." I kept my hand in his, gesturing behind me with my other hand. "I think I saw your car getting towed outside? You might want to check that."

Yup, gullible indeed.

Sloan's face fell, and I took a step back as he rushed to the door, barely able to squeeze his frame through. "Oh, shit, come on. I missed *one* insurance payment."

Not wasting any precious time, I pulled the first door open and moved on quickly when I found nothing but empty space. I had more success with the second one, and it took me a full-on minute to pull my jaw off the fucking floor at the sight that was waiting for me.

Serena's ass was up in the air, her hands around her legs as she stretched them, her head almost touching her toes. Seeing her bubble butt out in the air like that was all the ammunition my dick needed to grow into a semi, and it probably would have progressed into a full hard-on if she hadn't heard me close the door.

She kept the same position, her voice fleeting through the slight gap between her legs. "Good morning. I already started out with some of the pre-workout stretches."

I almost didn't want to respond because she'd freak out once I did. Alas, we had to get this show on the road.

"I can see. And what a glorious view it is," I drawled, and she locked up before whirling to me, her face red and probably not just because of her previous position. I leaned against the threshold, crossing my arms as I examined her. Flushed, feet bare on the Greatmats, hair smooth and shiny and ready for my fist around it. I might've had a dream like this once or twice. "Please don't stop on my accord. I suggest you continue with the downward dog next. That one *really* gets the blood flowing."

Blowing her strands out of her face, she sent me a scathing glare and stared at the empty hallway behind me as if expecting to see someone there. "What are you doing here? Where's Sloan?"

"Sloan was busy," I said.

"So he sent you instead? How awfully convenient." She raised a brow.

I shrugged, turning the lock and pocketing the key, much

LICK OF FIRE

to the distaste on her face. "Very. Seems like there's no way out for you either."

"It seems like you think I'm not strong enough to get the key from you." She squared her shoulders, and I grinned. This would definitely make a great script for a porno. Plenty of them centered around wrestling content, and I was confident she couldn't take the key from me.

So it was a win-win situation.

I got to feel her on me, and also what I wanted.

"Oh, you're more than welcome to try, Siren." I slid my phone out, setting up the timer. "You have two minutes. When your time is up, you're giving me the chance to talk whether you want to or not."

"Yeah, right—" she protested, but I cut her off.

"Your time starts now."

I clicked the start sign, and there was a pregnant pause as she battled the uncertainty in her. Ten seconds went by until she realized she was losing precious time, enough for me to get a firm hold around the key.

Serena rushed for me, and all I saw was a tiny blur of brown as her limbs found me before the rest of her did. Her fists hit my chest like she had some extra energy she needed to exert, and it actually fucking hurt, more so because of the damage Saint had already caused.

"Stop. Calling. Me. That." Serena perpetuated every word with a hit. "I'm not your Siren."

Okay, so that didn't win me any brownie points, especially after that painting fiasco. I didn't respond and just let her have at it. There was a lot of bad blood between us and frustration that was scary to deal with, so it led her to desperately reach for the key, her vicious claws marking my skin when she couldn't reach it.

"Why aren't you saying anything?" she asked with a frustrated sigh as she hopped up. Her chest brushing against mine was enough to bring me to my knees, but I needed her to listen to me more than I needed sexual satisfaction.

"I'm saving all my words for the end."

"You're that confident you're going to win?" she challenged, her tongue peeking out as she tried to reach my hand. It was kind of entertaining, really, like watching a little chipmunk trying to climb a tree and failing miserably.

"You have"—I glanced at my phone in my other hand—"fifty seconds left, and have made no progress, yet. I'm fairly confident I will."

Taking a deep breath, Serena stopped trying and took a step back. Puzzlement coasted over my face because she didn't give up easily, and I was about to ask what was wrong when a concerning smile spread across her face. It was a touch evil and a ton sinister as she approached again, in measured steps, her hips swinging seductively. All my blood rushed south when her hands lay flat on my chest, not aggressive, a touch soft actually, as they itched their way up.

I raised a brow, confused by the change of tide, but before I had any time to digest it, I doubled over in pain when her knee connected with my lower abdomen.

"What the fuck, Serena?" I grunted as we both lowered to the ground. Me because both she and Saint had really done a number on me today, and Serena because she was attached to my left fist like a leech, up to the point where she was drawing blood too.

"There were no rules in this. I can play as dirty as I want," she whispered in my ear, half on top of me now as we lay on the floor. Her boobs hung across my face, and the urge to bite them over her shirt was as primitive as my caveman ancestors pulling their women by the hair. If I remembered correctly, though, Serena quite enjoyed that, so nothing was off the table. Especially since we could play dirty.

Riiing, riiing, riiing.

The sound was like music to my ears, and just like clockwork, when the stinging got too much.

I swept my finger over the screen, a smile spreading on my face as I looked at her perplexed expression. "Time's up."

Not wasting a single second, I did open my hand, but just as Serena gasped, reaching for the key, I threw it as far as I could, and then I was on her. Serena yelped as I flipped us around, and my mouth almost dropped open when I settled between her legs, and her hair spread around her like a dark halo. She kind of looked like a fallen angel, but that wasn't the case. There was nothing holy about her. Serena Laurent had come straight out of Hell. To entice me, break me, fucking own me.

Her long lashes fanned over her rosy cheeks as my hands locked onto her wrists on either side. There were endless possibilities of what to do with her stunned form, but I settled for taunting her for the embarrassment gliding over her skin in an array of goosebumps. "What's the matter, Siren? You don't like being caught between two hard places?"

My hips pressed harder on hers, and she could feel all of me as her eyes rolled to the back of her head before snapping open with a glare. "You're sick."

"You like me, anyway." I *tsked* like she was a naughty child, tightening my hold. She really didn't want to know what happened to naughty girls. My eyes drifted over her heaving chest, and a smirk unfurled on my face. Or maybe she did...yeah, she'd fucking love it.

"Liked. Past tense," she spat, using her core strength to raise her upper body and get closer to me. A calculated smile —one meant to break and not repair—took over her lips. "The only thing you inspire in me now is my gag reflex."

"Really?" I leaned down, my gaze stuck on her lips. I wanted to kiss the curve of them, dip my tongue between them, and prove her wrong by conquering her inch by inch. "Let's test that theory, then."

"What do you me—" Her forehead bunched in confusion, but I didn't let her finish.

I rushed down, closing the space between us. My blood pounded in my ears, and my heart threatened to fly out of my chest when I finally felt her lips on mine for the first time after ten years. Ten *fucking* years of missing this...*us*, how phenomenal we were together.

Serena turned to stone beneath me, her movement ceasing as we sank into each other, and I took the time to explore her again like a hidden continent. I laid her flat on her back and slid her arms over her head, holding both her wrists with one hand as I let the other coast over her velvety skin, and attached it to the side of her face as I pecked her lips—*yes, pecked*—softening her up, easing her into it until she came alive like I knew she could.

It took everything in me not to grip her hair and kiss her the way I knew. The way I wanted to, with tongue, teeth, and a ton of grit. The urge burned through every cell in my body, yet I just pecked her. Once, twice, three times, until the kisses turned longer, and I felt her breath coast over my damp skin in utter surrender and disbelief.

"This means nothing other than I'm physically attracted

to you. Mentally, I still hate you," she said in a broken whisper, and my chest tightened as I nodded, my lips rubbing the same lie back on hers.

"I hate you too. Maybe a little less than I did a week ago."

And then we both kept our mouths open, and I took her. Wildly and furiously, making up for all those times when I was almost granted access. I razed all those memories to the ground with a branding kiss, one she would remember for the rest of her life. My hand delved into her hair, and I yanked her to me like a savage. Her limbs crawled around me like ivy, and I pried her mouth open all the way, demolishing her walls from the inside out.

Our tongues crushed like they were bound together by a gravitational pull, teeth clunked in a messy but heart-filling way. Our union was exquisite and gauche at the same time, something only the most morally gray of musicians could capture in their songs because what we had—that soul-crushing attraction, the kind that made you choose Hell over Heaven—wasn't gifted to ordinary people. Only to the worst of us, to hurt us because every touch, every place we connected, felt like a thousand mini abrasions on my skin that torched my flesh and invited me deeper into the gloom because the pain was too good to pass up.

Serena's urgent whimpers gliding over my tongue encouraged me to work harder. To open my mouth all the way and force her head to the ground as I literally ate her up. I licked the corners of her lips, biting and tugging her flesh until it became tender and sensitive. Our faces smashed together as I sucked her tongue in my mouth, and the kiss kind of stopped being... well, a kiss and ventured into tongue fucking territory.

My hard-on was painful against her pussy, and I ground myself on her, giving both of us some much-needed relief. We moaned at the same time, lips ungluing, as we stopped for a second to smell the roses. The scent of sex and desire crawled into my nostrils as I looked down at her beautiful face. Serena was gorgeous, her face fresh, skin smooth, and lips full and red, bleeding a little bit because of me.

I licked a bead of blood tenderly as if she was a wounded animal I needed to tend to, and she shuddered in my arms, lashes coming apart to reveal those swirling browns that brought me to my knees on more than one occasion. She was tiny and breakable under me, and I realized how easy it was for her father to manhandle her. While I believed men and women were equal, we had the unfair advantage of bodily strength. Of course, there were exceptions, but not in Serena's case.

Anger roiled in my bones, and I rubbed my nose on hers as I kept the movement of our hips steady. "If I could, I'd raise your father from his grave just so I could kill him again."

The bastard got to die in prison, a fate that was too kind for him, in my opinion. According to news outlets, both he and his mistress—Eliana's mom—"killed themselves," but we all knew it was someone higher up pulling the strings. They knew too much and needed to be silenced. The only ones I felt bad for in this story were the two girls they hurt the most with their actions, Serena and Eliana, and the kid Claire miscarried in prison because of stress, I imagined.

"Because he kept me away from you?" Serena asked. One of the rare times vulnerability shone through her, and it fucking cracked me in two.

"Because he abused you," I said harshly, inky darkness

settling in my veins. "I'm far from a murderer, but the thought of anyone hurting you has the power to turn me into a serial killer."

I didn't realize what I'd said until it was too late. Both our eyes went wide as my words rang true in the air because I would do anything to keep her safe from anyone but me, apparently. Unknowingly, my hold slightly loosened on her hands, and she used that advantage to lay *me* flat on my back. Air rushed around us as we switched positions, and she had the upper hand now.

"Why? If you hate me, you should like seeing me in pain," she said curiously, her eyes running over me, gouging for my reaction. "Actually, I know for a fact you do. You're very good with your words, Alsford, but I'm not twenty anymore. I've had plenty of men spew so much bullshit to get me to have sex with them. It's like I have a built-in radar for lies now."

The fact that she used plural verbs made me see red. I didn't even linger on her calling me a liar and went straight for the kill. "How many of them succeeded?"

"Enough for me to learn a few lessons." She swept her messy hair off her face and scoffed when I didn't try to hide the jealousy on my face. "Don't get that look with me. You'd bedded half the town by the time we got to college, even my best friend one time, if I remember correctly. Kind of makes me regret not sleeping with Leo."

That last sentence signified the end of her position on top of me, and I snarled as I shifted up *a-fucking-gain*, this time not giving a shit if I hurt her as her body knocked against the floor. I let her feel my full weight, and she clawed her fingers on my forearms in retaliation. Her ponytail was holding on by a thread now, and I used it to guide her head to mine.

"You made me feel worse than dirt, Serena. You turned me down every chance you got. Never. Not once were you clear about where we stood, and while I know why now, did you expect me to hold my dick and pine over you, just waiting for the day you might come around?" There was nothing humorous about my smile as we resorted back to what we always did best—hurting each other. "A pussy is a pussy, and if not yours, there were plenty of available ones around that got the job done. Maybe not as well, but good enough."

She bared her teeth at me, and if I wasn't holding her head, she would've probably bitten me. "You're disgusting."

"Look at who's being a hypocrite now. I don't remember you being a virgin either when we fucked. In fact, you were quite experienced." My thumb made its way from her chin to between her breasts, and I lay my palm flat, addicted to the rapid pound of her heart. "Tell me, was it me you used to wish was fucking you? Was it my head between your legs and my hands kneading your tits you dreamt about?"

Her face got painfully tight when I grazed the underside of her breasts, a small gasp parting her lips, but she didn't reply. Her gaze coasted over my shoulder to the ceiling, as if trying to forget my presence.

"It's okay to be honest. I did," I continued, my lips following a path on the arch of her nose before biting the end of it, enslaving her attention. "Caroline was the only blonde girl I'd ever slept with back then. It was easier to imagine it was you when they had brown hair."

The sentence echoed around us, and I didn't know what sprung this sudden rush to spill all my secrets to her—even ones that were as fucked up as this. Truth was, it drove me crazy knowing someone else had seen everything that was supposed to be mine. It made me want to tear their eyeballs out and make a smoothie with them.

"My God, do you realize how toxic that sounds, Ares?" she asked, but wasn't deterred when my mouth ghosted hers for a second time, even reaching up as if to sip from my lips. It meant she wouldn't mind being buried by my type of toxic. In fact, she was looking forward to it, judging by the way her tongue peeked out as if tasting my breath on her.

I groaned, a pained sound coming from deep within my chest as I made to close in on her again, but we both froze when we heard footsteps on the other side of the door. Then, at the twist of the handle, awareness trickled into Serena's eyes as she realized how close we were to being caught by her trainer.

Grunting, I hit the floor hard as she threw me off, sitting up immediately as if she had springs in her ass. I watched as she undid the rest of her ponytail, fingers flying to fix her ruined hair as a knock fleeted from behind the door.

"This was a one-off, a moment of weakness because of past memories. It can never happen again," she ordered, sounding more like she was trying to convince herself than me.

"No." I sat up too.

"What?" she demanded, getting onto her knees and looking for the key.

"It will happen again." I guided her gaze back to me by gripping her chin, not giving a shit for the knocking bastard outside. I could work her out so well she wouldn't need to step foot in the gym again. "Think about it, Siren. The only time we get along is when you're on your back and my dick is inside you. And after everything, you're still physically attracted to me, and I to you. We could fool around sometimes, as long as it takes to get rid of this pent-up energy between us. No strings attached, of course."

I hadn't even thought about what I was saying. My words were mostly inspired by how well her body fit against mine after wrestling with her for the past fifteen minutes. I wanted more of it, more of *me* lost in *her*. Even though I didn't trust her, I couldn't help craving her. The pure male need coursing through my veins ever since she'd stormed back in my life had me rubbing one out, morning, noon, and night.

I guess one could say I didn't see the fault in an... enemies with benefits arrangement. I knew what to expect of her now better than I did years ago. There was no chance I'd catch feelings beyond just physical ones.

Her hardened irises melted under my proposal, but another knock and a *"Hello, is anybody there?"* took Serena away from the moment completely as she got on her feet, rushing to get the key and whispering, "That's absolutely insane."

I followed, hot on her heels, boxing her against the wall next to the door. "He can knock the door down for all I care. We're not opening it until you give me a clear-cut answer."

"I can hear voices," Sloan spoke from the other side, clearly agitated, and Serena squirmed. "Open up. This is not funny."

One heartbeat.

Two.

Three.

We stared at each other unblinkingly, and she finally relented, wringing her hands together before pushing against my chest. "Fine. Fine. But if this complicates our deal in any way, we're pulling the plug."

A rush of satisfaction washed over me, and I let her open the door, watching her trembling hands struggle against the lock from behind as I slowly let the fact that I could tap *that* anytime I wanted to settle in.

Fuck, this would be so much fun. What if I even stopped thinking about her entirely when she left the second time around? It could've been physical all along. Men did tend to linger on things they couldn't have, and Serena was like a shiny new toy I hadn't gotten much use out of.

She finally unlocked the latch after much fumbling, apologizing profusely. I almost rolled my eyes at how fake it sounded. "So sorry, Sloan. We've been trying to get this door open for a while now, but it was jammed. It seems like it just needed a little bit of force from the outside."

"Ah, that's okay—" He cut himself off, his eyes narrowing in suspicion when he saw me. "Alsford?"

"Sloan." I nodded, and his eyes turned hard as I stood behind Serena, pressing her back to my front by circling her waist with my arm. An awkward smile pulled on her lips, and her nails dug into my skin in warning.

I wasn't trying to hide anything, much to her dismay.

"My car was not getting towed, by the way. No car was," Sloan said slowly, piecing two and two together.

"Is that so? I'm glad to hear everything worked out." My voice sounded bland to my own ears, and the pins and needles I felt from Serena's horrified gaze on my face made me smirk as I faced her. Dropping a peck to her cheek, I squeezed her ass discreetly, and she swallowed down a curse as I took my leave, winking at her over my shoulder. "See you around, Amelia."

Not even the disappointed look Saint graced my puffy lips and messy hair with when I returned could ruin my mood, but it wasn't all sunshine and roses as the thought that I was way in over my head floated in the back of my mind.

What if she destroyed me for a second time?

Would I survive it?

CHAPTER SEVENTEEN
SERENA

"Where have you been?" a dark voice asked from behind me, and the water I was drinking got stuck in my throat as I emptied out my glass in the sink.

The ticks of the clock echoed like shots in my ear in the partially lit kitchen; perhaps the only thing I was grateful for —being able to hide my fear in the dark. Starlight shining through the windows glared over the countertops as I turned to face my dad. It illuminated half of his face, too, enough to highlight the anger in his eyes as he stood sentinel behind the island in the middle, watching every nervous twitch of my fingers like a hawk.

"We had a study group meeting at Caroline's house." I accounted for my whereabouts with half-truths. The study group dispersed a while ago, but I spent a few extra hours driving aimlessly along the coast, looking at the waves and weighing the pros and cons of pressing the accelerator and diving straight for them.

"I told you to be home by eight because I wanted to talk to you," he spoke through his teeth.

And that's precisely why I didn't come.

I should've expected he would still be awake after twelve, though. After all, the devil never sleeps.

"I'm sorry. We lost track of time." My smile was tight as I made my way to the exit, my arms prickling with a sense of danger as I grazed past him. "On that note, I'm a little bit tired, so I'm heading to bed early. We can talk tomorrow."

What were the chances of him letting whatever it was he wanted to torture me with go until tomorrow?

Zero to fucking none.

I got my answer immediately when my father's hand found my forearm, and he dragged me back. I hissed when my lower back slammed against the island and breathed out fire as my brown gaze battled with his calculating blue one. I didn't know what he was, either a narcissist or psychopath, but he sure was one of those because there was no shred of empathy or love for his own flesh and blood in his eyes.

"I've given you many liberties, Serena, but if you start disobeying me, all your privileges are going to be cut off just like that." He snapped his free fingers in the air, his angry breath blowing my hair away from my face. "Do I make myself clear?"

My form trembled, craving to rebel. Sometimes it felt like a scream was trapped in my throat, big enough to make me lose my voice for a week if I let it out. It had been there ever since my mom passed, and my father got free rein on ruling my life.

It was moot, though; I'd tried speaking out before, and it didn't lead me anywhere... Well, that was a lie. It did almost lead me somewhere: the hospital.

"Yes," I gritted out.

He nodded in an appraising manner, and it made me feel like an obedient dog. "Was Leonardo Bianchi with you today?"

"Leo's major is different from mine. Obviously, we're not going to study together." I took great pleasure in lacing my voice with sarcasm, and he showed his aggravation by tightening his hand around my arm. It hurt, but it was a pain I was used to. My father wasn't the kind to get physical, so at least I dodged a bullet there, but he was the kind to push you around and leave fingertip marks on your skin.

"Seems like you are never together," he observed, and my heart beat in the base of my throat. One thing I gave my father credit for was that he didn't give up, beating a dead horse, even though it was clear it was long gone.

"Yes." Yes, we aren't because we don't like each other. I held back what I truly wanted to say, knowing that kind of answer wouldn't fly. "Yes, we are. We're great friends."

"Friends," he spat out the word as if it was offensive. If he only knew we weren't even that as of late. "Why not something more? Do you think you're too good for him?"

I knew better than to reply when his eyes ran over me like I was a bug he wanted to squash under his boot. Worthless. He wasn't looking for a solution. He wanted to bring me down. He was very vocal about how he disliked that I got my mother's features, and I wondered why they ever married if he hated her this much. I wondered what happened between them for him to behave this way, but some things were better left unsaid.

My mom was the only true parental figure I had, and seeing her from his perspective would probably ruin that. That was why I never dug too deep.

"I'll tell you what you are. You're not enough." *He enunciated the words with all his heart, and I could tell he truly believed them. I was never enough in his eyes. I was an average student, too short, too dull; nothing about me was exciting—his words, not mine. I was a disappointment through and through. "But do you know who is, dearest daughter of mine?"*

My heart turned into ice in my chest right before cracking down the middle. I considered not answering again, but he yanked my arm, despite the fact that it hadn't been too long since he weaponized the same person against me.

"Who?" I forced out, digging my nails in the wood behind me to combat the growing pain in my arm.

"Eliana Roux, since they've moved in together and everything." His scowl spread like cancer on his face, and I blanched. Eliana had one-upped me one more time, not knowing that her happiness meant my demise. "Dye your hair blonde, wear fucking blue contacts, or start going to the gym more. I don't care what you do, but we're not losing the sole heir of one of the richest families in the States to some bimbo with no manners."

Eliana had more class on her little finger than he had in his entire body, but I didn't let him know that. She'd cared more about me as my friend than my own father. I guess he didn't completely hate me since he was yet to suggest any limb lengthening surgeries.

"But they love each other. How do you expect me to come between that?" I asked through my teeth, stressed out to the max with all his expectations of me.

"Love," he scoffed, throwing his head back in a humorless laugh. "Love is nothing more than a social construct created to make people subordinate. *Those that believe in love are stupid. No child of mine is going to be stupid.*"

I blinked up at him as if in a trance, processing what I was hearing and trying to keep my dinner down. Any hope I had of reasoning with him was already slight, but it completely fizzled out when he admitted he didn't even believe in love.

He was a fucking psychopath, and I was so deep in his web, there was no escape.

A light illuminated the hallway, and both of our gazes snapped toward the source when Claire's sleepy voice floated to the kitchen. "Carter? Is everything all right?"

I studied him carefully to see how his demeanor would shift with his current fiancée, but other than the softening in his voice, his face remained unflinching. All harsh lines and a pursed mouth. "Yes, I'll be right there."

His tone was commanding when he turned back to me, whispering in my ear as if he didn't want oh-so innocent Claire to hear. Those two were made of the same cloth. "Find a way to win Bianchi over, or there'll be hell to pay."

He released me harshly, and I couldn't hold back a pain-laced gasp as my spine banged hard against the cutting granite edge on my spine. My breath caught as a result, and I'd never felt more alone than when I watched my father exit the kitchen with me trying—and failing—to pass oxygen to my lungs.

Blinding headlights broke the trance of calmness that blanketed the sleepy suburban community. A car, I realized, my lip trembling from the chill carried in the night air and cool surface of the step I was sitting on. A sleek black Audi appeared through the dark haze, speeding its way toward me. Save for the wheels kicking the gravel on the driveway, the engine was completely silent, so it must have been a hybrid.

It was the first time in a long time I'd seen Ares behind the wheel as opposed to on a saddle, and a zap made its way through my body. There was something so alluring about watching him exit a two hundred grand car with messy *just rolled out of bed* hair, slacks, a T-shirt, and a thin jacket, clearly tired but still present because I'd asked him to come.

"What the hell, Serena. It's fucking three in the morning." His breath fogged up slightly in front of him as he jogged over, his eyes scanning me twice as hard for signs of distress now that his headlights were off, and the streetlights were too weak to reach us. Ares sunk to his knees in front of me, palms pressing into my cheeks in order to feel my temperature. "What's wrong with you? What are you doing sitting in the cold? Your lips are blue."

"It's sixty-five degrees. It's not that cold." I tried to pull back but ended up sneezing, right on his face.

Okay, so maybe it was a little bit cold, but I didn't hate it. I appreciated the touch of frost seeping into my skin. I almost hoped it would form a protective layer of ice around my brain to keep out all the horrible memories that came from that one dream tonight.

Ares's expression was unimpressed, and I missed his hands on my face when he removed them to slide out of his jacket and settle it over my shoulders. The motion was natural to him because he'd done it a thousand times before. He always gave me his clothes when I used to be cold, and just like all those other times, butterflies swarmed in my belly at having his ocean scent surround me.

I didn't understand how it felt like home when he stood against everything a home should be. He was fickle; he'd throw me out the first chance he got, and he didn't love me anymore. I didn't think he ever did. Maybe he just wanted to fuck me all along, like he said at the gym.

"It is when you're dressed in nothing but a short night-dress and thin coverup." He rubbed my shoulders as if he wanted to instill heat in my body, and my eyes burned as I blinked and looked at the cracked pavement below. I didn't like it when he was nice to me. It made it hard to remember why I hated him all along. "What's the matter, Serena? Why did you call me here?"

I shrugged. "I wanted a tour of my mom's house."

Ares paused his rubbing, and I held my breath, not ready for him to ask any more questions at the moment. It was a crazy thing to ask of him. I'd called him hysterical after waking up from that dream, told him to meet me at the house he was holding over my head, and hung up before he could even say anything in return.

He probably thought I was a nutjob.

"Before the crack of dawn?" he asked incredulously.

"Yes," I deadpanned, as if it was the most logical thing in the world. "Will you show me around?"

"You're fucking crazy." Ares's hot palms slid around my neck, tugging my jaw up, his concerned eyes boring into mine. Whatever he found there, in combination with my pounding jugular, told him it was too early to dig, so he sighed tiredly and relented. "Let's go."

245

Half an hour into the tour, I'd forgotten all about my dad and less than stellar past. The remnants of that nightmare only lingered on a thin sheen of salt that encased my body after I woke up drenched in sweat. I was too busy trying to ignore the way Ares made my skin buzz with electricity. I didn't know what had gotten into me when I agreed to his proposal, but it was fucking bad considering how our last hookup ended. What was even worse was that I couldn't stop thinking about a repeat and that had the potential to be catastrophic.

Ares and I could never happen. There was too much he didn't know. He'd loathe me twice as much if I let this progress more than it already had if the truth ever came out. And it was bound to because secrets had a short shelf life.

Breathing deep through my nose, I relied on my mother's memory clinging to the barren spaces to calm me down. The house was very much like a blank canvas, empty and a little bit dusty. There wasn't a lot to take in, save for a wood fireplace embedded into the living room wall and shiny vinyl floors. It hadn't changed much from the pictures Sam had shown me, despite the numerous owners it'd had since my mom's family.

I ran my hand over a beige wall as we toured the upstairs rooms, and if it wasn't for Ares being with me, I would've lasted all but five seconds on this floor before running downstairs out of fear of being chased by Bloody Mary. Apparently, they'd only thought of installing light bulbs on the main floor, so we only had moonlight and our phones to aid our vision.

"This was my mom's room. My grandparents didn't have enough money to get her a proper piano, so they bought her a keyboard. I have a picture of her playing, and it was set up in the corner right there underneath that window." I pointed to the awning windows, and Ares shone his flashlight that way.

"Was she the one that taught you how to play?" I could hear the tenderness in his voice, and it made me blush. What a sight I must've been. Daddy and mommy issues roiled together to produce a severely troubled individual.

"She taught me the basics. Early on in her marriage with my dad, he got her a Steinway grand piano as an anniversary gift. After she spent like a week fawning over the African pommel wood, she sat me down, and we had daily lessons that then turned weekly, and afterward monthly, and finally ceased completely the more their relationship went south. She stopped playing altogether by the end."

"Did you love playing as much as she did?"

"Not necessarily. I was decent at it, to say the least. I continued taking classes only because I liked that it was something we had in common." I sat on one side of the built-in window bench, folding my legs underneath me, and Ares took the other, turning the flashlight off. It was a cramped space, though, and I could still make out each individual lash on his eyes this up close. "Overall, my genuine interests were much more similar to my father's. I remember being a kid and looking forward to becoming a criminal defense lawyer, just like him."

"But you ultimately didn't."

"No, I changed my mind later on." I shook my head.

"Why?"

"I guess I kind of questioned if all the fucked-up cases he dealt with on a daily basis were the reason why he ended up being the way he did. It was a well-known fact he dealt with the worst of the worst, and it's often said that criminals are a product of their environment, so I didn't want to go down the same path."

Given that I already had a history of bloodshed, I didn't even allow myself the benefit of the doubt.

"You are nothing like your father, Serena." Ares's voice carried a tone of fierce conviction. "Just because you had similar interests doesn't mean you also had similar mindsets. You didn't do his bidding voluntarily. He forced you into it."

I bit my cheek, diverting my gaze to the single-story houses spread out in the neighborhood. It was crazy how segregated Astropolis was. You could drive five minutes north, and all of a sudden, you wouldn't be able to see past the tall gates and bushy hedges. My parents came from completely different worlds.

"There are a lot of things you don't know about me, Ares. They say the apple doesn't fall far from the tree for a reason, and both my foundations are pretty rotten to begin with. My mother's substance abuse trickled down the bloodline. How can you be so sure my father's evil won't?" A cool sweat broke out on my neck at the thought, even though it was paranoid. I acknowledged that, yet the fear remained.

It was common sense not to share your weaknesses with your enemy, but the lines blurred when that enemy was Ares Alsford. The only way he'd even back off was if he saw all my darkest parts.

His pointer curled underneath my chin, bringing my face forward, so he got my undivided attention, and my lips parted at his words. "You had a shitty run in life and resorted to drugs to feel better. You're not the first or last person to do so. And the fact that you're proactively trying to be everything he wasn't speaks volumes—" Network paths of an overactive mind shone beneath his irises as he cut himself short and dropped my face. I braced my hands beside my hips and took in the sneer on his lips with curiosity. "You know what? I'm not going to be your therapist at four in the morning. Why are we really here, Serena? Give me the truth."

What the hell?

Every muscle in my body tensed at his one-eighty attitude change, and perspiration coated my palms as I answered. "I had a shitty dream about my dad and wanted to feel closer to my mother."

"Wrong."

One word.

Five letters.

More than enough to get me mad.

"Excuse me?" My voice was too high-pitched for my liking, so I cleared my throat before continuing. "Do you know how I feel better than I do?"

"Siren." His tone held notes of a warning, and the hair on the nape of my neck rose to prominence when I realized I was in the presence of the predator version of him.

My back pressed against the molding behind me, and I gave an uppity huff, crossing my arms in order to mask the embarrassment coursing through my veins. So much for not giving in. "Fine. I wanted to see you."

"Why?" he pressed.

"To tell you your proposal is stupid," I lied. "You took advantage of the moment we had and my clouded headspace, and it's never going to fucking happen."

"Wrong again." He cocked his head as if he was enjoying watching me struggle to find the right words.

"Well, why don't *you* enlighten me then, since you seem to know more."

Famous last words.

"Gladly, Siren." He took my bait, promising to chew it up and spit it back out. "You had a bad dream you wanted to forget about. I was the first person you thought about when it came to helping you do that. You didn't like the fact that I live in your head rent-free, so here we are with you trying to push me away for..." Ares threw his hands in the air, his laugh a bitter symphony. "Well, fuck me, I've lost count of how many times you've tried to do that."

"I-I—" I stuttered, my heart crushing violently against my rib cage. I paused, sucking in a mouthful of air to collect myself. My chest caved inward as I looked at him through my lashes. "Stop reading too much into things, Ares. Your imagination knows no bounds."

Ares's brilliant whiskey gaze shone with mirth, and I felt naked under its casual perusal. He worked his sight from my thighs over my quivering stomach, lingering on my pebbled chest, and finally got caught on my neck. My skin soared to sky-high temperatures when his rough palm dragged over my collarbone and circled my throat.

Our noses almost met when he pulled me closer, tightening his hold, but that wasn't the reason why I stopped breathing altogether. He wasn't the only one with a wild imagination, and mine was acting pretty inappropriately at the moment.

He was right.

He had the perfect tool to make me forget.

But I was scared—no, fucking terrified of going through with it, because no matter how good I knew it was going to be, what came after would suck. Like it did the first time.

"Are you challenging me, Siren?" His thumb smoothed over the hollow of my neck, and I memorized the movement of his lips as if in a trance. "Because you and I both know I'd excel in proving you wrong."

His face was shrouded in shadows, just as dark and promising as his words were. A chill snaked its way up my spine when he caught the web I hadn't even realized I was weaving. Maybe unconsciously I was egging him on to make the first move, put me out of the misery of overthinking.

Our foreheads touched, and when his breath hit my open mouth, my bones ached as if they'd been dried up, drought for more of his touch. Those rough hands on my body could replace all the horrible memories of the past years with some good ones.

Sex with Ares was not gentle or tender—but that wasn't what I wanted. I wanted passion, warmth, and reciprocated attraction. I wasn't just another glory hole to him. He'd confirmed it yesterday. And while I should've been creeped out by that little comment, I wasn't. Because imagining it was Ares touching me every time I'd had unwanted hands on my body made my dark times a bit lighter.

I wasn't in any better of a position to judge.

But I *was* in a better position to pull the plug. You couldn't cure an obsession by delving deeper into its waters. You had to claw your way out.

"There's nothing to prove." Reaching up, I touched his hand on my neck, sliding my cold fingers around his warm wrist. I pulled, yet he only buried his face beneath my ear, his shoulders shaking as he chuckled like he found my resistance weak.

The hitch in my breath when he tugged at my earlobe with his teeth gave him all the confirmation he needed. I was a phony, and he could see right through me.

"Lay on the floor, Siren." His rough voice pressed against

my skin like it wanted to sink into me, sending my heart into overdrive.

"What?" I asked, not quite sure I'd heard him correctly.

"We both agreed to a deal, so I'll give you what you dragged me here in the middle of the night for," he said as he ripped his hand from my neck and face from my hair, raising a long brow.

"I never signed anything."

His arms tensed, the cropped sleeves straining over his muscles, and my mouth watered. "You do not want to fucking test me right now, Serena. On the floor, legs spread."

"I don't think—"

"Good." He cut me off with a bark, his teeth gleaming with a condescending smile. "This won't require you to think, only feel. Why are you still sitting?"

CHAPTER EIGHTEEN
ARES

I saw the lump in her throat move up and down. Her skin glowed like white satin under the moonlight, soft, smooth, and pleading to be tarnished by my hands, teeth—anything it took to leave my mark on her.

Unsure eyes lingered on mine, and I invited her to test me and see where it led as I abandoned the bench and towered over her. Serena kept pulling a lot of shit because I was letting her get away with it. But tonight was more for me than it was her, and I wasn't going to be moving my mouth from her cunt until the whole neighborhood heard her scream.

She needed a reminder of who I was, and if she insisted on getting herself in trouble, at least I'd know it was intentional. Little Serena wanted me to punish her. It was like foreplay for her. I could tell from the way her jaw flexed in anger at the tone I took with her, but she melted like butter under my command, sliding her ass out of her seat and moving to the floor.

Defiance marked her gaze as she raised her chin up at

me, yet I didn't meet it. I was busy staring at her generous rack. Her tits looked gloriously plump from this angle, and my skin hummed with the urge to rip apart the lace flowers decorating the neck of her décolletage, pull her hair in my fist, and work a nipple stiff in my mouth.

"Flat on your back," I ordered, my voice clear of any emotion as I circled her. I pulled one side of her hair over her shoulder from behind, and her head veered in my direction, tracking me like a scared deer.

I moved to her front, waiting expectantly, and she glowered at me, fear and rebellion making her movements sluggish and slow. But anticipation won over until she was ultimately level with the floor, even though it could've used a pass of a mop. She didn't care, though, and neither did I as I lowered myself to the ground in front of her knees, clenched tightly together. The dark red skirt of her nightgown contrasted against her pearly skin, inviting me to pull it up with my teeth and explore what was beneath it.

"Good girl." I grinned, and her leg twitched when I ran my hands underneath her calf, massaging it before removing her shoes. They ended up somewhere in a corner of the room, and I fought really hard not to yank her legs apart and take what was mine. "Now, part your knees for me, baby."

My jaw ticked and my dick pulsed as she warmed up to the picture I was painting. I was an impatient fuck, especially when it came to her, but I wanted her to be in it as much as I was. It would be harder for her to lie about not liking this if she took initiative.

Placing her elbows underneath her, she hooked her gaze on my face as her skirt slid down her thighs when she opened her legs hesitantly. They parted like the gates of Heaven, and I almost fucking whimpered when the sight of her bare pussy greeted me. It was dark, and I couldn't make out much, but I knew for a fact there was nothing covering it. I mentally kicked myself for not equipping the house with lights because her cunt deserved to be admired.

"You're fucking bare, Serena? Someone was eager." My palms glided over her legs, and they quivered with adrenaline when I smacked her inner thighs, her head falling back. Grabbing onto her flesh, I forced her knees open wider and scooted her down, letting some spit dribble from my mouth to her pussy. "What do you want first, my fingers or my tongue?"

A small tremor rocked her body, her nails leaving crescents on the wood as she struggled to maintain eye contact. Her head was heavy, and if she wasn't wound so tight, she would've been pliable to any extent. Serena was by no means submissive, but from what I remembered, she loved getting dominated—at least in the bedroom.

"Don't be daft. I just don't like sleeping with underwear on. It has nothing to do with you." Her voice came out like a hiss when I continued massaging her ass cheeks, thighs, and again her inner thighs, my thumb skirting next to her lips, teasing her with a ghost touch. Serena's breaths got more pronounced, and her chest caved inwards as she struggled to get her next words out. "And tongue...please."

I should've done what she asked since she said please, right?

Yeah, no.

"My palm it is," I said with a smile, and she yelled out when I took a swipe at her pussy. It was my turn to hiss when I then smoothed my saliva from her hood to her opening, finding her already soaked without my assistance. She was so ready, my thumb slipped inside of her accidentally. A loud moan fell from her parted lips, and I cursed, my cock seeping in my boxers. "Such a compulsive little liar. Your body betrays you, Siren. It's trembling for me. We have to train your mouth to stop spewing bullshit, though, don't you think?"

I switched fingers and pushed in and out of her tight channel with my index while I used my thumb to work her sensitive area near her groin. Serena's lashes came together, breasts swaying inside that freaking nightgown I was getting tempted to tear down the middle more and more as her chest heaved with unregulated breaths.

"Or we could train yours to work more and speak less," she teased, but there was an edge of frustration there too.

I pulled out completely, coming down on her flesh again with my palm. It echoed twice as loud because she was so wet, and I did it once more just to hear the filthy sound again. I knew she enjoyed the sting of the pain. It registered as pleasure in her brain, and she confirmed my theory by biting her lip bloody to hide a cunning grin that threatened to take over her mouth.

"Is that a smile on your face? Do you enjoy the pain, Serena?"

"Only when you make it better afterward," she admitted, wetting her lips.

"How do you want me to make it better?" I taunted, playing clueless just to piss her off. And it did. Her palms turned into little fists, and her eyes rained fire on me as if she wasn't the one fighting this mere minutes ago.

At least I'd done one thing right so far. She'd abandoned any inhibitions because she craved anything I could give her. It boosted my confidence and the elevation of my dick to new heights. There was nothing more exciting than getting it on with the star of your wet dreams, knowing she wanted you as irrevocably as you did her.

"I want you to soothe the pain with your tongue, Ares," she replied, bold as a woman lost in her desire. There was nothing but pure need behind those eyes, and elation coursed through my body when I realized how much power I held over her.

At last, I'd cracked a part of her shield, but as much as I'd love to keep taunting her, I was barely able to control my drool at the scent of her arousal in the air. Eyeing that fucking nightie like it wronged me, I pushed the crazy idea of ripping it to shreds down, as I didn't want her to drive back home naked.

I stopped rubbing her with my hand, and she whimpered at the loss, but I wiped the excess juices on her navel, tugging at her skirt until it exposed more of her stomach. "Get that nightdress over your tits. I wanna look at them while I'm eating you out."

She did me one better and took it off entirely, shimmying her arms and letting it fall into a heap over her head, exposing her pink, coin-like nipples. Her entire body was magnificent, and I could tell she'd worked hard for it by the slight outline of a four-pack on her abdomen.

A chill snaked over my skin, and I dropped to my haunches as if tied to her pussy by some invisible force. She was wretchedly stunning, and I wanted to reward her for nothing else other than winning the genetic lottery.

"Gorgeous, Siren. Show me why you deserve your nickname, baby," I said as I licked the wet trail I'd painted on her navel all the way to her bare public bone. I shuddered at the bittersweetness that exploded on my tongue, already hungry for more, as I pried her puffy lips open with my fingers.

Serena watched me, her face a picture of fascination and pain as if she deemed my talking breaks personally offensive. "Scream while I make you come with my mouth on your wet cunt."

Done with any more conversation for the immediate future, I dove forward, sinking my tongue in her pretty pink opening and groaning so loud it sent the floor shaking underneath us. Serena's moan of relief was immediate as I savored her taste, sliding between her folds and nibbling slightly on the engorged flesh like I wanted to take a bite out of her. Honestly, that wasn't far from the truth; sometimes kissing didn't cut it. I wanted to squeeze her, pound into her, and leave teeth marks all over her body to satisfy the beast inside me that couldn't get enough.

I wrapped my arm under one of her thighs and held her to me as she arched her back and squirmed when I closed in on her clit, sucking the little bundle of happiness hard. Serena threaded her fingers in my hair, tugging just as hard as I was sucking like she wanted to detach me but also couldn't get more. True pleasure was so intense, it teetered the line between discomfort and euphoria, that straddling ground that drove so many people off the edge.

I eased the pressure on her nub, nibbling and kissing around her pussy and inner thighs again and teasing her little hole with the tip of my tongue. She moaned when I did that, and I did it again, savoring her taste and tightness. My cock bulged, and I continued eating her while I undid the button of my jeans and pulled the zipper down, giving my dick some space to breathe.

She was delectable, like well-preserved honey only my taste buds got to taste. My head could be glued to her pussy for days on end, and I wouldn't complain. I'd flick and tease her clit just like I was doing now until she creamed all over my face.

"Oh shit, Ares," her voice got higher, speech more slurred, and she dropped to the floor completely, giving up any semblance of control.

Pinpricks of pain decorated my scalp from her tight grip when I tugged my head up to look at her fat tits, and suddenly my hands felt severely empty as I watched them move in tune with my bobbing head. Snaking my arms under her thighs, I pushed her legs over my shoulders and groaned into her as I palmed both of her girls, twisting her nipples.

"Yes," Serena screamed, her hips shooting off the floor. She was even more exposed to me this way, and I sucked harder on her flesh, rubbing my scratchy chin on her soaked lips to get her more sensitive. It worked, as her stomach quivered, and I slapped one of her tits just to watch it jiggle. "Holy hell, don't stop, please. I'm close, so close."

I did stop.

Her eyes remained closed, but after a moment, pain was etched across her face, and she blinked them open. She found me watching her.

"Have I ever told you I love how you taste?" I grinned sheepishly, pressing a tiny kiss to her clit.

"No," she breathed, eyes wide in disbelief, and I made a mental note to compliment her more.

"Well, I do. You taste like honeydew on my tongue. It makes me want to eat you out for hours on end." I licked a path from the end of her pussy to the hilt, coating my entire tongue in her juices like it was my favorite thing in the world. And at the moment, it was.

"You like honeydew?" she asked, and I chuckled, stretching her clit out in my mouth. Her eyes rolled to the back of her head, and the harder I twisted her nipples, the harder I sucked and licked, syncing with her breathing, the faster her lungs bottomed out.

"Fuck, I'll take that as a yes." She shook, her short, shallow breaths wracking through her body. "Oh my God, Ares, I-I'm coming."

My eyes burned, and I was desperate to blink, but I couldn't take my gaze off her. I kept my face buried in her cunt as I fed off her, watching her skin glisten with perspiration as her stomach shook and her mouth dropped open in bliss. Dinner and a show. Eating her out was about to become one of my favorite pastimes because the view from my knees was so glorious. The combination of moans and whimpers escaping her mouth was a dirty melody I wanted to play on repeat.

I eased up when she started to calm, and my ears began picking up sounds again when her thighs let up around them. She slumped back down with a satisfied sigh, and the sound traveled straight to my groin. I was stiff as a flagpole when her hand fell from my hair as I kissed my way up her stomach, dipping my tongue in her belly button and plumping up one of her breasts before taking her pert nipple in my mouth. Serena whimpered, her hands coming to wrap around the back of my neck. I switched sides, running one hand down her length, encouraging her to dig her heels into my back.

"Goddamn, Serena." I popped her breast out of my mouth, trailing kisses up her neck and over her jaw. It seemed like I couldn't stop kissing her. Touching her. I was in the moment, but at the same time, it was like a part of me was peeking in from some sort of parallel universe, shocked that I was getting to hold her, feel her skin against mine, taste her for a second time. "I wasn't even down on you for a full five minutes."

I hovered over her, brushing a stray lock off her forehead, and cupped her flushed cheeks as she worked herself lazily on my erection. Her eyes were bright and as clear as the sky on a hot summer day. How I longed for some light right now, to see every detail of her face and every emotion running through her gaze.

"It's been a while, okay?" she whispered against my mouth.

"How long?"

"Since a man made me come, or since I've been touched?"

"Both." I ground harder against her, trying to distract myself from her answer in case it wasn't what I wanted to hear.

She took a deep breath, and her chest rubbed against my shirt. Feeling her nipples cut through the material was a different type of heaven. "About five years on the second count, and..."

"And?" I pressed when she trailed off, lingering over her lips but pulling away every time she tried to capture my mouth with hers. The answer mattered to me more than I cared to admit, and the deep-seated joy that bloomed in my stomach from her first answer didn't have any place being there.

She blew out a frustrated breath, screwing her eyes shut. "You were the last man to ever give me an orgasm. I do flick the bean regularly, though, so don't go feeling sorry for me. It's just not the same."

I paused, the world spinning around me as her words centered me. They grounded me before blasting my ego through the motherfucking stratosphere. I couldn't have heard her right. There was no way I was the last man to ever give her an orgasm. It had been ten freaking years since we'd slept together.

But looking down at her, the tension on her face was evident as she confided in me. And I couldn't help but sink down and claim her mouth with a brutal kiss. I was the one shaking right now, two different parts of me clashing like yin and yang. One rejoiced; the deeply rooted possessiveness in me over her was fucking ecstatic that only I had made her feel that good, but the other one felt dirty. Unworthy.

The woman in my arms, the one that came apart on my tongue barely two minutes ago, and was oh-so eager to return the favor with how she clung to me, had been through the wringer. First by losing her mother to suicide at a young age, exposing her to the ill intentions of her father, who had no qualms about stepping over her to get what he wanted, then by suffering through a drug addiction with no one by her side, and finally with a lackluster love life that rivaled the likes of my own.

It cut me up inside thinking about her with another man, but she didn't deserve to spend so many years in solitude. It was true—the only person I'd ever loved was Serena, but I opened myself up to other people as well, to a certain extent. Despite those relationships not working out, they made me feel guilty. I didn't deserve to have a warm body next to mine at night when she spent hers alone, all because I never searched for her—because if I had, if I'd gone after her one more time after her father went to jail, I could've spared us years of loneliness.

I poured all my frustration into our kiss, and she opened up for me like a flower in full bloom. We had all the puzzle pieces, but we couldn't figure out how to put them together. And so much time had passed, a future for us wasn't even feasible anymore. Too much contempt ran rampant between us.

She'd left. I was too tired of chasing.

We only had now, and even though our expiration date was yet unknown, I had to do the most to protect not only me but both of us from those pesky things called feelings.

"Ares," Serena mumbled against my lips, her adventurous fingers catching on the elastic of my boxers. Her hand slipped inside, and our breaths mixed as we both gasped at the same time when she palmed my hard length, giving it a firm pump. "Get a condom and fuck me, already," she complained, and I went cross-eyed, thrusting against her hand.

Serena made quick work of spreading the precum that had gathered on my crown down the rest of my shaft by rubbing up and down my length while I tried to get my last three remaining brain cells together to form a cohesive thought.

"Fuck," I muttered, wrenching my mouth away from hers. "I don't-I don't have any condoms. I was in a fucking rush, so I didn't think to bring any. But I could pull out?"

"No." Serena shook her head immediately, her hand stilling on my dick. "No condoms, no sex."

I slammed my jaw shut, hating myself with a passion at the moment. I didn't make a habit of stashing condoms in my pocket, but I'd always have one on hand after today. Her wet and soft folds around my finger had given me a small preview of what my dick could've been experiencing right now, and even though she knew her way around a hand job, I needed more.

"Fine," I retorted, and ripped my shirt over my head.

She screwed up her face in question. "Why are you getting naked then?"

"Because I wanna feel your tits rubbing against my chest when I make you come for a second time. Things come in packs of twos or more in this house." I forced her hand to start moving again by pumping my hips and delved between her slick folds, getting her ready for another round by slipping a finger in. "I'm not letting you go with one measly orgasm."

I ate up her groan, letting it hit the back of my throat as a second finger found the wet heat of her tight cunt like a fucking magnet. We both picked up a rhythm, syncing our strokes to each other. The only reason I was able to hold myself up right now and not crush her under my weight was by some grace of God.

"My poor mother must be horrified up there." She choked on a breath when I curled my fingers inside of her in a come-hither motion, stroking her inner walls.

I smirked, giving both of us some space by biting her fleshy breast. "You mean working your hips against my fingers so you come faster is not good daughterly behavior?"

"Ares?" She tugged at my hair, forcing my gaze up.

"Yes?" I grunted.

The witch squeezed my dick so hard it sent a shot of pain to my balls. "Shut up."

"Duly noted, Siren." I lapped up at her breasts, and a cry echoed across the walls along with the squelching sounds of her pussy, and the rubbing of my flesh. A thin sheen of sweat covered both of us, and she resembled an ethereal mermaid with her long hair all swept up on one side and some strands stuck along the lines of perspiration on her forehead.

Annoyed, I dropped my forehead on her cleavage, so consumed by her, by her talented hands and face and body that were like eye candy to me, I nearly blew before her. "Sometimes, I hate looking at you, Serena. You're so fucking beautiful. It's unfair. How the fuck am I supposed to resist you?"

"Beauty is not everything," she breathed.

"In this case, it is. No strings attached, remember, baby?" I reminded her, feeling the need to lower the intensity of this hookup. My dick hadn't even been in her, and I was already acting pussy-whipped. "I don't think about the soul behind those big eyes while I'm finger-fucking you. All I think about is how good they would look with tears spilling out of them while I force my big cock down your throat and fill your mouth up with my cum as it drips down your throat."

Pain etched across her features, and I bit down on my tongue so hard the taste of metal bloomed in my mouth. I couldn't go soft, for her sake and mine. "Ares don't—"

"Don't what?" I spoke over her. "Paint you as nothing more than a hot piece of ass? That's all you are, Serena. I would've dropped everything to be with you years ago, but you didn't want that. You threw every vow we made in my face and left, so while I admire your beauty, I don't trust you. Not a word that comes out of your mouth." I inserted a third finger, stretching her so tight, her eyes filled with unshed tears. "Now come all over my fingers like an obedient little girl, and then lick them clean. Prove to me this A-class cunt can get down and dirty."

Her nails sunk at the nape of my neck in her attempt to hurt me back, but we were both damn near hyperventilating at this point. Her center was like a slip and slide, and a searing heat collected at the base of my balls. I managed to hold my release back by five whole seconds before we came at the same time. She was the wave, I was the rock, and we collided.

My cock pulsed in her hand. White spurts of cum decorated her wrist, and her walls clenched tightly, sucking me in deeper as the sweetest kind of exhaustion set in; one you became addicted to. It crashed and burned all around us as our heads floated away from us in a fog of questionable decisions and past regrets.

Her hands left my body, and I opened my eyes to find her face set in a scowl, very unlike someone that had just orgasmed. Her full brows were slammed together, forehead bunched with lines of anger as she held herself up, holding on to my nape and removing my fingers from her pussy.

Getting close to my mouth, she whispered three sentences that were as powerful as a nuke going off in my brain. "Don't fucking touch me. Don't fucking talk to me. Don't fucking *breathe* on me." She shoved at my chest, and I dropped on my ass next to her, stupefied. Slamming the ground, her voice turned an octave higher with every word that escaped her mouth. "There's a clear line between light degradation and disrespect, and I will never, fucking *never* allow someone to treat me like that. Just because I'm willing to let you between my legs again doesn't give you the right to talk to me like I'm a third-class citizen whose sole purpose in life is to be fucked into oblivion."

All the pleasure that was crammed in my soul evaporated in seconds, sizzling the air with misery. I shoved my dick back in my boxers and zipped up my pants as she found what she was looking for in the dark—her nightgown, and pulled it on, hiding her magnificent curves from me once more. Not that I blamed her, but I was doing what was right.

"The less special and the more sexual I make this, the less likely it is for either one of us to get attached," I offered, explaining myself.

"Trust me to protect my own heart, Alsford. You might like twisting facts around and painting yourself as the victim, but you're not fooling anyone." She bared her teeth at me, and they gleamed even in the dark. "That night at the cottage happened solely because Leonardo asked you to take me out. Did you really believe I would sit around to suck your dick while you plied me up with all the words I wanted to hear and simultaneously ranked me at the bottom of the totem pole? I was never *anyone's* number one priority. No one ever looked out for me first, so when even you played me for someone else—yes, I left. And I would do it all over again, especially since you weren't even there when I woke up."

Now that was some bullshit if I'd ever heard some.

That was what she thought all this time? That I only took her out because of Leo, that my promises were some sort of pretense because I'd chosen him over her?

But of course, she did. Serena didn't have faith in anyone other than herself, and while I understood trust issues were to be expected when your own father threw you under the bus, it didn't lessen the sting. I'd spent the whole of my teenage and some of my adult life being there for her, making myself available when she needed me.

I couldn't help but chuckle. What a load of good that had done me.

Serena growled under her breath, thinking I was laughing at her expense when, really, I was judging myself.

"Let's get some things straight, Serena." My tone was dead calm, and her spine stood ramrod straight as if she was ready to take mental notes and counterstrike anything I said wrong against me. "One, with or without Leo, I was planning on taking you out. You were—*are*—mine to take. Always have been. So sue me if I jumped at the opportunity to be the one to keep you safe while Leonardo wreaked havoc over your father's life. If I hadn't put you first—if you hadn't been my number one priority, I would've left you home to watch while he caved your daddy's head in. But I didn't want you to witness that kind of violence. I didn't want you hurt in any way, shape, or form."

My heart squeezed painfully at the end of my speech as if someone was extracting the things I'd dreamt of saying for a while now with their fist wrapped around the organ in a vice grip.

Serena's chest rose and fell sharply, stunned into silence for five whole seconds as if she wasn't expecting my outburst. Shaking her head, she tried to gather her wits, but her eyes were glassy, and even *she* didn't really understand what she was saying, her brain playing catch up and trying to put two and two together. "You should've told me, given me the choi—"

"I did what I thought was best. I protected you the only way I knew how to—in my arms. One would have to tear me apart to get me off you if you were in danger." I pushed hot air out my nostrils forcefully, trying to regulate my heartbeat. "And as for not being there, I drove to the nearest town to get us some breakfast. Imagine my surprise when I came back and found nothing but empty space."

To say it sucked was an understatement.

I'd planned on waking her up the *fun* way, and then fuck, I didn't know. We'd ride off into the freaking sunset. I should've known better, though. I should've expected she'd make everything harder than need be.

"I—" She tucked her hair behind her ears, gaze zigzagging on the floor and slowly climbing up my marbled form until it reached my face. The panic I found there was so raw it layered an extra touch of frost over my limbs. "That can't be it. What about leaving me a note? Or a text, or anything?"

"Excuse me, if I thought leaving for twenty minutes wouldn't be a big deal, and you'd probably still be asleep by the time I got back since I had you awake for most of the night." I pushed a palm through my hair, pulling at the roots.

A stormy expression clouded her face, despair and disbelief moving through her near-black eyes like lightning breaking up the darkness of the night sky. She braced her hands on the floor in front of her as if she couldn't support her weight and gulped before she asked, her voice thick with unshed tears, "You really mean it, don't you? You never gave up on me?"

"How could I when you used to be my entire world?" I spat, thinking about what a fucking laughingstock I'd been, pouring all my devotion into her when I'd never seen an inch of it returned. Anger rattled my bones as our sordid past resurfaced once again. Gripping my abandoned shirt tightly in my fist, I rose, sidestepping her. "I was patient with you for so long. It amazes me how you believed I would be so willing to give up everything I worked so hard for the second I got it."

Serena twisted to follow me with her eyes, and her heaving filled my ears as she breathed like the room was running out of oxygen. I refused to look at her, giving her my back, but one way or another, guilt dug at my insides at getting her so worked up. I was so fucking torn I didn't even know what emotions I was experiencing. They all ran through me like zooming cars on a racetrack.

I needed some space. Time to breathe, as I felt like I was suffocating in this tiny room. Her scent was everywhere, on my beard, my fingers, embedded in my damn brain.

Veering around, I grabbed the door handle, but she wheezed on the floor like she was on the verge of a panic attack, and I paused, knowing how it was to be the recipient of one of those all too well.

"W-Where are you going?" she stuttered, and my jaw locked.

"I'm leaving. Isn't that what we do when things get tough?"

"No, Ares, please don't," she shouted out, and my skin burned when she wrapped her arms around my naked torso and buried her face in my back. I thought I felt the telltale sign of regret pouring out of her in the form of silent tears staining her cheeks and my back. Her voice shook, and my body froze. "You said we had a deal, and I need you. I need you to just hold me, please? I always needed you. I realized that when I saw you again right on this driveway, and my heart almost beat out of my chest at the sight of you after all these years. I breathe easier when I'm around you."

My eyes shut of their own accord as I listened to her beg and tell me all the things I wished she had before I went through all the shit I did, be it because of her, my parents passing, or the loneliness that clung to every facet of my life like an unwanted guest. I stayed still, listening to the rapid rise and fall of her chest in the quiet room, when all I wanted to do was scream at her and shake her for believing the worst of me.

It technically wasn't her fault. She was conditioned to be that way, but I'd let her walk all over me one too many times, and if anything, felt the need to get my own little revenge for once.

"Tough luck, Serena." I freed myself from her arms, and my heart hurt when she dropped by my feet as if I was her anchor and she couldn't stand on her own. I forced my body to freeze and not take her in my embrace like I craved to. My whole body itched, but I stood my ground, wanting to teach her a lesson, and didn't turn. "Where were you when I needed you? I wasted my twenties, my parents died, and I had to go through it alone. I watched all my friends get married and get their happily ever afters, while I couldn't keep a relationship if my life depended on it." I chuckled darkly. "A simple *I'm sorry* won't fucking cut it this time around."

I twisted the handle, despite her crying having picked up a storm. The fresh air that flowed all around me was as refreshing as it was damning. I shoved my shirt over my head, but every step I took outside and into the hallway felt weighted down like a hundred-ton Orca was pressed on me and holding me back.

One.

Two.

Three.

Ten steps in, I'd made it to the edge of the staircase when I stopped. My head slumped. Hearing the sound of her sobs coming out stronger now made the bile swell in my throat until I felt sick to my stomach. Cry after cry, she didn't stop, and worry twisted my heart up in knots.

I couldn't fucking do it.

I couldn't descend the stairs. She deserved better. *We* deserved better. Mistakes existed for a reason, to teach us a lesson in life, and I was proving I hadn't learned anything by repeating them. I was tired of fucking heartbreak and heart loss and wasn't even sure who I was punishing when leaving hurt me as much as it did her.

A growl escaped my mouth, and I punched the wall once for good measure before turning on my heel. The pain didn't even register, and it only took me five total steps this time until she was in my vision again. My shadow stretched on top of her like an omnipresent being, and her head snapped up.

"Ares?" she asked in disbelief, crumbled in a ball on the hardwood floor. Her tear-stricken face did funny things to my chest, and I damn near tackled her flat like a linebacker with how I rushed to her.

"I'm trying to be mad at you," I said, but every word felt redundant on my tongue as I breached her orbit. My knees cracked on the floor, and I knew I'd be a mess of bruised limbs tomorrow, yet I couldn't find it in me to give a shit when I shoved her in my chest, holding the back of her head and hovering my lips on the crown of her hair, pressing a fierce kiss there. "But, God, baby, you are tearing me apart right now."

"I'm sorry. I'm sorry. I'm sorry," she repeatedly cried, her tears staining my shirt as we came apart on the floor. Serena lay on top of me this time, and I bet her ribs ached with how hard I was pressing her down on me like I feared she'd disappear and this moment would flow away from us. "This is so much bigger than us, and I caused it. It's all my fault."

Worry twisted up my stomach in painful knots at the depth of her words, realizing there was much more I was yet to know. Her voice held a bucketload of agony as she struggled to regulate her breathing, and I smoothed my hand on her head, trying to calm her down. I didn't ask any questions, didn't pry, just held her like she'd asked, and let us have this moment.

Hell would come loose eventually, but not today.

Right now, we needed to heal, and that could only be achieved in each other's arms.

CHAPTER NINETEEN
SERENA

I have to catch a flight at nine to Dubai to oversee a project. I'm not leaving you. I'll be back in a week. We'll talk then.

—Ares

He'd made sure to leave both a note and send a text stating his whereabouts this time, and my eyes welled up with tears again the following day. Despite having soaked Ares's shirt with how much I cried on him that night.

I'd never hated myself more than I did when he left the room. I thought I'd really done it. I successfully drove away everyone that genuinely cared for me, all because I was impatient, because I couldn't have waited a little bit longer for him, and because I avoided him like the plague after the fact. For a second, I didn't want to believe what he'd said. I'd genuinely preferred the original version of our story. That way, everything I'd been through the past few years hadn't been for nothing.

Ares Alsford had always been the root cause of all the bad in my life; my mind's go-to person to blame for everything. Even then, I was aware that placing all the responsibility on his shoulders wasn't fair, but I wasn't looking for justice. I was looking for a scapegoat. Someone to split the guilt with so I could stomach my reflection in the mirror.

When he shattered everything I thought I knew, the ground opened up beneath my feet, and all I wanted was for it to swallow me whole. I couldn't help but apologize to Ares over and over when he came back. I was shell-shocked at his generosity when I shouldn't have been. I was the selfish one between the two of us. He was the perfect one.

The one I didn't deserve.

The hurt in his voice was so raw, it made an incision right down the middle of my heart until I was bleeding all over him. The flow of regret hadn't stopped the whole week he'd been away. Whenever he wasn't in my sight, there was this emptiness inside of me waiting to be filled by his presence. Even though I had one of the most intense cries of my life last Friday, I also had the best night's sleep in his arms. I was stiff as hell in the morning, waking up on the hardwood floor, but there had been no nightmares, and that was all that mattered.

He'd come back today, and I still hadn't heard a thing from him, so instead of staying at home and freaking out, I'd jumped on the chance to head to a masquerade ball when Elsa asked me to accompany her. Did it completely erase my anxiety, though?

No, and that became apparent when I rechecked my phone for the thousandth time as we left the red carpet, and

Elsa expressed her annoyance by sighing heavily. I cringed, dropping it back in my green clutch, and smoothed down the tulle of my dress as I faced her.

A whole bunch from the millions club were in attendance. I knew because I recognized some of them in the herd-like crowd heading inside the venue, but Elsa and I held our own. She had on an orange gown with a slit down her thigh that hung over her curves like running water, complementing her dark skin tone and enhancing her points of interest (i.e., her boobs, that I also couldn't stop staring at along with every other male and some females in attendance that walked past us) with that bustier neckline. And I wore a fluffy black dress with a shimmery green cast that caught the light of every chandelier in the opulent ballroom.

Luxury was dripping off the walls of this place—literally. The white walls were decorated with gold crown moldings at every corner, and the lights seemed so heavy from all the crystals, I was uncomfortable walking underneath them. Thank God, the room wasn't air-conditioned to the point of it being frigid, as was usually the case with such places. Otherwise, I, in my thin spaghetti straps, would've spent the night shivering.

"How did you even get invites to this event?" I asked, my head doing a three-sixty to take everything in as we dropped off our bags and got a ticket. A makeshift bar was nestled in a corner, but I doubted there was anything non-alcoholic on the menu, seeing as the median age of the room was probably forty and up.

"Oh, I met this guy." Elsa shrugged, and I raised an intrigued brow, glad she was moving on, and we could forget the whole double date fiasco.

"Do tell," I urged, linking her arm through mine as we

slowly walked to get a drink. Notes of expensive perfume overpowered the air, and I resisted the urge to scratch my nose, as that would entail removing the black metal mask that shielded me from the familiar faces that kept standing out.

"Honestly, there's not much to tell. He's hot as hell, but when we're not fucking, I'd rather tape his mouth shut."

"That kind, huh?" I *tsked*, sucking in air through my teeth. "Where did you meet?"

"A legal conference about four months ago. He works for the Goldberg firm and couldn't stop boasting about it the majority of the time we were together, but he's loaded, so this will be a fun short-term thing. We're going wine tasting in Napa this weekend, all expenses paid by him," she said with a smile, but it didn't quite reach her eyes, and I gave her my best *tell me what's going on* expression.

"Why do I get the feeling that you like him for more than just his money and dick?"

"He's a huge ass and spoiled..." Elsa said, sounding like she was actually trying to convince herself. "But he's also incredibly driven, and I respect that about him. Nothing is going to come out of this, though; he's in his *I will fuck anything with a pair of nice tits* phase."

Well, now I understood where her hesitation was coming from. He was young, cocky, successful, and by the sound of it, a manwhore. Basically, a heartbreak waiting to happen.

"Yikes, how old is this guy?" I asked when we reached the bar, fully equipped with illuminated amber countertops. My obsession was so bad, the color reminded me of *his* eyes, and my palm itched to reach for my cell phone again.

I scanned the menu quickly to distract myself, confirming that indeed the only thing I could have was bottled water, either still or sparkling. I got the latter, just to spice it up a little, and I bet if my old German pen pal could see me right now, she'd have proud tears streaming down her face. Let's just say, I was a tiny bit mystified when she told me that most Germans preferred sparkling to still water, and I might've told her it tasted like TV static...It made sense in my mind at the time.

"My age," Elsa replied when the bartender placed a dry gin martini in front of her and looked at me weird before handing me my water. My palms slickened against the plastic as we faced the conversing crowd, leaning back on the countertop. Adults that didn't drink were often seen as weird. "But it's okay. I'm using him as much as he's using me. There's nothing to worry about."

"As long as you're having fun." I took a sip, combating the sudden dryness in my throat. Elsa's face was perplexed as she toyed with the lemon twist at the edge of her glass, deep in thought.

Yeah, I had a feeling this wasn't as simple as she was making it out to be, but I didn't have the right to warn her off, not after the whole Ares thing. It was a wonder she was still friends with me. I guessed it partly had to do with me moping around for the past week, and she took mercy on me. She didn't have to invite me. She could've taken Elliot. Siblings were like default plus-ones.

Out of my peripheral vision, I saw a man striding toward us, wearing his smirk as an accessory, his icy eyes locked on Elsa's behind. I couldn't see his face because of the mask he had on, but his hair was a stunning shade of gold.

I scrunched up my face when he didn't seem to be stopping any time soon, my mouth dropping open to warn him off, as he surprised Elsa by weaving his hands around her stomach. She tensed, but relaxed when she heard his voice.

"Ms. Marrel," he purred, a low sound that even sent flurries of excitement in my stomach. Damn, he was tall.

Ares is taller, my brain chimed in, and I held an eye roll back. Sometimes, it felt like I had a devil on one shoulder and an angel on the other. Unsurprisingly, the devil won most of the arguments.

"Being a lawyer and all, one would expect you'd know not to touch random people like that. It's a sexual harassment lawsuit waiting to happen," Elsa chided in a mocking voice, lighting up in his presence. She removed his hands from her waist, but he kept one wrapped around her shoulders, pulling her to his side.

His smile was all pearly white teeth. "I knew it was you the second I saw the arch of your a—"

I cleared my throat, unimpressed and maybe just a tiny bit jealous, stopping him before he ended his sentence. I'd never had that—the full-on boyfriend experience, someone that wanted to claim me loudly and proudly. I lost my virginity at a college party because I was tired of hauling the dreaded V-card around and was cruising on mindless hookups ever since. I wasn't allowed to be in a committed relationship for apparent reasons. The one person I dated seriously for a short while was my drug dealer. He supplied me with free drugs—or so I thought until he sold me to pay for them.

It was ironic, really, like getting hit by an ambulance.

My neck flushed when the man's frigid gaze turned to me, a calculated smile on his lips as he looked me over. "And who do we have here?"

"Aaron, this is Amelia Duante, my coworker and friend,"

Elsa introduced, motioning to me, and my hands curled into tiny fists when I heard his name. It all clicked in place in an instant, but she still went ahead and confirmed it for me. "Amelia, this is Aaron Goldberg."

My expression soured under my mask as if someone had shoved an entire lemon in my mouth. "Goldberg?" I asked the question mindlessly, hanging on to a sliver of hope that maybe I'd heard wrong.

It was pointless. He looked...well, like himself, and from how Elsa had described him, he acted exactly like himself too—like a pretentious douchebag. I threw Elsa an *oh, girl, you're so fucked* look, but she was too busy making googly eyes at him.

Short-term thing, my ass.

"You've heard of me?"

Oh, you have no idea.

"Here and there," I answered tightly, shaking his extended hand.

"Mostly good things, I hope."

I raised a cool brow, wondering if I should ask what happened to the girl I'd seen him with last, but decided against it. For all his faults, I didn't see what he could gain out of Elsa. Maybe he truly liked her for her.

"I think you already know the answer to that." I settled for a neutral answer, but he'd already lost interest in me, snatching a flute of champagne from a passing waitress.

"Touché." He winked, his self-awareness below zero, and cocked his head at Elsa, already tugging her away. "Come. Papa has been asking to meet you."

God, what type of grown-ass man said papa?

The Goldbergs had strong German roots, but the word felt weird coming out of Aaron's mouth, considering the only reason he passed his language classes was because of hefty donations from his family. I bit my lip, resisting the urge to ask him what the hell his father wanted with Elsa, promising to grill her about it later. Things were serious if *Papa* Goldberg was getting involved.

I was giving him the benefit of the doubt, but I wasn't suddenly flushing his conniving nature from my mind.

"It's fine, Elsa," I responded to the silent question in her eyes. "Go. I need to use the restroom, anyway."

"I won't be long," Elsa promised over her shoulder as Aaron dragged her away, not wasting a single second.

And there I was, alone once again, my eyes boring into the gin martini Elsa left behind. I didn't yearn for alcohol like I used to anymore. My throat didn't scream with the need to feel that familiar burn as the liquid swished down my esophagus. Something had changed today, though, and every noise and moving body blurred in the background as a bead of sweat made its way down my spine.

Would it be so bad?

To take a sip or two?

It could help me loosen up, help me sleep better, and keep the dreams at bay. Visions of knives, bloody palms and thighs. I'd managed to get over most of the things I'd experienced in my lifetime, and there were a lot. It was like my brain exploded like fireworks whenever I treaded near the extensive memories of my father or all the men that'd hurt me after him, protecting me by keeping me blind. But there was this one thing I kept coming back to. One thing I couldn't forget. And learning that I was the cause of it all made my ribs ache like a bullet had shot clean through them.

I stared, and stared, and stared until blackness rimmed my vision, and my hand gave in to the temptation, raising to bring the glass to my lips. Just thinking about having to tell Ares made me reach for it faster, but just before I got to touch it, my hand was knocked out of the way, a broad chest in an expensive white tux moving in my field of vision.

"You need to leave," a deafening male voice curled in my eardrums, stark in warning. "Right now."

I jerked back, my breath lodging in my lungs as I stretched my gaze up to take in all of him. And there was a lot to take...like pounds of flesh and a ton of inches of height succeeding mine. I got a crick in the back of my neck when I finally reached his face, finding similar features to Aaron's. If it wasn't for his swirling gold eyes popping out of his gray mask, I would've thought they were related or something, and he was here to muscle me out because they knew who I was.

"Excuse me?" I broke our stare, finally letting his words filter into my brain.

He crossed his arms over his chest, and if I thought he was built before, he resembled a tank like this. I took a small step back as he asked, "What are you doing here?"

Unease melted in the pit of my stomach like butter, and I raised my chin haughtily, not letting him scent my fear. "Do I know you?"

Are you here to kill me?

I'd had a few murder attempts in the past, but they usually didn't start off with a warning. I let my arms loose by my sides, realizing that that wasn't the case. Sam had everything on lock. Him not having contacted me in a little over a month meant things were progressing smoothly.

"I sincerely hope you do, Laurent," he muttered, and my heart would've frozen over with fear at him calling me by my real surname if he hadn't removed his mask a second later, reaching to untie it on the back of his blond head. "I saw you at the gym while you were too busy ruining his life for a second time."

Despite feeling unwanted, relief hit my system like a Mack truck as Saint Astor's marble-like skin and berry red lips avenging his friend's honor registered in my head. I understood where he was coming from, but simply the fact that it was *him* speaking out of turn, considering his heavy-loaded past, had me busting my mouth open and forgetting my filter somewhere in Neverland.

"Is that judgment I hear in your voice, Astor? Are you really accusing me of ruining someone's life? How many hearts have you broken, and how many marriages have *you* split?" I spat, my voice harsh, making it clear I wasn't letting him bulldoze into me. "Just because you're married now doesn't make you Mr. Clean or give you the right to tell *me* what to do."

He didn't ask how I knew about his marriage. He was probably used to people being clued into every facet of his life. Saint was Astropolis's Golden Boy, after all; his business was plastered across every front page in the nation. Everyone either hated him or wanted to fuck him.

Saint Astor was a polarizing figure and too used to getting what he wanted by the sounds of it.

"You're right. I'm as far from Mr. Clean as one can get," he ground out, his molars crushing together and jawline sticking out in anger. "But at least I've never been cruel enough to string someone along for half of their life, and on top of that, swoop right back in and ruin things just when they get their shit together."

My chest caved in at his deductions, but he wasn't telling me anything I wasn't already aware of. His words acted like fresh scratches on old scars. I'd beaten myself up enough about this situation, so much so it sometimes felt like I was losing my grip on sanity.

I *should* have gotten my head out of my ass and spoken to someone about how my father treated me and the things he demanded of me. I *should've* lingered and heard Ares's side of the story. I *should've* paid more attention to my mother. I *shouldn't* have taken that beer or the white line I was offered just because I was curious about the aftereffects.

There were so many things I'd change if only I could turn back time. There was a cost to not following your heart, and that was spending the rest of your life wishing you did. So, unfortunately for Saint, I was done taking orders from others. I was over the isolation that clung inside my head like the walls of a mental torture chamber.

It might've been selfish of me, but I didn't care. I was going after Ares if he'd have me. I always fought for the wrong people when only one person deserved my devotion. That had stood by me through thick and thin and hadn't spewed a single word of judgment when the whole world rushed to brand me as a slut, homewrecker, and bitter cunt.

Ares *fucking* Alsford.

The final choice was in his hands, not mine. I was a goner and would do whatever made him the happiest, be that sticking by his side or leaving the city, our deal be damned. I didn't need a house within the vicinity of my actual home— one I'd be barred from entering.

Rolling my lips in my mouth, I didn't give Saint the satisfaction of answering. I was standing on sliding ground. There was nothing I could say to improve my case. The only way was down. Turning in my red stilettos, I started for the bathroom, but Saint hooked my elbow in his firm hold and pulled me back with little effort.

Growling under my breath, I struggled to get free, yet he didn't let up. Leaning low, he whispered words in my ear that made my blood run cold, "He doesn't want you, not really. You're just a pretty little thing he can't have, and all men love the chase. Just turn your head a fraction on the left, and you'll see what I'm talking about." I did, and the view that greeted me was like a sucker punch to the gut. "He's happy without you. Don't ruin that for him. If you ever cared for him, you're going to leave him alone, Serena."

He was here.

Ares was here with someone else.

I let Saint support my weight despite my better judgment as a splitting headache unfurled in my head. My lashes fluttered as I watched him glide along the dance floor with another girl in his arms, looking all dapper in his suit. He didn't have a mask on like most people, and it made sense. Ares carried a wave of mystery wherever he went. He was kind but detached. Fun, but could turn colder than the Arctic in the blink of an eye.

No one would tell him anything for not sticking to the dress code.

It was like someone forced my heart through a meat grinder as I took in his fingers curled possessively around her waist, pressing his body into hers as she smiled up at him, chatting him up. The fact that she was relatively attractive, too, didn't help. My mouth dried up when I got a vision of storming over there and body-slamming her to the floor.

Was this the Sonia Bella talked about?

I was no stranger to violence, and the impulse to snatch her up by her split ends won me over as I threw Saint off me.

I'd only felt this revolted once before—when he slept with Caroline. Did I deserve it? Yes. Would I let anything of that kind happen again? Over my dead body. Saint forgot that I knew Ares better than he did. He'd be *safer* with Sonia, not happier. And Ares preferred battle hymns written in blood over holy water and soft hallelujahs.

I more than cared for him, and that was why I wasn't going down without a fight.

"Go to hell, Astor," I said over the sound of Lana Del Rey's voice, walking away with brisk steps. All he'd done was egg me on further, so that was a mission failed on his part. I wasn't falling for mind games that sounded like they'd come straight out of the mouth of a sixth grader.

The staccato of my heels against the ground echoed across the room. It felt like I was stepping on nails as I weaved through the dancing bodies. There was nothing more poisonous to one's soul than bitter jealousy, and I was currently drenched in it.

Why didn't he call me when he came back?

Why was she the one he met up with first?

Had I given him too much time? Enough to get over me and all the complications that came with me?

Questions plagued my mind—not all ones I wanted answered. They accompanied me all the way to the happy couple, according to Saint, and I came to a standstill in the middle of all the couples. I should've been more concerned about causing a scene in such a public place, but I couldn't find it in me to care.

Dread mixed with anxiety, but I turned rigid, as if encased with a layer of hardened lava when Ares spun her out and reeled her back in, preparing for the eventual crash. They both cursed when it happened, going with the crowd favorite—fuck. As if in tune, they faced me at the same time, and I got to see the very second all the words died on Ares's tongue, already watching him like a hawk.

He blanched, losing all color, as if I wasn't supposed to be witnessing this. An immediate frown coasted over his features, turning them more severe than they already were. The sharp angles of his face created natural highlights over the hollows of his cheeks, contrasting harshly against his chestnut-brown eyebrows and tousled hair.

My stomach clenched as I realized just how good he looked in his three-piece suit, and I was close to ripping off Sonia's fingers one by one when I saw them tighten over the fabric to balance herself.

"May I cut in?" I asked, going for a civilized approach. If that was going to continue depended on how long Ares took to get over his initial shock and drop her like a hot potato. Sensing my gaze on his arms, they dissolved from her waist as if put in hot water.

"And who are you?" Ms. Sonia curled a brow as she turned to me, her tone snotty, face pinched with annoyance.

"I'm—"

The bitch that's about to cut you up if you keep rubbing your ass against my man.

Fucking hell, had I just thought of Ares as my man? Fondness had overpowered any remaining hatred I felt for him last Friday, but I was yet to pinpoint when that fondness had turned into straight-up possessiveness.

Ares read me like he could the back of his hand and intervened before I could finish the sentence. "She's a friend of mine, Sonia. It's fine."

Friend.

My temper flared, coming alive inside me like a separate

entity. I wasn't going to lie. It was shit being on the receiving end of the same treatment I'd spared him with for our entire history together, running away from labels with general proclamations. The one thing that pacified me slightly was Sonia rolling her eyes at us as she shoved her way past me.

She didn't believe him.

A bitter laugh fell past my lips as I replaced her in his arms. He pulled me close—closer than he'd been with Sonia, but the edges of my heart remained jagged as we coordinated our steps, moving in tune with each other. "So we're friends now? I guess I should start handing out hand jobs to more of my male friends, if that's the norm."

A deadly smile spread across Ares's face, painful looking as it stretched from ear to ear. "You do that, and your male friends won't live to see tomorrow." My breasts ached as he smooshed us together so tight, I could only breathe in his air. A hint of Sonia's vanilla lingered on his tux, but it still didn't stop me from inhaling his ocean musk with urgency after being deprived of his scent for a week. "I agreed to take her to this event before you were even back. It's not a date. Her family's hosting this whole thing, and I donated quite a bit to the cause."

I shrugged at his explanation, my gaze bouncing to the direction Sonia had disappeared off to. "No need to explain. It's not like we are together. You can do *whoever* you want."

Great, she could add bighearted philanthropist on her list of attributes, whereas I didn't have much to show for anymore. My budget was limited these days, but I liked volunteering at some local women's shelters every other weekend.

"Serena, unless you want me to kiss you until your mask melts off and everyone sees who decided to pop in for a hello, it's really not in your best interests to piss me off." His mouth descended until it was next to my ear, his breath trickling down my neck, making heat spike through my core, and I almost dared him to do it. "Who are you here with?"

My chest tightened as I glanced around, taking in our surroundings. Dozens of people, and yet, it felt like we were the only ones in the room. His energy crackled through the air, tangling with mine in the most delicious way possible. I peeled my dry tongue from the roof of my mouth, swallowing my nerves down. "Elsa, but I might as well be alone. Goldberg is monopolizing all of her time."

"Gabriel Goldberg?" His eyebrows spiked when he stared down at me. "Isn't he like balding and in his seventies?"

"Not Gabriel, his son, Aaron. Hairier, younger, but just as repulsive."

"Hm..." A grin sneaked along his lips, and my knees grew weak at the way his handsome face lightened up with desire. "It turns me on when you get competitive."

"Ares." I fingered the lapels of his suit, fighting off the anxiety that had taken residence in my mind. I needed to get this show on the road, so both of us knew where we stood. This state of limbo was bound to come to an end after fourteen years of yearning. "We need to talk."

Seriousness bled into his gaze, and I recognized that he wasn't as eager about getting answers as he once was. I didn't blame him. I'd made it explicitly clear that whatever I had to say wasn't going to be pleasant.

Nodding his chin toward wide doors leading out to the garden, he looped his palm around the back of my neck in a dominating hold that had my heart spinning like crazy. "Come on, I need a smoke."

I let him lead the way, and he shielded us from all the thrashing bodies around. I caught two pairs of eyes peeking at us the whole way there, and a smile danced on my lips on purpose. Saint and Sonia didn't have to know that I was on the verge of throwing up.

Fresh air filled my lungs as we stepped outside. The manor-like hotel stood on several acres of rolling greenery, and an artificial lake stretched across it like a mini sea. A gazebo with a round metal roof was tucked on one end, and Ares didn't stop until we were surrounded by its lush Greek pillars, crawling with ivy.

Removing his hands from my body, Ares reached for his breast pocket, pulling out a pack of cigarettes, and I breathed in deeply before he soiled the space with that retching smoke. His lighter came on, and his eyes haunted me in the dark, caressing every exposed part of my body as if he wanted to smoke me out exactly like he was doing to the cancer stick perched in his mouth.

My hands twisted together, and I placed my hip on the wrought-iron railing. "Did you have a good time in Dubai?"

"Terrible," he deadpanned.

"Oh, why's that?"

"It's a materialistic and superficial city with a peak dog-eat-dog mentality." He walked closer, purposefully blowing out a plume of smoke on my face, and I coughed as I glared at him. "Also, didn't help that you were in an entirely different time zone and didn't text me once."

"I was trying to give you some space," I explained, and despite my history with substance abuse, if there was one thing I despised the most, it was cigarettes. They stunk up the place.

Noticing the distaste in my expression, Ares groaned as

if fighting some internal war, but gave up and dropped the cig on the lake below us. Leaning down, he worked my mask loose, and I gasped when the metal clattered against the ground. He switched our positions, so my back was facing the ballroom, and bent over until my upturned nose brushed against his straight one, and I shook from the need to reach up on my tiptoes and kiss him.

I'd missed him. This whole week he'd been away reminded me of how barren my life was pre coming back to Astropolis.

"You've already given me a decade's worth of space. I don't need any fucking more, Serena," he said in a broken whisper, and a shiver shot up my spine.

"What are you saying?" I shuddered, willing my brain not to get too excited too fast.

I had no doubt in my mind I was the one for Ares, and he was it for me. It was absurd to think otherwise, given the time we spent obsessing over one another. Our souls were a mere reflection of each other at this point after soaking in our sins and seeing them through the end.

Desire and apprehension raced for first place in Ares's gaze. His fingers flexed by his sides, and I wondered why he wasn't touching me when he was usually so generous with his affection.

"*You* wanted to talk, so talk." Drawing back, his guard raised piece by piece, stitching together to protect his heart. A heart I'd stomped over one too many times, and it was coming back to bite me.

I masked the tremble of my lips by scrubbing a hand down the length of my face. I couldn't expect him to give me everything without offering a piece of myself first. "I'm not going to deny it—I held a lot of resentment for you over the years, and you already know why...well, mostly."

"Mostly?" His eye twitched.

"You know the root of my resentment. A lot more went down afterward as a result of that, though, things I'm not comfortable discussing right now. But I will; I'll tell you everything because you deserve to know, and as much as I'm dying to ask you for a second chance, I can't—*not yet.*" The words rushed out of me like a waterfall, and if we were alone, the whole truth would have unraveled thread by thread. It weighed down on me, and despite being terrified at his reaction, I was eager not to carry all this alone. "You need to have all the facts before you make a decision."

Warmth spread through my veins, his hold on my forearms singeing my skin. My head snapped up to meet his eyes as if drawn to them by an invisible magnet. I saw the lights of the lake illuminated there, along with a tenderness that softened up my limbs like melted butter.

"Baby, I've never been able to tell you no before. What makes you think I'll start now? You could've kicked a puppy, run over a grandma, sidetracked a school bus, and I still would've found a reason to defend you."

Suddenly, my vision blurred.

"That is kind of concerning, Alsford," I tried to say, but my words came out wrangled when a loud sob burst from my mouth, and I doubted he got any of it. God, it felt so good hearing him say that, even though I hadn't merited that kind of blind devotion, and I was sorry he was stuck with me.

"I don't care what anyone else thinks. As long as we're happy, no one else matters." He tugged my chin up, wiping the wetness that had pooled under my eyes with the pads of his thumbs. I probably had trails of mascara running down my cheeks, but his gaze burned through mine like he couldn't get enough of me. "Being away from you feels like hell; being near you and not being able to touch you whenever I want or kiss you in front of whomever I please is torturous. I can't pretend to hate you anymore because of shit that happened years ago."

Tears flowed faster now, his confession sealing the cap on a box full of toxic emotions that had reigned terror over my heart for too long. My bones turned to jelly, and I sank into his arms like a deflated balloon, all my fight evaporating from my body.

"I'm tired of fighting this too, Ares," I admitted, licking my lips while staring at his. Ares's cupid's bow was so prominent I wanted to trace it with my tongue.

A shattered exhale escaped him, and he pressed his forehead to mine. "You don't know what hearing you say that does to me."

"I think I have an idea or two." I closed my eyes, soaking him in. They snapped back open a moment later, the tension between us coiling so tight, the smallest feel of his skin on mine set me off. "You *can* kiss me, you know? No one can see my face from here, and I had my mask on inside the entire time."

I didn't have to speak twice.

A growl rumbled from deep within his chest, skipping over the still water next to us as his lips claimed mine in a toe-curling kiss. I opened up eagerly, fully surrendering, giving both of us permission to take what we'd always longed for. The ash on his tongue combined with my salty tears commemorating a perfect union of two wholly imperfect individuals that somehow found the solace they needed in each other's arms.

All of his deep, toxic, and slightly unhinged pieces called to me, and I embraced them by delving my nails into his scalp when he tugged me up, his palms getting a feel of my ass. We made out against a pillar next to some thorny rose bushes, like two high schoolers groping by the bleachers while the rest of the class looked on, horrified. We weren't that out in the open, but whoever *actively* searched for us could see that he was as much lost in me as I was in him.

"Take the rest of the week off work. Come to St. Pete with me. I want us to be free of Astropolis for a little while," he propositioned after detaching his mouth from mine. Our clothes shifted as we heaved, trying to catch our breaths. "We'll eat a bucketload of shrimp, drink a year's worth of *non*-alcoholic cocktails, and have so much sex you'll need assistance walking the next day."

My core contracted like it really liked that idea, and if I led a normal life, I wouldn't have thought twice about it.

"As tempting as that sounds, I can't," I said sadly, tightening my hold when he tried to withdraw. "I'm not allowed to leave the state. I'll tell you all the gory details later," I rushed to explain.

As much as I wish I didn't, but we're starting with transparency.

He sighed and held on to his self-control by a thread, giving me a different alternative. "Cape Cod, then? I have a boat there. We could sail to the nearby islands."

I paused, smoothing my palms over his five o'clock shadow and pecking his pouty lips. My ears were met with a satisfied male groan as he squeezed my ass. "Are you sure, Ares? I'll be happy if we spend the whole week at your house. I don't need anything fancy, especially if being there is going to stress you out."

I hadn't asked about his parents, but that didn't mean I hadn't looked them up. I knew how they'd passed, and I hadn't brought up the conversation because I didn't know whether reliving those memories two years later would be pleasing.

"I'll be fine," he dismissed my concerns, quickly—*too quickly*. "We're doing it right this time, Serena. Wining, dining, and the whole shebang."

"Does that mean I should make you wait for at least three dates?" I smiled.

"Yeah, no. We *are* skipping that." Stealing one last kiss, cool air rushed all around me when he straightened up, and I missed his warmth immediately. "Unless you don't feel ready, of course," he relented in a dejected tone, his fingers fixing the spaghetti straps of my dress.

"Ares, there's nothing else I'd rather be doing now than you." Holding on to his forearms, I reached up, managing to nip his pillowy bottom lip. "The harder your ex glares at me, the hornier I get."

"Serena..." he growled at me, reaching down to swat my ass, but I evaded his hold, a giggle bursting out of my mouth. He stopped dead in his tracks as if the sound had a physical impact on him, and the look he gave was one of pure need, making me look all the more forward to tomorrow.

"I have to go find Elsa. I'll meet you at your place?" I asked, picking up my discarded mask off the floor and tying it over my face again.

"Still won't give me your address, Siren?"

"I swear, it's for a good reason." I gnawed on my bottom lip.

"Fine, be there at six am, sharp. Otherwise, I'm leaving your ass behind. It's a two-hour drive."

"Yessir." I saluted, and a smile split his lips. It did funny things to my chest, and I took a reluctant step away from him, only to be stopped short.

"Oh, and Siren?" he asked, his fingers clasping around the stem of an overgrown white rose next to him, pulling until he worked the flower loose. He strode in my vicinity, and sweat made my skin slick under the metal when he hooked it behind my ear, winking. "Don't wear any underwear unless you want me to rip them off you."

CHAPTER TWENTY
SERENA

"My God, what did you put in here? Rocks?" Ares asked, his brown hair teeming with gold highlights under the morning sun. His muscles bunched with effort as he carried both our suitcases down a row of white boats at the Kingman marina. They increased in size the farther down we walked, rocking slightly as tiny waves marred the surface of the crystal blue water.

It was the perfect sailing weather, and almost no people loitered around at this early hour. It was just me, Ares, the seagulls, and this lingering tightness in my heart as I watched his bitable ass shift in his navy Ralph Lauren swimming trunks.

"It's a whole week away. Did you expect me to only bring two T-shirts and a bathing suit?" My strappy sandals smacked on the deck as I hurried to keep up with him.

"Yes?" he replied in a tone-deaf tone, his mouth pursing as he reconsidered, and relented, "Okay, maybe two T-shirts and a dress since you're a woman and all."

The vein in my forehead ticked. "I can't pinpoint exactly why, but I found what you just said low-key offensive."

"You've been on the internet for too long. People there always find something to be offended by." He winked at me, stopping abruptly in front of a monolith of a boat.

My eyes widened as I took in the catamaran's beauty. The glossy red finish of the hull was well-kept and unmarred by the salt water, with sleek blacked-out windows on either side. The yacht spoke of elegance within the purity of its lines. It was vast yet concise, with a main deck made of light Oakwood and two extra stories with an open floor plan and panoramic windows that offered you a three-sixty view of the surrounding world.

"This is *us*?" I managed to unglue my lips, scrunching the skirt of my flowy white dress in my fists. I hadn't been on a boat this big in so long. My ears buzzed with excitement.

"Yeah," Ares confirmed, holding both suitcases in front of him so he could fit down the narrow bridge. Placing them over the transom steps, he trudged back to me, offering his hand, so I was more balanced on the wobbly walkway.

"What the hell, Alsford? You said you had a *boat*." A serene grin lit up his face at the giddiness in my voice. "This is a yacht."

"Tomayto, tomahto, Siren. A yacht is still a boat, just fancier," he shot back, his hands circling my waist as he lifted me in the air and placed me on the deck.

"She is beautiful. Like a high-end Manhattan apartment on the water," I said, letting him lead the way. My fingertips rolled over the silver railing, the rays reflecting on the water and warming my skin despite being protected by shade on the lower deck where the cabins were. "I can't believe I'm saying this since I'm not the best swimmer, but I missed the ocean. The scent of salt in the air, and the feel of the sun against your skin."

"Not the best swimmer is an understatement," he scoffed. "I just realized how ironic it is that I call you Siren when you almost drowned me during spring break senior year."

"I thought I saw a shark!" I defended my case, my cheeks heating at the memory of attaching myself on his back like an octopus.

"So you decided to push me down in order to save yourself? Thanks, that makes me feel so much better now." He rolled his eyes, stopping in front of the master cabin.

"Stop being dramatic, Alsford." I reached over him, twisting the handle so he could enter first and finally unload our stuff. "I panicked and decided to hold on to you because you were the one I trusted the most to get me out of there."

Fluttering my eyelashes at him, I stepped inside, and while the bedroom took up the entire front of the yacht, Ares was on the tall side, so he had to slant his head which put him in the direct line of fire of my honeyed gaze.

"Those Siren eyes will get you nowh—" I licked my lips, and he stopped talking as if transfixed by the movement. He'd made it a point to touch me as little as possible since the morning, like if he did, he wouldn't be able to control himself, and my bones wept to feel the pressure of his calloused hands.

"Fuck, who am I kidding? They'll get you anywhere." Scrubbing a hand down his face, his front brushed mine as he headed for the door again, and my nails sunk in the fleshy part of my palms in disappointment.

Twisting at the waist, my nipples hardened at Ares's thorough bodily scan, his energy whipping around me like a lightning storm I wanted to dive into, uncaring of the after-math. But just when I thought he'd give in to the swirling lust in his eyes, he shook his head, ducking under the door. "Settle in, Serena. I need to go start the engines."

My middle squeezed when he left, and I dropped onto his king-sized bed with a huff, my hands stretching wide on either side of the burgundy duvet like a starfish. Neither of us had breached the topic of what we discussed yesterday, and I got the sense that he wanted a few mindless days of fun, to just be together without any worries. We'd never had that, and my utmost priority right now was to indulge his wishes... and relieve the ache in my core.

I sat upright again, my mind working in overdrive and crafting all kinds of elaborate plans to seduce him. The thrill of the chase made things all the more interesting anyway. And I'd brought along the perfect tools to do so in the form of bikini bottoms with strings so thin they practically disap-peared inside my butt.

The floor shook beneath my feet when Ares powered the yacht, and I smiled as I got to work. Within the next twenty minutes, I'd neatly folded all of our clothes in the built-in closet, and something about seeing his monochro-matic clothes next to my colorful two-pieces and gowns had my heart singing with domestic bliss. Before getting ahead of myself, I changed into my lilac swimsuit, putting my hair in a long braid to combat the heat, and took a tour of the kitchen in the galley while Ares steered us out of the marina. The mini fridge was stocked with fruits, and I made both of us a quick berry parfait, layering yogurt with granola, banana slices, strawberries, raspberries, and topping it all off with a drizzle of honey. Taking advantage of the DeLonghi coffee machine, too, I loaded up everything in my hands and wobbled to the second floor, trying not to drop anything.

"A little help, please?" I said when the back of Ares's head came into view. He was sitting on a cream couch in front of all the controllers. The fine dusting of hair on his chest greeted me when he whipped up to get his food, and I resisted drooling in my coffee when I saw just how built he was.

The urge to lick each pec on his toned stomach was overwhelming when his gaze swam with arousal as he took in my new state of undress. Seeing as the boat was cruising through open water, though, we both bit our tongues and dropped back onto the couch.

"I made your milk just the way you like it...with a side of coffee," I snipped as he took a sip, smiling around the bite of my parfait when I saw that his pinkie was out as if he was drinking tea with the Queen.

His pink tongue licked along the seam of his lips when his gaze floated to my chest first, then my face. "Thanks, baby. It's my second favorite thing to drink."

"What's your first?" My forehead wrinkled in question.

He set his half-full cup on the dash, fiddling with a little nob beside the steering wheel, cool as a mint, when he said, "Your cum."

A violent cough exploded from my chest, and I almost snorted a raspberry out of my nose at his unexpected response. "Ares," I hissed, hitting his rock-solid forearm, and his flat belly shook with silent laughter. "Don't say shit like that while you're steering a boat."

I knew most modern boats had an autopilot these days, but he seemed to be enjoying being more hands-on with the whole process. So I stewed beside him when I could've easily distracted him from the task at hand in less than five seconds, keeping myself busy by scarfing down my yogurt and staring at the blue horizon.

"We'll be anchored in about ten minutes, a little bit offshore from Lambert's Cove." Ares pointed in a direction, and I pretended like I knew what he was talking about. "It's a protected ocean inlet, water as cold and salty as the ocean, but the surface is nearly as still as a lake, so we won't have to battle waves and sand in every bodily crevice."

I nodded, but my attention was snagged by a small picture on his right glued on the white wood beside the two throttles. The gold in his eyes melted when I purposefully leaned over his lap to get a better look at it. My breasts slid over his trunks, and his dick twitched underneath them as if saying hello.

I hid my smile by angling my head toward the photograph, seeing a lanky young Ares standing in the middle of his parents. His mom's hands were on his shoulders. All of them were sporting huge smiles with a Disney castle in the background. My heart squeezed at how happy they looked. Out of all the people I'd surrounded myself with since first grade, Ares was the closest to his parents. To see them being ripped away from him so brutally knocked me sideways.

Swallowing the lump in my throat, I tried to lighten up the atmosphere with a joke. "Oh my gosh, I'd forgotten what a cute kid you were. The braces?" I swung my head, and my braid bounced on his chest. Wildfires ravaged his gaze as he stared at me, and he rolled my braid twice in his fist, arching my neck up, grazing my chin with his lips, and making warmth spread like molasses through my chest. "Very becoming," I whispered, finishing my sentence.

Neither of us seemed to care that the boat basically

steered itself as his other hand reached out to my back and pulled at my legs, so I slid right into his lap. But there were no possible collision points as far as I could tell, so I trusted him not to neglect his duties unless he was sure we weren't in any danger.

"Why do I get the feeling that you're mocking me, Laurent?" His deep voice bounced off my hot cheeks, and I circled my arms around his broad shoulders, feeling his heart beat in tandem with mine.

"I would never." I blinked rapidly, a picture of innocence as his palm started rubbing up my legs, shooting shivers of pleasure straight to my core. "You turned out very handsome. I'm very thankful to your parents for the braces and probably the thousands of dollars they spent on dermatologist visits."

"That was a backhanded compliment if I've ever heard one." He delivered a swat to my fleshy thigh and nipped at my chin when I giggled. "I'm convinced you crave my palm on your skin at this point, Siren."

His palm on my skin, his mouth on my body, his ring on my finger...I craved anything and everything he was willing to offer. But the thing I craved most at the moment was to lessen the burden of sorrow hanging heavily in his heart. I hadn't seen a genuine smile on his face not once in the past two months, and I was determined to change that.

"It's okay to miss them," I said on a serious note, trapping his devastating face between my hands. A glimmer of all the pain he carried resurfaced, and I was able to see all the broken fractions of his soul as clear as day. His arms tightened around me as if seeking reassurance, and I gladly complied. "It never really goes away, especially when they leave before their time, but don't let grief consume you. Remember all the good times you had together, and try to keep their memory alive by maintaining traditions. What were some things your parents loved doing?"

Smoothing my thumb along the dark line of his scruff, Ares's eyes closed, relaxing under my care. "Dad actually loved sailing. He refused to use a captain whenever we took the boat out and insisted I get my boating license as soon as I was of age. And Mom..." His face wrinkled in thought, and I gave in to the need to peck the little line between his brows. Ares's fingers dug into my flesh in response, his intelligent gaze hooking on my lips when I pulled back. "Well, my mom was really into embroidery stitching, and last time I tried to do that, I bled all over the white cloth."

My grin stretched from ear to ear when I imagined him stitching. Ares Alsford was a man of contrasts. He had a whole ass Harley collection yet liked his coffee sweeter than his waffles, and now a horror movie buff that tried his hand out at stitching in his free time.

I wanted to hug Quinn so hard for making him comfortable in his masculinity.

"From what I remember, you're much more like your mom than dad. Sweet, caring, and full of so much love to give, it spills out of you in waves. Being in your presence feels like stepping in a ray of sunshine," I admitted, the tip of my nose brushing his in an Eskimo kiss. Such an innocent move when his hard-on pressed against my thigh and arousal flowed freely down the center of my legs.

Our breaths interlaced, and it seemed we were both down to explore all sorts of kissing options when our mouths slanted and lashes fell heavy. So close, we were so close, but a millisecond away from connecting...I was robbed of the feel of his mouth on mine when I was dropped back onto the couch, my hair assaulting my face and my shriek scaring the fishies in the process.

Ares met my shocked expression with a Lucifer smirk, straightening up and sipping the rest of his coffee, unaffected like the large bulge in his trunks was a figment of my imagination. "Stop distracting me unless you want us to drown, Siren."

ARES

The glare of the sun was doing little to nothing to curb my gaze from following Serena's jiggly ass cheeks around as if they were two magnetizing globes. They were practically hanging out already, only a thin strip down the middle, and a little triangle at the hilt of her ass obstructed my view.

"It's cold," she squealed, holding on to the railing as she dipped her toe in the ocean, retracting it almost immediately. "Too cold." Her eyes sought me out, dipping over the planes of my stomach and heating up when they saw that I was still hard as a rock and doing nothing to hide it. "Although, I suppose you could use a dip in cold water."

"I sure could, Siren." I smiled, sauntering down the stairs and joining her on the stern. "Right after you."

Her eyes widened, smelling my intentions a second before I put them forth. "No, no, no. Ares, don't you dare. I will get in at my own pace." Her loud voice echoed over the peaceful tide, and she tried to duck away from my hold, but I had her securely in my embrace in an instant. Her stomach quivered beneath my fingers as she screamed, "Ares, no!"

I jumped.

Our bodies flew in the air, and Serena's shriek turned into a gurgle when we broke the surface of the water with a big splash. I positioned myself beneath her, so I took the brunt of the fall, and the plunge was painful, like I had smashed right into concrete.

Cold concrete indeed, because despite it being the middle of August, the water was fucking icy. Twisting in my arms, Serena swam up again like her lungs were running out of air, and I followed closely behind.

"I fucking hate it when you do that. You know I could've gone into thermal shock, right?" Her hands slapped the water, eyes blinking fast to get rid of the salt in them.

"Now, who's being dramatic?" I chuckled, sweeping the hair off my forehead before widening my arms. "Come here, baby. I'll warm you right up."

She refused my offer by making a little triangle with her hands and pushing until a little makeshift wave hit my face and salt went into my lungs.

"Oh, now you're asking for it," I growled, paddling over to her. I trapped her squirming body in my hands and shoved her head underwater, all with a smile. Call it a little light revenge for her stubbornness.

We'd been teasing each other relentlessly the whole day, and I didn't expect to like the torture she inflicted on my poor dick. But seeing her face light up with a vixen smirk and her bending over a certain way, so she drew my gaze to her assets, did wonders for my ego. Not that it already needed to climb any higher, but every little gesture was appreciated where Serena was concerned.

The tension between us charged up the water with a dangerous electric current I would let destroy me if it meant having her wet, half-naked curves pressed against me for the rest of my life. I couldn't remember a time I was happiest than now—a full half an hour of diving and swimming laps with Serena, letting her climb on my back like a monkey to catch her breath when she got tired and kissing her underwater because she wanted to recreate those corny couple pictures on Pinterest or some shit like that.

Not that I was complaining—not at all. Holding the railing on either side of the stairs, I pushed my body up, licking a drop of saltwater dripping down her ass and squeezing her tender skin between my teeth. Serena sucked in a sharp breath, her narrowed eyes locking in on mine as I smiled at her from below.

"Let me help you up," I offered, giving her a well-placed push.

"You didn't help anyone but yourself to copping a feel," she pointed out, her gaze roaming over me as I shook my head, spraying droplets of water in the air that sparked up the atmosphere with mini rainbows when they caught the rays of the sun.

I shrugged. "Not my fault, Siren. You're wearing a thong. Your ass has been basically inviting me to touch it the whole day."

"It's a Brazilian bikini," she corrected in a haughty tone, not reaching for a towel, and I got the idea that she was waiting for me to dry all that delicious tan skin off. "Besides, I thought you said you'd rip off my underwear if I wore any, so I was trying to be accommodating."

Accommodating, my ass.

She was trying to get me to fuck the insolence out of her, and I'd completely forgotten why I was fighting it in the first place. I'd had enough taunting from her to last me a lifetime. So, kick-starting my legs, I shoved off the stern, bending at the waist and locking her ankles behind my back. Serena held on to my shoulders to combat the sudden shift in gravity, losing her breath at a faster pace, her pussy flush with my stomach.

"Swimwear does not constitute as underwear." I gave her a lesson in undergarments as I carried her to the cabin, planning to peel her clothes off with my damned teeth. "The only time you'll be naked in the ocean is only on a private island with no boats in sight for at least twelve nautical miles off the coast."

"So possessive. I don't think I like you telling me how to dress," she complained, but her hips were already seeking some friction from my abs by shifting on them like I was a surfboard she was dying to ride.

"And I think you're going to love it when I tell you to *un*dress." Once inside the room, I threw her on the bed, shutting the door behind me, so no chilly drafts bothered us. She bounced on the mattress with a yelp, nails looking for some grip by scrunching up the cotton sheets. We were about to make a mess with all the saltwater still on us, but seeing as there were four more cabins on deck, I couldn't care less. This was going to be messy either way; my shaft was throbbing for release, and I wasn't even inside her yet.

Serena's jaw locked when I slid my trunks down, my balls tensing and my length growing rigid under her languid stare. There was this weird shift in my stomach one could easily confuse as the fluttering of butterfly wings, but I recognized it for what it truly was—licks of fire rushing up the walls of the careful self-restraint I'd built, burning them down for the one girl I'd allow to do anything to me.

"Get that top off and crawl to me, Siren," I ordered, my

peripheral vision growing dark as if my eyes were a telephoto lens solely capable of focusing on her.

My hand glided over my dick, and I started stroking as she untied her bikini top, taking it off torturously slow. She unwrapped her tits like she knew they were a present, I waited to see with a bated breath every time we were together. Her pink nipples were like my personal chew toys, the fullness of them making me go cross-eyed at how fucking magnificent she was.

Ass up in the air behind her, a fake bashfulness entered her gaze like she was a blushing virgin about to have her cherry popped as she edged at the foot of the bed on all fours, where I towered over her. "What are you going to do to me, Mr. Alsford?"

"What's done to every obedient whore, my little scream-er." My hand slid behind the nape of her neck, dragging her into me until she was mere inches from my cock. Her tongue peeked out as she stared at the drop of precum staining my head, and nerves made my heart burst with delirium until my rib cage bruised from the inside out at the pounding rhythm it had adopted. "I'm gonna fuck your mouth, and then you."

Serena's perfect, pouty lips parted in expectancy, ghosting over my tight foreskin, but I waited for an indication of confirmation from her before proceeding. Her eyes flashed with warmth, recognizing it, and at her little nod, I surrendered to the prison of my addiction, going by the name of Serena Laurent with a relieved sigh, and shoved her head forward until my dick was enveloped fully by her wet heat.

"Shit," I drawled, my head lolling back, stars flooding my vision at the fucking out-of-body experience that was having her mouth on me. The walls of her throat felt like the perfect home around the tip of my cock, constricting and trying to further aid my intrusion.

Serena's little hand encased my base, and we moved like a well-oiled machine. I thrust my hips forward, and she conceded to the dominance of my hand, ruining her wet braid by white-knuckling the hair at the base of her scalp. She choked every time I pumped my erection in her mouth, and I became attached to her struggling sounds prompting me to go harder.

Nostrils flaring, I looked down at her. My abs tensed at the masterpiece of a woman swallowing down my cock like she was starving for it. Her pink lips stretched around my girth, eyes closed, a little hum coming from the base of her chest and vibrating my cockhead as if she loved my taste as much as I did hers. My mind took a mental snapshot of the moment, committing it to memory.

"Look at me while you take my dick. I want to see those watering Siren eyes on me while I hit the back of your throat," I instructed, and she blinked up at me in an instant, the corners of her eyelids overflowing with tears. I almost came right then and there, and I had to cease her movement completely to regain some of my stamina. I pressed her nose against my pubic bone and held her there for a good ten seconds.

Serena slapped my thigh, her vision growing hazy by the lack of oxygen, and I let her go with a wet pop, my slobbery cock glistening from her saliva. Dribble coated her lips, a thin layer connecting her to me, but I couldn't give less of a shit as I bent down, kissing her mouth with an unparalleled sense of urgency. I tasted a bit of myself there, my flavor lingering like a brand on her tongue, and I got the crazy idea to spoon-feed her my cum in case any other asshats felt compelled to put their mouths on what belonged to me in the future.

"Fuck, it should be illegal to look that good with spit and precum running down your chin," I groaned under my breath, stretching tall over her again. My dick bobbed against the back of her hand as she used her palm to wipe at her mouth, her curiosity rolling over me as I reached for the over- head compartment. "Is your pussy all wet for me, beautiful girl?"

"Like a slippery slope," she confirmed with a filthy grin, and I fumbled to find the condoms I'd brought faster. The universe took mercy on me, and my fingers stumbled across the sharp edges of foil. Retrieving it, I dropped the small square by her knees on the mattress and her brows laced in question at the red wrapper.

"Roll the condom on me, and get it nice and lubricated so I can fuck you with it," I said, and a small laugh bubbled out of her sore lips when she traced the tiny designs on it. I couldn't even pull myself away from her face for a single second to see what had her so entertained.

"Why are there strawberries on the packaging?" Serena asked, and my belly convulsed with amusement. She ripped the little foil with her gleaming teeth while waiting for my answer, and I held back a grimace when I saw the light pink color of the inside.

I'd love nothing more than to feel the walls of her sex clinging to my bare cock, but I couldn't demand she take birth control. I was aware that shit had a long list of side effects, and if losing some sensitivity was all I had to suffer through, then so be it.

"Even though the only thing I want you savoring while sucking me off is *my* taste, you insist on using condoms, so I got us some strawberry flavored ones." I hissed when she grabbed me again, gentleness flying out the window with the way she squeezed the one-eyed monster begging for a sliver of her attention. "I want you to enjoy being on your hands and knees as much as I love watching you there."

"So thoughtful," she hummed against my crown as she worked the latex down my length, taking an experimental lick, her flat tongue peeking beneath my engorged flesh. My hands tightened on the drawer's handles when she smacked my dick across her cheek, once, twice, before sinking the whole thing in her mouth again.

Despite every emotion known to mankind running rampant in my brain at the blatant display of her experience when it came to sucking dick, one reigned supreme. Fucking *appreciation* at the way she knew what she was doing, at how much she enjoyed going down on me. I bet she felt like a goddess, seeing the amount of restraint it took not to come down her throat every time she hollowed her cheeks and I hit the back of it.

I'd fucking rob a life for her if it meant I got to experience the extensive TLC she was performing on my dick every day from here on out.

"Mmm..." She swirled her tongue over the sensitive slit on my tip, a Cheshire grin pulling at her lips. "It does taste good, maybe even better than you do."

Right, that's it.

She's had enough fun.

Running my hand down her braid again, I used it to detach her from my cock like a leash. Gasping, her body flailed in the air as she dropped ass first, back on the mattress. It was my turn to crawl to her, unable to remove my gaze from the curvy bronze lines of her body, flaring out on her chest, pulling in at the middle, and then opening back up again as I propped her thighs over mine, settling between her legs.

"You're going to pay for that," I said, carrying out my threat by ripping her vexing bikini bottoms off. Her eyes squeezed in pain, but exhilaration was present there too once fresh air flowed to her sopping pink cunt.

Her naked chest puffed out with challenge as she replied, "I'm counting on it, Alsford."

The weight of my hard length settled on her swollen flesh, our second heartbeats basically in sync wherever we connected. A vortex of heady sensations ravaged my insides like a category five hurricane as I grasped Serena's chin, ensnaring her fleeting gaze with mine.

"Keep one thing in mind, Serena." With my other hand, I worked the elastic band on her hair loose until it popped free like a dark halo when I forced her head on the pillow, gripping her throat tight. Her nervous gulp tickled my palm, but I held firm, making sure my next words imprinted in her mind.

It was all fun and games until I got hit by a revolving door again.

"When I sink into you this time, I'll be the last man ever allowed to take you. When you need your pussy filled, you come to me. When you need your pussy licked, sucked, and slapped, you come to me. When you need someone to talk to, someone to hug you and hold you, you'll do all that stuff with me," I commanded, my voice grave with the importance my statement carried. Fierce possessiveness colored my tone red, but there was something deeper coiling underneath. Something that had been there since the first time I saw her. I'd tried to tell her once, but she shot me down, and I wasn't ready to get the exact words out just yet. But I was basically paraphrasing them at this point, hiding my true intentions under complex sentences, laying the ultimate decision at her feet. "Are we on the same page? No more running away. I can't do this for a second time, baby. I can't live without you. It doesn't matter what you have to tell me."

I made it clear yesterday that I didn't care. Whatever it was, we'd face it together, not apart. Not anymore.

A tidal wave of feelings broke on Serena's face, and what was painted there had a sharp pain searing across my chest. My beautiful girl was in disbelief that someone was willing to tie their life to hers, to want to listen to her, to be there for her without judgment because she was fucking worth that and more. It was obvious her mangled soul had gone through a lot, but it shone like gold in my eyes. All those jagged scars added to her beauty by providing depth to her character.

With shaking hands, she cupped my face, breathing a word that would've made me kneel if I was standing up. "Yes."

A blinding inferno raged, and all I could see and feel was pure fire coursing through my veins and spiraling around us like a tornado as I captured her lips with mine. Tugging her hips up, I positioned myself at her entrance and, with one firm thrust, slammed myself home after so many years of heartache and longing.

Our mouths fell open at the same time, spilling sounds I was unable to hear over the blood roaring in my ears. Her pussy clenched around my dick, adjusting to the thickness, and I jerked inside her, her tightness tampering with my sanity. I pulled out all the way before slamming to the hilt again, then did it a couple more times until we both floated down from our dream-like state, and every ridge of my cock registered in her brain, her pleasured whimpers flooding my mind.

My head dropped to the juncture of her neck, too heavy for me to keep up as every sensation known to mankind surged inside of me. My hips matched the intensity of my feelings, and I pushed into her so hard I thought I felt the still boat start rocking ever so slightly.

"Holy shit, baby," I managed to utter, barely able to string two sentences together. "You feel so fucking good. *So right.*"

"No more running away, ever," Serena groaned as I licked along the shell of her ear. Her fingernails dug into my shoulder, and her hips rose to meet mine. "You're my everything, Ares. The one that always made me smile when I was feeling down. The one always by my side when everyone else tried to bring me down," she continued, her acknowledgment making my torn-up heart rattle against its blackened cage. "The first and last man I ever loved."

I gasped in her ear, and her lips sought the corner of my mouth out, pressing a tender kiss there that held as much gravity as her admission. "What did you say, Serena?" My thrusts lessened in power, but she kept the movement of our bodies going, all whilst divulging her thoughts, letting her truth out like ripping a Band-Aid off.

"I love you, Ares." Her words grounded me. They destroyed me as she littered the side of my face with kisses, one more drugging than the other. "Your body, your cock, your mind, the way you fuck me. I've never been able to get over you. You're a force of a man, and I'm obsessed with everything that has to do with you. I'm in love with you, baby."

I love you, Ares.

Oh, how she undid me with one sentence. A sentence that irrevocably tied her soul to mine with an impenetrable metal lock. I returned one of her many kisses, fueling all things that sat on the tip of my tongue there. Passion collided, and need and love overflowed out of both of us.

I couldn't say it back, not yet.

Not because I didn't reciprocate her feelings, because I did. But we both had things left to discuss, and whatever it was that pumped fear into her whenever she thought about opening up to me would be flushed away the second I showed her I accepted her completely.

"No." I wrenched my mouth away from hers, stilling her hips and mine at the same time when I felt the beginning of my release crest inside me.

"No?" Her brows bunched, confusion splayed across her expression.

"I've been inside you for barely five minutes after ten fucking years. You're not going to make me come prematurely," I complained, and her eyes softened, that beautiful smile of hers making an appearance.

"I'll take anything you give me." She sucked on the skin of my neck, grazing the start of my scruff with her bottom teeth, before biting my chin playfully.

Shit, could she be any more enticing?

I was trying to hold myself back, but just being in her presence made me want to explode.

"Don't settle for scraps from anyone, Siren. Least of all me," I said harshly, hoping the lesson sunk in her head. "I'm planning on handing you the world; anything you want, just ask for it, and it's yours."

Her eyes moistened, and she struggled to get the friction

between us going again, despite my hold on her hips barring her movements. "Right now, all I want is to come."

Growling low under my breath, I promised myself nothing but burned beans for a week straight if I ruined this, and flipped us over, sitting her fully on my dick, my view from below as glorious—if not more so, than it was from above. Serena's eyes rolled to the back of her head as a result of me being balls deep in her, her hips gyrating lightly, trying to get used to my encroachment.

"Then ride me, baby. Milk my cock with your tight cunt," I demanded, and her hands fell on my chest, pushing her breasts out as she worked herself up and down my length in a frenzied fashion that had heat pooling at the base of my stomach.

"How's that?" she asked, a little moan escaping at the end of her question.

"Perfect, Siren. You're fucking perfect," my voice echoed loudly, betraying the depth of my craze for her. Holding on to her waist, I started pistoning my groin up at hers, balls slapping against her ass with every inward stroke. "Lean down and grab the headboard. Let your tits bounce on my face."

She followed my instructions to the T, smothering me with those fun bags I'd use as my personal pillows every night if given the chance. I pulled a nipple in my mouth, staring at her distraught face, pleasure filling every crevice of my body at all the concentrated jubilation I found there.

Up, and then down.

Up, down.

Up, down.

I got a good rhythm going, and her breathing got heavier and deeper as her clit benefitted from my picked-up pace, rubbing against my skin. Her hair smacked the arch of her ass when I upped the suction on her breasts and controlled her speed by digging my fingers into her thighs.

"Fucking hell, you're something else, Ares Alsford." Her scream bounded across the room, and I closed my eyes, letting the moment soak in. All the love she showed me today filled up the cracks of my heart.

"*Your* something else. Only ever yours," I confessed, because no one else had ever owned me as wholly as she had. No one else had ever owned me other than her period. It didn't matter the marathon I ran every day to distance myself from her. It had no end.

"Shit, babe, I—" Serena started, but I silenced her with my lips on her sweaty forehead, closing her in on my embrace, our torsos sliding together.

"Shh, I know, Siren." I smoothed a hand down her long strands, and she collapsed entirely on top of me. Our releases crested at the same time, and I gave her the green light, so we came together. "Let go, beautiful. Come apart on my cock."

The sound of our skin slapping mixed with her moans until she tensed and then exploded. Her pussy walls clenched around me, urging my balls to tighten, my muscles seizing until they ached. Cum pulsed through my shaft, my cock jerking wildly inside of her as she pulled everything from me.

All I had to give, Serena Laurent took, but this time she showered me with her love and affection too.

CHAPTER TWENTY-ONE
SERENA

F our days passed in the blink of an eye.

As usual, when I was with Ares, all of my worries muted in the background. They paled in comparison to what he brought to the table. Everything Cape Cod had to offer—you name it, we did it in a few short days. From eating eccentric ice cream scoops heaped on fresh, buttery waffle cones for breakfast every morning to taking a glimpse at what the ecologically fragile peninsula held by boating across its waters, seeing seals flop on tidal flats, and even a whale come up for air.

We mostly coasted along the Upper Cape, and while I really wanted to pass through a cranberry bog, harvesting season wasn't until much later, so the view wouldn't have been all that exciting. Instead, Ares took me horseback riding on the beach while the sun set, and it was one of the most liberating moments I'd had in a long while. Feeling the wind shift through my hair, sand grains rub against my skin, and Ares's sweet kiss when the last embers of the sun died off was pure magic.

The first hit came as Ares and I were climbing the stairs of a lighthouse he used to sneak into all the time as a kid, and my phone buzzed in my purse with an incoming call from Sam. I declined because it wasn't a great time and swiftly slipped it back in my purse, but not before noticing I already had three missed calls from him.

I hadn't been on my phone at all lately. Ares had been keeping me pretty busy with extracurricular activities both outside and inside our cabin. I lived and breathed him. It didn't matter that he hadn't said he loved me back because he showed it every time he made sure I'd had enough orgasms. I lay boneless beside him every night, so deep in sleep, I could've missed an entire tsunami. It was domestic bliss at its finest. The yacht had all the necessary equipment a standard apartment would, and even though we spent most of the day exploring and having fun, at night, I refused to step foot outside.

I cooked, and he offered to help, but I declined, saying that I was too young to die of a fire yet, so he took it upon himself to thank me by trading in his dessert and having *me* instead. Afterward, we fought over what movie we wanted to watch like old times before settling for an ambiguous mystery film and forgetting all about it ten minutes in by making out on the bed middle-school style.

I was not looking forward to heading back to Astropolis tomorrow afternoon, and today would mark whether I was going to be doing it alone or not. We both got swept up in the excitement that was being together for the first time ever, and we functioned as if we'd always been a couple. I put off the nasty part of this trip until the very last moment, but the music had come to face me earlier than I expected, and I needed to rip off what I had to say like a Band-Aid sooner rather than later.

"Are you okay back there?" A few steps ahead of me, Ares twisted his head, worriedly looking at my heaving chest. "You sound short of breath."

"That's what usually happens when one has to climb up four flights of stairs," I snarked, holding on to the concrete wall as we neared the top. A thin sheen of sweat covered my body, and I was worried I'd catch a cold with how drafty this place was. Random air currents would raise the edges of my powder-blue skirt, and my whole back was exposed in my halter top.

"I offered you the option of a piggyback ride, did I not?"

"You're not carrying me up; I'm heavy, and we could fall and plunder to our deaths." I motioned behind me to remind him of the scary set of spiral stairs just waiting for a misstep so they could swallow us whole.

He rolled his eyes, still not facing forward, as if stumbling never crossed his mind. "You're about as heavy as a hobbit, shortcake."

"No." I wrinkled my nose in distaste. "I like Siren just fine. That nickname is not catching on," I continued when he opened his mouth to argue, but soon we were both distracted by the light spilling out from the top of the stairs.

Ares let me walk into the lightroom first, and despite being slightly exhausted, I didn't stop as I passed by the huge lightbulb in the middle—maybe even bigger than my head— my gaze dancing around the open space surrounded by quadrilateral windows. I finally came to a stop by the glass near the catwalk, the small balcony beyond the lightroom. The views were dramatic, and even though all I saw the past few days were sandy dunes and endless choppy turquoise waters, they still managed to rob me of my breath.

"Wow." My voice echoed across the empty space, and Ares's warmth pressed against my back as my head fell on his chest when his arms circled my exposed midriff.

"Beautiful, eh?" he asked, splaying his fingers on my stomach. There wasn't a moment in the past few days where he'd stopped touching me. It was like he needed to have his hands on me the whole time. "Leo and I discovered it while tailing Isabella on one of her dates one time. You can say she was less than pleased when we burst right into the lighthouse shortly after them. They thought they'd been caught by a guard or something."

Laughter rumbled up my chest at his serious tone, despite the thought of having to face Leo and Eli eventually, making me slightly lightheaded. Ares was super close to them, and I had a sinking suspicion they wouldn't be too pleased when they found out about us. Based on the facts that they had, their feelings would be more than valid. I hadn't been the nicest person to Eliana at the time, but I'd been drowning under a pool of problems, with no one around to teach me how to swim. So, repairing my broken relationship with her had never been at the forefront of my mind.

Our friendship was amazing while it lasted. The kind every young girl dreamed of until teenage hormones hit and razed everything to the ground. Couple them with an overbearing father and conflicting interests from third parties, and you had an unsalvageable mess on your hands. But I didn't need to be friends with them. All I wanted was for them to accept me, so Ares didn't feel compelled to choose between us. I didn't want him to lose his best friend, and I didn't think I could bear losing him either.

"What kind of creeps crash a girl's date, Alsford?" My heartbeat fluttered when Ares's pinkie slipped past my skirt, his whole hand following suit and meeting nothing but soppy, naked skin. I'd listened to his instructions, making myself always available so he could get his pleasure and provide me with mine too.

He groaned, his chin meeting the crown of my head, and I widened the distance between my legs, so his fingers got to sweep through my folds more easily. Ares's index quickly found my clit as his middle finger gathered some of the wetness at my core and glided it over the rest of my pussy, getting me ready.

"I'll let you know, the guy's intentions weren't pure, and Isabella was just fifteen," he argued his case, and I released a very unladylike snort, as I spread my palms on the windows in front of me, not giving a shit about staining the glass with my handprints. He moved in slow, measured circles, honed in on my reflection, his other paw kneading my breast until desire splintered the air around us, embedding in my system with every unregulated inhale.

"Your intentions are pure *filth*," I shot back, my stomach jumping when his hand disappeared from my pussy, but my body lit up like the fourth of July when he spun me around, pressing my weight into the windows.

"We're grown-ass adults, Siren," he rasped into my ear, bunching my skirt below my waist, unzipping his pants in the process, and hoisting me up. I squealed when the glass whined under my weight, and held on to his shoulders. "And if I feel like fucking you against a window until it breaks, I will, because you're mine to do with as I please."

"This place has probably seen more ass than a public restroom stall." My top and bottom lashes met when his tip poked at my entrance, lining up against my sensitive nerves.

"Possibly. I've heard it's quite a popular spot with the locals."

"You bring me to the nicest places." I laced my voice with a heavy dose of sarcasm, my legs starting to tremble on his either side with impatience.

I needed him inside of me. Now.

"It's just a pit stop, Siren." I felt his smirk against my skin, his hands pulling my ass cheeks apart, leaving me exposed to all the humid air inside the lightroom.

"To where?" I moaned in frustration when he kept teasing me with his head entering me the slightest bit and leaving me craving more.

"Heaven," Ares replied before sliding all the way inside, his hips flush with mine.

I gasped, butterflies flying from my pelvis and up to my stomach, locking my ankles behind his back to pull him in closer. Our chests were flush, my soft breasts rubbing up and down his hard pecs as he pulled out and thrust back in. His harsh breaths spread over my neck like a balm reaching into my soul and pulling all the scattered pieces together bit by bit as he set a steady pace, working me on his dick with impressive core strength.

"If there was a dumbest person of the year award, I'd win it," he said, touching my back on the glass, despite my fear, and plummeting into me faster and harder. The unease sprouting in my belly got flushed out by a bigger fire growing larger by the minute. There was a tiny balcony outside anyway. It wasn't like we were going to fall.

"Why?"

"Because there was a time when I thought I'd be able to outgrow this obsession I have with you if I fucked you a couple more times." He laughed bitterly, and blood beaded like broken ruby particles on his neck, pooling under my nail beds. Ares visibly got off on the pain, his gaze growing heavy —darker as his hips met mine like cresting waves crushing aggressively against the shore. "But every minute I spend inside you just makes me want to live with my cock buried in your pussy for the rest of my life. Why are you so addictive, Serena Laurent?"

A loud moan flowed out of my mouth. He made me feel so good in my own skin. So confident and *sane* because I could never stop thinking about him either. It was like he was an extension of me.

"Shh, baby." A wicked grin lit up his face when he saw how close I was getting. "There's a guard that comes to check on the lighthouse every now and again. We wouldn't want him catching us before I make you come."

"I can't—" Another moan escaped as my vision grew blurry. "I can't hold it in."

"Then bite down on my shoulder, Siren," he instructed, and I did, my teeth sinking in his cotton shirt as my walls squeezed his hard length tight, trying to milk every drop of cum out of him.

"Say it again," Ares demanded, and I smiled so lost in my pleasure I could barely see straight.

"What?" I mumbled.

Ares swatted my ass, and that was what sent me over the edge, catapulting me into utter oblivion. "Don't play dumb, Siren. Tell me you love me. I want to hear you say it again."

"I love you. I can hardly call my heart my own because it's so full of you," I screamed out so loud probably every person in a ten-mile radius heard me, as I gave in to the burn in my lungs, my middle winding tighter and bursting into an array of grays and blacks behind my eyes as I rimmed the edge of unconsciousness. My head grew fuzzy, walls contracting around Ares's cock while he continued his rough pace, before joining me a second later on the other side of the aisle with a tortured groan muttered in my ear, exploding inside of me.

Somewhere in the mess of limbs and bodily fluids, his lips found mine in a tender kiss that ripped my heart open and pumped it with so much happiness it was overwhelming.

The crash and fall from the artificial heaven he'd put me in came a little while after us, though, when I felt something dribble down my thigh, and the realization of what had just happened dawned on me.

Ares Alsford had just fucked me without a condom for a second time.

And he finished inside of me—*for a second time.*

CHAPTER TWENTY-TWO
ARES

Serena went limp in my arms.

Even though I was holding her up, her lips stiffened against mine, and her weight turned dead as her legs fell limply by my thighs. I detached my lips from hers, the space between my brows wrinkling when I caught the haunted expression in her eyes. Every trace of an orgasmic glow was wiped off, giving way to terror.

"Serena? What's wrong?" I asked, and she blinked a couple of times as if trying to see past the fog clouding her head. A dark aura settled over both our shoulders, and Serena bit her trembling lip, her eyes filling with tears.

"Let me down," she ordered, her fists colliding with my chest in order to get away from me. "Let me down, *right now.*"

A sob broke free, and I removed my hands from beneath her ass, slowly sliding my dick out of her and letting her fall to the ground carefully. I was stupefied when she didn't even let me fix her skirt over her lap, instead pushing me away like I disgusted her. My heart swelled in my chest, going into overdrive as tears started silently spilling down her cheeks like a broken faucet.

What the hell did I do? The question assaulted my brain as I tucked myself in, and she adjusted her clothes with shaking hands.

"What's wrong?" I pierced through the fog of silence, and her revolted gaze found mine, sending a shot of shivers down my back.

That look...it was the same one she'd graced me with when I cornered her in the parking lot. Hatred tinged with fear.

"What's *wrong*?" Serena parroted, mimicking my tone. Her high-pitched voice echoed in the empty lightroom, and when she gestured to her legs, a pang of realization hit me, twisting up my insides in a tiny million knots. "Can't you see? Your *cum* is running down my leg."

"I-I—" I stuttered, inhaling in through my nose and out.

Dammit, I've done the one thing she is vehemently against.

I pinched my eyes closed, trying to avoid the sight of the white liquid on her pressed-velvet skin because it fucking turned me on when it shouldn't. Serena didn't want it, and I should've done everything to respect her wishes. Instead, I got lost in the moment. "I'm-I'm so sorry, baby. I forgot to put a condom on in the heat of the moment. I'm so sorry. I didn't mean to do that."

I backed my apology with as much remorse as I could, feeling bile rise up my throat when she crossed her arms, facing away from me as if not able to bear the sight of me. Gaze fixed on the abysmal ocean, beyond the rugged cliff where the lighthouse stood, she didn't make a move to wipe me off her skin. There was nothing we could use up here other than our own clothes. I'd sacrifice my shirt, but something told me my hands on her was the last thing she wanted right now. So I stood a few inches behind her, staring at the back of her glossy brown locks, trying to dig a hole in the ground with my shuffling feet to keep from getting close.

"You can't go around getting lost in the heat of the moment," Serena chided. "How many times have you been inside one of your exes without a condom since you're so forgetful?"

"Never. I never forgot with them." My response was immediate, ringing true.

There had been no one else that made me lose my mind like Serena. I was usually controlled, my movements measured with cold precision, trying to extract as much pleasure from my partners as I could. But with Serena, everything was frantic. Urgency oozed out of every pore in my body, as if I'd die if I didn't get inside of her soon enough. It made me hasty, my memory sloppy.

"Oh, so I'm the sole recipient of your memory lapse. Lucky me," she huffed, irony permeating the air.

"Serena, I'm truly sorry," I murmured and tried my luck by getting closer to her, resting my hands on her hips. She turned into a solid block of ice beneath my touch but didn't push me away, so I considered it a small win. "Come on, we'll just get a Plan B pill on our way to the boat, and I promise you I'll fucking glue a condom on my dick."

"Yeah? Well, where were you the first time I needed a Plan B pill?" She spun around, her brown eyes glossing over with every shade of pain in the emotional rainbow.

My brain turned to mush as I tried to decipher what she meant, but came up blank. "What?"

Serena gathered my hands in hers, not because she

needed the attachment, but because she was looking to hurt me with her white-knuckle grip. I let her exert her energy, numb to any physical pain she had to offer. It was much better than the emotional one anyway, muting my receptors with a suffocating blanket.

"This isn't the only time you forwent using a condom with me, Ares," Serena spat, cocking her head at me as if I was slow and needed special instructions to function. "Where were you then? Why didn't you hunt me down to shove a Plan B down my throat then?"

"I-I assumed you were on the pill when you didn't ask me to put one on." My chest rose and fell faster when I realized how stupid that statement sounded once I said it out loud. Truth was, I hadn't even thought about protection when I had her the first time, but neither of us were virgins, and I'd caught her talking with her friends once about contraceptive methods, so I just...I didn't pay it much mind.

Serena's lips stretched with an empty smile. "Well, you know what they say about assuming."

"What are you talking about, Serena? Did-did something happen?"

Fuck, I'm stuttering again.

Why am I stuttering so much?

It must have been a byproduct of my pulse flying through the roof. My veins pumped blood faster when she pressed her back against the glass, keeping a vice grip on my wrists and pulling me to the dirty floor with her. Our knees met on the ground, and it was all I could do not to pull her on my lap and erase the affliction from her expression.

"A lot happened."

"Like what?" I asked through my teeth, unsure if I

needed an answer. Intuition was telling me what was about to come out of her mouth next would tear me apart.

"What do you get when you mix a sperm with an egg, Ares?" Her question was hollow, and her next words slashed down my throat like an ax perched at the base of my neck, plundering toward me with enough force to detach my head from my body. "*A baby.*"

My bones froze over, turning into a solid block of ice. One punch to my arm and I would've shattered on the ground, pieces of me scattered all over the place. They'd need decades to collect all of them.

"No." I shook my head, trying to pull myself together. The only thing that motion contributed to was making me more lightheaded, a vortex of different conclusions frying my brain up like scrambled eggs. "You didn't—did you..."

"What are you asking me?" Serena's sharp voice revitalized my determination to get to the bottom of what she was saying, and I gathered all my strength together, slumping forward, disbelief and dread coloring my tone.

"Were you pregnant? Do I have a kid?"

"Well, having sex without a condom does have its consequences," she said conversationally, prompting me to snap to action.

Twisting my wrists in her hold, I switched our positions, and I was the one holding on to her now. Her eyes flared with fear at the severe scowl on my face, and I tried to take it down a notch by setting my lips back in a straight line. "Give me a clear-cut answer, Serena."

She worried her bottom lip between her teeth, her gaze flighty as she took three heady breaths before pinning me with a stare and changing my entire perspective on life with two hushed sentences. "Yes, and no. I was pregnant with your baby, but it was never born."

My jaw went slack, my heartbeat filling my ears until I wasn't able to hear anything else over my labored breaths.

Pregnant with my baby.

Serena Laurent had been pregnant with *my* baby. My little son or daughter, and I wasn't finding out until ten years later.

Pregnant. Pregnant. Pregnant.

The word played in a continuous loop in my mind, like a car speeding down a racetrack with broken brakes, having to circle back and forth a thousand times until it ran out of fuel.

I stared hard at her exposed midriff, my hand hedging forward without an elaborate thought process. All I wanted at the moment was to feel where my baby had once been, and in between all the thoughts shuffling through the open tabs in my head, one reigned supreme.

Why was my kid never born? It had to have been at least eleven by now.

"Oh my God." Relief flooded me when Serena let me touch her, her palm closing in on mine, our fingers looping together on her flat belly. I imagined it swollen, a beautiful Serena glowing with pregnancy as I kissed her womb over her skin, deliriously happy at us becoming a family of three. But the dream dissipated when I blinked again, and my eyes stung with what could've been if I hadn't let the inadequacy I'd felt fester into abhorrence and gone after her. "Did you have an abortion?"

My head snapped up to catch her answer, and despite the fact that I would've loved being a dad, I wouldn't have blamed her if that was the decision she'd taken. At the end of

332

the day, it was her body, her choice, and she'd had no support system. Serena's face held grief, sadness, and a myriad of other darker feelings. I felt like I was staring at a broken mirror, but the biggest piece...it held vehemence.

"No abortion," she said forcefully, pressing our hands tighter together on her stomach as if the idea physically made her sick. "I didn't even know I *was* pregnant until one day my stomach suddenly started cramping, and blood, unlike period blood, rushed between my thighs. I miscarried six weeks in."

It was like someone pulled the plug, and my brain emptied out of all thoughts. Loss crashed into my heart with the air of a thousand armies, making it its stomping ground and laying an eternal claim. Without tact, I dove forward, Serena's shock reverberating down my mouth and through my system when I kissed the delicate skin of her stomach.

"I'm sorry. I'm so sorry, Serena." A few stubborn tears rolled down my cheeks, and now we were both crying as her warm hands cradled the back of my head, a gasp befalling her lips when she felt the wetness on my face. "Why didn't you tell me? You were still here when it happened, no?"

"I'd been alone for so long at that point, shunned by everyone, and I also thought you'd left me, so I didn't see the point in telling you. It would do nothing other than hurt you..." She trailed off, rolling her fingers through the strands of my hair, trying to calm both herself and me down. "Or maybe elate you. I didn't even know if you wanted kids."

"Something like that would've never made me happy. Never," I barked, straightening up. Serena's eyes widened at my abruptness, and I brought my face flush with hers, kissing her mouth, our tongues tasting the saltiness of each other's tears. "I want everything with you, Serena. All you have to offer. Were we young? Yes, but we would've made it work."

With her hand on my neck, Serena pushed me back, determination running through her gaze, and I felt an after-shock coming when her cheeks pinked and her mouth dropped open like she had more to say. I didn't know how much I could take, but I'd rather keep all the hits closer together than spread out over time.

"That was kind of the beginning of it all. The initial scratch that started the bleeding," she started, streamlining the rest of her sentence. "Shortly after I graduated, I moved to Boston, and as you know, started dealing with some heavy drugs after getting mixed up with the wrong people. One of those people was my boyfriend at the time. He was a junkie that owed a lot of money to the wrong people, and he..."

"And he?" I urged softly, despite not liking where this was going.

"And he sold me in order to pay it back," Serena breathed out, her grip tightening on my throat as if she needed to feel me, to distance herself from the memory. My jugular pounded beneath her fingertips, violence pulsing through my veins and painting my vision blood red. "On the eve of my twenty-fifth birthday, he told me he had something exciting planned and drove me to suppos-edly one of the hottest clubs in town. The area seemed sketchy to begin with, but he'd promised me free coke, and I was already buzzed, so I didn't notice where I stepped into."

"What happened?"

"I had a bag forced on my head, and next thing I knew, the world went blank before I woke up tied to a bed. My head was pounding so hard and the world around me was so grainy, I didn't even realize what was being done to me until it was too late."

Out my nose and in through my mouth. I tried to breathe normally, but my body buzzed with erratic terror for her, savagery unlike anything else I'd experienced, distilling my blood until it was made out of revenge and brutality.

"Where did you step into, Serena?" I prompted, my middle bottoming out when she confirmed my worst fear.

"A brothel I wasn't allowed to leave," she pushed out with a heavy sigh, her shoulders dropping a whole two inches as if some sort of invisible weight was lifted off her. "I was forced to do a lot of things I didn't want to do. It's all better now, but I had to go through extensive therapy to get to this point. I still don't like it when men touch me. Your touch has been the only exception for some reason."

"You were raped?" I fell back on my ass, not even being able to keep it together for her. "You were forced against your will more than once?"

Concern marred the lines of Serena's face because of my reaction, but she nodded as if wanting to move past this dark time in her life already and couldn't do so without me knowing the truth. "Yes, I was high during most of it, so I mostly remember pieces of the puzzle, not the whole thing." Her eyes squeezed like what she did remember was enough to give her nightmares daily, and she shrugged. "You can almost call it poetic justice. What was done to me was nothing, unlike the things my father subjected Isabella to. At least I'm still alive."

The veil of anger parted slightly, allowing for disbelief to filter through.

Justice? Where the hell did she see the justice in this?

Not even Leo would've considered this a favorable

outcome, and he was the one that held on to grudges the fiercest out of everyone in our friend group. In fact, if I called him up tomorrow and asked him to help me find every bastard that put his hands on my girl, torture them until they bled out, and bury them in unmarked graves, he would. No questions asked.

"There is nothing fair about this, Serena. When will you stop comparing yourself to your father? You are not to blame for *his sins*," I said as a plan started forming in my brain. "What was done to you was cruel, and everyone involved in it deserves to be punished, starting with the cunt of an ex-boyfriend of yours that I will rip limb from limb."

Viciousness crawled over my bones like slithering smoke, and Serena's pupils dilated, scenting the truth blanketing my statement. She'd just given me a new purpose that I would see to it because the only other alternative was letting the people who hurt her walk away unharmed, and I couldn't have that. I'd die before allowing that to happen.

"He's dead already." She crushed all my dreams with three short words. "Overdose. When I got out, I went to look for him to...I don't know, make him pay, I guess. But he was already dead, and deep down, I was grateful for it because I didn't want to stain my hands with blood again."

"Again?" I repeated her last word.

Her eyes strayed on the cracks of the wooden floor as if she wanted to crawl there and hide away. "My pimp had an attachment to me. He was the one that would put up with me the most. I was difficult to deal with, and most men didn't want anything to do with me, but he...he enjoyed breaking down my walls." She shuddered at the memory, and I got a vision of me tearing the heart off a faceless man's thorax. "I was turning out to be more of a liability than an asset, though, and once I caught him talking about planning to off me, I took matters into my own hands." Her long lashes slammed into her brow bones as she looked at me dead in the eyes, ripping off the final Band-Aid. "I killed him before he killed me, then escaped out the window."

Bile rushed up my throat, and I couldn't help it. I ripped myself from her, ducked next to the fixture holding the largest light bulb I'd ever fucking seen, and puked my guts out on the floor.

Failing to hold it together, as I'd failed her time and time again.

No wonder she'd hated me for so long.

SERENA

Enough was enough.

My nerve endings were on high alert after Ares puked his breakfast out on the floor of the lightroom, and despite him insisting on being fine, when he clearly wasn't, I steered clear of saying anything more until we'd gotten back on the boat. Even though Ares's reaction was as bad as could be, I didn't think it was because he was scared of me or because he viewed me as a murderer. It was more so the fact that my past experiences were as bleak as could be. And when you cared about someone, you felt their pain as if it was your own.

The proof was in the pudding. I threatened him with bodily harm when he made his way to the driver's side after exiting the lighthouse because he was in no position to drive, yet he still kept his hand perched on my thigh the whole time

I cruised on the road as if needing to assure himself that I was fine—I was there with him. His eyes were glassy, like he was lost in his thoughts, but he set the temperature just the way I preferred and instructed me to stop next to a pharmacy on the way home when I missed. Without a word, he jumped out of the car and saved me from the mortification that was asking for a morning-after tablet by doing it himself.

"Stop taking care of me. I should be taking care of you." He sulked after brushing his teeth, and I placed a charcuterie board on the table, telling him he was only allowed to have the crackers and nuts.

"I'm okay," I said, hopping next to him on the two-seater and popping a dried plum into my mouth. He didn't let me have personal space for long, didn't even look at the food, and slid so close I was pressed against the armrest, inhaling the scent at the base of my neck with a shudder, like he needed it to calm himself down.

"How could you be okay after everything?"

"I've had five long years to chew on what happened, lots of psychologist appointments, and group therapy discussions," I admitted. I'd be a mess otherwise. I wrung my hands together in my lap, seeing the dried-up blood underneath my nails. Fucking hell, I'd mauled him. "I don't think I'll ever be totally fine, but I'm okay."

Ares's hand came underneath my knees, and my lungs bottomed out when he placed my legs on his lap, twisting and massaging my skin until I was pliant in his hands. "Please tell me it got better after that."

The look on his face told me he was ready for round two, and I blew out a large sigh, expelling all my hang-ups. This walk down memory lane was understandably less than pleasant.

"Well, the first year afterward was rough. My addiction got worse, and you already know how that ended, but it did get better after Sam entered my life." His hand stilled, and I rushed to explain to my jealous man. "Sam's my uncle, my mom's brother. Somewhere along the line, he started working for the FBI and looked for me. He was the one that rushed me to the hospital when I overdosed and has been taking care of my case ever since."

Which reminded me that I needed to call him.

"Your case?" Ares questioned, resuming his massage.

My head fell back on the couch as tingles spread all over my body. He knew what he was doing: taking care of me like he said. Always taking care of me, and with every new word I uttered, I relaxed even more, despite the heavy-loaded topic at hand.

"Yes, it's an open investigation; the people that kidnapped me, essentially, have done this to a thousand other women before, sometimes even underage." I shuddered, and he worked the tighter knots on the arch of my foot. "I provided them with the names and physical descriptions they needed, and in turn, they gave me protection. That's why I can't leave the state and why I changed my name. Most of the people that are after me have been caught already, so the rules on what I'm allowed to do have relaxed by a ton, but I still don't have my full freedom yet. Sam says they're closing in on their last lead, so everything might go back to normal by the end of the year, though. I'll be able to travel, and well, live without fear."

The veins on his neck protruded once my reality took shape. The things people watched in movies or in documentaries—I was the real-life embodiment of that. It was a tough pill to swallow, and if he didn't feel like sticking it out with me, I'd accept it. It was a lot to ask of anybody.

"I do understand if you want to put a halt to this—*us*; dating me is not safe at the moment." I tried to gulp all the oxygen I could to stop myself from crying when he didn't answer immediately. "That was why I wanted to give you all the facts before you made a decision."

"What decision, Serena?" Ares asked, his tone grave when I turned to avoid the discomfort of eye contact and rejection. Reaching over, he enveloped my face with one big palm, tugging me down until I sat comfortably on his lap. My hands found his shirt as hope bloomed in my chest at the earnest expression that mirrored mine. "There has never been any decision to be made. I don't have a choice in the matter. You've owned my heart since the moment I first saw you, and I'd rather die than have to live without you. But I don't fucking think I deserve you."

"What are you talking about?" I sputtered as he progressed with his last statement. "Of course, you deserve me."

"Do I, Siren?" He smiled grimly, abandoning my face to shove a hand through his brown strands. "Where was I when you were going through literal fucking hell? Too busy throwing a pity party for myself and dancing to the tune of the world's smallest violin. Goddamn, I even called you a whore—"

"Don't," I cut him off. "Don't let my past affect what we have now." I shook my head, his heartbeat thundering beneath my skin. "If I didn't like you calling me that during intimate times, I would've stopped you. Trust me to set my own boundaries, Ares. I love it when you call me that because it pleases you, and whatever makes you happy makes me happy. That's how love works. And I don't care about where you were. I only care about you being here for me now. We've both done a lot of shit we're not proud of but prevailed despite all of that."

"I love you too." His voice rang loud, leaving no space for doubts. I knew already, yet I gasped regardless. Ares showed me he loved me every single day, but hearing him say it filled me with so much joy I could write twenty love sonnets with the added adrenaline. "Even though you beat me to the punch and said it first, I *felt* it first. Loving you hasn't been easy, but only because it has been from afar. I need you to put me out of my misery and say you'll be with me, Siren. Today, tomorrow, forever. No more time apart."

A sweet taste spread in the back of my mouth when Ares's determined gaze pierced through my inhibitions, and imaginary birds chirped a jovial melody in my head when he offered me everything I wanted on a silver platter.

My breath puffed out over his face, and I blinked through the dusty fog in my brain, making sure that this was indeed real. That my dream man craved every piece of me as much as I did him. "Today, tomorrow, and forever, Ares. No more time apart," I agreed, diving forward to cement our words, but Ares stopped me with a finger on my lips, stretching my bottom one out and retreating with a refreshing chuckle when I tried to bite him.

"Before we seal this deal with a kiss, I need you to agree to a couple of terms." His Crest-white incisors came out in a smile meant to charm. "Number one, I need you to stay with me. At least until this whole situation with the FBI is sorted out. I can't promise I won't do my best to seduce you into staying longer after that, though. I do have some *big* things in my arsenal that could convince you otherwise." Ares adjusted me between his legs, so I *felt* what he was talking about.

"It's not safe—" I tried to argue past the lump in my throat, but his blank stare told me he wasn't really giving me a choice in the matter. I was either going home with him, or he was staying with me. There was no way he'd leave me out of his sight now that he knew I was in danger. "Fine. What's number two?"

"I'm going to need Sam's number, to thank him for being there for you when my head was so deep in my ass I couldn't see straight, and because I have big plans for those still after you," he announced, his smile transitioning from charming to threatening. "And they involve cutting off their heads on a public square for everyone to see for daring to touch you."

CHAPTER TWENTY-THREE
ARES

"Why did you lock yourself in the bathroom?" Serena blinked in question, her eyes a molten brown so sweet they reminded me of the inside of a brownie bite.

The fact that she'd been forced to push herself beyond her limits and take a life to defend hers tormented me daily. There wasn't a moment since we came back from Cape Cod about two weeks ago that I didn't feel my heart squeeze with guilt at everything she'd been through and was still going through as a result of someone else's evil.

She could be dead for all I care.

The mindless words I'd told Eliana came back to bite me in the ass. I wished *I* was dead for not going after her. I wished I'd experienced what she had, so she didn't have to. But most of all, I hoped I could raise her pimp from the dead just so I could kill him myself by detaching his spine from his body, and get my hands on anyone else who touched her, cut their dicks off with a chainsaw, and then follow along with the rest of their limbs.

But if wishes were horses, beggars would ride.

So, to curb even an inch of my bloodthirst, I finally convinced Serena to let me speak to her uncle despite her being on the fence about it for the past week. It took a lot of special treatment on my part, i.e., thorough full-body massages, paying special attention to the bundle of happiness between her legs, making up with Elsa as she was turning out to be a prominent friend in Serena's life, and taking the time to pick her up from work every day on one of my bikes because she liked the feel of the wind shifting through her hair.

A woman after my own heart.

"Have you ever heard of personal space, Siren?" I moved her robe-clad body from the bathroom's entrance, taking in her puffy face and erect nipples, begging me to suck them through the pink satin.

It was seven in the morning on a Saturday, though, and we both needed our fuel. Serena introduced me to these San Francisco Bay coffee capsules that were a game-changer. She even made me purchase caramel and white mocha syrup to showcase my inner white girl—her words, not mine. And fuck, I did because it was about time I embraced the chink in my alpha male armor—I didn't like the taste of coffee but liked the effects of caffeine.

"No," Serena replied, hand resting on my bare abs as I led us downstairs. "I learned from the best." She gave me a pointed look.

I chuckled, kissing the crown of her head. "Fair enough."

I *had* been all up in her business since she moved in. I was even reconsidering signing off her mother's house to her because I didn't want her to leave, even if I kept finding her hair everywhere. Some might say we were moving too fast, but I thought we were ten years too late.

"So what did Sam say?"

"That he thought I was a wonderful man and couldn't wait to meet me."

That he would castrate me if I hurt Serena and would promptly run a background check on me.

Serena's uncle was a peculiar man, to say the least, but fiercely protective and just as regretful as I was for not getting to her sooner, so we tolerated each other.

"That definitely doesn't sound like Sam." She tugged at the hair on my chest, suspecting my lie. "He yelled at me for over an hour, just a week ago, for telling you."

"He told me he regretted it today." I shrugged, turning the kitchen light on.

No, he hadn't.

He'd actually made it really clear he didn't like my involvement with snippy replies to my every question about Serena's case, but he sure did shut up and listen when I told him what I was thinking. We'd been in contact every day for the past few days, finalizing a plan.

"Why aren't you telling me?" Serena stomped her foot on the ground when I powered on the SMEG coffee machine. "You two have been talking a lot lately."

Turning, I found her worrying her lip and decided to pull her in for a good morning kiss, feeling her muscles liquefy. It was all tongue and teeth, and her body melted, pressing against me until there wasn't even a fraction of space left between us. Placing her on the counter, I indulged myself by inhaling as much of her orange aroma as I could and settled my body at the juncture of her thighs.

"You've worried enough, baby. Let me worry about you

for once." My gut clenched tight when she shivered, her mask splitting in two and revealing a very emotionally tired Serena. "Please," I whispered, littering the underside of her chin, neck, and décolletage with pecks when she nodded. Working the knot of her robe loose, I ignored the coffee maker and decided she was going to be the first thing in my mouth this morning.

"What are you doing?" Serena moaned as if she wasn't scratching my scalp already, forcing me lower. Her gaze was heavy, but it didn't stray away from me, watching with fascination as I dragged my tongue flat over her puffy nipple, like I was the lead actor in her favorite porno movie.

"Tasting you." My tone was matter-of-fact as I skimmed my lips over her silky skin, small goosebumps springing in my wake, stopping when I reached her panty-clad pussy.

With a vicious tug of my fingers, the material ripped, and I didn't even bother feeling any guilt. I told her what would happen if she had underwear on that I hadn't bought for... well, myself, whenever I felt like unwrapping her like a Christmas present. She chose to defy me because she didn't like making things easy, and I couldn't complain. I enjoyed working for it.

"You're distracting me from my line of questioning," she complained, almost ripping my hair out when I brushed my nose over her glistening lips, inhaling the tang of her arousal.

"Is it working?" I pressed an open-mouthed kiss against her center, securing my arms around her thighs and scooting her forward until she was perched on the very end of the counter, ready for my taking.

She licked her lips, locked in to where I was spreading my tongue flat, starting from the bottom of her pussy to the hilt, closing my lips when I got to her delicious clit.

"Fuck, it is," she choked out, jutting her hips in an attempt to get closer.

I complied, suckling greedily at the bundle of nerves like she was all I needed to survive. No coffee. No food. Just Serena rubbing her cunt's juices all over my face, her flavor bursting on my tongue like my favorite fruit.

Her stomach quivered under my forehead, her eyebrows knitting together as her legs shook, muffling my ability to hear anything else except for her labored breathing. Her clit swelled in my mouth, pulsing like a live wire as I swiped my tongue over it in fast but measured movements.

"Holy hell, Ares," she panted, tugging on my hair so hard, pain lanced inside my brain, but it paled in comparison to the pain my dick was in at the moment, so fucking hard it could break glass.

Eating her out was so satisfying; I'd made it a point to do it at least once a day, even if we were busy with work. She loved it, loved having my mouth on any part of her body, but especially on her pussy, and I didn't blame her. Not when she let me choke the hell out of her by sliding my cock down her throat as far as it could go and drank down my cum with a pleased smile at the end.

I strained against my shorts and groaned, working quicker to bring her to her release. Stretching her clit in my mouth, I gave it a good pump, once, twice, until she started screaming out my name over and over again at the top of her lungs. I let my tongue glide over it, drawing little figure eights, toying with her sensitive nerves when she broke, her face fracturing with ultimate contentment.

Her voice fled the premises as if she didn't have any power anymore, her mouth parting with a silent scream, thighs tightening around my head like she was trying to suffocate me. I slurped at the cum that rushed down her lips as her back arched, prolonging the sensations of her orgasm.

Freeing one of my hands, I opened the drawer next to us, retrieving a condom, and I heard her laugh as she came down from cloud nine. I lifted my mouth from her soaked folds, just in time to catch her giving me the stink eye, her naked breasts looking like they needed my mouth on them as she tried to catch her breath.

"What the hell, Ares? You've stuffed condoms here too?" She gasped. "The kitchen is supposed to exist for cooking and eating only."

"I do eat *you* out here, occasionally," I said sheepishly.

With a roll of her eyes at my corny line, she reached over to deal with the elastic of my shorts as I ripped the package open with my teeth. Like you kept the utensils for your food within reach, I needed condoms within mine. We weren't ready for babies yet—I was still trying to process the loss of what I'd essentially never had, but it still hurt, like a thorn wedged in my heart. In the future, though, I would love nothing more than to have a little mix of Serena and me running around. When it was safe, after I'd done everything in my power to eliminate anyone that was a threat to her.

Just when Serena had reached inside, her fingers grazing over my dick and making it twitch wanton for attention, the doorbell rang. The loud noise punctured the air drenched with lust and need, and our eyes clashed, her hand freezing, and I felt like I was about to blow.

"Let's ignore it," I whispered, as if whoever was on the other side of the door would hear me all the way from the kitchen. "I'm not expecting anyone."

"No, it could be my food delivery." Serena shook her head, and I almost wept when she removed her hand completely, patting my length with a *poor you* expression I was going to make her pay extensively for when we were alone again. "I ordered some groceries, and they're supposed to arrive today."

"I told you my chef takes care of that." I blew out a frustrated breath as she cinched her robe closed again, dropping the wrapper on the counter next to her.

"Well, I *like* taking care of it, so sue me." She propped her lips on mine in an apologetic kiss before hopping off. I didn't even see the point of having a chef anymore since she monopolized the kitchen every time he was here. I'd caught Gerard giving her the stink eye once or twice. "I'll answer. You see to *that*." Serena motioned at the tent in my pants. The material was stretchy, and it did nothing to hide my erection, since I wasn't even wearing boxers. "And come help me bring the stuff to the kitchen."

She was already moving to the exit, and I stared at my sad buddy, wondering what to do with him. Rubbing one out was out of the question when I heard the heels of her feet skipping to get the damned door. There was no way I was sticking my dick in ice either, so I shut my lids and tried to think of anything displeasing to get this erection down.

Grandmas in walkers, murderous hippos, cannibalistic birds.

The nasty images played like a reel in my head when she unlatched the door open, but what really propelled the de-escalation of my dick was the voice that floated into the house, a touch rough and a ton smokey belonging to a smooth bastard that was used to always getting what he wanted.

"Surprise, motherfucker. Why haven't you been picking up your ph—" Leo stopped abruptly, and my eyes slammed open, my body burning as hot as an iron skillet left forgotten on an open stove when he uttered a single word next, a lot like Joe Goldberg would, "You!"

SERENA

My smile fell from my lips in a matter of seconds, eyes growing to the size of tiny moons when I befell who was standing across from me. My heart pitter-pattered in my chest, and a lump grew in my throat, making it difficult to swallow.

Leonardo Bianchi.

Leo.

The guy my life revolved around for so long. The guy I spent countless nights awake for, plotting and planning on how to win him over to appease my father. The guy I tried to fall for to make things easier but couldn't because I had my sights set on his best friend. His name had been in the forefront of my brain for so long, it was as if it was carved there with a quill, but looking at him now, I found that I hadn't missed him one bit.

There was no doubt in my mind he was an amazing husband to Eliana and an incredible father to Bella. Leonardo had always been fiercely protective over his own people, but when you stood on the other side of the aisle, it wasn't so nice. The thought of being his enemy sprung shivers up my arms.

"Me," I numbly replied, soaking up his gray cigar pants and polo shirt the same vibrant green as his eyes. The mop of curls on his head was unruly as ever, and save for a few added wrinkles around his mouth and eyes, his face was exactly the same too.

"Serena?" His gaze stretched from the tips of my red-painted toes and up to my face, and I blushed under his examination because I was fucking naked under my robe, thanks to Ares. Leo's face was struck as if hit by a thunderbolt when he repeated the question. "Serena Laurent?"

No, I'm her long-lost twin.

Thank God I was prone to filtering my words after living with a psychopathic father because that answer wouldn't have gone over well. Crossing my hands over my chest, I pursed my mouth, trying to gather my wits. Fuck, I knew the time would come eventually, but I was yet to feel comfortable enough to face all the people from my past.

"In the flesh. Hi, Leo." The late August breeze carried my words to him, and even though it was starting to get nippy out, there was a pregnant pause as we stared at each other—well, more so Leo getting re-acclimated with my presence that came like a bolt from the blue.

He'd driven all the way here for Ares, but he'd gotten me instead. Not really a two-for-one special to be excited about.

Somewhere down the line, the silence and disbelief morphed into anger so potent I could taste it on my tongue and feel it brushing against my arms in a static caress that was looking to electrocute. A labyrinth of long-buried memories unveiled in his eyes, and he was confused as to which direction to take first. Leo and I had been at the very least friends for a little while, but all that got flushed out the moment our objectives changed. Based on the darkening of his irises, though, it wasn't one of the good ones.

"What the fuck are you doing here? Where's Ares?" he spat, feet digging on the ground like he was about to charge at me. My back was wet with perspiration springing up in an instant from the stress of the impending showdown, but Leo barely gave any time to respond before shoving past me and pushing inside the house, shouting up a storm. "Ares! Ares!"

Cursing under my breath, I shut the door, going after him. I was jogging, trying to keep up with his long legs, and by the time he stopped in front of the kitchen, I'd gained too much momentum and slammed into him. Leo regarded me with so much disgust one would've thought I was covered in ticks, and I immediately distanced myself.

"Leo," Ares cleared his throat, a few feet away from us now.

He'd probably heard Leo's voice and rushed to intercept, but while doing so, he'd neglected to throw the half-open condom away, and of course, that's where Leo's gaze strayed first, then at Ares's disheveled hair and naked chest, and my skimpily tied robe.

Shit, we looked like we knew each other very well, in the biblical sense. And we did. We'd fucking dusted the passages about Sodom and Gomorrah enough times to paint the town red.

Leo puffed air into his cheeks as if lost for words before his still vibrato rippled across the room. "Give me one good reason why I shouldn't lose my shit right now."

Ares's mouth twisted into a smirk that screamed trouble, so I inserted myself before he said anything he'd regret. He had an *act first, think later* approach that wouldn't bode well for him in the long run. "We can explain."

"I think it's pretty self-explanatory." Leo didn't spare me a look, pinning his best friend with a hateful glare. "Are you fucking her? How long have you known she was back?"

Both of them took a step forward, almost meeting at the

threshold, and my breath caught at the thundering glare on Ares's face. They were both so similar they looked like brothers, save for the difference in eye color, gold clashing with green, Ares's slightly bulkier build, and Leo's few extra inches in height.

"If you want the conversation to remain civil, I suggest you hold your tongue, Leonardo." Ares cocked his head, and a chill raced down my spine at the promise in his voice.

"You're defending her? You're defending her from *me?* Your fucking best friend." Every time Leo blinked, I could see the shifting emotions—surprise and fury fighting for the number one spot. "What, she opens her legs for you, and you suddenly forget what a shit of a human she is? You conveniently forget how she tried to break Eli and me up, almost sent Eliana to the hospital, and had you on the back burner for years?" He angled his body toward me, the vein on his forehead pulsing as he reached me in two short strides. I didn't even feel his hands closing in on my forearms, the weight of his words hitting me like a ton of bricks. "What did you do to him? What fucking lies did you tell him?"

His shaking made my teeth rattle, and I didn't know if it was seeing me with Ares that had him so revolted or just seeing *me* in general. He'd left me alone after my father went to prison. Both he and Eli did. I reckoned they were too tired to keep up the game our parents had started, but they didn't want me near, and that was understandable. Even knowing the truth, I didn't crave a connection or forgiveness from them. Being in Leo's presence brought back a period of my life I wasn't all that nostalgic for.

I knew what I was getting myself into by getting involved with Ares, though. Leonardo had always been a big part of his life, and as protective as Ares was of me, I knew losing his friend would cut him deep, and I never wanted to be the cause of his sadness.

"If you don't remove your hands from her body, I will remove them from you."

Out of my peripheral vision, I caught Ares rushing for us, but Leo's hold was lax enough for me to be able to slip away and place myself between them. My back plastered against Ares's front to lock him in place. His nostrils were wide, his hot breath sliding down my face, and I had to jam my heels on the hardwood floor to keep from slipping.

"Ares, calm down. He doesn't know," I muttered, pushing him back in the kitchen.

Leo's hard as steel eyes were on me, probably wondering what kind of witchcraft I'd performed on his friend to get him to turn against him, his knuckles white by his sides. Steeling my spine, I kept my voice hard as granite as I faced off with him.

"I think you might've suspected already that your father had something to do with me kissing you on my birthday, but he didn't act alone," I started, my voice falling into a cadence like I was getting ready to tell him the bedtime story of his life. Walking deeper into the kitchen, he followed me as if tied by an invisible string. I motioned to the stools underneath the island, where Ares was already pulling three out as if in tune with my thought process. "Take a seat, and I'll tell you the rest."

Much to my dismay, Leo did, and right there, I discovered another way he'd changed since I knew him. If this had happened years ago, he wouldn't even have asked for an explanation, much less stuck around for one. He would've run with his own conclusions, all because he hated my father, and therefore, by default, he hated me. But now, he remained still as Ares and I settled next to each other, our arms brushing like a united front. He sat across from us, taking us in with a barely contained fire in his eyes.

Fatherhood must have really changed him because his muscles bunched with the effort it took to restrain himself when I started talking, explaining the real-life soap opera that had been my life. I started with how I believed Eliana had been aware of our parents' affair, and she hadn't told me. I was mad because if I had known, I might've been able to prevent my mother's death. And finally, I went forth with exposing my father's permanent hard-on for Leo and his questionable ways of encouraging me to pursue him.

Leo's cheeks pinked when he heard about his starvation techniques, and my chest puffed. I wasn't particularly fond of the twinge of pity in his eyes, but it beat the embarrassment I felt after one of his many rejections. Him learning I could barely tolerate him most of the time vindicated me. I would've never gone after someone else's relationship, not if my father hadn't twisted my hand when it came to Leo and Eliana.

I made sure to highlight that, stretching my words out until they were embedded in Leo's brain. Ares caressed the curve of my back with his thumb during the whole process, encouraging me silently. My throat was parched after all the talking, but something told me it wouldn't be wise if I asked him to bring me a glass of water. Seeing Leo simply shake me rattled him so hard, he was ready to knock him out.

I felt like I was in the middle of a dick-measuring competition between two predators. One wrong move on my part, and they'd dive over the island to attack each other. Spirits ran high, and Leo was conditioned to think the worst of me for years, so he was having difficulties accepting my version of the story.

"So what you're telling me is that you essentially knew that your father was to blame for Isabella's murder since he was so hell-bent on using his own daughter to keep Eliana and me apart." Leo scowled, and I spoke fast, cutting off his train of thought before it had time to fester.

"At first, I thought he wanted me to be with you because your family was the wealthiest in town, and my father would settle for nothing less than the cream of the crop. When he picked up on your relationship with Eli, his mask started to slip, and that's when I realized." I twisted my thumbs on the marble, nerves ramming my gut because I hadn't told anyone this. Not even Ares. But I didn't see the harm in admitting it now. Carter Laurent was dead. There was nothing he could do to me from beyond the grave. "I searched his office for any clues I could find and came across a binder with some peculiar locations. I didn't know exactly what they were, but I handed them off to the police regardless, and well, a week later, they had sufficient evidence on my father to make an arrest."

Both Leo and Ares's breaths hitched at my confession. It was like I pulled some invisible plug, and every noise ceased for a couple of seconds. Even the birds outside stopped chirping their morning melody.

Leo shook his head, a laugh lacking any humor bubbling out of his throat. "No, *my* dad found—"

"The rest of the girls that had gone missing around the same time your sister did?" I finished his sentence. "It wasn't like they ever saw my father in person. He wasn't the one actually kidnapping them. He just gave the orders. Hence why their testimonies weren't enough to bring him down or link him to any crimes; they needed more concrete proof."

"If that was the case, they would've told us," he argued.

"I asked for my involvement to be kept a secret." I shrugged, ruining all his counterpoints. It wasn't my intention to spar with him, simply to bring the truth to light. "They used the locations as a guide to try to find a physical link between him and them, but not as evidence. It was never brought up in court because the second my father saw the binder, he would've known I'd betrayed him, and I didn't want that. Even behind bars, he had connections, and at the time, I was solely dependent on him. I couldn't afford the kind of protection you did."

"Why am I even surprised?" Ares breathed, looking at me like I was the entire ocean in a drop. Leo faded in the background, the pride on Ares's face making me slightly dizzy and delirious with love. "You're amazing, Serena Laurent."

God, I wanted to jump him.

The air between us sizzled with untapped chemistry, coercing me to lean entirely against him and his palm to weave through my hair until he was pressing his lips on my forehead.

A gurgling sound came from Leo's direction, as if watching us together made him want to hurl. I cringed, trying to disconnect from Ares, but he didn't cave to appease Leo and tucked me into his side.

"She's a liar." Leo's palm crackled against the marble slab. "Just like her father. The sooner you remove your rose-colored glasses, Ares, the better, or it's not going to end well for you."

"Are you threatening me?" Ares asked with a deadly

calm, his pecs flexing under my cheek, and he felt hot like he didn't understand why Leo didn't take my word for it like he had.

It was clear to me. The reason stood in the parallels of the relationships I'd built in the past with both men. They sat on opposite ends of the spectrum. The only thing that tied Leo and me together was revenge and bad blood. When that dissipated, so did our rocky friendship. Whereas Ares was...he was my soulmate. There was no other way to explain the invincible draw or why we gelled so well together. He was my missing piece, my better half. He was inclined to see the good in me.

It would take time for Leo to come around.

"Never. You're my brother. I'd never hurt you," Leo said incredulously, kicking his chair out and pointing his finger at me. "But she—"

"She's my girlfriend, and I love her." Ares's arm turned into a steel band around me. Heat melted my insides into goo, and I bit my lip, my gaze bouncing between them. "We live together. If you hurt her, you hurt me."

The feeling of a win diluted inside of me until I couldn't recognize whether I was enjoying this moment or not. There was only one direction our meeting was heading toward today, and that was south. It didn't matter how many times I tried to smooth out the bumps along the road. Healing took time.

"Fine." Leo's shirt stretched under the strain of his muscles, his stature growing formidable as he rolled his shoulders, nodding once as if respecting Ares's wishes. "Your fucking funeral, Alsford. Don't come to me when she leaves you high and dry," he said and then left just as abruptly as he'd shoved his way inside, leaving behind him a wind of despair.

Ares stared blankly at the space where Leo had been, like if he tried hard enough, he could make him materialize again. Cupping the side of his face, I turned his head to me, my heart splitting in two at the poorly masked melancholy I found there.

Dammit, this was what I was trying to avoid.

"I'm so sorry," I apologized.

I was the guilty party in this, despite my best intentions.

Ares squared his shoulders, dragging my hand to his lips, and kissed the inner part. "You have nothing to be sorry about. It's not your fault he's a hothead."

The blame game never ended well, so I relented.

It didn't mean I was giving up, though—quite the opposite. Leo's weak spot stuck out like a blot on the landscape. I knew exactly who I needed to poke to get him to see reason.

CHAPTER TWENTY-FOUR
SERENA

"You're going on another trip with him?" I choked on a sip of water, scanning a flighty Elsa who was shoving the last bite of a cream cheese bagel in her mouth. We were having brunch after work at a little corner café we frequented next to our building with cute bistro chairs and white wallpaper full of pink and red flowers. The whole place was very cutesy and looked as if it was vomited on by the Goddess of spring.

"I know, right? I'm acting stupid, but it's like I can't say no to him." Elsa spoke in between bites, scratching the back of her neck. Her hair was up in an elegant bun, so I currently had a full view of her pinkening skin under the weight of my judgmental stare. "I've decided to live in the moment and see where it takes me."

So that was what happened to "we're just having some fun."

Goldberg must have really known how to put his dick to good use if he'd managed to suck all the sense out of Elsa. They were already planning a second trip after the one in Napa ended with multiple orgasms in one night. She was the *get married and have kids as soon as possible* type, and Aaron was, well, the exact opposite. Not to say that she didn't have all the necessary assets to get him to reconsider, and I sincerely hoped that was what he was doing, or Elsa was in a straight trajectory toward heartbreak town.

I sighed, tossing my brown locks over my shoulder. I was letting it go. I wasn't the relationship police after all. Sometimes the more you interjected yourself into a matter, the further away the other person drew from you. "What did his father want? You never ended up telling me."

"Just to meet me. He thought it was cool that I was also a lawyer, but made it pretty clear that he believed I was wasting my degree working where I am now." She rolled her eyes, placing a couple of tens on the table to cover the entirety of the bill before I could stop her. I'd invited her out as I was waiting for my...date, for lack of a better term to show, so it was only fair I paid, but Elsa wasn't having it as she slipped her wallet back in her purse and settled the strap over her shoulder. "Ugh, the superiority complex made me mad like you wouldn't believe."

Oh, I would. I've been around enough people with a superiority complex. I can fill ten diaries full of nasty experiences with them.

I made a mental note to give Elsa a crash course on all the darned ways rich people made you feel less than, but subtly...I didn't want to blend my past with my present. The people that knew Amelia Duante would continue knowing Amelia Duante. Serena Laurent was reserved for family only. I didn't worry about anyone else other than my immediate circle recognizing me. A long time had passed since my father went to jail. I trusted most of them had moved on already.

"But anyway, Elliot is here to pick me up. Are you sure you're fine? Your friend still hasn't shown up." Her gaze wandered around the busy café, and I felt my body temperature rise at the thought of who I was about to meet with.

I glanced at my hot chocolate on the round table. I hadn't gotten anything to eat since I didn't think I could stomach it with my nerves on high alert, but I probably should've gone for something iced.

"Yeah, I'll be fine." Nodding, I extended my arm for a side-hug as the store's bell chimed in the background. Elsa's earthy perfume sunk in my loosely buttoned dress shirt when she reached down. "Have a fun weekend, but keep a clear head," I whispered sternly in her ear, and she winked when she pulled back in a *you got it* manner.

"See you later, Amelia." She blew me an air kiss, and I waved goodbye, dread pooling underneath my chair like pitch-black soot. Elsa's chatter was comforting, distracting me from what I'd willingly subjected myself to.

Dealing with Leo was one thing. My father was who he was, but my conscience was guilt-free when it came to the green-eyed man. Leo wasn't the villain in my eyes, but he sure as hell wasn't a victim either. Eliana was a whole different ball game. My cheeks flamed whenever I remembered what a cunt I'd been to her, spreading rumors and making it my life's mission to get her to feel even an inch of the stabbing pain plaguing my body.

If it wasn't for salvaging Leo and Ares's relationship, I most likely would've put off our impending reunion indefinitely. Embarrassment held my heart in a vice grip, and my brain pulled short whenever I tried to come up with something to say to her. I didn't think a simple apology would cut it. Yet she still went ahead and agreed to meet with me after I stole her number from Ares's phone, and I wondered if it was out of pure curiosity or if she genuinely wanted to see me after all these years. After all, they didn't say time heals all wounds for nothing.

"Why did she call you by your mother's name?" A reluctant voice filtered through my eardrums, and my neck cracked with how quickly I whipped around to take her in.

Wincing, I resisted the urge to rub the back of it, Eliana's presence already making me strive to be the most elegant version of myself. Even back at the ripe age of twenty, she exuded an aura of maturity, her experiences hanging over her head like crown jewels collected after each successfully learned life lesson. At thirty, she was more put together than ever in her neatly pressed silver suit and Dior saddlebag. Blonde curls framed her oval face, and her complexion sparkled under the fluorescent lighting of the room, brighter than her ocean eyes.

She had that glow about her, one that spoke of a fortunate life.

"Eliana?" I mumbled, like I needed to confirm it was actually her.

A smile that hadn't been pointed at me since before we went off to college graced her bubblegum pink lips, and some of the anxiety eased off my rigid posture. Already a much better start than Leo.

"Hi, old friend," she greeted, and I prolonged my blinks to get rid of the stinging in my eyes. If there was one thing I hated from my character progression, it was my innate ability to tear up at the darndest of moments.

"Hi." I chewed on my lip, cocking my head toward the

chair Elsa had recently vacated. "Um, would you like to take a seat?"

"I'd love that," she said, and I felt like I was in a trance as the waiter came in to collect Elsa's plate, took Eliana's order, and she looked at me expectantly. "Well?"

"Ugh..." I thought back to her question, not really fond of diving into all the gory details, and settled for the very top tier of the cake. It would take a while to build up to full transparency. "I decided to change mine when it closed more doors for me than it opened, so I chose Amelia Duante. It made me feel closer to my mom."

"Oh, do you want me to call you that?"

"No, Serena is fine," I cleared up. "When we're alone," I added as an afterthought.

She nodded, and an awkward energy buzzed about the place as we re-acclimated with each other's presence. Conversations and laughter flowed from the tables over, but silence stifled the space between us as Eliana took the time to learn the contours of my face again. I used to hate having her eyes on me; the disappointment that swirled beneath her blues was stifling, but it wasn't present this time.

"Did you go blonder?" I decided to take the lead, a warm-up for the eventual cataclysm.

"You're the first person that actually noticed." Her fingers delved into the back of her hair, and she gave the buttery strands a shake. They settled over her shoulders in shiny waves. "I had to. Leo found a silver hair on my head after one of my kids almost swallowed a Lego the other day. So I totally know who's causing me to age before my time."

"Bella?" I laughed, her name flying out of my mouth before I had time to come up with a reason for how I knew.

"No, my youngest, Matteo," she corrected with a shake

of her head, her mouth pursing in thought. "You know, Bella did tell me she'd caught Ares with a woman named Amelia the other day, apparently *much prettier than Sonia*. I should've put two and two together, eh? It would've been weird for Ares to start dating anyone with your mother's name."

My fingers itched to grab a napkin and rip it apart, but I placed them around my hot chocolate even though it burned my skin, wanting to match her coolness. "She's very clever."

Eliana gave a gracious grin to the guy that delivered her cappuccino, and I ducked my head to hide a smile when he stumbled, walking away. "Too clever for her own good sometimes. She gets sent to the naughty chair at least once a day."

I chuckled because that was the exact vibe I'd gotten from her. A little rule breaker in the making, the exact opposite of her mother. When we were younger, I was the one that always dragged her into shit, and she tagged along because she couldn't say no. "I had a feeling you'd be a strict parent, always a stickler for the rules."

"This feels a bit surreal," she voiced, her porcelain cup clinking as she placed it back on the table after taking a sip. "Sitting across from you, talking normally as if nothing ever happened."

We'd definitely slipped into a conversation with no sweat. I didn't know what to expect after the blowup with Leo or if he'd even told her all that I said, but judging from her relaxed stance, she was probably clued in. Eliana wasn't an angel, even though she came damn close. She bit strategically and didn't rush the process, unlike her husband.

"I take it Leo caught you up with what I told him. I doubt you'd be all that willing to meet otherwise, and I don't blame you."

"He did, but I'd still meet with you regardless, even if what you had done was out of your own volition. I wouldn't have been as friendly, for sure, but I would've liked to know you're all right." She tied her hands together like a diplomat about to give a speech, and I held my breath, hanging on to her every word. "I looked for you, you know. Hired a P.I. to find you and imagined the worst when he got back to me with no information. Obviously, I must've been scammed since you're sitting right across from me, as healthy and put together as ever."

Surprise staked claim across my face, my mouth falling open as I digested what she'd said. I'd never thought I'd hear something like that from her after everything. It felt a lot like she was telling me tales of dark magic and fire-breathing dragons.

"Why? I was fucking horrible to you." My voice was an octave too high, and I continued in a lower timbre to divert attention. "Why would you want me to be okay?"

"I've never prayed for anyone's downfall, Serena, and I wasn't going to start with you. I've dreamt about bitch slapping you more times than I can count, I won't lie," she admitted with a twisted smirk, as if the visual brought her satisfaction. "Being on good terms with you was amazing. You were definitely cruel, but even being on bad terms with you was better than nothing at all."

"I'm sorry." I rushed into my apology, almost cutting into her speech at the end, and her eyes widened, mouth freezing in a half-open position. I'd had the chance to apologize before, but I was too lost in my own vanity. I viewed apologizing as a sign of weakness when, in reality, it took a great deal of character to admit your wrongdoings. "I know it's just words, but I'm truly sorry for everything, Eli. You and Ares were my two biggest regrets—the way I left things with you two. I hated that I believed the worst of you without confronting you about the situation first—*non physically.*"

I shuddered at the memory of our altercation. I didn't remember the whole thing. I was high as a kite, straight out of a Halloween party, but my father's scowl was imprinted in my mind, promising hell when he got called to the detention center after the cops arrested me.

It was *that* bad.

Eli reached across the table, taking my hand in her warm hold, her eyes full of benevolence I didn't deserve. "I believe you, Serena. I've experienced firsthand what Carter was capable of, so many things fell into place when Leo told me what you'd said."

I blew out a breath that was lodged in my throat. For the first time ever, I was grateful my father's reputation lived up to who he truly was. It meant my words didn't fall on deaf ears and made my explanation believable. "At least one of you does."

"He'll come around. I'll talk to him," Eliana reassured, patting my hand before biting into the tiny cookie they'd brought as a supplement to her drink.

I blew on my drink before gulping half of it down, quenching my thirst. "Thank you. I didn't want to come between him and Ares."

"He was just caught off guard and possibly a little annoyed when he realized Ares would choose you over him any day, as if he didn't almost make Saint eat shit once because he was making fun of me." She rolled her eyes at his shenanigans, waving her hand in the air as if it was old news and hitting me with an onslaught of questions she was dying to know. "When did you come back? *Why* did you come back? You and Ares are even living together now, so it must've been a hot minute."

I shifted in my seat, sticking to as much as I was comfortable divulging at the moment. It wasn't that I was ashamed of what I'd been through. I was fucking proud of everything I managed to overcome when the odds were stacked against me. But experiences like these shaped the way people saw you, and I didn't want to be pitied by Eli. Maybe further down the line, I'd tell her, but for this first meeting, we were sticking with a brief summary.

"We actually have only been a couple for about a month, give or take. Things are moving fast, but they make so much sense. It's like I know deep in my bones there's no one else I'd rather be with." I tucked a strand of hair behind my ear.

Ares had given me the choice to move out when it was safe, but I didn't know whether I wanted to. I was getting addicted to falling asleep in his embrace every night, protected against anything and anyone. A few days ago, when I'd come home stressed from work, he'd pulled all the furniture in the living room aside and danced with me to help me relax until we both rolled on the carpet with exhaustion. The other night we decided to break in the Jacuzzi in his backyard after I told him thinking about Sonia and him in it together made me mad with jealousy. He assured me I was the only one he'd held his breath underwater for and the only one whose ass he'd slapped red afterward while taking me from behind in the hot tub.

"She's a thing of my past. You're my future," he gasped in *my mouth as I squeezed his dick to death by clenching my walls around him.*

"And you'll do well to remember that," I groaned, *sweeping up his lips in a possessive kiss.*

My cheeks heated under Eli's knowing gaze, and I shook my head to get rid of the memory. "I came back seven months ago because I decided to take a job offer and ran across Ares three months in, so it has been a hot minute, but not *that* long."

"You seem happy," she observed.

"I am, deliriously so," I confirmed with a firm nod.

"Then it doesn't matter how fast things are moving. You've known each other forever. No need to prolong your happy ever after when both of you guys were forced to spend so much time apart."

Eliana and I shared a grin for the first time—in a long time—on the same side of the battlefield. I used to have a crush on Leo back when I had barely hatched, but I fell in love with a new guy every day in my earlier teenage years. It was nothing serious, certainly not something worth throwing my best friend under the bus for. Having Eliana see me for who I truly was, not the role I was forced to play, healed a part of me I didn't realize was severed.

CHAPTER TWENTY-FIVE
SERENA

"Honey, I'm home!" I screamed at the top of my lungs after kicking the door shut behind me, a huge smile plastered on my face. I'd always wanted to do that, and now I had someone I could do it to.

Today was a success.

The reconnection with Eliana had been instant, like the strike of a match. It might've started out as me approaching her to fix Ares's relationship with Leo, but we'd stayed longer than expected, rebuilding ours from the ground up. She'd been excited when I told her I was an actual lawyer now, and I loved that she'd pursued her dream of opening her own ballet studio instead of sticking with college when she very clearly wasn't into it. We had a lot of catching up to do; we hadn't even set the entire foundation yet, but I was confident we'd get to it.

"In the living room." Ares's voice floated down the hall, and I slipped on my pink fuzzy slippers before racing to greet him with a kiss.

"Hi, baby—" I stopped short when I saw who was standing next to Ares in front of the electronic fireplace. As soon as September rolled in, that thing had been in full use, and even though I liked the toasty atmosphere it provided, right now, it was stifling me as the orange fire helped cast a daunting shadow over *his* frame. "Sam," I muttered, not knowing how to feel about his presence. It usually meant one thing: trouble.

"Serena," he acknowledged in return with that familiar grumble of his, cocking his head. "You don't look all that excited to see me."

"No, I just wasn't expecting you." Shaking my shoulders loose, I glared at Ares when I passed by him and hugged Sam. The scent of fresh pine tickled my nose, helping me ease up a bit as I pulled back, frowning. "I didn't know you were coming."

Despite my uncle's glare, Ares's hands knotted together over my belly button, pressing my back to his front and kissing my temple in a hello. I squirmed as Sam studied him like he wanted to rip his head right off, but remained put nonetheless. This gathering was a lot like I imagined meeting your significant other's parents for the first time would be. Except they'd already talked on the phone, but that did nothing to quench Sam's distaste.

"Yeah, you've been rather busy lately, moving in with random men after less than a year of dating." He crossed his arms, the light of the fire deepening the prominence of his frown lines. "Didn't I tell you to stay out of trouble?"

"Please don't start. I told you I've known Ares since kindergarten." Sighing, I leaned sideways so Ares would stop kissing the side of my face just to make Sam uncomfortable. I could practically feel his smirk on my skin when Sam growled under his breath.

"It's okay, Siren. He's just joking; deep down, he loves me way too much, and this is his way of trying to hide it," Ares reasoned, and Sam barked out a laugh.

"You wish, Alsford. You cost me at least ten grand on surveillance equipment with this move, and it's much harder to hide the cameras in this type of neighborhood." He gazed outside the massive windows taking up the entirety of the living room wall.

There was nothing but grass for a few yards, ending by Ares's recently installed wrought-iron fence and gate. The neighborhood was one of the safest in Astropolis, so he hadn't felt the need for the added security...until I happened.

I could see how it could've been much harder to find hidden nooks and crannies, but also, what the hell had he just said?

"What do you mean?" I took a step away from Ares, breaking away from his embrace. Needing to sit down, I placed my ass on Ares's sturdy coffee table instead of the sectional because it was the closest. Both of them towered over me like opposite ends of the same coin. "Was I being watched in my old apartment?"

Sam nodded grimly. "Twenty-four-seven security; I didn't want to take any chances. There were about a dozen cameras pointed toward your apartment building entrance, so we could capture every angle and maybe one or two toward your balcony and outside your door."

"Wha—" My mouth dropped open and closed like a fish, and I blushed, thinking about all the things they could've witnessed. "Why wasn't I made aware of this? At any point, I could've stood in front of the balcony in a compromising position!"

"Because you would've protested like you're doing now. Besides, you didn't." Sam shrugged like he'd dodged a bullet, except what about all the times I could've picked my nose or had a bad day, and it showed, or invited someone over I didn't want them to see. *Or* simply wasn't fucking comfortable with the idea of being watched.

This had to have been the case in all my previous locations too.

"That still doesn't make it any better!"

"Come on, babe, he was trying to protect you," Ares coaxed, his big palm rubbing between my shoulder blades as he squatted next to me. The motion made my tense muscles fall in line again, and I bit my lip, looking at him like he'd betrayed me.

I preferred when they weren't getting along.

"I hate the two of you together," I confessed, and narrowed my eyes when I saw that Ares was trying to hold back a grin, poking his chest. "You know they're probably watching us now, too."

"Would you rather get murdered while I'm not looking?" Sam asked drily, sucking the air out of the room with the reality of my situation.

As the years passed, the attempts made against my life lessened. I'd gotten comfortable with my new daily life, forgetting all the times a member of the agency had shown up at my door late at night, forcing me to shove all my belongings in a tiny suitcase as fast as I could.

"No." I cleared my throat, trying to make it easier to swallow. I massaged my forehead with the pads of my fingers, sensing an incoming headache as I shifted my gaze between Ares and Sam. "So why are you gathered here? Does it have something to do with Ares whispering away on the phone when he thinks I'm not looking?" I said, giving a sheepish Ares an accusatory look, although I didn't hate that he'd kind of taken over the communication side of things.

Ignorance was bliss, and I trusted him with my life.

"Carlos Peña made some ATM withdrawals under one of his aliases in a bank not too far from Astropolis. We have sufficient proof to believe he's closing in on your tracks, and we thought to expedite the process." Sam balanced his weight by leaning on the wall next to the fireplace and crossing his ankles.

That name, I recognized it.

Max had called the man that was plotting to kill me by that name, and it made sense he was the last one standing. The underworld was full of minions. To get to the head of the game, you had to set off a domino effect and catch the small responders first.

"We've jailed all of his inner circle and active accomplices, so he really has no support anymore or hopes for gaining back what he's lost. He only wants one thing, and that's—"

"Me," I finished his sentence, staring blankly at the fireplace, my trepidation rising as high as the flames.

"He can't have you, Siren." Ares squeezed the back of my neck, his voice as deadly as the edge of a blunt knife. "We're going to be one step ahead of him this time. The hunters, not the hunted."

"How?" I met his magnificent gold stare, my chest warming at the determination I found there.

"What's the best way to lure a predator?" Sam met my question with one of his own.

Ares's answering smile made my blood run cold. "With bait."

ARES

"I'm scared." Serena's shoulders glistened as she stretched her arms wide on the edges of the Jacuzzi, the fizzing water eating away at the wonderful view of her boobs—deliciously naked because that was the only way she was allowed in here.

I proposed we took a dip after Sam retired for the night to relieve the stress both he and I caused her, but even after ten minutes of the jets hitting us from every direction, she was wound tighter than a ball of barbed wire.

The plan was as followed: since soon-to-be-dead Carlos was already hot on her heels, we thought we'd give him what he wanted...or at least make him believe so. Lure him out of his hiding place with an anonymous tip-off of Serena's location and arrest him as soon as he steps foot on the premises. It would all be very public—at a concert I was planning on attending for a hot minute. We wouldn't even get to see him if all went as planned, and I would make sure it did. Over my dead body would Serena have to suffer another day in the presence of low lives like the likes of him.

I thought I was against the death penalty, but there was nothing I craved more than for it to be legalized in Massachusetts at this very moment. So, while we were starting with an arrest, a finger slip and a shot in the dark weren't out of the question if Carlos so much as squirmed. Abuse of power was the root of all evil, but sometimes it was exactly what was needed to fight those that were wasting our oxygen reserves, and I couldn't wait to be the one to pull the trigger.

"There's nothing to be scared of, Serena. The plan is foolproof. We'll be surrounded by police at all times. It'll be like having your own secret service at your beck and call," I assured, floating up to her and shoving my face in her neck, breathing in the oranges that drove me wild on the daily. "And I'll be there too. Right by your side."

She wrapped herself around me like a squid, her breasts sliding down my sternum and driving my cock to nestle between her ass cheeks. "You're not really making your case stronger. I don't want you within a mile of people like Carlos."

"Too bad, Siren." I blew on her skin, smiling when she shivered and rammed herself harder against me. "The only way you're going without me is over my dead body."

"Sam could probably arrange for that to happen." I could hear the smile in her voice, so I couldn't even be mad that she was plotting my death already.

Moving backward with her still glued to my chest, I sat on a little step underneath the water, spreading my legs wide in the water and placing her in my lap.

"Close your eyes, my wicked little Siren," I instructed, ghosting my lips over her high cheekbone, turning her down when she went in for a kiss.

She narrowed her eyes at me. "Why?"

Because I wanna ogle you while you're not looking.

"Just do it, and think about all the places you'd love to travel to once all this is over." I squeezed her ass playfully. "I'll take you anywhere you want. Close your eyes and tell me what you want to do when we get there."

To my surprise, she didn't fight me on it. There was a

stunning sunset behind us, yet I couldn't remove my eyeballs from the strands of hair plastered on her temples, the droplets of water gliding down her creamy skin, and her long lashes fanning over her rosy cheeks. The gazebo the hot tub was placed under was disturbing some of the quickly diminishing soft light, and it made me want to knock it down in order not to miss any details.

"For Christmas this year, I want to go to the Santa Claus Village in Lapland. See Santa's reindeers, kiss you in the back of a husky ride, and go on a snowmobile adventure. I've never been on one."

She painted a very vivid picture, and all I could think about was the snuggling in our assigned cabin portion of the trip. Fuck, why was my head constantly in the gutter? Probably because all I needed was one stroke, and I'd be inside of her, but sex was a temporary solution to a long-term problem, and I had to take my time to alleviate some of her worry.

"As long as you don't go near any ski equipment, that sounds wonderful to me." I winced, remembering how when it came to sports, she ranked at the bottom of the barrel. "Where else?"

"Venice, Italy for Valentine's Day to eat gelato on the back of a gondola, but before we get there, I want to stop by Casa di Giulietta in Verona and write her another letter. It's supposedly the setting for Shakespeare's famous tragedy, *Romeo and Juliet*."

"Shakespeare never even visited Verona, and that story is purely fictional, so Juliet having an actual house there is the epitome of the modern world's money-grabbing techniques."

She cracked an eye open to pin me with an unimpressed stare. "You told me to close my eyes and imagine; don't ruin my dreams with your cynicism."

"Fine." My thumbs brushed against her underboob, and her lashes fluttered shut again, this time with no encouragement from me. I continued a path over her ribs, memorizing the contours of her body. "What did you even say in your first letter?"

"Oh, I sent several." Her lips twisted in a smirk. "All detailing how obsessed I was with Leo and his beautiful green ey—"

My fingers stopped their soft detour on her skin, digging into the sides of her stomach until she was squirming with laughter, and leaned as far back as she could to get away from my tickle attack.

"I'm kidding! I'm kidding!" She giggled, and the sound coupled with her arched back thrusting her tits out of the water did wonders at making all my blood rush south.

My breath whooshed out of my lungs when her laugh lines hit me straight in the heart as I let up and tugged her back closer. "It's too soon to be making such jokes. Give it ten more years, and then we can talk about it."

Yeah, no, even after a century, I didn't think I could stomach the fact that there had even been a possibility of a world where Leo and Serena ended up together.

First of all, because she was mine.

And second of all, because she was. Fucking. Mine.

Serena cupped the side of my face, and I wasn't even embarrassed as I nuzzled her palm, pressing a kiss there. "All I talked about were my favorite pair of gold eyes, turning as hot as scorching lava whenever they saw me and how much I wished I could give in and finally make him mine. How much I wanted to stop pretending you didn't interest me." My organs did melt away at her rushed statement like I indeed had lava flowing through my veins. Hotter than the one that melted Pompeii. "And now, I want to thank her for making that happen and giving me one of the best endings I could've asked for."

Serena leaned in as if about to make contact, but she just hovered over my mouth. So I saw to it to bite her delicious pout until she released another giggle and tried to escape my cute aggression.

"I don't want to lose my happy ever after before it has even properly begun, Ares." Her forehead creased, and I pressed an actual kiss to her damp hairline this time.

She'd get her happy ever after. After this weekend, she'd never have to worry about another thing again.

"You haven't even asked me whose concert we're attending, Siren."

"Whose?"

"Do you remember your favorite girl from the Astropolis Children's Home?"

"Arta?" My lips curled into a smile when she slithered farther away to get a good look at my face. Her features lit up, hands smacking the fizzing water like an overzealous baby seal and drenching me with drops of water. "No way."

"Yes way." My grin turned wider at the disbelief she projected. "I own some shares in a big record label group in L.A. and made sure to put a word in. She's very talented, and her first album this year was a major success."

I also couldn't let her fail, or I'd be failing you.

Even when I hated Serena, I felt the need to do right by her.

Serena sniffed, her nose wrinkling up adorably. "Out of fear of sounding repetitive, I'm not going to tell you I love you again."

"You kind of just did." I chuckled, and it didn't matter how many times she said it. I wouldn't get tired of hearing it.

Placing her head on my shoulder, she sighed happily as I drew circles over the skin of her back. "I think I'm going to start taking birth control so we can stop using condoms."

My hands stilled. "Are you sure?"

"Yes, I want no barriers between us, not anymore. And if anything unplanned happens, then we'll face it together. Right?"

"I'd love nothing more," I croaked, clearing my throat when my voice came out hoarse.

I'd already cried in front of her once. I wasn't going to do so twice in such a short span of time.

Being inside of Serena bare, watching my cum spill out of her pretty pink pussy was enough to make my dick weep, but hearing her say she was open to the idea of a baby made my heart fucking soar in my chest. It wasn't an easy feat after her miscarriage, so it meant I must've been doing something right to rebuild her trust in me.

We stayed locked in each other's embrace for a little while, and her soft breaths hitting my collarbone, coupled with the incredibly warm water and pressure of the jets, almost lulled me to sleep. Serena was totally at ease in my arms, too, somewhat more at peace with attending Arta's concert.

My ringtone broke the peace of the moment, and I groaned as Serena detached from me so I could get my phone. I glanced at the screen, my brows hiking up.

"It's Leo," I whispered, which was ridiculous since we were all alone. There were only a few chirping grasshoppers left, tucked away into the trees that were probably gonna stick it out until the beginning of October.

"Answer it." Serena bounced in the water, and mini waves lapped at my abs as a result.

Sighing, I did, even though the bastard deserved to sweat it out a little longer. "Hello."

"Hey." His grumpy voice greeted me, and I waited for him to continue. I thought I heard him *oomph* through the receiver as if someone had elbowed him in the gut, and he relented. "Do you and Serena want to come over for lunch next Saturday?"

Not quite the apology I had imagined, but even this probably took a lot out of him. I looked at Serena, her tongue peeking out eagerly as she awaited news.

"Are you free next Saturday for lunch at Leo and Eli's?" I asked her, despite knowing she was. I wanted to make Leo wait, even if just for an extra few seconds.

She nodded eagerly, and I sighed again before confirming our attendance. "We'll be there."

"All right. See you then," Leo heaved, and then the line went dead as if he couldn't get off the phone fast enough.

I pulled my lips in my mouth, placing my phone by the lip of the Jacuzzi again and rolling my shoulders. If he thought I was letting him off the hook like that, he had another thing coming.

Come next Saturday, he was apologizing to Serena, or so help me God, we'd both end up in the hospital.

"Well, his temper tantrum lasted shorter than I expected." My gaze sought out the smirk on Serena's face, and I raised a brow in question. "Did you have something to do with it?"

She shrugged, a vixen-like expression plastered on her face. "I might've met with Eliana. After all, *beside* every great man stands a great woman, and you always do as you're told, right, baby?"

We had matching smiles on now, and I slowly bounded over to her, ready to do *exactly* as I was told. "Put me to work, oh great woman."

Her hand soaked the curls on top of my head as she pushed me down. "Hold your breath, my love."

CHAPTER TWENTY-SIX
SERENA

The crowd was alight with excitement as the lights went down, and slowly five projector beams focused on the middle of the stage. Cold sweat ran down my spine, but I downplayed my nervousness by gazing at the remote-control luminous bracelet on my wrist that suddenly flashed a bright pink. We were positioned in the middle of the arena. A few rows up from the main floor where everyone was on foot, right next to the aisle, in case we needed to make a quick escape.

Ares's thumb ghosted over the silicone band and engulfed my hand in his, tugging it up and pressing his lips to my knuckles. His eyes shone like uncut obsidians in the darkened stadium, and a puff of air fell from my mouth at the intensity I found lurking there.

"Don't overthink," he chided, and I let my gaze roam around us, spotting at least five potential agents in the throng of people. I could very well be wrong, since their job was to blend in. Ares scraped his teeth over my fingers gently, and my attention snapped like a rubber band back to him, finding a Cheshire cat grin perched on his lips. "Enjoy the moment, Siren. You're about to listen to someone that can scream even louder than you did last night."

Heat flooded my cheeks, and I retracted my hand. "Sometimes, I can't tell whether I like it when you call me that or not. What happened to cute nicknames like princess, angel..." My mouth pursed as I pondered over it. "Sunshine?"

Ares rolled his eyes. "Next, you're going to tell me you prefer *baby* more."

It was pretty generic, but it beat being called Siren because I was fucking loud in bed.

"I do," I said, but my voice was weak even to my own ears.

"You're pretty when you lie." Those talented fingers of his skimmed to the edge of my blue sundress, and I almost swallowed my tongue. "Your neck flushes this gorgeous pink color, and all I want to do is taste it with my tongue and trace the edges until I find the blush's end line."

"Ares, stop," I hissed, my palm colliding with his on my thigh to stop the little path he was paving upward. He dug his fingers in my flesh as a response, and my whole body started pounding to the low beat that had started playing in the background.

"Why? If you don't want me to call you Siren anymore, then prove to me you can be quiet."

My eyes bugged when I realized what he was getting at. "Absolutely not. There are a lot of eyes on us right now, even if we don't see them."

"Is it that, or are you scared you're gonna lose?" Ares's lips rose, just at the corner.

"God, I hate you." I'd lost count of how many times I'd

told him that, but unlike the first few, there was barely any bite behind my words now.

"Mm-hmm." He smiled, keeping his touch on me at all times, immune to the chant of the crowd when a little underground door slid open on stage. "Then Siren it is for the foreseeable future."

Licking my lips, I gave up because there was no winning with Ares Alsford and cocked my head to the stage, saying, "Shh, it's starting."

My leg was still tingly from the contact, but it was comforting, and he'd successfully managed to help me loosen up. A very intense pop beat sent the ground underneath my feet shaking, coming to a complete halt when a little thing appeared in the center decked out in a black leotard and tights that sparkled under the lights.

"Holy hell, she looks so different," I gasped, my gaze roaming over what I could capture since we weren't glued to the stage. Almost everything was the same, but the air of confidence and maturity that hung over her shoulders gave her a different appeal, one of a compassionate adult as she gave the brightest fucking smile I'd ever seen to her fans, and they all went wild as her melodic voice started seeping through the massive speakers.

"Considering she was six years old when she got adopted and you last saw her, I'd say that's to be expected." Ares leaned in to talk over the loud music.

"She was actually seven, smart-ass," I bit back, not being able to take my eyes away from her. Her midnight hair swung around her in tune, with the fan hitting her face as she held an impressive note. "She has really grown singing wise, too."

"Tell me about it. Connecting her with the right people

might've started out as a favor, but so far, it has been a really lucrative investment," Ares said, and I felt so old next to all the screaming kids while complimenting her style.

"Just how many industries are you involved in?"

"A few." He rolled his lips in his mouth. "Real estate is lucrative, but I like having other stuff to fall back on."

That made sense.

Perhaps if my father had had something else to fall back on, he wouldn't have gone to such great lengths to rob other people of their money.

"I want to invest too. Will you help me? Show me the ropes?" I didn't know where the wish came from all of a sudden. All I knew was that I wanted security. I wrung my hands together in my lap, looking at him through my lashes. "I don't have your kind of capital. I don't mind starting small."

The way his eyes softened when he looked at me made me pant. "Siren, my money is your money. You could blow a hundred grand a day, and I wouldn't care. I'll happily lend you as much as you need to build your investment portfolio and never ask for it back. And I'll help you all you need."

"Thank you, but I wanna do this with my money. I'd feel too bad if I blew yours in a crappy investment."

"We'll talk about it later." He dismissed my words, angling his body back toward the stage. "Now stop talking about money at a fucking concert, Siren."

"Are you okay?" I asked as Ares squirmed in his seat for the thousandth time, crossing his long legs and almost knocking his boot on the person in front of us.

"Yeah," he panted, very clearly not fine when he squeezed his thighs together.

Arta had disappeared somewhere offstage, probably to change outfits as the guitarist performed a solo, working through the notes with expert precision.

"Ares, what's wrong?" I pressed, and he heaved a loud sigh.

"I have to fucking pee."

"Then go to the bathroom?" I asked rhetorically, the space between my brows bunching.

"Come with me." He spun to face me in sharp, jerky movements, his leg bouncing on the floor. I met him with a horrified expression. "Come on, I've seen you pee, and you've seen me pee before."

"Yes, but usually not in public restrooms where there might be other people who are not comfortable with having me around," I whispered feverishly.

"Who cares? They'll live."

"Go, I'll be fine," I said through my teeth, aware as to why he refused to leave. But it was fine; it had been more than an hour, and nothing had happened. We were waiting for Sam to contact us any minute and tell us it was safe.

"No," he gritted out, falling back into his seat.

I rolled my eyes, trying to keep the edges of my lips from lifting by taking a long, loud slurp out of my Coke cup. "You know, holding your urine for too long can cause urinary tract infections."

"Ah, shit." I watched his eyes roll to the back of his head when I purposefully did it again. Ares shot laser beams at me through his eyes before a devious smirk developed on his face, and he swung his head around so fast, I thought I heard a crack. He fluttered his lashes at the girls behind us who stared at him, flabbergasted as he greeted them in a low sexy tone, "Hi, ladies."

Confusion swam through my muddled brain as I glared at his profile. The group of three girls released breathless smiles and returned his address simultaneously, like some sort of telepathic triplets. "Hi."

"Do you mind keeping an eye on my girlfriend? I need to go to the bathroom really quick, and I don't want her to feel alone." His soothing voice had the exact opposite effect on me, and my mouth released a strangled sound that was drowned out by the music.

Twisting at the spine, I dug my nails into his hairy fore-arm, but he didn't budge as I addressed them. "No, that's fin—"

"Of course!" they cut me off, little moons in their eyes as they nodded, eager to do his bidding.

"Thank you, girls." He winked at them, and just like that, all of his charm bled out as he swooped down to kiss me, the lines of his face taut like the thought of staying away for just a few minutes stressed him out.

"I'm going to kill you," I murmured against his lips, not understanding his intense reaction when he had been cool as a witch's teat the whole evening.

"I love you too," he replied back with a wink and shot out of his seat, leaving as fast as his feet would allow him to without sprinting. Which was pretty freaking quick since he reached the exit in a few seconds.

I heard a dreamy sigh behind me, accompanied by, "He's so fucking sweet."

"Why are the hot ones always taken?" the one from the far left added. I couldn't see them, but I could sense the direction of the flowing voices, my cheeks pinkening at the domino effect Ares set forth, but my chest also puffing with pride.

Yup, Ares Alsford is fucking hot, and he is fucking mine.

"I don't know, but he definitely gives off big dick energy."

"He's probably rich too. Did you see the Rolex on his wrist?"

"Really? I didn't notice. He was dressed pretty modestly."

"Yeah. It's usually the broke ones that love to show off the most."

They shot sentences rapidly between themselves, and even though I was invested, now *my* bladder grew uncomfortably full. I cursed myself for downing that Coca-Cola cup like my life depended on it to prove a point.

I shifted, squeezing my legs closed, but it was of no use. The drummer had taken precedence now, and I felt each of the loud bangs straight to my urethra. My gaze bounced over the mass of people, searching for anything inconspicuous, but nothing caught my sight. There were men and women swaying to the tunes and chatting as animatedly as they waited for Arta to make another appearance.

Shit, I also had to go.

"So what you're saying is I have to go after guys with a crappy fashion sense?" one of them asked, sounding perplexed, and I scoffed as I grabbed my phone from Ares's cup holder, getting on my feet.

What she needed to do was go after someone she genuinely liked. If they happened to have no social media accounts or a big desire to boast, those were all pluses but not prerequisites. Relationships didn't work with checklists.

"Hey, where are you going?" the redhead in the middle asked and my eye twitched at her tone, her eyes rolling down my body like she was assessing me. "Your boyfriend told us to watch you."

Her gaze flicked to my face again, like she wasn't impressed with what she found, and I resisted baring my teeth at the teenager. "Well, lucky for me, I'm capable and don't need adult supervision."

I left it at that, even though I heard them muttering *bitch* under their breaths. I'd been called worse, plenty more times. Getting into catfights used to be one of my favorite pastimes when I was their age, so I didn't pay them much mind. It was like a rite of passage for every girl until they came to a realization that other women were their friends. Not their enemies.

It was a tight fit trying to get past the rest of the seats. You had to mobilize an entire line of people to fit through and perform some acrobatics over the ones that refused to budge, and when you finally freed yourself, you had the matter of a tiny crowd gathered underneath the bleachers to get through.

Ares had made it look so easy; they parted like the Red Sea for him, but I was bumping shoulders left and right trying to pass through, seeing as I didn't have the advantage of intimidation through towering over everyone in height. At one point, I was shoved from behind, tumbling forward so hard I hit my forehead on someone's jaw, causing them to cry out.

I pulled back, my eyes watering at the ache that spread underneath my browbone. Hands reached out to steady me, and I apologized, "Oh, I'm sorry I—"

I shut up.

My eyes widened, and my heart stopped.

A thick layer of sweat formed instantaneously on the

surface of my skin when I was met with dark brows, a tan skin complexion, a slightly hooked nose, and sneering lips. The hands wrapped around my arms transitioned from supportive to feeling like metal shackles, ready to tie me down as *he* tore into me.

Carlos.

No.

No way.

This wasn't happening. Sam promised me this wouldn't happen. *Ares* promised me this wouldn't happen.

Past trauma gripped my throat, and I struggled to get my bearings straight as the stench of sweat wafting from his form filled my nostrils. He smelled foul, like the life I tried so hard to leave behind. My chest heaved, and I tried to catch sight of anyone rushing for me to help me.

There was nothing. No one.

Bile made the back of my mouth sting, and I realized I'd have to do this alone. I'd trained for this. I could do this. I could take him.

"You will be if you don't do as I say." His voice slithered under my skin like a reptile, and it took about five seconds for my fight-or-flight reaction to kick in, but I didn't choose one or the other. I went for both as I twisted in his hold, but at the same time tried to punch his chest with my fists. In response, it took two for him to totally immobilize me by shaking me in place and whispering on the side of my face, "Don't even try it, little girl. I have a bomb strapped to my chest, and the timer is already running. Unless you want to die and take hundreds of others down with you, you will walk."

I froze, my blood turning blue in my veins, something heavy settling in the bottom of my stomach. I tried to find reason, but I couldn't see past the chaos in my brain and around me.

This wasn't it, right?

I wouldn't die.

Why had no one planned for the possibility of Carlos bringing weapons?

"I don't believe you." I held on to a sliver of hope, having experienced the vanity of men like him first-hand. They loved themselves way too much. "A man like you would never take his own life in the process too."

His chuckle made my stomach roil with unease, and I shifted to get as far away as possible from his nasty breath. He had hit rock bottom, and if a bug-infested hotel room was a look, he was sporting it right now, so far off from the decked out in luxury bordello owner he'd been a few years ago.

The mighty had fallen, and despite my perilous situation, satisfaction mixed with the terror in my chest.

"Bold words coming from a bitch that ruined my entire business. You want us to stick around and find out?" he asked, and my gulp was painful as the inside of my body pruned up when he shoved me forward, and I obliged. Alarm was tattooed over my every movement and constrained in my arms as I was being kidnapped in a venue full of people, but no one noticed. "That's it, keep it going, and don't try anything funny. I'm the only one that knows the combination to turn it off."

I wasn't going to punch the hell out of him just yet. There were children, mothers, and so many young souls around, I'd be vetoed out of Heaven with no second thought if I allowed for such damage to ensue. But when we were alone, past the long hallway leading to the exit and out to the parking lot where he was heading, it was game over.

Nerves lit up inside of me, and a million electric shocks spread over every hair on my body, but at the thought, I didn't care.

I'd rather die than let him have me again. If there was one thing I knew he wouldn't do, it was a swift death. So I was going to take matters into my own hands and take him down with me, like I did Max, until he couldn't hurt anyone else ever again.

Ares would understand.

He had to.

"From the very first moment I saw you, I didn't like you," Carlos confessed, and I bit the inside of my cheek until blood flowed to balance out the fright in my system and not let it show in his eyes.

I wouldn't give him the pleasure of seeing the devastation slamming against my every crevice until I had trouble focusing as he dragged me through wide spaces. His hand was firmly locked under my armpit, and the music got fainter by the second.

"Bummer, and here I did my best to form a good impression." I plied my tone with enough sarcasm to feed an army. Not giving up, never giving in.

"Oh, I'm going to enjoy this. I've been waiting five years to get my hands on you." He sounded animalistic, a pure evil smile spreading his already thin lips into two tiny lines.

"Are you mad I killed your boyfriend?" I countered.

"Max?" A sharp laugh escaped him, and for being so quiet, his voice rang loud in my ears. "You did me a favor, sweetheart. I was planning on getting rid of him for a while. Honestly, if you'd just kept your mouth shut, you would've lived a free, happy life. I wouldn't have thought about you twice. You were a fucking low-life prostitute, not fucking worth my time, but then you had to go and get the feds involved."

His steps got quicker, and I was figuring his time was running out as he became rougher once we burst outside, the night air capping around us. I came into the parking lot with the love of my life, and I was exiting the parking lot and life by leaving him behind.

God hadn't been gracious to me, and for a good reason, but the biggest blessing so far had been leaving Ares far away from this whole ordeal. I knew my death would be like looting his heart out of his chest, but he was young. He would rebuild and replenish without me.

Without me. Without me. Without me.

Those two words wreaked havoc in my brain, and tears lodged themselves at the base of my throat, but I held on to the anger as we weaved through parked cars. The less people we saw, the bolder I got. "I'd rather die than let the rapists you protected roam free and allow you to harm more girls."

"And what do you think happened to the ones you left behind?" He swung me around in front of a white van, and I almost got whiplash by the force of the jolt. In the fluorescent lighting of the parking lot, I got a true feel of how far gone he was, in his jeans that seemed like they'd never seen the inside of a washing machine and the dried-up food and blood on his plain white shirt. But most importantly, the look in his eyes...it was that of a crazed man as he cackled, piercing me straight in the heart with his next words. "I had to get rid of any liabilities, and it was most unfortunate when a fire burned the whole building down due to some faulty wiring."

My mouth dropped open, any false pretense of strength I tried to hold on to evaporating in thin air. "No."

"Yes." His nod felt like a very sharp blade cutting through my soul, and pieces of it started drifting in the wind like accumulated sawdust. "In the process of trying to ruin me, you killed every single girl in that house and, in a few minutes, yourself. Me? I'm still in my fucking prime. I'm going to rebuild everything I lost. You're just a dumb bitch that destroyed a bunch of lives in order to get revenge. So really, who's the bad guy here, me or you?"

A loud whirring noise buzzed in my ears until I couldn't hear a whisper. Exertion, like I'd never felt before, hit me like a Mack truck, and I couldn't breathe, let alone fight him, as he picked up his pace again toward the van. The entire purpose of the suffering I'd endured for the past several years disappeared in a few seconds, leaving me null and void.

"No, she didn't, and now you're not," a low, dangerous voice uncurled from our right belonging to the man I owed my life to. Carlos spun in place, stilling when Sam filled his vision, formidable as ever, with his buzz-cut hair and cognac eyes. "Those girls got out safe and sound. No matter how you paint it, you're the sole loser in this ordeal."

A whoosh of relief escaped me at the exposure of Carlos's lies, but it was short-lived when I remembered the literal ticking bomb strapped to his chest.

"Sam, leave! He has a—" I tried to warn, but his hand came around my chest, his other palm covering my mouth, fingers bruising my cheeks until I couldn't get a single word out.

"Listen to her," he crooned, but Sam remained in place like a well-trained soldier. "There's no way either of you are walking out of here alive if you stay."

"The only one that's not walking out of here is you."

My eyes closed as a tsunami of terror swept through my

mind when Ares's voice joined the mix from the left this time. It was like the final nail in the coffin when he came into view, his gaze seeking mine like a moth to the flame, promising dire consequences when I tried to speak, but nothing but muffled mumbles came out.

"You brought your whole posse with you, huh?" he growled in my ear, and I so craved to scratch the fuck out of his face until I clawed his eyes out, and the confusion on Sam's face when I didn't fight back was prominent. After all, he'd been in a few of my self-defense classes.

I couldn't do it, though, not at their expense.

I wouldn't let my two favorite people die because of me.

"She did," Sam answered the question directed at me, and I tried to plead with him through my eyes when I saw him reaching for a handgun behind his back. He pulled it out regardless, and I felt like a lost cause.

"And if you don't let her go within five seconds, I will shoot every major artery on your body and fucking watch you bleed to death with a smile on my face," Ares added, him too holding an identical gun in his hand, his eyes like deadly shards of black ice.

He was telling the truth.

He'd kill Carlos for me and enjoy it, but he wasn't aware that in the process, he'd be wiping all of us out.

Carlos's body trembled behind me, and I dug my nails in his forearm to get him to let up so I could use my mouth. "You'll still shoot me if I do."

"We're not going to shoot you, but you are going to get arrested. What do you prefer, Carlos? A life in Hell or a prison cell?" Sam served him with an ultimatum, and I didn't even know who was shaking more at the moment, me or Carlos.

Sam hadn't accounted for a third option.

Carlos, taking us all to Hell with him.

His scream of frustration bounced across all the empty cars, and in an unprecedented move, I found myself hurtling toward the ground when Carlos pushed me roughly. Shock entered my system as air flowed all around me like static pulsing over my skin.

My hands flailed, and gravel bit into my palms and bare knees when I tumbled onto the ground on all fours. Searing pain filled every pore in my body, and I groaned as I tried to shove it all down, spinning on my ass toward the action.

"We forgot to specify," Ares said as slowly but surely both he and Sam backed Carlos up into the white van by standing in front of me. They were in tune almost, and I marveled at Ares's perfect gun-holding position, both his hands thrust in front of him in a dominant grip. "The prison cell *is* going to be situated in Hell."

"No, Ares, don't! He has a bomb!" I tried to inform them, but it was too late.

A round of rapid gunfire drowned out my words, and I cried out in my elbow as I tried to shield myself from the explosion that was about to ensue. My biggest fear in life came true—failing my loved ones—as death knocked on my door.

White noise violated my ears, and a bright flash like lightning striking on a field, suffocating everything with its brilliance. Everything turned dark, and I was blinded. Blinded by despair as all that I worked so hard to gain went down the drain from the pull of a trigger.

So this was what hell felt like.

Explosions were still going off in the back of my brain, coupled with the added sound of anguished screams experiencing the deepest of suffering. My heartbeat ceased for a second before it started beating again, way too fast to be in the mortal world. The atmosphere around me was *enraged*. The violent energy washed over me, its stunning intensity overwhelming me, causing my senses to tumble down along with the rest of me.

An earthquake built up inside me from my core and then outward until the crushing weight lifted, and something familiar registered in the back of my mind. A touch crushing me to a chest drenched in that familiar ocean scent that sent my distress scurrying. My teeth clashed, and suddenly the screaming stopped as if pulled by a plug, and I grasped that it was me all along...I'd been the one screaming.

"It's okay. Shh, it's okay, Serena. Everything is fine." A palm rubbed up and down my back soothingly. My head was tilted back, and I was met by an order. I immediately obliged. "Open your eyes, Siren. Look at me."

Breathing ragged, my wild gaze swiveled around the dead of the night, stopping when I found him. He hovered over me, deeply troubled as he shook my shoulders, his T-shirt decorated with splatters of blood.

"Ares?" I whispered, my voice hoarse and cracked. When I blinked several times, and he still filled my vision, I touched him, my hands roaming all over his chest, neck, and face with spiraling panic. "H-how... Ah, he had a bomb. Are we dead?"

I stumbled over my words, the normally striking lines of his face seeming fuzzy as my vision still swam, and my brain tried to catch up with my current reality.

Tension crept over his jaw, and it was as if I fell back to planet earth, crashing and burning when I heard his next statement. "There was no bomb, Serena. We're very much alive. It was a bluff."

A shudder worked its way down my body, and every limb tingled as I crushed myself back into Ares's warm arms. They enveloped me wholly, taking me in and providing all the strength I needed right now. My vision widened enough for me to see the grotesque view of Carlos over his back, a fountain of blood rushing out of his chest, plastered against the van dripping with his essence.

Bile rushed up my throat, and I had to shove my face back in the crook of his neck not to throw up. "You killed him," I said numbly, the gravity of the situation not escaping me.

"We both did," Sam appeared over Ares's shoulder, his voice holding notes of a complaint as if I wasn't giving him enough credit. I saw men in dark uniforms rush all around us, and my pulse skyrocketed as I held on to Ares protectively.

"This isn't fucking funny, Sam," I hissed, a tremor rocking through me. "What's going to happen to Ares? To you? This wasn't self-defense."

The knowledge that this had the potential to go further south than it already had grounded me, and I didn't know how it was possible to be crushed any more than I already was.

"Says who? The cameras were shut off, and no one's going to take the side of a traffic ringleader. The facts are what we make them to be." Ares gripped the back of my hair gently, bringing my face in line with his. His eyes shone like shards of brilliant amber, fierceness pulsing through his following statement. "It's over, Siren. It's done. You're free now, completely and totally free."

Free.

Completely and totally free.

I'd finally beat my past—with help—but I'd beat it before it beat me.

Everyone who had previously hurt me was dead, and none of them went peacefully.

My face scrunched, and the beautiful view of his face blurred as tears spilled down my cheeks before I could stop them, the buildup of emotions flowing out of me. My thoughts were like scattered wisps of smoke, but through the haze, I managed to put two and two together.

"You didn't really need to go to the bathroom, did you?"

"No, I didn't." Ares confirmed my theory, swiping at the wetness that collected on my face tenderly, so fucking tenderly it made my heart weep at the lengths he'd gone. At the lengths both he and Sam had gone, not to just arrest Carlos, but completely end him.

"You got blood on your hands for me." My exhale was frayed, tattered.

Ares nodded, not a hint of regret on his face, only sheer love as he gave me the softest of kisses, uncaring of the disarray surrounding us. "And I'd do it all over again if it meant avenging you."

EPILOGUE
ARES

Three Years Later

A piercing cry pulled me from my slumber. I shifted on my elbows in bed, body braced for an intruder, when it happened again. A shrill, whiny noise attacked my ears, causing an exhausted Serena to groan beside me, hiding her face underneath her elbow as she rolled onto her back.

The desire to just fall back on the mattress and sleep through the noise was as enticing as taking a bite out of a forbidden apple, but duty called, and I loved my kids way too much to ever do that to them. They'd be making it up to me once they grew up a little, anyway. I was always my parents' errand boy, and it was a tradition I intended to keep going in my household as well.

"I'll get it," Serena muttered tiredly, and I glanced at the digital clock by my bedside table, seeing that it was almost three in the morning.

"No, sleep. I can handle it." Swooping down, I plucked

my wife's hand from her face and placed a kiss on her forehead, breathing her in, and nuzzling her temple, fueling my
serotonin in a few seconds. She turned at the last minute, her
lips catching mine in a brief, hot kiss before she leaned back,
her smile never lackluster even at this ungodly hour.

"Honey, you can do plenty of things very well." Her gaze
strayed to my naked chest, illuminated by a soft nightlight
we left on, so we didn't stumble on our way to the nursery.
Liquid heat followed her path, and I straightened when it
was clear she wasn't going back to sleep. "But nursing babies
is not one of them, seeing as you lack the necessary equipment to do that."

"Is there no pumped milk in the freezer?" I asked, and
we both threw our covers off simultaneously, climbing off the
bed and into our awaiting slippers. It had been four months
now since the twins were born, so we had our routine down
to a T. Not to mention the number of times we practiced
before they'd even arrived.

And Serena even had the audacity to be offended after I
called her a helicopter mom.

"There is, but this way, we'll get them to fall back asleep
faster. Plus, my boobs feel heavy," Serena complained, and I
took the liberty of getting an eyeful of her delicious girls as
she tightened her robe. They'd gotten so much bigger during
her pregnancy, and I couldn't seem to tear myself away from
them. I was as obsessed with her tits as my kids were. Her
eyes narrowed, catching my stare as we both stumbled out
the door. "Don't even start."

"I didn't say anything." I grinned, remembering how she
got mad at me the other day for having a weakness for the
cowgirl position the past few months because having her
chest shoved in my face while I worked her on my dick like

there was no tomorrow felt like stepping into fucking heaven.

And not just for me.

I knew for sure she loved it too. My Siren had never stopped being my little screamer. Even in inconvenient times like this. But I'd found the solution in stuffing her panties in her mouth, so she could be as loud as she pleased.

"You were thinking it," Serena countered, forming mini squares around her chest with hands to emphasize her following point. "This is a no-go zone for the time being."

We stopped in front of the nursery, where most likely our daughter—Penelope—held her nightly crying concert while her brother slept through it, waking us up all over again, approximately an hour after his sister fell to sleep. "We'll see how you feel about that when they're leaking and heavy this weekend, and you'll be an ocean away from your babies."

I opened the door, giving Serena's ass a good squeeze as she walked in first, making a beeline toward Penelope.

"Ugh, don't remind me," she said, a smile taking hold of her pouty lips as she came to stand above our daughter's crib, who immediately, upon seeing Serena, started kicking her legs out. "Shh, my love, you're going to wake your brother," Serena cooed, her voice dropping to a whisper, even though Alexander could sleep through an earthquake. My son liked his beauty sleep. Penelope immediately quieted when in her mother's arms, as Serena clutched her against her chest like she was the most precious of treasure. "Yes, Mommy is here. Mommy is here to make it all better."

The baby talk was like catnip for my little girl, and my heart gave a little squeeze inside my chest at her happy gurgle. I passed by Alexander's crib, roaming my gaze over the blond tuft of hair on his head, exactly like his sister's, and his fists, curled tight in his sleep, just to check on him before joining Serena on the beige rocking chair. I pulled a stool out, sitting right next to her, and Penelope sought me out as she latched on her mother's boob, making grabby hands, and quieting down when I handed her my finger, her chubby rolls flexing as she grabbed ahold of me.

"Do we have to go, Ares?" Serena sang the same tune for the thousandth time. The pearl in combination with the diamond on her ring finger glittering as she supported Penelope's tiny head, smoothing her thumb over the light dusting of hair. "I don't want to leave my babies alone so early on."

It all began last week when I surprised her with tickets to Iceland so we could visit that Blue Lagoon place she'd been talking about nonstop. It was a freaking geothermal spa, but with the way she was resisting, you'd think I was taking her to explore the Sahara for two days.

"They won't be alone," I reasoned with a sigh. "They'll be with Leo and Eli, Siren. They too have two kids; they already know the drill."

Despite Leo's initial rocky start with Serena, they'd smoothed things over. They weren't the best of fucking friends, but it didn't matter. She and Eliana were once more as tight as they used to be in their early childhood, and we saw both of them nearly daily. They trusted us enough to hand their kids over whenever they needed to travel, and we were available since they were both pretty paranoid about nannies, and I didn't blame them. The thought of leaving my kids behind with strangers made me want to hurl. They were unnecessary as long as you had people around that were eager to help you out, and other than my wife, there was no one in this world that I trusted more than Leo and Saint.

"Yes, but you know how Matteo gets a little too over-excited when he's around the twins," Serena countered.

"It comes out of a place of love. You're overthinking things. Plus, he gets distracted easily every time Aria visits, and her belly is bigger than the last time. He doesn't understand what the hell's going on."

Serena giggled softly at the picture I painted, remembering the way the four-year-old's eyes popped when Aria started showing. "Have you seen the way Saint's eye starts twitching whenever someone tries to feel the baby?"

"I don't blame him. I don't get people's fascination with touching a pregnant woman's bump," I said, and Serena rolled her eyes.

"Of course, you don't. You were even more overprotective than he is."

The corners of my lips tugged up, and I shrugged. "I don't know what you're talking about."

Her eyes turned to slits, and I marveled at her beauty even when she was glaring at me. Her wavy caramel hair sat smooth down her back, and her complexion glowed even more, if that was possible, after she'd given birth to our kids. "Oh, so you've conveniently forgotten how you wouldn't even let me *approach* the girl at Sam's barbecue party because you were scared it was going to explode?"

I lost the war against my smile, and a full-blown one spread on my face. We gifted her mother's house to Sam when he decided to move back to Astropolis because it used to be *his* house as well, and Serena could visit whenever she wanted. Plus, we didn't need it, and we wanted to thank him for everything he'd done for us. Years ago, when I told him I couldn't stand the thought of Carlos drawing another breath, he pulled all the stops to make it happen and kept me out of trouble.

Cameras were shut off, and with self-defense cited as the reason for his death, no one raised an eyebrow when they looked at Carlos's questionable record. Sometimes you had to fight corruption with corruption, and I had no regrets about it to this day. There was no greater joy than seeing Serena and my kids safe, sound, and comfortable under my roof.

"It was a gas grill with a propane tank. I was being *cautious*. There's nothing wrong with that. Besides, Sam agreed." I rubbed Penelope's soft skin. She was still latched on, but she was getting drowsier by the second, those heart-melting hazel eyes hiding behind prolonged blinks.

"Dropping Sam's name during an argument makes you automatically lose an argument," she stated haughtily.

"Who's drafting up these rules?" My brows met, and I chuckled.

"The mother of your children." Serena winked, adjusting Penelope in her grip when her boob fell out of her mouth. "Happy wife, happy life—isn't that what they say? You're not supposed to fight me."

A rumble wrecked my stomach, and I joked, "My soul is laid at your feet, Siren, for you to stomp on as much as you want."

"You're so corny." Serena burst into a fit of giggles, and a second later, another cry circled through the room as if Alexander had had enough of hearing us talk for the past ten minutes. My wife snapped her mouth shut, guilt etching on her features, but it was what it was. Better he woke up now than later.

Sighing, I left both my girls behind and got Alex out of bed, tracing his scrunched-up nose with tenderness.

"Hey, little man." I rocked him gently as Serena made space on her other arm, and I fixed both of them in her hold before taking a step back and staring at my perfect daughter, son, and wife, my chest swelling with gratitude over my blessings. Moonlight drowned all but the brightest stars, and with an aura made of pure fire, my family, our entire lives, stood apart amongst the masses.

"You never fail to take my breath away every day." I sunk to my knees, my eyes latched on Serena *Alsford* now, my soulmate and the girl that held a stake in my heart for as long as I could remember. So many things were viable to break us apart, but against all odds, we made it and got two tiny angels out of our union. "Thank you, Siren," I breathed, and her eyes closed in surrender when I attached my forehead to hers, both our faces angled toward our kids.

"For what?"

"For making me the luckiest and happiest bastard on Earth and gifting me two of the most precious gifts." I kissed her mouth softly with every ounce of affection I held in my heart for her, and she melted against me. Exactly like the first time our lips met. I got to live and build a family with the love of my life. Not many people achieved that. "I promise to always cherish you and them."

THANKS FOR READING!

If you enjoyed Lick of Fire, please consider leaving a review! Your support means the world and helps other readers find books.

Join Clara's Firehearts Facebook group for exclusive excerpts, giveaways, funny memes, book talk, and more.

Scan the code to join the group:

ALSO BY CLARA ELROY

City of Stars Series

Kiss of War #1

Vow of Hell #2

Lick of Fire #3

Sting of Ice #4

Scan the code to read the books:

ACKNOWLEDGMENTS

I've been wanting to write Ares and Serena's story for so long, and I'm so happy with how it came out. I know many readers had their reservations about Serena, but I hope I did you proud. It was always the plan for her and Eliana to reconcile, seeing as I don't like pitting women against each other in my books. Especially when all the people that help make my author dreams come true are a group of incredible women.

The biggest thank you goes to my sister for always encouraging me and not judging me (much), even though I might go days without leaving the house just to finish a book.

My parents who never fail to mention how proud they are of me. My family is my biggest support group, and I'm so grateful for them and for the fact that none of them are readers because I'm not letting them get within a mile of my books.

My amazing beta readers, Ariel and Mia. Thank you so much, my loves. Your input is greatly appreciated, as well as your friendship.

So many amazing bloggers, bookstagramers, and book-tokers who constantly shower me with love. Thank you so freaking much, guys. Your support means the world, and I've made so many incredible friends in this community.

Thank you to my incredible editors, Erica and Mackenzie, for making my job so much easier and my words so much cleaner with their expertise.

My lovely cover designers, Kristy Still and Books and Moods, for bringing my vision to life with their talent!

The RONA writers for always being there when I need someone to turn to for advice and encouragement. I love going through this self-publishing journey with you, ladies. It's amazing to see all of you flourish and achieve your author goals!

And of course, thank you to all my wonderful readers. Thank you for all the heartfelt messages you send me, for asking for more books, and for changing my life. You guys make my dreams come true every time you pick up a book of mine, and I'll keep writing them for as long as they make you happy.

Always grateful,
Clara Elroy

ABOUT THE AUTHOR

Clara Elroy is an Amazon Top 100 best selling author of romance novels that make your heart clench. Her love for reading began when she was a young girl, and would lose sleep because she wanted to read "just one more page." Clara lives for reading and writing about flawed and relatable characters. She loves making sparks fly between stubborn men and the badass women that make them kneel. When Clara's not typing away at her computer, you can find her with her nose buried in a book or writing biographies in the third person.
Yeah, she's cool like that.

You can find Clara at these places:

Website:
www.claraelroy.com

Newsletter:
https://bit.ly/3voOhiz

Follow on Amazon to be alerted of her next release:
http://author.to/claraelroy

instagram.com/claraelroyauthor

facebook.com/claraelroyauthor

goodreads.com/claraelroy

bookbub.com/authors/clara-elroy

Made in the USA
Monee, IL
14 July 2022

99762201R00236